# Beneath a Colesberg Sky

Jeffrey Whittam was born in Lancashire, England in 1947. His formative years in Southern Rhodesia were spent fishing, hunting and exploring the wilderness. Still in his early twenties, Jeffrey became a prospector of note and sold his first gold claims in 1973. For the best part of the bush war, he fought with the Rhodesia Regiment's 10th Battalion. He now lives in the wilder reaches of Lancashire's fell country with his wife, two sons and three dogs. Beneath a Colesberg Sky is his third novel.

Also available in paperback:

Sons of Africa
Empress Gold

# BENEATH A

# COLESBERG SKY

## JEFFREY WHITTAM

COCOPAN

This edition published by Cocopan Publishing 2017
ISBN: 978-0-9573665-7-2

For
VICTORIA
My most precious, flawless diamond

The urge to turn her horse about uncoiled as some visceral snake from the pit of her stomach, for from across that denuded stretch of the Great Karoo the rabid wolves of desperation were already running to meet her. Smoke from a thousand fires clung to a broken landscape and towering above it, churned from a vast and open wound in the earth's crust were those billowing clouds of powdered Kimberlite; as yellow, ochrous fingers they reached upwards for over a thousand feet, deep inside the heart of that darksome Colesberg sky...

# I

# Port Natal, September 1, 1870

# -1-

A girl on the very brink of womanhood inclined her head and looked sideways along the deck of the anchored sailing ship, *Eudora*, her attention captivated by the appearance of a young man at the railing no more than ten yards or so from where she was standing. Though his stature was slight and his face portrayed that sallow complexion begot of ill health, still his eyes glowed, alive and fire-like, indomitably drawn to his first sightings of Natal's intriguing coastline. She sensed in him the urge to see beyond those deep forests, beyond those rolling hills to some far hinterland, and the wistful smile on his face was that of a man who had at that very moment set his cap to some strange and torrid love affair with Africa.

'You're English...?'

'And you, young lady are most obviously very young, very precocious and judging by your accent, very American.'

The girl, unperturbed by the man's brusque rebuff stood to her full height and brushed a ribbon of green silk away from her face.

'And proud of it, mister. Where are you headed for?'

'Not quite sure. My very first time in Africa, though I have it on good authority that my brother has settled himself to a portion of land some fifty miles in from the Port of Natal.'

'Sod buster then?'

Amused by the girl's lack of guile the stranger turned to face her. He put her age at fifteen – sixteen at a stretch, certainly no more. He spoke slowly, a trait he had learned from his mother. *Put people at their ease,* she had advised him, *or you will learn little of their intent.*

'My brother Herbert would not applaud your labelling him a sod buster, young lady. However, purely as a means of satisfying your insatiable curiosity, the answer to your question is yes – my brother grows cotton, the Umkomaas Valley I believe.'

The stranger tipped his hat to her; an onshore wind plucked at his hair and like a bird's unruly nest the unkempt mop fluffed and ruffled about his ears. Lured by growing curiosity, the girl moved closer. It was then she noticed his eyes – ice blue – bled from that of a winter sky. Though in stature he appeared as softly built, still there was a strength in him that she could not fathom, a mindset way beyond his years, that of a man to whom others would unwittingly be drawn.

'What do they call you?' The girl dug deeper, her womanly need to know already nipping at her throat. Her eyes flashed Celtic green, symmetrically placed about a perfect, pixie nose. Her hair was the culminate jeweller's setting, the colour of raw native copper it flounced and flashed as an exquisite auburn mount to those emerald eyes, and though she had tied it back still it wrapped about her cheeks and flew where it would with the wind.

'You first, though with eyes and hair like yours, I would assume you to be of Irish parentage?'

'Kathleen,' she acknowledged his guesswork, 'Kathleen O'Rourke. My father hails from Donegal.'

'Your mother...?'

'Dead.'

'I'm sorry.'

4

'No need – wasn't your fault, she drank too much. Fell off her horse, all liquored up the sheriff said.'

'Sheriff...?'

'Back home,' she nodded her head, 'Dakota Territory. Sheriff McLennan. My Pa sent for Doc Jeffries, but it was too late. We buried her that same day before the death rot set in.'

'It would appear you do not miss her?'

'Nope.' She held him with dispassionate eyes. 'She was a bitch. Beat me reglar-like and mostly for nothing, just 'cause she felt like it.'

The stranger smiled, wider and softer this time. The girl's accent intrigued him.

'I can most definitely empathise, seems that we are not too unlike.' He held out his hand. 'Cecil John Rhodes of Bishop's Stortford, England; son of a vicar, raised in fear of God Almighty and the restless disposition of my father's birch. Seventeen years this last July birthday, banished to the colonies for a so-called reparatory cure to ill health and my apparent lack of regard for my parents' Calvinistic lifestyle.'

Kathleen, though her response was tentative, accepted the pleasantry.

'My father warned me against fraternisin' with strangers.'

'And out here, I believe you would do well to heed his advice. Trust no one and keep faith only in your horse, your dog and your gun; that is, aside from God and your father of course.'

He cut short the handshake and then pointed shoreward, like hers, his own curiosity already had the better of him.

'That's a big piece of land out there, you still haven't told me which part of it you are bound for?'

'Gold country. My father's a miner; fossicker, some folks call him.'

Her reference to gold scurried insect-like inside his collar, raised the fine hairs at the back of his neck, his interest now that of a man brought to the boil by a hint of

5

new adventures. In the ship's meagre saloon bar, stories of untold wealth were eagerly set upon and devoured by gullible listeners, and for a ready supply of free liquor, cash-strapped carousers would roll out endless tails of good fortune, one upon the other. It seemed that Africa had opened her vaults to all comers; more gold nuggets and diamonds than all the pebbles scattered the length of England's rugged shoreline. Men were flocking from far afield as Australia and the Americas, migrant Cornish tin miners were already working reef whilst others prospected the first hints of alluvial diamond deposits some five hundred miles west of Rhodes' port of debarkation. His voice cracked and wavered between a sometimes, reedy falsetto and the more expected, deeper intonations of the young man.

'He knows how to mine, then?'

Kathleen nodded her head. She liked him; unlike those of other men, his smile was placatory and she sensed in him no untoward intentions, perhaps even a slight inexplicable alignment with her own femininity.

'Knows enough to get us by or reckon we would've starved by now. Why'd your folks give you that funny name?'

Rhodes smiled at her forthrightness.

'We all have our personal cross to bear and mine is a name some might choose to ridicule; nevertheless, they do not forget me. Rather a memorable name than the commonalty of 'our Albert' or 'our little William'. The name Cecil John Rhodes, I think you will agree has a certain exciting ring to it?'

Again, Kathleen nodded her head. His eyes seemed even bluer than before. As busy fingers they felt inside her head. His words, though concise and well enunciated sometimes flurried too fast, too clever for her to understand him fully.

'Changed my mind,' she said, 'your name's not funny, I like it.'

'Likewise to Kathleen O'Rourke,' Rhodes levelled the

playing field, 'splendid name.' He sprung the lid on his Hunter. 'Almost nine o'clock. An hour at the outside and they will be sending their boats to ferry us across the bar. We must ready ourselves for the onward journey.'

Once again they shook hands. He noted the shape of her fingers, long but not too slender, the nails short but not too chewed upon, her grip, like that of a boy was strong enough to take up the pick or shovel or even the rifle if called upon to do so. Now her eyes were more vibrant than the forest-greens behind her, he saw in them that solid, indomitable spirit of the adventurer and though their meeting was still within the bounds of its first half hour, already he had well acquainted himself with this young American and he knew that in some distant time their paths would once again collide.

Kathleen slipped his grip on her fingers.

'I'd best be going then, been nice talking. God grant us all strength enough to find what we're looking for.'

Rhodes tipped his hat to her.

'Time, that fickle master of all our destinies shall be the decider of that, young lady. I have it on good authority that a pair of your hardy, fossicker types have chanced upon rich showings of alluvial gold, somewhere close to the Blyde River; might well be worth your mentioning that to your father.'

'I will tell him, and thank you, Mister Rhodes. I hope your brother's cotton does well for you. Reckon you would make a better fist of things through fossicking though – same as my father. More excitement in digging up gold and diamonds than busting your back fighting off cotton jiggers – just a thought, mind.'

She smiled at him; perfect teeth, high, freckled cheeks. From behind those flouncing fiery tresses the eyes of a grown woman glittered intently. Laying aside the chance acquaintance, she nodded politely and turned on her heels.

'You've been gone for almost an hour.' Kathleen's father met her before she reached the companionway. He looked beyond her to the man at the railing. 'Saw you talking to the stranger. Not sure I agree with that.'

Kathleen stepped back up to the ship's side; she scowled her annoyance at lengths of discarded timber riding the ocean swell.

'Then I will say nothing of the gold men are finding, for chance that what he told me may well rile you up even more, father.'

'What're you saying?' Jim prompted her, 'mind that lip of yours young lady.' Before he could caution her further, Kathleen had turned to face him, grinning – then chuckling. Iridescent shades of green stirred by laughter and sunlight was the colour of her eyes.

'What's his name?' Jim's annoyance softened; already wrapped around her little finger, he allowed her the moment.

'Cecil Rhodes and don't you dare say anything awkward, father.'

He brushed past her and positioned himself at the railing, less than a yard away from where Rhodes watched with eager eyes for the first signs of a ferry boat putting out from the shore. He held out his hand, his intentions exploratory.

'Jim O'Rourke, Kathleen's father.'

Rhodes lifted his eyes from the ocean; in awe of the American's stature, he stood closer in to the railings and with his foot to the lowest bar, vainly he levered his height by an extra inch.

'Cecil Rhodes,' he accepted the outstretched hand, his grip light and lissom; the American's firm, big-boned and calloused. 'Your charming daughter and I were discussing the pros and cons of our landing in Africa. She mentioned your earning a living from mining?'

'I've done a bit,' Jim relaxed his grip, his mistrust for the stranger he now saw as unfounded, 'small placer deposits, mainly.'

Rhodes nodded his head. Like Kathleen's father he was

hungry for information.

'Then what I heard would suit you amicably,' his eyes glittered, 'these placer deposits? Forgive my ignorance, Mister O'Rourke, but would I be right in comparing them to the taking of gold from your Klondike riverbeds?' Like those of his daughter, Jim's eyes were a deep, Irish green.

'Near enough,' Jim said, 'the Black Hills don't give up their gold easily. Good ore when you find it, but patchy as hell – pot luck. On a good day a man can take out twenty ounces and more; next day she's gone, disappeared, and if the rain holds off for more than a month, not near enough water to feed your sluice box.'

'Gold and dry riverbeds,' Rhodes smiled ruefully, 'I have heard of the phenomenon, a cruel combination, Mister O'Rourke. However, from what I have been told, some hundreds of miles to the north of where we are disembarking men have already found first sightings of the precious metal in tributaries feeding a certain, Blyde River; also, for nine tenths of the year I believe there is water there in abundance.'

Rhodes' attention was suddenly diverted to a group of people further along the deck, their excitement spread and quickly he located its point of origin.

'The boats are coming. We should get a move on if we are to be amongst the first to set foot on dry land. Might I suggest we make the crossing *en masse*, Mister O'Rourke? Your insights to the art of mining gold have most certainly snared my interest.'

# -2-

The boat was rudimentary; wide-bottomed, jury-rigged with a small sail and clattering rowlocks. Four Zulu oarsmen set to the task of making landfall, all of them powerfully muscled, all were sweated up from britches belt to their glistening peppercorned heads and to Kathleen, all seemed bigger, blacker and more intensely overpowering than a Dakota winter's night. As they worked the heavy oars they sang the songs of old Africa, it was then that Kathleen found herself enchanted, enraptured even by the deep, bass thrum of that single, ancient voice. The helmsman noted her interest and quickly he intervened.

'Pay no interest to the blackies, lassie. Give 'em an inch and they'll have your arm off.'

'I like their singing,' Kathleen rounded on him, 'what's the harm in that?'

The helmsman scowled at her, angered by the rebuke his lips curled down at the corners and his nose, where it stuck out from his whiskers, Kathleen likened to the bulbous, sunburned snout of a Wessex pig.

'Don't know much about the Zulu, then. Have yer innards out as quick as look at you they will. Killers they are, savages every one of them. Partial to a piece of white meat if ever they gets the chance.' He winked an eye at Kathleen's father. 'You being a man of the world will know what I mean, I'm sure.'

Without warning he spun around and lashed out with his boot. Not breaking his rhythm on the oar, like a boxer, the Zulu ducked away from the blow and from under his breath, growled abuse at his overseer. Again the boot lashed out and struck the wooden bulkhead just inches away from the Zulu's knee.

'Keep your eyes to yerself you bastard savage or I'll have your four pence worth of wages.'

10

The Zulu lowered his gaze. Now was not the time. Shocked by the unprovoked act of violence most of the passengers lapsed into silence and stared fixatedly at the oarsman. Like frightened whitebait they shoaled together; mouths open, eyes wide, pale-faced and flaccid. Put to the spear, their bellies would pop like over-ripened figs in hot sunlight, but it was the helmsman he wanted… eyes first – flick them out with his thumbs – leave them dangling. With the razor edge of his spear he would open the white man's belly to the flies; left alive and entangled by his own entrails the *mabunu*, white pig would scream to his god for death to come quickly.

'Brazen heathen is all that they are,' the helmsman went on cursing and without shame lowered his gaze to the neck of Kathleen's blouse, 'never know what's going on in that filthy mind of his; keeps their womenfolk naked as the day they was born, they do.'

A single drop of sweat clung to the tip of his nose. Kathleen stared at it, willing the wind to gust it away.

'Best to keep 'em in their place, missy, you'll do well to remember that or they'll be at yer like dogs. I feeds them only a little and pays the bastards even less. That way when McKinnon speaks, the savages listens, or they'll sleep the night with empty bellies.'

Kathleen twisted sideways in her seat. Ocean water hissed against the hull, gulls dipped at its surface, close as they dared to the boat. Discarded, shore-borne flotsam folded in with the wake. She glanced sideways at the Zulu oarsman and smiled innocently; the acknowledgement was a mere flickering of the eyes before they were forcefully turned away. Above those of the others the Zulu's voice soared, and again, to Kathleen it was the rolling, velvet thunder of some far-off ancient storm.

'So where are you headed for?' The helmsman turned to Jim O'Rourke for an answer.

'Soon as we have supplies we head inland; north I reckon, gold country is what I'm after.'

Jim watched his face for signs of recognition.

'Around the Blyde River; heard there are good pickings to be had from the streams up there.'

McKinnon nodded his head and adjusted the lie of his tiller to suit the swell. The water was blue-green and blood-warm.

'Heard so, myself; long way to go if there's little or nothing though, and a long haul back if yer down and out on yer luck, matey.' He shook his head and spat a stream of tobacco juice over his shoulder. 'Diamond man myself.'

He swung his attention onto Cecil Rhodes.

'Thinking of trying my luck again, the Free State river diggings, same as that brother of yours.'

'Herbert...?' Rhodes leaned forward; surprised that McKinnon knew his name and even more intrigued by the man's reference to his brother's whereabouts. 'What do you know of him?'

'Know the man to speak to, nothing more. Told me you were on your way from Blighty. Heard your name mentioned. Showed me a likeness of you and him back home. Never still, always on the move, he is. Bit of a flibbertigibbet if my memory serves.'

'These river diggings...?' Rhodes pushed for information, 'good or bad, what did you make of them?'

'A year ago this next month,' eagerly, McKinnon took up on the subject, 'gets into your blood; put six months and every penny I possessed into searching for those bastard stones.' He shook his head at the memory and again, a stream of brown spittle shot from between his lips. Behind the boat, gulls screeched and fought each other for fish heads and rotting ribbons of shore-borne offal.

McKinnon reached inside the folds of a lightweight khaki jacket and from his waistcoat fob pocket drew out a battered silver timepiece.

'Plenty of small stuff and a couple of twenty-pointers, nothing to shout about. Found enough for me to pay the Kaffirs' wages and to feed myself from what was left, but

12

the big ones are there alright,' now his eyes glittered, 'I could smell the beauties; felt them burning holes into the soles of my boots I did.'

He sprung the watch's lid and held the timepiece close-in to his face.

Fixed to the fob ring, set to silver clasps and each to a separate silver chain were three, octahedral crystals of pure carbon, each no bigger than a green pea. Like the practiced hypnotist, McKinnon wittingly enthralled his audience. Allowing his hand to rock in time with the boat's slight yaw and dip, cleverly, he displayed the diamonds, twisting them full-on to the sunlight for best effect.

Veiled by the natural opacity of their uncut state their splendour remained subdued, though still the gems were able to release a fine show of colour; soft hues of pale lemon and open sky, as if they were indeed drops of stolen sunlight.

Fascinated, Kathleen was unable to tear her eyes from the precious stones.

'Might I hold them?'

McKinnon opened the clip that held the bauble to its fob ring, and where the chains were joined together, slowly, between finger and thumb he spun the tiny chandelier. As shards of broken rainbows the gems showed off their intrigue. Kathleen held out her hand.

'Just for a moment. I give you my word, boatman, I will not drop them.'

Reluctantly, McKinnon placed the stones in her palm; he was loath to lose them, for they were the first of those he had taken from the riverbed and through his cunning and the quickness of his tongue, many times had they won for him a night's free drinking and more often than not, the compliancy of some not so eager woman.

'Seen 'em ten times big as these,' McKinnon grinned at her, 'drives men mad, they do.'

Enthralled by the gems' reaction to sunlight, Kathleen studied them intently. Two were the colour of a pale, winter's sunrise; the third, half as big again and by far the brightest of the three was now a tear of blue rain to the girl's pink, upturned palm.

'Big as grapes,' McKinnon exaggerated and leaned in closer to Kathleen's place against the hull, 'the devil's luck is what yer needs to find them though. Hides them where you least expect.'

'How would I know a diamond when I see one?' Kathleen asked him, and without showing her revulsion for the stink of McKinnon's breath she carried forwards her eagerness to learn. 'In the riverbed, what do you look for that would set them aside from stones worth nothing?'

'Like the feel of fair skin to your fingertips,' McKinnon growled, and by lowering his voice, shielded his devilish intent from Kathleen's father. The girl was young, her face angelic and her body, lithe and long-legged, like that of a young filly ready to take its first run at the paddock fence. Not the straining of the oarsmen, nor the screech of squabbling gulls distracted him for one single moment from the sweetness of her tone. Voices roared inside his head and in the very pit of his stomach there awakened a terrible iniquitous need for release.

'I want to learn,' Kathleen held her nerve. 'The feelings you told me about, tell me more.' She caressed a single stone between her thumb and forefinger. 'Feels like soap...?' she encouraged, and then McKinnon, snatched back from some fantastical land of make-believe, nodded his head to her.

'And that it should, missy,' he licked his lips, 'slick as eels but hard as the devil's claws. Scratch anything they will, nothing on God's own earth any harder than that stone yer holding on to.'

Kathleen held the crystals aloft and like a purveyor of fine jewels allowed the sunlight to ignite their innermost fire.

McKinnon reached out his hand for the stones.

'Something else to tickle yer fancy.'

14

Like that of a lizard, the pink tip of his tongue parted his lips. He reached over the boat's stern planking and with a cupped hand scooped up a measure of sea water.

'Watch closely now,' he told Kathleen and wetted all three gems, 'tell me what you see.' Again he dipped the diamonds. 'Watch the water,' he insisted. 'Watch the water, girl and tell me what you see.'

'They stay dry,' Kathleen realised, 'the water does not stick to them...?' She looked at him for an explanation. 'Why is that?'

'Can't tell you,' McKinnon told her, 'just that I know that it happens; a mystery, same as them always feeling cold. Some say the devil himself made them that way before scattering them in rivers for fools like me to look for.' He clipped them back to the fob ring and pocketed the watch. The landing stage was now less than a hundred yards away. McKinnon put the tiller over, shouted instructions to the oarsmen and stood erect with the stern mooring line coiled and held at the ready.

Kathleen turned her concentration shoreward. Most of the buildings were roofed with tin, their walls put together with baked brick and bonded together with mud and cow dung. Everywhere the trees and grass were lush, thick and greener than any she had ever seen. Behind her, on the opposite side of the natural harbour, a lighthouse straddled the highest point of what the helmsman had referred to as the Bluff; the whitewashed beacon was the only one of its kind to be found anywhere along the entire length of Africa's eastern shoreline.

'Watch yer personals once ashore and keep yer children close and yer purses even closer,' McKinnon shouted over the excitement, 'or the Kaffirs will have them both off yer.' He gloated over the power he wielded. 'One of them to roast and the other to spend on women and liquor.'

The chatter eased, replaced by apprehension and mute excitement. Only yards away from Africa, and after so many weeks at sea this boatload of pink-skinned settlers stretched their necks for a better view and on shaking legs yearned for the feel of solid ground beneath their feet. McKinnon put out the mooring line and soon enough the boat was tied up solid to her allotted place on the staging.

# -3-

Kathleen looked about her; the crowd was thick with mysterious black faces, different smells and different sounds. She moved closer to Cecil Rhodes and touched his shoulder.

'Should there be someone here to meet you?'

'My brother, supposedly.' Rhodes screwed his eyes at the dust and strong sunlight. 'Never was one for punctuality, though. Works as and when the mood takes him, otherwise quick to show an interest in the crown and anchor board and a goodly filling of grog whenever he gets the chance.' He smiled at her and his eyes sparkled. 'May have changed for the better, but I doubt it, Herbert and his addictions were always hard to prise apart.' The smile spread to a wide grin and he pushed back his hat to leave a pale band across his forehead. 'Have to say though, that I love him dearly. If Herbert is not here to meet me, then there will no doubt be other, more pressing business interests in need of his attention. A pot of gold perhaps, some treasure map or whatever fanciful dreams he conjured up from the night before.'

Kathleen, intimidated by the differences of this multi-coloured boiling pot, took to the protection of her father; all around her, shifty-eyed urchins drifted in and out of the crowd. Hawkers shouldered baskets filled with exotic fruits and squawking fowl and the air was thick with the aroma of Indian spices, that of dampened earth and the piss from a hundred people steaming off of it. In with all

16

of this, held by a slow breeze was the permanent smell of curing fish, wafting in from rows of rickety smoking racks further along the shoreline, determinedly the alien smell of smoked fish coated the lining of Kathleen's throat.

Most of the *Eudora*'s passengers were now ashore, like sheep they moved as a single organism in search of shade; pale-skinned and heavily rashed with prickly heat they were all of them at odds with Natal's extreme humidity.

'Over there!' Kathleen directed Rhodes' attention. 'The man with the whiskers, he's waving to you. I reckon he knows who you are.'

At the crowd's extremity and standing upright from the driver's seat of a stationary Cape cart, a middle aged, portly gentleman caught Rhodes' eye and like a ship's signaller, vigorously he waved his arms, gesticulating for him to come across.

'Wait here for me,' Rhodes told her, 'let's find out what he's after. I would appreciate you and your father keeping an eye on my personals.'

Rhodes made his way back from the quayside. Kathleen followed his progress and was aware of him and the bearded stranger talking animatedly. Within those next few minutes, Rhodes' baggage was whisked away by grinning Indian boys, their actions carefully orchestrated, their every movement continually overseen by the man on the Cape cart. Rhodes' arm went up.

'He's calling us over, Pa.'

Without waiting, Kathleen picked up as much as she could carry and fought her way forwards. Already the sun had burned the back of her neck and forearms. Sweat had dampened her hair so that it lay plastered flat against her forehead.

Fitted with tempered steel springs and sleek, rubber-shod wheels the Cape cart projected an aura of speed, comfort and lightness of build and was at that moment being given the once-over by a dozen or so appreciative onlookers. A white canvas duck hood shaded the cart's upholstered

17

leather interior and a matched pair of bay geldings stood patiently to harness. Rhodes' portmanteau and other personal packages had already been loaded and easily they filled the width of the cart's rear seat. In front, Rhodes himself sat smugly alongside his benefactor and from his allotted emplacement took in everything. Herbert, Cecil's older brother had been unable to make good his promised welcome, for having been cursed with that fickle spirit of the adventurer had some weeks prior to the arrival of the sail ship *Eudora*, been lured away from the mundanity of growing cotton by other supposed, more lucrative horizons.

Filled with wonderment, Rhodes' eyes were never still. His senses jarred and struggled for points of recognition, but found few. Strange tongues, overpowering smells, those of rotting fruits and heady spices, and even the air itself seemed heavily laced with a thousand untapped adventures. With a woman's guile, from behind a line of thickly wooded hills the hinterland crooked her finger and smiled for him to venture onwards into the unknown; it was there that his eyes settled and in that alluring smile he found those first glimmerings of his life in Africa, those first slender threads of his own fate were already unravelling before him. However, driven by excitement and that sudden urge for him to journey inland, his chest tightened, constricting his airways. Recognising the debilitating effects of his malaise he calmed himself and turned his attentions back to the comparative timidity of his listening in.

Dr Peter Sutherland leaned sideways from the driver's bench; his balding pate glistened with sweat. He focused on Kathleen's father and from a forest of facial hair, his words, though invisibly formed, tumbled out.

'Pietermaritzburg old boy, sixty miles or so from where we are standing. Enquire at any establishment along the main street and you will be given directions to our home, Gardenscliffe. Mile at the most from your intended route

– a firm bed and a hot meal await you both.'

Kathleen's father contemplated the offer, the sun was at its zenith and with the back of his hand he wiped the sweat from his forehead.

'I would think myself presumptuous, sir. You barely know me?'

'Nonsense! I insist. My wife and I would be most perturbed if you rode on without overstaying for at least one night. Duty bound, old boy. You're new to Africa. Any help and good advice from a fellow chum should be accepted with alacrity.'

'I meant no disrespect.'

'None taken old boy,' he leaned closer, 'didn't catch your name, or may have forgotten. Memory's not what it used to be?'

'O'Rourke,' he held out his hand, 'Jim to my friends.'

Sutherland accepted the offering and returned the handshake vigorously. 'Mine's Peter. My wife and mentor whom you will meet later, is called Jane.' He patted his stomach. 'Too damned good in the kitchen and a more compliant companion a man could never come by.' He swivelled sideways and like some owlish schoolmaster, peered at the young man sitting alongside him; pale and pink and neatly wrapped in braided jacket and stiff white collar, subdued by the goings on around him, Cecil Rhodes resembled the bookkeeper's dowdy clerk.

'Sun is what you are short of lad, and goodly amounts of fresh air.' He pressed the reins to Rhodes' fingers. 'Hold on to them; quietly mind or you'll have us half way home minus our hats and baggage.'

He swung round and like a weather vane caught by a sudden gust of wind, again the arm shot out.

'Forgot to mention, old boy, second name's Sutherland – Natal's Surveyor General-cum-geologist-cum-general dogsbody, take that as you will.' He spotted Kathleen. 'Your daughter, I presume?' Armed with a convivial smile he looked to her for acknowledgement. Kathleen nodded her head, unperturbed by the impromptu introduction.

'Kathleen, sir.' She fixed him with those green eyes. Sutherland saw the cheek in them and warmed to her.

'Make sure of your father's dropping in, young lady. Two girls of my own, you know. Without a doubt you will mix in well.'

Kathleen dipped her head politely.

'I look forward to meeting them, sir.'

'And so you shall,' he promised, 'so you shall – enough fresh lemonade and sticky buns to feed the entire Zulu nation.'

He turned back to Kathleen's father.

'You'll be staying here to purchase transport and so forth?'

'Horses, rifles, and such like,' Jim concurred, 'from experience, what would you advise?'

Thoughtfully, Sutherland gazed outwards from the shoreline.

'Accommodation first and foremost old boy. Suggest you look sharp, the steamship *Cambrian* will supposedly be dropping anchor in the roadstead later this afternoon. If she has made the journey without mishap, every boarding house along the waterfront will be filled to bursting. A good night's sleep and an early breakfast and then get yourself along to Jooster's sale yard. Tell that idle excuse of a proprietor it was I who sent you or the scoundrel will double his prices. You're new here, prepare to be taken advantage of and watch your purse – in the shadow of every honest man walks a dozen quick-fingered villains. For the Queen's silver they would willingly bleed the veins of their own mother.'

Jim laughed at the analogy.

'Sounds more like the backstreets of Dublin.'

'Far worse if the pickings are good enough. Nevertheless, should not take any more than a few days for you to find what you're after. Again, be careful of what you purchase. For your weaponry stay away from the exotics; stick with the better known calibres. Couple of good fowling pieces will prove invaluable and with the right load, besides bringing food to your table will prove more than good enough to knock down any attacker at twenty yards.'

'I cannot thank you enough,' said Jim.

'Save your energy, lad. Avail yourself of the road north before the rains break or you'll be up to your fetlocks in mud and blood-sucking insects; jars of embrocation in case of bites and stings, add them to your list, a dozen at least. I'll warrant you will both be grateful for the relief they bring.'

He tugged at his whiskers.

'Forgive me for asking, but would I be right in assuming you have funding enough for your venturing inland? A good wagon and sound oxen will knock a fair sized hole in any man's pocket.'

'We have come adequately prepared,' Jim smiled, 'enough, at least to see us through these next twelve months.'

Sutherland brightened. 'Splendid! Then I will leave you to it.' He took back the reins and pointed his whipstock at the waterfront. 'That's your way, old boy.' He winked an eye at Kathleen. 'And don't forget your stopping over, young lady. I shall keep a sharp eye out for your arrival.'

'I shall make certain of it. Your daughters' names, sir, how do you call them?'

'Elizabeth and Charlotte; Charlotte is the eldest and somewhat of a tearaway, same age as you I should imagine. Little Elizabeth is the gentler of the two and the apple of her father's eye.'

Sutherland turned his attention back to Jim.

'Almost forgot. Seek out a man who knows a thing or two about horses. Pay him for the information if need be, or the beasts will be dead and rotting alongside the road within a month of your leaving.' He sensed confusion and elaborated. '*Ngana*, old boy; horse sickness. Purchase with caution; salted horses only. Wheedle out the Boer horse trader and buy your stock from him.'

'How will I know him?'

Sutherland smiled at his naiveté.

'The eyes, man; dark as the devil's on All Hallows' Eve. They have the wilderness in them. When you make your acquaintance with the town's *Meneer* Jooster, I'm sure you will understand.'

He settled a battered old Homburg squarely against his ears and nodded politely to the newcomers.

'I'll be getting along then. Two days full journeying and three stops to rest the horses. Damned nuisance,' he wiped a trickle of sweat from his brow, 'damned long way and most of it uphill old boy. Take it slowly or you'll beggar your horses before you reach the half way mark. Make sure you find me out once you reach the town of 'maritzburg. Drop in on us, Jim, I am sure you will find the experience much to your liking.'

Without waiting for a reply he gathered the reins and turned his team towards the beginnings of a rutted track. Rhodes leaned out from the cart; looking back, he waved his hat and shouted his farewells to Kathleen.

# -4-

'How long will you be wanting to stay?'

The proprietor's eyes were small and rat-like. In the lamp's guttering half-light, though less than middle-aged, the woman standing across from Jim was now the wheedling shrew. Eagerly she sniffed the scent of coin from his breeches pocket.

'A week – no longer,' Jim told her.

'Just you and the girl?'

'My daughter.'

'Of course.' Her eyes shot sideways and settled on

Kathleen. 'How old?'

'Fifteen.'

'Two adults, then.' She wrote slowly, the nib of her pen sparsely loaded with Indian ink; claw-like it scratched their details along a vacant line in the register.

Her eyes came up and levelled with Jim's.

'Your name? Can't be too careful, fly-by-nights cost me a pretty bob or two; at least until my husband catches up with them.'

'O'Rourke. First name, Jim.'

She blew on the ink, intolerant of the time it took to dry. Like her writing, her eyes were jet black, those of a raven, Kathleen decided.

The woman waited, her pen poised.

'Any forwarding address?'

'Pietermaritzburg. The Surveyor General.' Jim saw the change in her and took advantage. 'Doctor Sutherland. We'll be staying with him and his family at Gardenscliffe for a week or so.'

She dropped her eyes, again she bowed her head to the register and the pen flurried. A single string of iridescent pearls, harvested from off the southern tip of Al Muharraq swung in time with her writing. Her hair, swept back from a pale forehead was fastened at the nape by a cluster of those same, pink pearls. Jim pegged her age at early thirties though in her voice he saw the steadfastness of a much older woman.

'Six shillings a day for the pair of you, including your breakfasts.' She glanced across the room at Kathleen. 'Will you be sharing?'

'Separate rooms,' Jim told her. 'When do I pay?'

The raven's eyes flashed.

'Half in advance, the rest when you leave. Simpler that way, saves for any unforeseen aggravation.' She pointed out a narrow staircase. 'Upstairs. Last two doors but one on the right; closet at the end and three pence extra for hot water.'

'The rooms...'

'Are clean,' she cut him short, 'roach-free and the sheets are fresh on this morning.' She held out her hand, palm upwards. 'A guinea, Mister O'Rourke, leave earlier and I'll refund you what's owing.'

She pocketed the money and looked past him.

'Your luggage, would that be all of it?'

Jim nodded his head. 'Along with the saddle, six pieces.'

She glanced sideways. An eager, olive-skinned Indian boy stepped from the shadows. His hair, slicked back from his forehead was thick and black and shone with oil pressed from the fruit of the coconut palm.

'The coolie will take up your bags. Tip the lad if you choose to do so, but not too much mind.'

Jim got the measure of him; barely reaching up to his shoulder, the boy appeared as weak in the leg and no wider across the chest than an English taproom whippet, but his eyes were bright and his smile willing. Two of their bags were eagerly gathered up and like a pair of rabbits to the fox's den were dragged inside the stairwell. Kathleen followed them up. The stairs were poorly lit and every step groaned and creaked like some ancient lugger beset by rough seas. She matched the spread of her hand to marks left on the wall. Some were twice the size of her own whilst others were small, tiny even – the hand prints of children, left there from their paddling upwards through the dark, one hand on the step, the other against the wall.

'This is your room, Miss – number nine and very close to the convenience.' The boy pushed back the door and dragged the cases inside. 'From here you can see the ships and everywhere along the street.'

He drew back a single curtain and left the window ajar. Salt air and sunlight poured inside the room; humid sunlight and windless heat bounced from off the tin roofs.

'I will now be fetching the other bags,' he told Kathleen. He grinned at her; his skin was a lustrous nut-brown, his teeth white as the lime-washed wall behind him.

Kathleen nodded her thanks and moved to the window. Waterfront smells rose up to her; sickly scents of rotting fruit and salt. Hot to her face she relished the sunlight; the sight of deep forests across the bay evoked in her an unexplained expectancy of this strange adopted land.

Still on the roadstead, the *Eudora* rode to anchor. A mile to starboard, after an eleven week voyage and having been becalmed for thirteen days in the doldrums, the *Monsoon*, a barque of some two hundred and ninety-six tons had, within that last hour put out her anchor. The tide was on the point of turning; slack and indecisive the water muddled amongst the stagings, discarded timber and old fruit rode the swell. Kathleen craned her neck and leaned from the window, less than a stone's throw away from where she watched, the waterfront bustled, readying itself for that next boatload of migrants to be ferried in from across the bar.

'What have you seen?' Kathleen's father knelt on the bed.

'Watching the people,' Kathleen told him. 'Reckon they're waiting for the next lot to come ashore. So many colours. Over there,' she alerted her father, 'black, white, brown and Chinese, I think.'

Jim watched with her. The waterfront had come alive. Different people, a dozen different races, all of them flung together by chance, united through common cause, all had but one thing on their mind – the wherewithal to scratch out a living.

Kathleen's arm shot out in front of her. 'Past the *Eudora*, Pa! Another ship – I can see her smoke.'

From out of the haze, the *Cambrian* loomed ghostly grey and compared to the sail ships already anchored off the Bluff, she was gargantuan and magnificent. From the far Cape she had taken the journey in a single stretch and now, though still some five miles out, she approached her final destination; the eager, iron leviathan.

'Sutherland was right,' Jim mused, 'there will be upwards

of a hundred souls aboard that ship. By tonight, every vacant room within ten miles of here will be spoken for.'

'Then we should move now, father, or our searching out what we need will be made all the more difficult.'

'What about something to eat?'

'Later.' Kathleen insisted and turned for the door. The woman in her had awakened and was eager to get things done. 'A couple of hours at best before the shelves are emptied. Besides your horses and guns there are a hundred other things for us to look for.' Excitement flashed in her eyes. 'The sooner we show our money, the better our choice will be. By tomorrow night there will be nothing left worth buying.'

# -5-

Jim noted the change in his daughter; she walked with purpose, her shoulders squared and with her head held high. About her face, her hair, gilded with African sunlight whipped as a copper mane to an onshore wind. There appeared a jaunty spring to her step and with each new turn of her head she discovered exciting, unfamiliar sights to marvel over and from them she chose her needs for their journey to the hinterland. Deftly she sorted through stalls and rummaged the shelves of a hundred waterfront traders. She haggled over price and more often than not came away more suited than the vendor. Quickly her basket filled and was just as quickly carried away and emptied; twice she returned to her room and her latest acquisitions were neatly laid in rows across her bed. Sewing needles and cotton thread, embrocation and cures for dysentery and fever were but a small portion of what she had bought.

'We need guns and good horses,' Jim reminded her, and

under sufferance, Kathleen followed her father away from bric-a-brac-loaded market stalls.

On Sutherland's advice, Jim made his way from the waterfront and a few hundred yards inland he found what he was looking for.

Big and built of rough timber and native stone, the trading establishment stood four-square to a background of thick forest. A large sign, emblazoned with Jooster's name and business credentials in black lettering had been nailed to the building's frontage. To either side were wide paddocks, fenced with post and rail and shaded in part by young mahogany and clumps of fever trees. A man's deep voice spirited out from the ether.

'Horses such as the one you are looking at, *engelsman* do not come cheap.'

'Nor did I expect them to. The gelding and the little mare – a fair price for the two of them?'

'Just the horses?'

'More if your prices match up to my expectations. I was told you are a man of conscience. Peter Sutherland, the Surveyor-General put me on to you.'

Hendrik Stephanus Jooster stepped from behind a broken cart, dropped his tools and waved for Jim to follow him inside.

Taller than Kathleen's father, Jooster leaned against the counter top, about his full lips, beard hair, dark as a starless winter's night ruffled from his breathing. The eyes, as Sutherland had warned were fierce and fanciful, flecked with gold at their centres and black as those thickly tangled curls about his chin.

'You have money?'

Jim nodded to the Afrikaner.

'Enough for my needs.'

'The needs of men are sometimes those of the devil. What are yours, *engelsman*?'

Jim tolerated the Afrikaner's banter. He needed information.

27

'The Blyde River, what do you know of it?'

The man's face softened and it was then, Jim recognised the Afrikaner's deep yearning for the wilderness. Slowly, Jim's eyes adjusted to the half-light of the trader's store. Stacked from floor to ceiling were a thousand items, shelved in orderly rows; bundled and priced, all of them were the accoutrements of the hunter, the farmer and the prospector.

'Elephant country,' Jooster reminisced and like a nodding bear settled his weight to the counter. 'Were I not a husband and father of four, perhaps I would go with you. Thirty years I hunted the banks of the Crocodile River for elephant teeth and buffalo meat.' Like those of a man besotted, his eyes half closed at the recollection. 'From the *Soutpansberg* to the river mouth, the valley was my home. The creek of wagons, *engelsman*,' wistfully, his gaze raised up to the roof, 'the stars at night and even more comforting than a woman, the feel of a long gun pressed against your side.'

'A man cannot live alone forever,' Jim argued, 'the power of a gun never falters, but the eye that sights the barrel grows weak and without a woman's hand on his shoulder, a man's aim will soon waver.'

Jooster threw back his head and roared at the analogy.

'I like you, *engelsman*. You make a worthy preacher. *Kom* – first we look to your fancy and then I take your money.'

Jim and Kathleen stood at the paddock fence and watched the Afrikaner exhibit his skills. Both horses stood quietly for him to saddle and neither one attempted to bolt or lash out. Jooster nodded to Kathleen for her to follow his lead and with the agility of a man half his size, swung up onto the gelding. With the lightest touch from his heels he coaxed the horse into a slow walk. Smiling from behind that great beard he encouraged Kathleen to mount up.

'Ride her, *meisie*. She will not hurt you, but beware, she is young and feisty. Sit with soft feet to her flanks.'

Kathleen ducked between the fence poles and without

fear she outstretched her hand for the filly to find her scent.

'You have ridden before?'

'Since I was three years old. I could ride before I could read and that's the truth.'

The filly nuzzled her fingertips; Kathleen took a hold on the bridle and with the filly's wide red nostrils close to her own, quietly she blew in her breath and the animal calmed. Unashamedly, she wrapped her skirt about her thighs, kicked off her shoes and lightly as a ballerina, swung up into the saddle. With her bare toes she found the stirrup irons.

'What should I call her?'

The filly whickered softly and cocked an ear at the sound of Kathleen's voice.

'She knows the name, *Umoya*,' Jooster told her, 'the Zulu word for wind.'

Lightly, Kathleen brought her heels to bear and the filly responded.

Jooster watched them; cast by shadow and sunlight to that of a single form, horse and rider jinked between the trees. With soft hands, Kathleen guided the filly away from harm and like the zephyr upon the surface of a lake they seemed to glide above the ground.

Jooster dismounted and stood alongside Kathleen's father.

'She is yours, *engelsman*. Sixty pounds and for another twenty, the saddle and bridle.'

'Horse sickness?' Jim brought the subject to the fore. 'Sutherland warned of purchasing unsalted stock?'

Jooster smiled at the inference. 'She was sired in the low country. Six months ago, along with her dam and six others I brought them south to Natal. Not a single one has died from that cursed disease. Travel no further north than the goldfields and you will suffer no losses.'

'And the gelding?' Jim looked towards the other horse, 'along with the filly – how much for the pair?'

'The same for the gelding,' Jooster told him, 'One hundred and twenty pounds for the both of them.'

'Your word on them making the journey? Save for feeding the dogs, dead horses are worth nothing.'

Jooster's face hardened. 'Only God Himself can see what lies ahead, *engelsman*. Hendrik Jooster sells only good salted horses. Leave them where they stand if you are not satisfied. By tomorrow night every horse within twenty miles of my yard will be sold, and for twice the price. Already there are two more ships waiting their turn on the roadstead.'

Jim extended his hand to Jooster.

'Your price is fair, and whatever it takes for a few days' feed.'

'And you pay me now?'

'I pay you now,' Jim agreed.

Jooster accepted the hand.

'You said there are other things you are in need of? *Kom engelsman*, Hendrik Jooster keeps many things in his store, not all of them are left out here for thieves to pick over.' He herded Jim towards the rear wall and looked to Kathleen for her to stay outside with the horses.

A solid mahogany door had been let into the stonework; Jooster threw the lock and pushed the door back on its hinges. The windows of the adjoining room were generously barred with iron and from between them, reluctant sunlight found its way inside. Jim stood at the centre of the room and silently, he stared in awe of Jooster's trade goods.

The room smelled of leather and lamp oil; it glittered with glass, steel and brass fittings and its wide shelves were filled to overflowing.

Along the full length of the north wall, rifles of twenty different origins and calibres stood stock to stock in their racking, the deep patina of oiled steel and old walnut drew Jim over. One particular piece caught his eye and like a moth to the flickering flame, he went straight to it.

'.44 Winchester carbine,' Jim nodded his head to Jooster, 'I would have picked it out from a hundred yards – had one stolen from my horse, back home in Dakota.'

Jooster lifted it down from the rack.

'She's a beauty, *engelsman*. Saddle-ring carbine, fifteen shot repeater.' He worked the loading lever and lifted the weapon to his shoulder. 'Not so good for buffalo or lions but for food on your table and knocking down Kaffirs at two hundred yards, she is perfect.'

'Ammunition?' Jim queried.

'As much as you can carry, brass-cased .44 Henry rim fire.'

He handed the weapon to Jim and watched him delight in the carbine's feel and balance. Like Jooster, as though it were an extension of his own arm, Jim worked the lever action and recalled from memory the smoothness and alacrity of its performance; the sounds and touch of moving steel thrilled his fingertips and the rifle's bronze frame glowed as old gold when touched upon by incoming sunlight.

'Yellow Boy Winchester carbine.' Jim gave reverence to it and with a lover's fingers he stroked the yellow, flat-sided frame that gave the weapon its nickname. The stock, where it had been fashioned to meet with the shoulder was finished in yellow brass and standing proud of that same walnut stock, a steel bar and saddle-ring were there for the soldier's clip-on shoulder harness. The barrel still glowed with that fine, grey patina of the nurtured weapon; in all, the rifle showed no outward signs of overuse.

'The scabbard I throw in for free,' Jooster added and smiled wryly, knowing full well that the deal was already done.

'How much?'

Without any hesitation, Jooster put the price to him.

'To you *engelsman*? Thirty pounds – the bargain of your lifetime.'

'More than twice the price when the weapon was new,'

31

Jim said, but nodded his head in agreement. The price was exorbitant, but fair; Africa was a long way away from the Winchester's birthplace. Again they shook hands and then Jooster pointed to where the shadows were at their deepest. 'Something else I think will tickle your fancy. The ship you travelled with, the *Eudora*, only a few hours ago, her captain brought me this.'

He led Jim across the room, struck a Vesta against the wall and held the flame to the wick of an oil lamp. The flame guttered, then held steady. He held the lamp at head height for it to cast a favourable light on the treasure.

'Is it not a thing of wonderment, *engelsman*? Only the second one of its kind have I held in my own two hands.'

This time, Jim did not wait for the Afrikaner to lift the weapon from its placing – the Sharps rifle, though of heavier build than the Winchester was at the peak of its magnificence. Unscarred, the barrel was still blue-black, clean as a prairie winter's night and there was more – a deadliness, a fearsome power, the ultimate killing piece and at a distance of eight hundred yards, the Sharps was just as adept at bringing down the running man as it was the great American bison.

'The barrel?' Jim asked and the without speaking, Jooster took the rifle from him. He worked the breechblock lever and held the opened weapon close-in to the lamplight.

'Look for yourself, *engelsman*. The barrel has been relined; no pits no rust. The gun is clean.'

Slick from lack of use, the rifling was free of any acidic residue left by burnt powder; three spiralled grooves gleamed bright as oiled glass from the ingress of lamplight. Centred on the rifle's left side, the letters DFC, the manufacturer's inspection cartouche, had been stamped into the walnut stock. Jim recognised it immediately.

'New model carbine,' he got in first, 'upgraded to take the latest .50 metal jacket cartridge.' He looked at Jooster and smiled. 'Tell me you have the cartridges to go with the gun and I'll take her.'

'More than three hundred brass jackets,' Jooster nodded and shot his price at Jim, 'seventy-five pounds including the cartridges, a fair amount even for an American. The scabbard I will make myself. By tomorrow night it will be ready for you.'

Jim nodded his head in agreement.

'Half now and the rest in two days.'

'What else, *engelsman*?'

'I take the Winchester with me; now, today.'

Jooster smiled. He could not lose.

'Half now and if you do not return our agreement will be over. I will sell my horses and the Sharps for a second time.' The smile widened. 'Watch your step and that of your girl. The waterfront at night is not the place to be when a ship the size of the *Cambrian* makes her landfall. Sleep with one eye open, dead men have no need of a horse, nor the need for a Sharps rifle.'

# -6-

By the following evening, every vacant room along the waterfront had been taken and more often than not, let for double the going rate. Boarding houses that for most of the year stood empty of clientele were now filled to bursting, and where the *Cambrian*'s crewmen collapsed dead drunk in blind alleys, there they were left – easy pickings for thieves, and rats the size of half-grown terriers.

'I'll thank you to leave the front door locked, Mister O'Rourke. After dark, those who wish to drink must enter and leave through the side door.' The proprietor pushed home the deadbolts, only then did she visibly relax and for the first time since his signing the register did Jim notice the faintest hint of a smile.

'Will you be taking a drink yourself, Mister O'Rourke?' The smile stayed. 'Or do all Irishmen abstain from strong liquor for chance the Lord Himself is looking on?'

She moved back behind the reception counter top and leaned on her elbows. Under the covering of her bodice her breasts were firm, like filled sails they rose and fell in time with her breathing.

'An acquaintance of yours has been asking after you. The ferryman, Mister McKinnon...?'

Jim nodded his head.

'What is he after?'

'Heard you were staying here,' she told him, 'said you were a mining man and a fossicker like himself.' She looked sideways along the corridor. 'He's in there now, thought you might find the time to take a drink with him.' Like the black brooch at her throat, her eyes glowed. 'I could join you Mister O'Rourke; nights when there are good sized ships anchored in the bay I find more interesting. A more varied clientele you might say.'

'Your husband?' Jim pointed out. 'He wouldn't take kindly to you being in there with me and McKinnon.'

'Your daughter?'

'Asleep,' Jim said.

'Then she will not begrudge her father a little time to himself, I'm sure.'

She took him by the arm and led him down the corridor. Strains of Waltzing Matilda filtered out from behind the heavily curtained door. 'Australian gold diggers,' she explained and momentarily, cocked her head for the music. 'Six of them up from the Cape and as luck would have it eager to lose a penny or two at my crown and anchor tables.'

'You still haven't told me your name,'

'Mary,' she told him, 'Mary McKinnon.'

Like shattered coal her eyes sparkled and in that small space between the curtain and the door she pushed him back against the wall; without hesitation she drove her tongue deep inside his mouth and with frantic hands worked her way inside his shirt.

'McKinnon's my husband,' she moaned, 'the door's locked from this side, and there's no need to worry, the bastard knows what I'm like.'

# -7-

McKinnon sat with his back to the wall, at waist-height a layer of grey tobacco smoke swirled about the room. Jim likened the smells to those that seeped from deep below the quarterdeck of the *Eudora* – the stench of human sweat and vomit; that of steaming piss and a hundred unwashed poor souls confined to steerage. Oblivious to the discomfort, McKinnon looked up from his place alongside the crown and anchor table.

'Mister O'Rourke, the American gent with an eye for our goldfields.' His face hardened. 'And my dearest, darling wife – what took you so long, woman?' His eyes dropped to the front of her blouse, the top two buttons had been left undone, with the slightest wink of an eye he acknowledged her conquest and then looked sideways. 'The big one in the corner, blonde hair; been waiting more than hour, lassie. Make sure he leaves with a smile on his face, as well as empty pockets.' He turned back to Jim. 'Sit down, Jim. Sit down, sit down. Your daughter not with you...?'

'Asleep.'

'Mary gave her the end room, only one with a view of the ocean. Pretty little thing,' McKinnon's eyes glittered, 'and sharp as a tack I'd say. What would she be now? Sixteen almost and going on trouble...?'

'She's fifteen,' said Jim, 'but with the tongue of a cheeky thirty year old in that fiery head of hers. More of her

35

mother in there than she realises.'

McKinnon grinned at the comment and lifted his arm. A Chinese girl picked up on the gesture, swept through the smoke and stopped alongside him.

'My bottle, Mei-Lien,' he hooked his arm about her waist, 'the special, McKinnon reserve, my darlin', you know the one I mean; and two clean glasses quick as you please.'

The girl bowed her head; however, stoically, like some obedient child she fixed her eyes on the far wall and waited for McKinnon's hand to exit itself from inside her skirt.

'Not one of my girls is more than sixteen years old,' McKinnon bragged, 'mixed themselves in with the coolie contract labourers; dress like boys they do to get free passage over here, but Mary picks them out for me; finds 'em down and out near the waterfront, grateful of a bed and food they are.' His eyes swung back on his wife. Already, her hands were well occupied below the level of the tabletop. 'Works well for the both of us.' He caught her eye and commended her actions with a slight nod of his head. 'I gets 'em young and in return my darlin' Missus McKinnon over there gets to fuck whoever takes her fancy.'

Mei-Lien came out from behind a curtain; she carried a black bottle and two thick-cast shot glasses. Mesmerised by the girl's slightness of build, Jim watched her approach; dressed in coloured brocade and delicate sandals she seemed to float above the surface of the floor. Doll-like, the Chinese girl extended her tiny arms and like a butterfly alighting a fragile flower, carefully she set down the bottle and glasses in front of McKinnon. For a moment, she smiled at Jim; tiny mouth, tiny rosebud lips, jet black eyes. Her hands were those of a child, her fingers slender, the colour of pale butter, like the ivory-coloured keys of the piano crashing away at the far side of the room. Intuitively, McKinnon picked up on the interest.

'A guinea for the night, Jim,' he winked an eye and with his finger and thumb made lewd, suggestive movements, 'like a squirrel's ear,' he grinned and took his time pulling the cork on the black bottle. Thickly swollen, but lubricated, the cork squealed away from its hole in the narrow neck. 'Trust me when I say that I know, Jim boy, been down there a few times myself.'

'What's in the bottle?' Jim asked McKinnon.

'Rum, laddie. Bit 'o the good stuff, black as ship's tar and thick as the devil's blood.' He poured both glasses full to the brim. 'Here's to good health and a bucket full o' gold for the both of us.'

McKinnon downed the rum in a single gulp. He smiled at Jim to follow his lead.

Jim complied and emptied his glass. At first, only the taste of sweet roasted spirit coated his mouth; thick with the juices of wild cane sugar harvested from along the banks of the Tugela.

'Good,' he nodded his head at McKinnon, 'sweet with a fiery edge to it, hot as hell on the throat, but very, very good.'

Again, McKinnon raised his hand to Mei-Lien. With a slight nod of her head she acknowledged his instruction and quick as a whippet she disappeared behind the curtain.

'Would you be the kind of man who takes a smoke, Jim?'

'If the company suits,' Jim countered, and already the warmth in his gut had reached upwards for his cheeks; even his ears felt warm, as if he were sitting outside in the heat of full sun.

Mei-Lien left an opened box of Cuban cigars on the table. The cigars were tightly rolled, their dark outer leaf still pliant and slightly moist to the touch. McKinnon reached inside and drew out a pair of thick, Ramon Allones. He handed one to Jim and leaned back in his chair.

'From your neck of the woods. Twelve weeks out from San Francisco, compliments of the skipper of *Dawn Star*.'

He clipped the end and tossed the silver cutter to Jim. 'Real adventurous gent; taste for the unusual and always quick to part with his money.' He held a lighted Vesta to the cigar and pulled evenly until the air about his head was thick with blue smoke, then slid the Vestas across the table and again, reached for the bottle. He refilled both glasses and with an experienced eye looked about him, assessing the monetary clout of his clientele. His wife and the blonde-haired sailor had already left the room.

'So you're a gold miner?'

Jim nodded his head. 'Last twenty years. Once a miner, always a miner; don't have a flair for anything else.' He leaned forward, filled his mouth with rum, swallowed and fired his first question at McKinnon. 'Going off what you have heard, what are my chances of finding gold near the Blyde? Yesterday morning, back on the boat, you said you knew the area.'

McKinnon shook his head.

'Stories, Jim, rumours. Africa churns out more than her fair share.' He picked up his glass and from between his lips, blew it full to the brim with raw cigar smoke. Trapped within the confines of the glass wall, as an inch thick layer of mist it floated there. 'Like I said, long way to go if there's nothing there. Reckon you'd do better working the rivers for sparklers, matey.'

McKinnon put the glass to his lips and whilst he filled his mouth with rum, simultaneously, he drew the swirling cigar smoke in through his nostrils.

'Watched a man sell on a big blue-white; size of a dove's egg and damn near colourless it was, came away with more money than most men would see in a lifetime.'

'So the clearer the stone, the higher the value?'

'The clearer the better, matey,' McKinnon's eyes glittered, 'fancies, they calls the coloured ones. Yellows and browns and black even, but it's the colourless ones that's wanted the most; fetches their finder the highest prices they do.' He winked an eye at Jim and smiled ruefully. 'It's the clear stones what throws out all the colours and shines the brightest, once they're cut that is. Clearer the stone, more's the sparkle, needs to be deep in the girdle though, enough for a good cutter to work his magic, but they're a hundred times harder to find, Jim boy. That's what London's high society ladies wants; a three carat colourless stone, bright as winter's starlight and there isn't a woman on God's fair earth who won't fall flat on her back with her legs open for any man willing to part with it.'

'And these stones – the good ones. You dig them out of the riverbed along with the gravel?'

'You're getting behind, Jim. Push your glass over.'

Jim did as McKinnon asked. His face glowed – warmed through to the back of his neck. Inexorably, a feeling of gentle quiet swept over him and now his legs were heavy, leaden things beneath the table. McKinnon's voice seemed little more than a whisper from far away. Across the room, a dozen or so of the *Cambrian*'s crewmen were shouting for their schooners to be refilled with beer.

'First you have to find the right gravel,' McKinnon explained, 'you look for the markers – garnets and jasper, pieces of petrified tree wood,' he clenched his fist, 'quartz pebbles and blood red jasper, sometimes big as bricks and smooth as babies' arses from rolling around in their kettles.'

'Kettles...?' Jim slurred and strained his eyes for focus. McKinnon's face floated ghostlike within a haze of cigar smoke.

'Walloping great holes in the rock,' McKinnon explained and like the paddles of a butter churn moved his arms in a circular, swirling motion, 'the old river picks up stones and grinds her way inside the bedrock, seen them holes big enough to swallow a coach and horses.' He rolled the ash from his cigar. 'That's where they are Jim boy, that's where you get your richest diamond gravel – bottom of the kettles. When the river's low the black buggers dig out the gravel and carry it back to the sorting table.'

His eyes flashed, his obsession with finding diamonds, like the lascivious, scheming woman had bullied her way inside the room, pulled up her chair alongside him and was now with soft, insistent fingers stroking his cheeks.

'Yer clears off the shit and small stuff and then screens what's left into different sizes.'

Now McKinnon's eyes were glazed over by the effects of his own liquor and recurrent diamond fever, that wild, insatiable look of the obsessive diamond hunter.

'Then you start a looking, Jim boy, long and hard until your eyes feels like they're bleeding.' He reached out and with a hooked forefinger sorted his way through an imaginary pile of fine gravel. 'Bit at a time, laddie. Slowly, slowly catchy monkey or yer'll miss the little ones; the ones that pays the Kaffir's wages and puts another month's bag of mealie meal under your cookhouse table.'

Jim didn't hear him; his eyes were closed, the part-smoked cigar slipped from his fingers. McKinnon picked it up and clipped off the end, half inch back from the ember.

'Then you pray to God for the big ones, matey. A pair of beauties the size of doves' eggs – Devil's Dice the diggers calls them.'

He dropped the half-smoked cigar into his top pocket and then reached across the table for Jim's sixth, untouched filling of black rum.

'I'll not be wasting good rum now, Jim. You'll not be needing this, my friend – not tonight laddie.'

He beckoned to Mei-Lien and on her reaching the table pressed a shiny shilling piece against her palm.

'Stay with him, let our friend here sleep as long as he wants.' He stroked her cheek with the back of his hand. 'Just you sit quiet now and keep your eyes on him. If he wakes up, you know where to find me. Quick as you can or I'll have you back on the streets where we found you.'

# -8-

In the half-dark, McKinnon inched his way along the entire length of the upstairs corridor and at the same time, listened for following footfalls on the stairwell behind him, making doubly sure he would not be disturbed before going down on one knee in front of Kathleen's bedroom door. He pressed his eye to the keyhole, careful not to touch the wooden panelling for every fibre of his body was shaking.

From the other side of the door the key had been drawn out, allowing McKinnon a clear view. Moonlight covered the bed and from the open window a slight breeze ruffled through Kathleen's hair. McKinnon tore his eye from the keyhole and cursed his own depravity, but he could not find the force of will to move himself away.

'Mother of Jesus Christ, forgive me,' he whispered, 'so young, so young; let the child alone, McKinnon.' But now there were other voices inside his head. 'One more look,' they pleaded with him, 'just one more look and that will be enough.'

Draped in moonlight, Kathleen's naked form was to McKinnon, that of a sleeping angel; the room in which she lay, softly veiled in that same ethereality. Her bed was the marble alter and upon it, devoid of any covering she was now the virgin adolescent, willed to him by the gods at the very moment of her first flowering.

With a life of its own McKinnon's hand reached inside his jacket pocket for the spare key. The feel of hard metal shocked his fingertips and inside his chest his heart was now the devil's pounding hammer.

'Just a few more minutes my darlin' and on my father's bones I swear you'll hear no more of old McKinnon.'

With his left wrist braced against the door frame and his finger and thumb positioned either side of the lock, he guided the duplicate key inside the keyhole. Like a surgeon probing an open wound for buried shot he felt his way deep inside the innards of the mortice lock. Only when the iron key was fully seated did his breathing steady enough for him to turn it full circle.

Through that first slight opening of the door, McKinnon took in that warm, puppy smell of young girl, and again his pulse raced and hammered. Gradually, an inch at a time he pushed the door inwards so that now he could hear the low sibilance of her breathing. With her arms and legs outstretched, to McKinnon, she was the epitome of some ancient, ritual sacrifice to the goddess Astarte. His arousal, thick as the girl's wrist twitched as a separate living thing inside his breeches and from beneath the hooded brow of his skull, his eyes bulged wide and white, enlivened by lust and raw moonlight.

From outside the tiny room, waterfront sounds drifted in through the open window. The tide was now at its highest mark on the stagings, the moon at its fullest – the slightest movement of warm air lifted a wisp of auburn hair from Kathleen's cheek and at the juncture of her legs, as a tiny, down-covered creature, the faintness of her adolescence nestled there. To McKinnon, that unsullied mark of her sex became the focus of all his yearning, the powerful culmination of all his wildest dreams and he was unable to tear his eyes from it. Her youth was the elixir, more potent than the rum he had consumed, more tantalizing than a thousand golden guineas, had they been piled there well within his reach.

Rising up from all fours, McKinnon steadied himself and wraithlike he moved forwards; as the circling vulture he loomed over Kathleen's sylphlike form and with practiced fingers, silently he slipped the brass buckle on his breeches belt.

Kathleen lay in a state of half-awareness. She had sensed the danger, but in that moment of semi-sleep, she dismissed the threat as fanciful – the remnants of unreal thoughts, surreal shadows traversing the moonlit space above her head. Through slitted eyelids she watched the shadows move, though there were no sounds except for the soughing of a sea breeze floating in through the open window.

The fingers of McKinnon's right hand encompassed her throat and now, bared of his breeches, quickly he covered her and with his full weight he held her motionless, pinning her to the mattress.

'There's no one to hear you, lassie. Call out if you dare and that same breath will be your last.'

Kathleen stayed silent, her eyes locked on to the darkened face in front of her own. At first, she was unable to comprehend what was happening, and then the stench of her assailant's breath was charge enough for her to fully recall the familiar face of the ferryman.

With his knee, McKinnon forced her legs apart and with thick fingers grubbed between her thighs for a way inside. Lost to the perversity of his excitement, McKinnon rolled his head to the side and closed his eyes; like some excited boar he grunted into her face.

'There, lassie. That's it girlie, open her up for me and I'll finish the job before yer wakes up proper.'

Kathleen steeled herself to the pressure of McKinnon forcing his fingers between her legs; those of his right hand tightened about her throat and now, at a point of wild delirium he raised himself onto one elbow and covered her mouth with his own.

Like an eel sounding the deepest, darkest parts of a warm pool, McKinnon's tongue forced its way between her teeth and thrust for the sweetest depths of Kathleen's throat.

Desperate for air, Kathleen bucked wildly and thrashed at the weight on top of her, and she reached down for the open space beneath her bed. With each new second the urge to bite down on him grew stronger, but she feared him lashing out with his fists so that she forced herself into feigning loss of consciousness. McKinnon sensed her weakening and tore his mouth away.

'Don't you go dying on me now, my pretty; you be the good little girl and give old Blackie what he's after.'

Kathleen allowed her thighs to fall open, and again, with desperate fingers she searched the space beneath her bed. McKinnon lowered himself between her legs – he sensed the change in her, compliance even. With slavering lips he found her pert pubescent breast and filled his mouth with warm flesh.

'I want you to,' she told him and to strengthen the subterfuge gritted her teeth and worked her hips with the expertise of a practiced whore. With a grinding, circular moving of her pelvis she met his thrusts with her own, as though his demands had unleashed in her some hidden store of wild perversion. Each sideways, upwards movement brought her that little bit closer in to the side of the bed.

McKinnon reached down between her legs and with trembling fingers guiding his thickened shaft to the soft and silky triangle at their apex.

'Sweet mother of Mary Magdalene, I swear you'll not be sorry! There, yes lassie; push at me now and as sure as my cock's thick as yer arm, quick as a flash I'll be up inside that virgin slit o' yours!'

Like the invasion of a hot iron, Kathleen felt him move to break inside of her and it was at that very moment her fingers found the walnut grip of her father's Colt revolver. The double click of the Colt's cocking hammer cut the excitement from him and within that same moment his ardour shrivelled away to nothing.

'Easy on that trigger, lassie. Out here in Natal they'll hang a girl just as quickly as they would a man back home on Bodmin gallows.'

'Get off me.' Kathleen growled at him; her chest heaved from lack of air.

McKinnon rolled away from her.

'No harm done, I swear it. Can't help myself, you see.'

He drew down the front of his shirt. 'The devil hi'self gets inside my head, lassie. Since I first saw you the deck of the *Eudora* I've suffered his voice inside my head.' He clasped both hands about his ears. 'I want to make amends, I swear it – on my dead mother's grave, lassie give this old fool a chance to put things right.'

Without lowering the gun, with her free hand, Kathleen drew the covers about her nakedness.

'The diamonds,' she shot the words between clenched teeth. 'Leave them on the table.'

'I could not part with them,' McKinnon pleaded.

'Nor I my innocence, but you would have taken it from me, McKinnon, without so much as a second thought.'

She raised the angle of the Colt's barrel.

'On the table, sir, or I'll take my chances with the law and blow out your brains.'

Reflected by the dresser mirror, the force of that full moon fell upon her face; her eyes, now black as shiny wavelets in the bay. Her skin, in that light, glowed with the bloodless pallor of the waiting hangman.

'On my count of three,' she goaded him, 'the diamonds, Mister McKinnon. Deny me one more time, and on your mother's grave you will be dead before you reach the door.'

A breeze whispered through Kathleen's hair. Rock-steady, the Colt's barrel stayed square-on to McKinnon's forehead. It was then he realised the closeness of his fate so that he fumbled for the insides of his jacket pocket and drew out his timepiece. Kathleen watched him unfasten the chain from its silver clip and lay his precious trinket on the table.

'Now get out of my room and if I were you I would be long gone by sunup. Just the smell of you will stand as enough reason for me to tell my father what happened here – he will not be so forgiving.'

Kathleen listened for McKinnon. Like the flogged hound he padded back along the dark corridor and then there was

45

silence. She rolled from the bed and closed the door; her hands began to shake and the nausea from what had happened rose as hot bile to the back of her throat. With trembling fingers she took up the key from the dresser, pushed it back in place and threw the lock.

# -9-

From forested heights above the natural harbour, Jim O'Rourke looked back along the rutted track they had followed outwardly from Natal's first grand port. Everything he gazed down upon ranked favourably against all the lands he had ever seen; it was the perfect vista, one to be taken advantage of by those who would one day stand as he now stood and through talented eyes, reproduce the very same on canvas. Beyond it all, the Indian Ocean sparkled, trapped between green forests and blue sky and as a protective arm with its spanking, snow-white lighthouse, the Bluff promontory pointed eastwards for the Pacific archipelago and the scattered lands of Australasia. He adjusted the wide brim of his hat to ward off that decreasing angle of sunlight and waited for Kathleen to bring her horse alongside.

'We should have stayed a few days longer; Jooster's trading store deserved more of our money.' He looked at Kathleen. 'Why the sudden urge to leave?'

Kathleen kept her eyes to the front, like her father she had dressed in a loose fitting shirt and men's breeches. Pushed inside her leather belt, her father's .44 Colt was now a permanent addition to her attire. A slouched drover's hat kept the sun from her face and her voice was rock steady, betraying nothing of her run-in with McKinnon.

'The sky's thickening up, Pa,' she looked westwards to a

convenient shoulder of thin cloud, 'old man Sutherland suggested we be clear of the road to Pietermaritzburg before the rain comes.'

She turned in the saddle and smiled at him, though inside, the anger McKinnon had left her with was still there. Like a wolf it would watch from a dark place for that chance to kill – for twenty years if need be.

'We can make better time of it over dry roads. The sooner we reach the goldfields, the sooner we find us that gold you're always talking about.'

Jim reached behind for the walnut stock of his Sharps rifle. Jooster had made a good job of the scabbard, matching it as close as he could to the colour of the Western style saddle; in opposition, the Yellow Boy Winchester had been holstered stock forwards, close-in to Jim's left knee. He narrowed his eyes at the haze and instinctively, reached inside one of his paired leather saddlebags for a five draw brass telescope; with casual interest he muddled amongst the miles they had left behind.

'Back there on the track, about where it comes out from the treeline,' he passed the spyglass over to Kathleen, 'your eyes are younger than mine; tell me what you make of it.'

Kathleen put up the glass and, working in reverse, tracked back along the way they had journeyed; through woodland and deep cuttings in the hillside and at under a mile distant she picked out urgent movement amongst the fever trees.

'Black man and a coloured boy. Might be wrong, but looks like they're in a hurry.'

'Look carefully,' Jim insisted, 'the Indian lad from the boarding house – the boy who carried our baggage...?'

'And the Zulu,' Kathleen realised, 'the oarsman from the ferryboat, I remember him.' She lowered the spyglass. 'Reckon they're following us, both of them are carrying bundles.'

'Then we'll wait here and find out soon enough,' Jim

decided and eased down from the saddle. 'Help me halter the horses, we'll make camp – edge of the forest where there's plenty of firewood.'

# -10-

'I am very pleased to have caught up with you, sir. Meneer Jooster said I must find the American man and his daughter and give them this most important communication.'

He handed Jim what was now a crumpled piece of paper and with some exuberance, eagerly he gave his own account of what Jooster had written.

'Meneer Jooster has a brother in Pietermaritzburg; also his brother owns a wagon and many fine oxen with which to pull it.'

Jim started reading; the directions to Jooster's brother were easy enough to follow. The wagon had been handed over in part payment of bad debts and the brother, according to Jooster, was eager to be rid of it. Jim looked up from the letter.

'Tell Jooster I will look in on his brother and if the wagon is in good order I will make my offer.'

The boy shook his head.

'Not possible, sir. We are not going back. There is nothing worthy of our remaining behind.'

'Then where will you live? What about the boarding house, your work with McKinnon's wife?'

Again, the head shook, more vigorously this time.

'That also is not possible. Her husband ran away for somewhere no one knows about; work on the ships, perhaps. Whatever his reasons it does not matter, his woman no longer has the money with which to pay for either one of us. We are as you would say, relieved of our employment.'

'Why?' Kathleen pushed the boy for answers. 'Why did McKinnon leave his wife?'

'I do not know, missy. But there was much noise and fighting; his woman took up her gun and shouted at him so many profanities of fuckings and blindings that I feared for my life and concealed myself beneath the stairs until it was over.'

Kathleen ignored the innocent obscenities and laughed openly. McKinnon's suffering she found to her liking.

'What will you do?' Kathleen asked him, and with imploring eyes the Indian boy looked up at her.

'Come with you, missy.' He spoke matter-of-factly and glanced over his shoulder to where the Zulu boatman watched from the shadows. 'Both of us; I myself will cook and clean and my friend, Zingeli, will shield your wagon from harm.' He beckoned to McKinnon's redundant boatman and then transferred his reasoning to Kathleen's father. 'He is a most fearsome adversary and a skilful hunter, Mister Jim sir. Besides his mother tongue, also he speaks the language of the Shangaan people to the north and besides that, through myself, Mister Jim, you will have at your fingertips the complete language of the Zulu people.'

'You understand Zulu?' Jim asked him.

'And the *Boeretaal*,' the boy emphasised, 'bastard Dutch – the language of the Afrikaner, also I am dabbing hand at cooking and have indeed brought with me my own selection of spices and interesting concoctions that will last a very long time – all the way to where we are going.'

Like Kathleen's, Jim's smile was unstoppable.

'What's your name?'

The boy's face lit up.

'Moosa is my name, Mister Jim, sir.' He outstretched his little arm, the colloquial twang and lilt of far-off Calcutta dominated his every word. 'And I am very pleased to meet you.'

Jim accepted the handshake; the hand was small and bony, but there was warmth there. From the perimeter of the camp, as some attentive black colossus, Zingeli watched and listened.

'Can he lead my oxen?' Jim asked the boy. 'Put it to him. Let me hear you speak his language.'

Moosa switched easily from English to Zulu and within that same moment, Zingeli's smile loomed wide and bright as the blades of his spears.

'Zingeli says he knows the ways of the oxen better than a man might know those of his own children.' The Zulu went on and Moosa translated. 'From his time as a boy of eight rainy seasons he has worked a hundred Boer cattle and their wagons between the snow mountains and the far place you have called the Cape. The Boers look upon these drivers of oxen as very important; they are the *voorloper* – those who walk in front. Where they walk the cattle will follow, where they sleep so will the cattle sleep and like the children of some great family, each one of them will bear a name; that of *Mpunga* the grey one, or *Mabalabala*, the spotted one.'

Kathleen looked at her father and nodded her head.

'They can only do good for us, father. I say we take them with us.'

'How would I know the good in a man who neither speaks as I do nor worships even the same God?'

The boy spoke hurriedly, afraid of losing momentum and just as quickly the Zulu replied.

'Zingeli says that wherever the spear of hardship falls, the lion lies down with the leopard and both are at peace. He gives you his word. There will be no mistrust between you. All that he asks is for a place to build his fire and space beneath your wagon for him to sleep.'

Moosa reached for the Zulu's hand, drawing him closer.

'Zingeli said that I must show you this, Mister Jim.'

In the half light, clad only in some white man's cast-off breeches, from the waist up and still sweated from the long climb, Zingeli's upper torso glowed black and hard as quenched iron. At the centre of his great chest, suspended by a fine thong of plaited leather, a tiny, silver crucifix no bigger than his thumbnail shone brightly as a star; an undisputable token of his belief.

'He is a Christian, Mister Jim. Like myself he will bring only good to your journey.'

'It may well be many months before you return,' Jim countered. 'What lies ahead, I know nothing of, and I can promise you little other than hard work; perhaps worse even.'

'We expect nothing more, Mister Jim.' Again the boy conversed quietly with Zingeli. 'He says, you are the father of our future. Where you go, we will follow. Your tears will be our sadness, your laughter, our joy; whatever befalls us we will rise above the misfortune and carry on.'

He took hold of Jim's hand. His smile widened, his teeth, white as *berg* snow; in the dimness of sunset they shone as stars upon the dark countenance of his face.

'Thank you mister Jim. God is great. May our journeying into the wilderness not be too damn bad.'

# -11-

For one last time, Jim O'Rourke and his daughter looked down from the hills above the Port of Natal, for to their front the track fell away and was flanked by thick forest and high ridges. To the both of them, the land they were leaving behind was more than beautiful; from the forest's edge, golden mist rolled down to the waterfront, where, as a moving lake it tippled into the sea. Early sunlight lit up the bay and at the highest point on the Bluff, the lighthouse, as a gloved religious finger stretched itself above the trees and pointed skywards.

'Last chance for us to turn back, two more days to reach Pietermaritzburg and after that...' Jim shrugged his shoulders, 'only the devil and God Himself know what we will come up against.'

*Eudora* was still there, anchored beyond the bar, gripped by the ebbing tide like some aggravated child the vessel rolled impatiently to her moorings. Kathleen shook her head and turned her back on the vista, enthralled by the uncertainty of what lay ahead.

'We go on, father. No going back and besides, I'm looking forward to meeting with Rhodes again.'

'The pair of you got on well,' said Jim, 'I like the man; pleasant company, well educated.'

'But as a man...?' Kathleen asked him, 'how do you see him?'

'Same as old man Sutherland,' Jim replied, 'first impressions are that his health is questionable, but a month or two of sunshine and he might well turn out for the better.'

'I think he will mend,' Kathleen decided, 'Rhodes is not the kind of man who would give in to his ailments, but as a cotton farmer,' she shook her head, 'he won't last long. Mark my words, a month or two at best and Cecil Rhodes will be gone from Natal.'

'In exchange for what...?'

'Gold or diamonds, same as his brother, Herbert; growing cotton will go sour on him; reckon on him going north, same as us.'

With the packhorse trailing behind on a long tether, they pushed northwards for the town of Pietermaritzburg. Kathleen rode alongside her father. To the rear, Moosa and Zingeli walked with their bundles slung about their shoulders, garrulous with relief they chattered like monkeys.

They made twenty miles that first day and an hour before last light camped where Zingeli found a patch of open ground, close to a small stream of bright water. Kathleen showed Zingeli how to knee-halter the horses and within minutes of them off-saddling, Moosa had cleared back the scrub and put together the makings of their first fire.

'Do you have food?' Kathleen asked him.

'Enough for three days, missy,' and respectfully, he withdrew and went to find Zingeli.

From first light of the next day they made good use of rested horses and easier terrain, whenever the forest opened, Jim freed his feet of the stirrups and took time to ease the stiffness from his back. Already, the indomitable peace of open wilderness had found its way inside of him, memories of past events and people who had driven him to leave America were falling away behind. His mind, like the way ahead was clear; mistress second chance, arms opened wide was waiting there to embrace him, and at forty-three he was more than ready for anything.

Without sign of human habitation, park-like forests rolled away to the north and east. Yellow woods and white stinkwoods towered above the shorter forest pear and bush willow, and from as far away as five miles the alarm calls of the vervet monkey echoed back from the where the canopy stood at its highest. Five days out from their making landfall, from the crest of a wooded ridge the O'Rourkes caught their first glimpse of Pietermaritzburg.

# -12-

The way into the town was well kept and pleasantly gardened. The houses, set back from the street were fringed with tall trees, many were concealed from passersby, hidden by thick hibiscus and riotous, flowering redoubts of colourful bougainvillea.

'What are we looking for, Pa?'

Jim slacked the pace and urged Kathleen to catch up.

'Small church on the right, we take the track running alongside it, give or take a mile the man said. Gardenscliffe is the only house out there.'

Kathleen's spirits soared.

'A real bed and home-cooked food. After three nights of hard ground and Moosa's curry powders...? Manna from Heaven, father.'

The town's origins and latter day influences were reflected in its buildings. Through the years, an obvious mixing of interests had embedded the town with an attractive quirkiness, and though the mark of the original Boer settlers still ran deep, the inevitable following-on of British colonists was now permanently established, and as if to emphasise the point, a contingent of Natal Carbineer rode past at a canter, their snow-white spiked helmets and blue uniforms handsomely shown off in the bright sunlight.

Jim found the building he was looking for; a small non-descript brick-under-tile place of worship. The door was wide open and the bass intonations of the *predikant*, the Dutch Reformed minister rolled as a spiritual wave across the street.

Kathleen peered inside as she rode past; though lit by light from the windows, still, the long room with its rows of hardwood pews appeared to her as melancholic, a place where the sufferings of long ago had somehow infected the very fabric of this sombre chapel. In foot-high lettering, the words *The Church of the Vow* emblazoned the wall above the entrance. Though she rode in strong sunlight, her skin shivered with gooseflesh, and from her looking inside the tiny church she felt the ominous chill of some past catastrophe reach out to her.

Peter Sutherland was waiting for them, his daughters, Elizabeth and Charlotte stood to either hand, arms linked with their father's; both were flaxen-haired, blue-eyed and willowy as the pampas grass that fringed the entrance gates. Charlotte, taller than her younger sibling reached almost to the line of her father's brow. Sutherland stepped forward and held the gelding's head for Jim to dismount.

'Not a moment's peace since we last spoke, Jim. My girls have been on tenterhooks watching for you. Come on inside, was afraid you might not find the time to make the detour. Tea, or a rejuvenating glass of Port old boy, and a hot bath for the pair of you; water's being heated as we speak.'

'My servants...?' Jim realised and looked to where he had left them at the gate.

'Already taken care of; they are both of them in good hands.' Sutherland nodded his head to Charlotte. 'My girls will take your horses round to the paddock. Dinner in a couple of hours; someone I would like you to meet. Sent word this very minute; took the liberty of inviting him to join us, I'm sure you will appreciate the experience.'

Both men craned their necks and were able to follow the girls' progress beyond the hedge. Kathleen was with them and from the way they shared the task of leading away the horses, to Jim it appeared as if his daughter had known the Sutherlands all her life. Peter Sutherland voiced his observations.

'That daughter of yours has changed already, Jim. Duck to water, old boy. Almost a woman; fitted right in from the looks of things.'

'Different girl to the one I brought over on the *Eudora*, Peter, and yes, like you, I too have seen a change in her.'

Entranced by the rural beauty of Gardenscliffe, Jim looked out across luxuriant gardens and wide, manicured lawns. Beds of brilliant yellow and blood red cannas slashed the sunlight and in their thousands, pink and white and mauve cosmos leaned their heads to the warmth.

'Your girls are lovely, Peter. You must be very proud.'

Sutherland's eyes twinkled.

'Best a man could wish for, old boy. Another year and every red-blooded suitor within fifty miles of 'maritzburg will be banging down my door.'

Charlotte, the eldest, walked with Jim's horse on a loose rein and though dressed in a pretty, summery frock her stride was that of a boy and on a strong though slender neck, her elfin face bobbed in the sunlight, brown as winter grass, her gaze inexorably fixed to the Colt in Kathleen's waistband.

'Have you used it?' she asked – in total awe of the weapon.

Kathleen shook her head. 'Not yet, but almost.'

'Tell us!' Elizabeth, the younger of the two piped out like a fretful sparrow and hurried to catch up, determined not to miss out on a single word. 'Why almost? What happened, Kathleen? Were the Zulus chasing after you?'

'You're being silly, Elizabeth.' Charlotte remonstrated playfully. 'We would have heard. Martha would have told us if there was trouble brewing.' She turned to Kathleen. 'Martha works for my mother; she's a real Zulu, does the housework and such. Mama sits in the garden with her horsey friends and does nothing, at least for most of the time.' She dropped her voice to a whisper. 'They all drink gin from her special teapot – she keeps it covered over, under the table. Last week when father was away, she fell in the garden; squashed a huge geranium with her bum.'

All three of them laughed, though it was more the dramatised shriek from Elizabeth.

'You should never use the bum word,' Elizabeth was quick to exploit the satire and with posh expression, theatrically she rolled her eyes skywards, 'ladies say, posterior, my dear – not bum.'

'Prefer bum', Charlotte insisted, 'no fun in the word, posterior. Or arse, even. Father uses the arse word when he shouts at Benson, the Zulu boy who does our gardening.'

Elizabeth muscled in closer, her eyes were fired up.

'We watch from behind the shrubbery. What does father say, Charlotte? Tell Kathleen what father says to Benson.'

Kathleen took an instant liking to them both. Charlotte

was of the same age as herself; somewhat aloof, but gentle and especially, quick-witted. Elizabeth was two years younger, freckle-faced and vibrant as a honey bee. Charlotte folded her arms across her pretend belly, emulating her father's flair for harsh reprimand.

'Get off your arse, boy! I don't pay you to malinger.'

Charlotte leaned further forwards, this time with her brow furrowed and fists balled against her sides.

'You steal my money, boy! I'm paying you for doing nothing...? up on your feet, boy before I kick your malingering little arse through the front gates!'

Elizabeth shrieked and made pretence of covering her ears.

'Sometimes, Benson runs away and doesn't come back for weeks!'

'But father always takes him back,' Charlotte countered and smiled at the recollection, 'a more compassionate employer or father one could never wish for.'

The girls off-saddled the horses and turned them loose in the paddock. Freed from the weight, as spring foals they flew like the wind.

Rested against Jim's western saddle and protruding from its scabbard, the Sharps rifle was quick to capture Charlotte's curiosity. She reached down and with the very tips of her fingers dared to touch it. The feel of polished wood sent shivers up her arm.

'Such a big gun, Kathleen, my guess is you have never fired it?'

'Not as yet,' Kathleen admitted and turned her interest to the smaller Yellow Boy Winchester repeater. 'This one's my favourite.' She offered the weapon to Charlotte. 'Hold it if you want. Be careful mind.'

With both hands, Charlotte took a firm hold on the weapon; immediately, a change came over her. The soft skin along her arms flushed with gooseflesh, and from inside her chest there came the excited, bird-like flutterings of her own heartbeat. She drew the gun into her shoulder, puffed a lock of gold-coloured hair from her cheek and aligned the iron sights with a patch of orange lichen on the far granite wall. Her balance was rock solid and with the flair of the naturally talented marksman she leaned into the shot.

'You must teach me,' she suggested, 'everything you know, Kathleen.'

'Then I will speak to my father, we can learn together.'

Charlotte lowered the Winchester and reluctantly, handed it back. Next to Kathleen's, Charlotte's hands appeared as slender and small boned. In sharp contrast, the former were strong and deeply tanned. For a brief moment, Kathleen felt the urge for her to reach out, but the moment quickly passed.

'Here comes Rhodes!' Elizabeth piped and tore off across the lawn to commandeer her favourite person, hair flying out behind, arms windmilling, wildly out of time with her legs.

With amusement, Kathleen watched Elizabeth's insistent efforts at manhandling Cecil Rhodes between the flowerbeds. Rhodes, without complaint, lightly dressed in open-necked shirt and worsted trousers allowed for him to be steered to where the others had gathered at the paddock gate.

'Good day to you all,' Rhodes warbled and rolled to a halt behind his captor, 'thought the relief column would never get through; been well and truly brought to boot by the Zulus!'

Rhodes tipped his head to Kathleen.

'Glad you made it, wasn't sure if you would cope. The road to Pietermaritzburg I found a little tenuous to say the least.' He assessed Kathleen's choice of clothing; particularly the Colt revolver in her waistband. 'And ready for anything, I see. You will be staying on with the Sutherlands for at least a few days I hope?'

'Depends on my father,' she glanced at Charlotte and smiled, 'but I think I might convince him, I love it here.'

'Your time on the waterfront,' Rhodes queried, 'we were doubtful of you finding accommodation at such short notice.'

'We managed,' said Kathleen and steered the conversation away from her run-in with McKinnon. 'What about yourself? Your brother's cotton farm, when will you start?'

'Soon enough,' Rhodes intimated, 'much rather stay on here for twenty years or so; being thoroughly spoiled.'

He looked past her, towards the homestead.

'Cook's rung the bell – we're being called in.' He grinned at Kathleen. 'Prepare yourself, more food than you can shake a stick at, and be warned, Kathleen, the old girl does not take kindly to those who cannot clear their plate.' He grasped the front of his belly with both hands. 'Fat as a Christmas turkey – a couple of days at Gardenscliffe and already my breeches are in urgent need of letting out.'

# -13-

The kitchen staff had adhered exactly to Jane Sutherland's instructions; the guest seating was precisely spaced to both sides of the homestead's yellowwood dining room table. The room, the largest in the house, had been well lit with candelabra; towers of silver and candlelight, and like the placement settings, were at equal intervals so that pools of soft light were linked each to the other, illuminating a full length run of pure white linen and London hallmarked silverware. On light chain, suspended from wooden beams of seasoned *hardekool* were an adequate number of brass lamps – planets of soft illumination, subtle enough to assist, rather than overpower the candlelight they gentled the room with an air of quiet sobriety.

Sutherland's wife seated herself directly opposite her

husband. From here they could watch, listen and converse equally with all who were at the table. Now in her forties and from her not so subtle predilection to an overindulgent colonial lifestyle, her once, hourglass figure had rounded out; her bosom now an ample cushion of flesh upon which she could rest her arms whilst napping away those balmy, colonial afternoons outside in the garden. From the crystal jug at her right hand, she topped her glass to the brim, supposedly with lemon water. From an inter-leading corridor, on silent, bared feet the servants appeared at either side of the table, without so much as a single word they left their salvers; dishes of steaming vegetables, boats of beef gravy and then, just as quickly, dispersed.

'Would you be kind enough to say grace, Peter?'

With bowed heads, everyone waited, committed to silence by Peter Sutherland's intonation and the metronomic tick of the room's long-case clock.

'For what we are about to receive, may the Lord make us truly thankful.'

'Amen.' Everyone droned. One seat was still empty. Sutherland's wife paused, her arm at mid reach for the roast potatoes.

'Rhodes not joining us for dinner...?'

'Feeling a little poorly, darling,' Peter covered for Rhodes's lack of appetite and nodded his head to Jim O'Rourke, 'problems with his breathing. Left him alone with Jane Austin's Pride and Prejudice and a generous helping of library port.'

Jane brushed the incident aside and swung her attentions elsewhere, her last thoughts already dispensed with. Her eyes fell on Jim.

'You must stay for as long as you like, in fact, I insist on your doing so.' She looked about her and quickly she went from face to face. Outside the walls, far thunder, like some disturbed mastiff growled over Gardenscliffe. 'A few more days at the very least. I'm sure that everyone here would agree...?'

Kathleen's face lit up and she nudged her father's elbow.

'Say we will, father.'

'And your wagon, Jim,' Peter rejoined the conversation, 'ample time will be needed for you to familiarise yourselves with its workings; damned hard job, old boy, all those brake blocks, chains and *disselboom* things; a lot for a man to pick up on.'

'Guess I'm outnumbered,' Jim capitulated. 'I accept your generous offer Mrs Sutherland. Until the wagon is ready then, and the cattle are of fit condition to pull it.'

'And you must call me Jane, if you wouldn't mind. I hate formality.' Her smile softened and with the zest of a ship's stoker and as reward for his decision, she loaded his plate with succulent, pink rosettes of roast sirloin. 'Should you decide to extend your stay with us, you will be more than welcome to attend our church gymkhana. Target shooting for prize money may well interest you. Big event you know; horse racing and beer tent second to none.' She dropped her eyes. 'Not that the latter would mean anything to me, Mister O'Rourke'

'Of course,' said Jim, 'though I'm sure there will be plenty of other attractions more suited to holding your interest.'

'Like gin and cake,' Charlotte whispered under her breath and Kathleen all but choked on her cauliflower.

'Charlotte...?' Jane Sutherland's hawkish glare fell on her daughter.

Charlotte tipped her fringe to cover her eyes and glared at the peas on her plate.

'Nothing, mother; I merely worried over the horses to Kathleen.' She abandoned her knife and fork. 'May I leave the table, mother. I've eaten too much and feel bilious.'

'I suppose, if you must. I'll have cook put something aside for you.' She focused her attentions on Kathleen. 'And you young lady, will no doubt be wanting to go with her?'

Kathleen nodded her head.

'If I may, Mrs Sutherland; whilst there's still enough light.'

# -14-

Jane Sutherland stood up from the table, she had sensed a presence, a movement outside and she strained her eyes for a glimpse beyond the window. To the north-west the sky was a mixture of puce and black and above the outlying storm-covered hills, unimpaired, thunder and lightning fell from the clouds. She beckoned to her husband.

'I think your celebrity guest has arrived, darling. Why you encouraged a man of almost seventy years to ride out here alone when it's almost dark and under threat of him being struck by lightning, totally confounds me.'

Sutherland winked an eye at Jim.

'Prepare yourself for some interesting conversation, Jim, but you will have to be tolerant of him, he's none too understanding.'

'Grumpy old bastard would be nearer the truth,' Jane chuckled and topped up her glass, adding a slice of lemon to the four already there. 'Hang on to your hat, Mister O'Rourke – spiritually, as well as mentally.'

She turned to her daughter, Elizabeth.

'Time you were not here, darling. Away you go before the whiskered angel of retribution starts spitting his fire and brimstone.'

Elizabeth sat fast and cursed the peas on her plate.

'Now, Elizabeth!' She pointed to the kitchen corridor. 'And tell cook our guest has just arrived. He knows what to do.'

The outer door rattled against its hinges, as though some

discontented soul were demanding entry. Peter crossed the room, drew back the bolt and swung back the heavy, mahogany door.

'*Dominee*! *Kom binne*, come inside, reverend. Jane was on the verge of sending out a rescue party; convinced the Zulus had run off with you. Excellent timing, old boy, another few minutes and the rain would have had you by the scruff.'

Johannes Paulus van Reenen stepped through the doorway, bowing his head for it to clear the lintel. Behind him, in the high vault of the heavens, lightning burned like cannon fire, for the storm was close now. Jane Sutherland stood on tiptoes and coyly, she turned her cheek to him.

'Good of you to come, Johannes, let Peter take your coat. Come and sit down and I'll bring you something with which to warm your soul.'

As a bemused, black bear, van Reenen shrugged off his calf-length drover's coat for Peter to take away and like the thunder outside, his voice rolled about the room.

'*Dankie mevrou*, I am grateful for your hospitality.' Dressed in black moleskin breeches, black shirt, heavy boots and winged collar common to the *voortrekker* pastor, to Jim O'Rourke, van Reenen was the ogre giant from Benjamin Tabart's fairytale Jack and the Beanstalk. Twice the bulk of other men, he moved with slow deliberation, but with power. Without diffidence he took up his place at the table.

Purposely, Jane had set a place for the burly Afrikaner directly across from Jim O'Rourke and now, with his elbows leaned to the table, through onyx eyes van Reenen measured the worth of the man sat opposite. His chair, though built of heavy stinkwood creaked under the strain, the legs were the great stone columns of Solomon's ancient temple and the seat was lashed across with leather *riems*, cushioned in scarlet brocade and heavily stuffed with horsehair.

'Tell me *engelsman*, do you believe in the resurrection – in

God Almighty?'

'As much as most men,' Jim cut back and readied himself for a spiritual drubbing. Without dropping his eyes, he carried on eating. The black bear nodded its head.

'It is right that a man should believe. Without belief, a man's soul is worthless; grist for the devil.'

Jane came back from the kitchen; the salver she carried was loaded with lamb and roast potatoes. Like a dove just returned to the cote she cooed and clucked for the bear's attention.

'Cook's speciality, Johannes. Your favourite. If God were to come amongst us now, He would surely fight you for it.'

'Bless you, *mevrou* Sutherland.' Momentarily, his eyes lifted and from amongst a forest of black whiskers there grew the first inkling of a wry smile. 'If ever your husband tires of your company, I will marry you myself.'

'Heaven forbid,' Jane chuckled, though many times she had contemplated van Reenen's beard against her bare flesh. His hands, big enough to span the plate from which he was about to eat were heavily calloused and thick with scars; the paws of an old lion. Her skin flushed with gooseflesh.

'Peter, my darling,' she signalled with her eyes, 'on the dresser, my sweetheart; the envelope if you would be so kind – and the bottle.'

She turned to van Reenen.

'A small token of appreciation, Johannes; a little something from us ladies at the gardening club.'

Sutherland handed the envelope to van Reenen; the bottle of brandy he placed in front of him.

'What is this?' Tentatively, van Reenen accepted the envelope and looked to Jane for an answer; titillated by her success she thrilled over the subterfuge.

'For the poor, Johannes, and for your conscience to decide how best to use it.' Her cheeks flushed. 'I thought the time for us to contribute was well overdue.'

64

He nodded his thanks to Jane and not without some reverence turned his attentions to vetting the spirit. Lit by the nearest candelabra, like Tugela mist, potent liquor swirled inside the bottle. Van Reenen turned his head and with his eyes, fervently he demanded the attention of Kathleen's father.

'My name is Johannes Paulus van Reenen. How do I call you, *engelsman*?'

'Jim O'Rourke. Call me Jim, it is enough.'

'A small name, *meneer.*'

'Plenty big enough for me,' Jim countered, 'easy enough for a man to remember.'

The Afrikaner's eyes sparked mischievously in the candlelight. There was resilience here; spirited, but misguided also, that of a man committed to what was right. Boers had little time for soft, pink-faced settler Englishmen, but this one was different.

'I hear you look for gold, *engelsman*?'

'That's what I came for.' Jim relaxed, the conversation was swinging his way.

'For a man and girl, and whom neither one understands the way, it is a long and perilous journey.'

Jim played the card he knew van Reenen was looking for.

'With God's guidance, reverend, we will learn as we go along.'

With powerful fingers, Jooster drew the cork and sniffed the bottle's contents.

'*Druiwedop*,' van Reenen recognised the smell, 'Boer brandy.' He smiled at Jim and his mouth flooded.

Like the moonshine distillates of America's Deep South the liquor had been home-stilled; the sun's awesome power and the melding of rich fruits were both there, locked inside the bottle. Peter Sutherland set a pair of glass tumblers down on the table.

'You both have much to talk about. Jane and I will retire to the library. Rhodes is waiting for us, we too have much to discuss.' He turned to the Afrikaner. 'Jane had the annexe guestroom made up for you, Johannes. To the back of the house; I will leave a lighted lamp beneath the awning to guide you in.'

'*Dankie*, Peter. I will be away before sunrise.' Again, he waved the envelope. 'And my thanks for this; God's blessings upon you both.'

\*

Even though Jim's plate was still half-filled with beef, van Reenen insisted on equal shares of lamb from the salver, so that they conversed through mouths full of steaming meat and roasted potatoes. Between them they drank the fiery spirit to well below the halfway mark and occasionally they glanced up at the windows, for outside the homestead, dark clouds had blotted out the moon. Inside, other than the low intonations of two big men, the quiet of the dining room held solid, tempered even more by soft light and high, exposed roof beams.

Jim saw in Johannes van Reenen a rabid need for the past to be talked about, so that he gave free rein to the Afrikaner's recollections and through the somnolence derived of the brandy bottle, he listened compliantly. Thunder and lightning added poignancy to the conversation, rain wheeled down from the hills and like gravel flung to the homestead's tin roof it lashed the metal sheets and flushed the gutterings clean of insects and leaf-fall.

'Thirty two years ago, *engelsman*,' van Reenen leaned forwards and lowered his voice as if God Himself might be listening in, 'December sixteen, 1838.'

He lifted his hands from the table and held them to the candlelight, the scarring to both hands was as extensive as it was horrific; slashed across by the Zulu stabbing spear.

'Less than five hundred Boers against fifteen thousand warriors, the might of the Zulu empire and I was amongst them, *engelsman*. Kaffir and Boer mixed together, screaming and cursing, laughing and dying, side by side with Andries Pretorius and Sarel Cilliers, this way we fought off the Zulu impis and with the Lord's help we rose up stronger than before.'

He paused, but just long enough for him to drain his glass and refill it.

'It was then that the man beside me spoke with a lion's voice, but the words I heard were not his own, they were indeed, the words of God Almighty.'

Again, van Reenen drank his glass empty, his eyes closed as though he were now aware that Heaven itself had opened up before him, damning and judgemental, too magnificent for a mere mortal such as himself to behold. Still with his eyes closed he quoted from memory, for he had said the words a thousand times before.

*'The battle is won, Johannes. Go now. Go into the wilderness and prepare yourself, for when the time is right, it is you who must administer to our people; you who must stand at the lectern and from it preach the word of the Almighty. You, Johannes Paulus van Reenen have been chosen to stand as God's holy emissary before the altar.'*

Van Reenen lowered his eyes and gazed about the room; those who no longer lived were there; stone-faced they gathered about the table, and there were those amongst them whom he could never forget. From their place beyond the veil they watched and listened and nodded their heads in agreement.

'The Church of the Vow,' he whispered, more for the sake of his own ears than for those of the man sat opposite.

Jim stayed silent; as yet there was place for no one else to speak. Through the power of his obsession and that of strong liquor, for that one precious moment, van Reenen had detached himself from all things earthly, and then, as if the wind had suddenly changed direction, his eyes turned back to Jim O'Rourke.

'Those are the words of Andries Pretorius, *engelsman*. In the eyes of the *Volk*, another man of greater standing they will never meet again.'

'You spoke of the wilderness?'

Van Reenen's eyes flickered.

'What do you know of the wilderness, *engelsman*?' He wiped his lips with the back of his hand then selected a fourth rib from the salver. 'Men go there to die; or to leave behind that which they no longer need.' With his teeth he stripped the rib completely and dropped the bare bone on his plate. 'A year and three months; one Boer, one Kaffir, two brothers alone in God's wilderness – we were inseparable.'

His eyes clouded with old memories.

'I buried him where he fell – close to the waterfall.' Where moments ago his voice had echoed bear-like about the room, it was now the voice of the quietened man. Jim saw the change in him and reached for the bottle. Without asking, he refilled van Reenen's glass to the brim.

'Perhaps the past is better left alone.'

'Always, the past is here with me,' van Reenen pressed the flat of his hand against his chest, 'like the *bedonnered* woman, she cannot be ignored. What Johannes van Reenen learned in a year, he will give to you in a single hour. There will be many times when you are glad of it.' He leaned back in his chair and reached for his inside pocket.

'From the bottom of that same waterfall, from beneath the great boulders that killed my friend, from the devil's pit, *engelsman*, these and many others we dug from the bed of a single river.' He straightened his massive fingers and allowed for the treasure to tumble forwards onto the table.

To Jim O'Rourke, what he gazed upon, through their size alone seemed to him more fanciful than real; nuggets of raw gold, each piece naturally twisted and misshapen, each was the colour of ripe corn and late sunlight, one the size of a gnarled plum, the other, larger and almost relic-like replicated the shape and size of a child's hand, fingers and thumb hooked inwards. When he lifted each of them up from the table, the leaden weight and warm patina bequeathed of their creation, was to Jim O'Rourke, unmistakable.

'Men would kill for these.'

'And many have done so,' said Johannes, 'where you are going, aside from the strength of a man's arm there is no rule of law. Not even the Lord's commandments can shield a man from the wrath of his brother. Not when the gold sickness is with him.'

The Afrikaner filled his lungs with new breath and looked across to the nearest window. For a long moment he listened to the night outside; the storm had reached the peak of all its strengths. About the homestead's stone chimneys the wind howled and the rain in all its fury whipped as a thousand angry flails against the roof sheets.

'I can never go back, Jim, what happened out there in the wilderness will always be mine to live with. That part of my life is finished and God willing will never be added to.'

He drained the last half glass of brandy from the bottle and nodded his head to the man sat across from him.

'Take them, *engelsman*, they are yours. The sight of them has poisoned my eyes for long enough. Put them in your pocket before the devil ties my words with knots and changes this old man's mind.'

Jim shook his head; van Reenen's insistence was foolhardy and irrational.

'I cannot accept. The both of us have had too much to drink, Johannes. What you are offering would stand as two years' wages, a small fortune in any man's eyes.'

'Listen to me, *engelsman*.' He leaned across and pointed to the smaller of the two nuggets. 'This one will cover the money owed by me to my native labourers. You will pay them for me, then both my debt and my conscience will be cleansed of this burden.'

'What are you saying?' Jim asked.

'There is work for both of them; the smallest we have already spoken of.' He reached out and with some reluctance he lifted up the second nugget of raw gold for it to catch at the candlelight. 'However, this one, the largest of the pair... I have weighed it myself, thirteen ounces of the devil's own gold, from the very pit where my friend, Piet Jakkals was killed. Enough money to purchase most of your needs for the journey northwards, for at least as far as the Blyde River; this will stand as money owed between us, as payment for your willingness to do what I ask.' He paused to catch his breath. 'For your help, *engelsman*, if you agree. Beyond what we have already spoken of, I will cede you all rights to my gold claims. I no longer have need of them. Johannes van Reenen has suffered enough of Lucifer's torment.'

Long minutes elapsed before Jim found strength of mind enough for him to speak.

'Why are you doing this? Whether or not you return to your claims, no one gives a damn.'

'And you are right, my friend,' he held up one finger, as a sign of his total commitment. 'Only God Himself would know, but that is enough. Perhaps, in the future, when people speak of Johannes Paulus van Reenen, they will speak kindly of him, and when the Lord looks down from the heavens, He might, within Himself, find reason enough to forgive me.'

He stood up from the table and as a black bear towered over Jim O'Rourke. From his breast pocket he took out a sheet of paper.

'On this I have written the names of those who worked the claim with me; five in all and as I have already said, one of them, Piet Jakkals, no longer lives. His woman lives close by at the base of the mountain, give his share to her.' He crossed the room and retrieved his coat. 'Also, *engelsman*, I have drawn for you the way to Peach Tree Creek. From where the spruit enters the Blyde River, you must follow the stream until you reach the waterfall, if the

70

kaffirs have not abandoned me, that is where you will find them. Show them my mark on the paper and they will know that it is I who has sent you.'

'Will I see you again before I leave?' Jim asked him.

Van Reenen smiled and nodded his head.

'The Church of the Vow, *engelsman*, if you feel the need before you take the road north, I will be there.' He held out his hand to Jim. 'If not, God go with you. Watch for the name, van Reenen, I have cut it deeply to many places along the road. Follow my mark and those on the map and if the Lord sees fit to spare you, He will light your way to the diggings.

# -15-

Warm mist clung to the treetops, the forest was breathing again. Streams were rushing, filled to bursting by early rains, but the ground about them had already started to dry and within that first hour of daylight the temperature climbed enough for it to suck that topmost layer of moisture out from the soil. Cecil Rhodes sat on the top step with his back to the homestead's front veranda, his eyes fixed to what was going on some four steps down from his feet. Without looking up he spoke to the girl seated alongside him.

'Never have I seen so many different creatures so rabidly intent on consuming one another.' He used the toe of his shoe as a pointer. 'For instance, that furry chap over there,' he drew Elizabeth's attention onto the murder scene; a large moth, big as his open hand with lifelike eyes displayed on each of its massive wings, 'not a cat in hell's chance of the poor fellow coming out of that alive.'

'Papa says in Africa everything eats everything,' Elizabeth qualified dispassionately, 'I think it has to be that way or the place will be all filled up with bugs and things.'

Rhodes smiled at the truth. With relentless determination the ants cut away the moth's wings and in columns of hundreds, the voracious, tiny creatures carried away choice dismembered bits; down the steps and across the hard-packed ground to their hole amongst the roots of an old poinsettia.

'You will be leaving us soon...?' Elizabeth intoned solemnly.

Rhodes nodded his head, touched by the innocence of her concern; the focus of his attention still on the moth.

'My dearest Elizabeth, you make it sound as though we will never again see one another.'

'The Umkomaas Valley is a long way from here; perhaps we never will.'

'Rubbish, girl, on horseback – couple of days at the most. You and your family will soon be sick of the sight of me.'

'Never,' she emphasized, 'not in all of my lifetime.' She turned to him and flung her slender arms about his neck, almost unseating him from the step. 'You are the sweetest, most caring man I have ever met and I shall never grow tired of your company.'

She released him and without embarrassment, lifted her face to his and placed a single, innocent kiss upon his cheek.

'That was from me and Charlotte, so you will never ever forget us.' Dejectedly, she slumped back down on the veranda step. 'Mother said you might well be leaving us sooner rather than later?'

'I have to,' Rhodes confirmed her suspicion. 'There will be work for me to do. My brother is away and no one seems to know when he will be coming back – if ever.'

The moth's bulbous body was dragged from step to step. Rhodes marvelled at the tenacity of those tiny insects. Nothing deterred them from the task of moving a weight one hundred times greater than their own. Every obstacle was either negotiated or forced aside, their determination to succeed was blatantly unequivocal.

Elizabeth watched with him, sharing Rhodes' fascination for the tiny caravan. Eventually, with what remained of their quarry held aloft, the ants delivered it into the hole and followed it down inside the earth.

'Lesson to be learned, Elizabeth.' Rhodes smiled at her. 'One's stature is of little importance. No matter how small or frail we might appear to others, it is our strength of will that matters.'

'Determination,' Elizabeth proffered – her expression sternly enacted to suit his, 'the will to prevail, to win the battle,' she raised a tiny, clenched fist aloft – her battle flag, 'whilst beset upon by terrible, overpowering enemy fire.'

'Bravo!' Rhodes applauded her efforts. 'Well said, that soldier!'

Her commitment to battle withered, but still the gleam of achievement was there in her eyes.

'Father told me.'

'Your father...?'

Elizabeth nodded. 'Because I'm the littlest, and therefore have to fight the hardest in order to succeed.'

Rhodes rested his elbows against his knees and relaxed his posture to match the unevenness of the steps. As they had done a hundred times before, his eyes found that furthest familiar point upon the horizon.

'I envy Jim and Kathleen. If it were not for the promise I made my brother, I would go with them.'

'Why do you say that?' Elizabeth asked him.

'For the excitement, the adventure, Lizzie,' Rhodes shot back at her, 'think of it, girl, how much there is for a man to see out there.' He pointed with his eyes. 'A wilderness so vast it would take an entire lifetime to realise even a tiny, infinitesimal part of it.' He shook his head at the grand scheme of things. 'Grow my brother's cotton I will do, and with a willing heart, but when the bolls are picked and bundled up for market, then I will hand the reins to Herbert and take my leave of farming.'

He stood up from the steps and held out his hand to Elizabeth.

'Come, we must find your sister.'

'If you left the farm, where would you go?'

He shrugged the stiffness from his shoulders and without hesitation, chose once more a misty break in the far horizon.

'Perhaps I will follow my brother to the diamond fields. Either way my path will eventually turn northwards, for as long and far as God sees fit for me to journey.'

# -16-

'I feel time is running out for us,' Charlotte whispered her regrets to Kathleen, 'two, maybe three more days at best. Or even less, perhaps,' she added as an afterthought. 'This might well be the last day that we spend together, ever.' She reached for Kathleen's hand. 'Even though we have known each other for such a little time, Kathleen, still I feel as if my heart is breaking.'

Hand in hand, two girls so much alike walked the periphery of the homestead gardens, both were lithe of limb and slender as young otters, both were at the very cusp of womanhood.

'I have a gift for you,' said Kathleen and turned face-on to Charlotte, reaching as she did so for the gold clasp at the nape of her neck. 'This was my grandmother's and I know she will understand my wanting you to wear it.'

Charlotte's eyes softened and like Kathleen, sprung the clasp on a gold chain suspended about her throat.

Without speaking they exchanged tokens of their endearment. Both were crafted from yellow gold;

Kathleen's tiny crucifix, the symbol of her Catholic upbringing and Charlotte's heart-shaped locket, a gift from her mother. Set at its centre with a single sparkling diamond, the precious locket spun on its chain of gold link.

'One day,' Charlotte promised, 'I shall come and find you.' She reached out, but with her eyes. 'Wherever you go, Kathleen, however long it takes.'

There was the rustle of small feet crossing the lawn and that magical spell so intricately woven was suddenly ripped away; fluffy seeds to a selfish wind.

'There they are!' Elizabeth came from between the flowerbeds at a full pelt. 'Rhodes and I have been looking everywhere for you! He's leaving Gardenscliffe, Charlotte! Tell him to stay, sissy. I do so want for him to stay – for a few more days at least.'

'Calm yourself, Elizabeth. Rhodes has things to do, a farm to run. We cannot insist that he stays when he may well have a crop to bring in.'

From his walk about the garden and his being without a hat to ward off strong sunlight, Rhodes' face was now brick-red; his lungs laboured for air so that he flopped down on the grass and found some shade. The girls, already used to his predicament, gave him time to recover before bombarding him with questions.

'Have you decided yet?' Charlotte asked him, 'whether or not you will wait for your brother to come home before you make your way to the diamond fields? Growing cotton is hard work, Papa said, but digging up the ground for diamonds proves to most men to be as dangerous as it is foolhardy.'

Rhodes thought for a moment, contemplating a line of sight to where the sky met with the forest. It would not be long before the clouds gathered; mid-afternoon, this much he had learned from his brief time in Africa. Though it was still at the very onset of summer, unseasonal, early rains had come upon the town of Pietermaritzburg from the north-west. Always after luncheon the sky would darken; with almost clockwork precision that's when the storms came.

'As clichéd as it may sound, Charlotte, it is sometimes necessary for a man to take control of his destiny. Success is always the product of some happy inclination. Without enjoyment, there can be no satisfactory outcome, without total commitment of interest, a man's endeavours will nine times out of ten, prove disastrous.' He smiled at all three of them. 'It would prove most advantageous for you all to remember that.'

'Are diamonds really as beautiful as they say?' Elizabeth mused and wriggled her way as close as was physically possible alongside her mentor. Rhodes shuffled uncomfortably and through habit, ran his fingers down inside the collar of his shirt.

'Some men would give everything they own, just to close their fist about a few, small stones. It is a sickness of the heart and mind, Lizzie; an incurable dilemma.'

'Be it gold or diamonds,' Kathleen added, 'that is why we are here.' She contemplated the stones she had forced from McKinnon, nestled to the deepest part of her pocket they were now, hers alone. 'For some, fossicking for either would be nigh on impossible to resist. It is all that my father knows and I wouldn't have it any other way.'

'Spoken like a true dreamer!' Rhodes chuckled and then, for the benefit of his audience, theatrically, he lifted his eyes to the heavens. 'Never will I settle to the fairest side of any hill. Never will its green and gentle slopes bear fruit enough to satisfy the heart of those who climb without regret, for a chance to witness land that lies beyond.'

'Who said that?' Charlotte pressed, 'a poet perhaps? Some famous bard I imagine.'

'I did,' Rhodes confessed and laughed aloud at Charlotte's look of bewilderment, 'pretty good I thought.' His attention was distracted and he looked beyond the tiny gathering. 'Your father, Kathleen, and from the brusqueness of his stride I would put money on his wanting to give voice to something important.'

Jim O'Rourke made short work of crossing the lawn. He nodded to Rhodes and then turned to Kathleen.

'Van Reenen sent word of twenty wagons departing the market square for the north road, two days from now.'

Kathleen rolled herself upright.

'Why so soon, father? We have spent so little time here.'

'I'm sorry, but we have no choice,' Jim countered, 'Jooster's brother will have our wagon ready and the oxen inspanned for sun-up, day after tomorrow.' He sensed his daughter's disappointment. 'Six weeks, before the next convoy of wagons leaves Pietermaritzburg for the interior. We cannot afford to miss out on the opportunity, my sweetheart.'

'I'll ride in with you,' Charlotte insisted.

'I'm coming, too,' Elizabeth piped, 'we can look on the market for fruit and things for the kitchen. I'll get some money from papa.'

'I too will be leaving the same morning,' Rhodes dropped his bombshell. 'I will accompany you for at least a mile or so; prior to my turning off for the Umkomaas.'

Elizabeth rolled her eyes at Rhodes' decision to leave.

'That's not fair; everyone's going! Back to boring old, nothing-to-do time. Mother promised you would all stay longer.'

'You're being silly, Elizabeth,' Charlotte admonished, but inside, besides her own regrets, other feelings were settling there, those of emptiness and yearning. She held out her hand to Kathleen. 'Walk with me, we still have an hour of full sun, let us not waste it.'

They walked to where the forest encroached on the garden, purposefully, but with sadness striding out between them. At first, neither Kathleen nor Charlotte could speak, not until they reached the very limits of Gardenscliffe. For as far as they could see, lush forest struck eastwards for the coast.

'Once you are settled,' Charlotte told her, 'then you must write.'

'As soon as I can,' Kathleen promised, and gently, without diffidence, she pressed her lips to Charlotte's.

# -17-

Settlers, like busy ants gathered in supplies, last minute purchases were quickly stored away inside their wagons; after today, they would rely on their rifles and the expected bounty of God's open wilderness for their livelihood.

Jim O'Rourke leaned from his horse and shouted instructions to Moosa, forced to raise his voice above the hubbub of the market square.

'Tell Zingeli it is time; the front wagons have started to move.'

He swivelled in the saddle and looked across to where Kathleen perched on the wagon box, her horse, tethered behind on a long rein pawed at the ground.

'I promised van Reenen one last visit before we leave. Zingeli will see the oxen onto the beginnings of our road; I will be up with you before you lose sight of the church spire.'

As an entire family, the Sutherlands sat quietly to the same Cape cart that had collected Cecil Rhodes from the waterfront. The girls were smiling, but the act was one of pretence, their gestures of farewell were stiff-limbed and without enthusiasm. All about the market square, oxen fought the weight of their yokes, eager to move; instinctively they lifted their eyes for the way ahead. Spurred by the whip and shouts from the voorloper they threw their heads and shook out slack from their trek chains.

With flooding eyes the sisters watched each of the

wagons lurch forwards in turn. Charlotte stood up from her seat and fearful of losing that one last glimpse she held her hand aloft, willing Kathleen to look back over her shoulder.

The air was thick with bovine smells, dung and dust. Trek whips crackled like rifle fire and a hundred iron-shod wheels rocked forwards on their axles. Jane Sutherland, without averting her gaze from the spectacle, reached beneath the woven lid of a wicker basket; her fingers found a small silver flask and carefully, she drew it out. Briefly, as a means of diversion she pointed out the unruly cavorting of young, untried oxen, and at the same time, with her left hand, surreptitiously she unscrewed the silver stopper. In the blinking of an eye she had filled her mouth, closed up the flask, slid it back inside the wicker hamper and again, as a means of subtle distraction sniped at her eldest daughter.

'Compose yourself, Charlotte. Sit down, girl. You're making far too much of their leaving. People are staring.'

On impulse, Charlotte jumped from the cart and though her mother called after her, within a space of a hundred yards she had caught up with the O'Rourke's wagon. She stretched out her arm and with urgent fingers fought for a hold on Kathleen's hand.

'Write to me, Kathleen! If there is at all a way. A letter; anything! Promise me! Swear that you will, Kathleen!'

Kathleen leaned from the wagon box; her hair was an auburn halo about the beauty of her face. In her eyes there was a deep and powerful sadness.

'I will, Charlotte! I will get news of my whereabouts sent back to you – I promise.'

The wagon lurched sideways from the off-side front wheel finding a deep rut in the track; the sudden motion parted their fingers.

Alone and with her hand still raised, Charlotte stood at the road's edge and watched the tented column snake from the market square; the wagons became trees and shadows and suddenly they were fighting to survive amongst the colours of the veld. On iron tyres the great turning wheels took them out from the town, away from civilisation, soon to be swallowed up by the wilderness.

# -18-

'So, *engelsman*, you have come to say goodbye?'

Johannes van Reenen watched Jim dismount and then gestured for him to climb the stone steps to the doorway. '*Kom binne*, come inside. It is good to see you again.'

'For a man of the cloth, Dutchman, you show little faith. I would not have left without saying goodbye.'

'And so should it be.' Van Reenen nodded his head in agreement and like winter leaves to the church's tiled roof, his great beard rustled against the front of his waistcoat.

'The Church of the Vow,' van Reenen whispered and gestured with open arms for Jim's benefit. The name departed his lips with sibilance; the stirring of berg winds over long grass. His eyes moved over the innards of that small church and for a moment, he was lost to some far field; the drum of Zulu spears on cowhide shields and the crackle of Mauser rifles were there, all around him, until reluctantly he freed himself of the illusion.

'Many things I have built myself,' he told Jim and now his eyes glowed contentedly, 'hands that once held the Mauser and the spear, have taken up instead, the hammer and the scroll saw.'

He reached out and with an artist's love of fine things ran his fingers over the deeply patterned frontage of the lectern.

'For the makings of God's church, there are none finer; no lesser woods will suffice. No greater trees ever stood as strong and pure as those that fathered these timbers.'

Though the church was small, the feelings Jim incurred from standing inside of it were monumental. Every pew, every wooden piece had been first envisaged through the sublime eye of the master craftsman. Olive wood from the Natal forests; hard and smooth as washed river stones, sometimes blended together with that unique, golden enrichment of the towering Cape yellowwood. He stood at the foot of the high pulpit and looked upwards to where on the Sabbath, van Reenen would stand and preach the Word to his faithful.

'Eighteen forty, *engelsman*. That is when it was made. Guided by the Almighty, two German master carpenters put together this perfection.'

As he had done a thousand times before, the Afrikaner appraised the structure of the great pulpit and marvelled at the exquisiteness of God's holy creation; though assembled by mortal hands it stood to van Reenen as miraculous and all magnificent, a symbol of triumph and acknowledgment of man's awareness of the Supreme entity and the acceptance of his own smallness.

Van Reenen held out his hand, and though he had known the *engelsman* for only those short few days, still, the corners of his eyes glistened.

'And now you must go before our talking makes a woman out of me. Walk with God, my friend; the place where you are going is of the heathen and the wild animal. Sleep with your gun close and when each sun rises, give thanks to the Almighty for your deliverance.'

# II

# The Hinterland

# -1-

With spirited faith in van Reenen's map, Jim shouted directions to Zingeli for him to put his span of twenty oxen to their new heading. Theirs was the only wagon out of the original twenty-four to break from the column and head north-eastwards, for the Boers had turned their wagons north by north-west; determinedly they had followed their beliefs; they sought out new lands, lands neither sullied by Zulu nor Englishman, a place of sanctuary, delivered by God Himself from the heavy yoke of British interference.

Moosa, Jim's self-appointed jack of all trades, walked abreast of the central pair. The Indian boy had muscled up, and his smile, whenever he spoke was as infectious as new sunlight. As he had done for those last two hundred miles, he walked without complaint amongst the trek oxen, and he learned from Zingeli the way in which to flight the whip. Whenever it was asked of him he urged the oxen forwards, putting the lash to within a hair's breadth of those lolloping silken ears.

Jim reined in his horse and from the lip of a long valley gazed outwards to where the track cut steeply into the banks of a lively river. Three times he checked the outlying features against those on the map and then, convinced of their matching up he nodded his head to Kathleen.

'Has to be the Blyde River, my sweetheart; fits van Reenen's description to the letter.' Dolomite hills, rounded and hump-like clustered around ravines and small valleys; the tops appeared as to be shorn of timber, but the slopes were green and lush as any Jim had seen in Natal.

'All of it tallies. The hills, the flow of the river, everything. Van Reenen has brought us right onto it.' He stood high in the stirrups for a fuller surveillance of his surroundings. 'Right on the nose, I would say; God bless the man for his seeing us safely through.'

Kathleen reached across the gap for Jim's saddlebag and drew out the telescope. Long days in the saddle had turned her skin to that same, deep, golden brown of the Boer frontierswoman and where once there had been soft flesh, pale and featureless, now those same limbs were firmly toned, strong and sinuous.

With the glass at its fullest extent she swept the hills and riverine glades for signs of human presence. She followed the crags, probing their secretive shadows for movement, and for as far as was possible traced the track-line until it disappeared inside the far forest. For the most part the forest was thick and untouched, but where the track rose up from the river for it to crest the far bank there were signs of recent human activity. Stumps, still oozing sap, stood out from trees that were left uncut. Felled saplings straddled the track, laced together with green bark and pegged to the ground where mud and the steep river banks were at their most cumbersome.

'There's our crossing place, Pa.' She pointed out the drift and then looked up at the sky; already, great cumulus thunderheads were gathering above the western horizon. 'There's bad weather coming. By nightfall the river could well be in full spate; I say we push on.'

'I agree,' said Jim, 'either we cross now, or wind up stranded this side of the river for God knows how long.'

Along that high ridge, the continuous grind of wagon

wheels had cut deeply into the hillside and, to the left hand, a vertical drop of more than a hundred feet fell to the gut of a boulder-strewn ravine. Kathleen turned the spyglass away from the river and only then, having lowered the angle of her searching did she discover some previous aftermath.

'Some poor souls never made it through, father. People have died out here, the gulley's filled with old bones and wagon parts.'

The carcasses had been stripped bare by scavengers and over time had been scattered in with broken wheels and splintered wagon beds; the sight of the devastation imparted in Kathleen a feeling of dark foreboding. There would have been little, if any time at all for those riding the wagon box to jump clear. Perhaps, like now, a storm had come upon the wagon train and at that point it would have been impossible for them to turn back. Burdened with heavy loads the rear brakes would have been wound fully on – squealing, smoking, even in the wet. The driver's eyes wide with fear and like some wrathful, biblical re-enactment, the sky would have been seething – alight with fire, the air itself filled with terrible thunder. Terrified by all of this the oxen would have gone berserk.

Kathleen sensed her father's apprehension and wheeled her horse in line with the gradient.

'We have no choice, father. We must go down before the storm gets here. Any more rain and the oxen will lose their footing; the wheels won't hold.'

Jim had already made that decision; he looked to the front and shouted instructions to Moosa.

'You and Zingeli; hold the oxen well into the hillside! Take them down to the river!' He turned to Kathleen. 'Stay sharp; we have come too far down the road for us to fail now.'

Moosa moved along the line of waiting oxen, touching his fingers to each one of them as he passed; coaxing them with soft words.

'Be strong, *Inhlanhla*, your good fortune must ride with us. And you, *Ungqongqoshe*, you are the first in line; our leader and strongest of all. Keep our wheels to the road and your feet to solid ground.'

Zingeli lifted his eyes to the heavens and like the beasts behind him, he breathed the oncoming wind.

'You have learned well their praise names, little Moosa *amaNdiya*. It will soon be time for you to walk as a man and take my place at the front.' He looked to the boy. 'The storm will be soon be upon us. Keep your whip and your god alongside you, for today you will need them both.'

Thick with heat and humidity, the air fell silent. It hung above the valley – still, yet menacing. North-west of that solitary wagon, the sky, already the colour of black iron had blocked out the sunlight, and the sounds from out of it were those of the growling lion.

'Stay behind the wagon,' Jim told Kathleen. He slid from the saddle and handed Kathleen the reins to his horse. 'I will stay with the brake or we risk a runaway. Whatever happens, keep clear of the wheels.'

Zingeli positioned himself between the lead pair of oxen. Head and shoulders he stood above them and with gentle hands he stroked their cheeks and coaxed them to where the gradient sloped away at a steep angle. One last time he felt for the tiny, golden cross at his throat and then, with dogged faith he intoned his own beliefs and took his first step forwards, onto the downslope.

# -2-

The storm struck with such ferocity that even Zingeli felt the need to turn his face from the driving rain. Fearful of the tempest, the oxen rolled their eyes and bellowed incessantly, and so close were the clouds that the tallest forest trees appeared to reach inside of them. Where once there had been blue sky and radiant sunlight, now there was a solid, overhanging wall of leaden grey, laced with bolts of lightning – cannoning thunder.

Jim walked in close as he dared to the yawing wagon and driven solely by his intuition, one half turn at a time he wound in the brake. The great iron tyres slowed and settled to wheel scars left by haulage contractors and earlier fortune seekers. Where the ruts were cut to their deepest, now the wounds were busy rivers of red slurry. Once below the surface, the slurry sought out old weaknesses, fissures in that upper layer of decomposing bedrock. Through the rains of a hundred summers these same fissures had been widened and driven deeper into the hillside, prised apart by powerful watery fingers.

With shoulders hunched against the rain, Zingeli fought his way forwards and shouted obscenities at the thunder. Kathleen held short rein to both horses and encouraged them with firm voice and all of her strength. A yard from where they walked, the dolomite jaws of that deep ravine enticed her and she stared down into them like a small child fixated by fire.

The track was trapped between that giddy, vertical drop and a high bank, and it was narrowed to half its normal width by the hillside's natural, right to left downward gradient. In her mind, Kathleen recreated that fateful moment when the settlers' wagons would have been bunched too tightly; their drivers terrified. From the muddied edge, a yard from Kathleen's feet, storm run-off leapt as a waterfall, out into the void, blood red with soil washed from the hillside.

'Kathleen!' Jim shouted through the melee, the sight of her standing so close to the edge frightened him. It would take little more than a sudden squall to spook the horses and unbalance her footing. 'Step away from the edge!'

This time, Jim's shouting caught her attention. She looked back at him and at the very point of her replying, deep beneath the wagon like some mythical giant being roused from a long sleep, the ground itself shifted.

Like that of mountain snow slacked from solid ice by spring melt, so was the sound of moving ground deeply hidden. There was neither sign nor hint of anything untoward happening, for the phenomenon was deceptive, secretive even. This awakening, at first was slight and tentative, then, taking momentum from its changing, as liquid slurry and from that weight of a full wagon travelling across it, the saturated earth shrugged free of its anchorage. With the soft sigh of an old woman, the ground relinquished its grip on the hillside.

The oxen lunged at the gradient, desperate to shirk the yoke – spooked by the earth's imbalance they fought with all their might against the brake. Then, as though intent on following the lumbering trek wagon on its journey down to the valley floor, running lengthways along the track, a yard left of its centre, the earth opened and the rain and slurry were gobbled down inside of it.

Flensed from the road's original plane by underlying subsidence, the track freed itself, and then, miraculously it settled.

For that smallest of moments, Kathleen, still with both sets of reins looped about her wrists managed to steady herself, but it was then that the horses lunged sideways and wrenched her off balance. Her legs, unable to compensate for that sudden movement went from beneath her, and only through her slightness of build was Kathleen spared the drop to the ravine floor.

Doll-like, by both wrists, Kathleen was left suspended against a sheer wall of black rock, the reins now stretched almost to the point of breaking free from their bridles. With braced forelegs and Jim's determined grip on the bit, the horses fought to right themselves, then mercifully the tremors ended. Compressed to stronger, more solid shelves of bedrock the ground settled itself to a new place. Zingeli ducked beneath the necks of the floundering horses and shouted over the storm for Moosa to take control of the oxen. He dropped to the ground and with his left hand locked to an exposed tree root, leaned outwards into the void.

'*Bamba isandla*!' He shouted out to Kathleen. 'Grasp my hand or die!'

Kathleen dangled there, helplessly, like a discarded marionette in mid-air, a hundred feet above the finality of the chasm floor. Without a foothold, she was unable to push herself higher and instinctively she feared that at any moment the softened leather might give way and send her spinning into the abyss. Close as he dared to his tipping point, Zingeli inched forwards on his belly; through fully extending his arm, he encouraged Kathleen to reach out for him. With one hand still grasping the tree root, he lowered his right shoulder and strained with all his being for a longer reach.

Through screwed eyelids, Kathleen stared up at him; slurry covered her face and now the images above her were blurred and unsubstantial. Zingeli's fingers, tantalisingly close, were less than one whole inch away from her own. In desperation, Kathleen swung her legs towards the sheer wall and with the toes of her boots found the solidity of the rock face. She judged the exact whereabouts of Zingeli's outstretched fingers and on her second attempt, found a toehold, a tiny open break in the rock. Zingeli saw her make the find and readied himself.

'Do it now! Push upwards!' he shouted down to her, for behind him, Jim was floundering under the strain of controlling the horses.

Kathleen favoured her right arm, though she was frightened that under the extra weight the leather would give. She forced herself into moving slowly and when the balance felt even, spragged the very tip of her right boot as firmly as she could inside the fissure.

One chance was all that fate would give her; with a prayer on her lips and with all the strength of her right leg she drove herself upwards.

\*

Just as quickly as the storm had come upon them, so did it wheel away to the south-east; mist boiled up from the valley and within that next hour, where iron and rock were exposed to the sunlight both were rendered untouchable. Jim held his daughter within the cradle of his arms, and with the width of his shoulders he sheltered her from the direct heat. Kathleen's eyes fluttered, then opened fully and she looked up at her father; the recollections of what had happened came rushing to her.

'The horses? The wagon? Are they...?'

'All of them safe,' Jim assured her, 'Zingeli and Moosa also. If it weren't for them I would have lost you.'

Kathleen struggled to right herself; with her father's help she regained her balance and looked about her. She massaged the stiffness from her arms and tentatively, probed the flesh and the joints of her wrists for damage. The runoff had disappeared; it was as if the storm had never been and where the track levelled out, as a bright ribbon, an eager river flounced and sparkled over the valley floor. On the opposite bank, an excited stream emptied into the Blyde; with his hand on Kathleen's shoulder Jim drew her attention to the tributary.

'Has to be the stream leading up to the diggings,' Jim pointed it out to her, 'from what I can make out the track runs alongside.'

'Zingeli saved my life,' Kathleen whispered, her mind still outside of the moment.

The Zulu was back with his oxen, he was aware of Kathleen watching him and when she smiled, it was enough.

# -3-

Moosa pushed a handful of dry grass and twigs in amongst the ashes and gently he coaxed new life from last night's pile of floundering embers. In the still, dawn air the smoke went straight up and those first tentative flames were soon to follow. Zingeli dragged over bigger pieces of dry timber and like every man who ever lit a fire, for long moments he watched the flames take hold, mesmerised by the changing colours, a willing victim of fanciful thoughts and old memories. Behind him, the trek wagon stood as a stark outline to the sky and within forty paces of the camp, where the river had spilled its banks, the land itself was strung across with a necklace of silver mirrors.

With the toe of his boot, Moosa pushed an iron kettle deeper inside the coals and from a box beneath the wagon, he took out brown sugar and a muslin bag filled with beaten coffee beans.

'Coffee water is ready and boiling in a few minutes Mister Jim, sir.'

Jim, already dressed, pushed aside the canvas flap and with both feet on the wagon box, took time to look around him. There was an air of expectancy about the camp, already the horizon had coloured and not far from where he stood, flocks of snow white egrets flurried blizzard-like above the forest.

Moosa dropped the muslin bag inside the boiling water

and stirred it with a stick; Jim breathed in the aroma and his senses flooded, then he recalled from that last night's fireside chatter how Kathleen had set her mind to hunting the river line for small antelope. As much as he tried to come to terms with it, her decision to hunt alone perturbed him.

He climbed down from the wagon box and waited for Moosa to fill his cup.

'Two spoons sugar, like you told me, Mister Jim, sir, very good – very sweet on tongue.'

Jim held the mug with both hands and sipped the coffee through a briar of six week old whiskers. The light was strengthening, almost as fast as his concern for Kathleen's reckless urge to bring in meat for the pot. The area was strange to them; the riverine forest, in places grew thick and tall enough for it to block out his view of the valley floor. There was no telling of what dangers might be lurking there. He beckoned to Moosa.

'Tell Zingeli to prepare himself; he will be going with her.'

'To where will he be going, Mister Jim?'

Jim shook his head at the foolhardiness of letting his daughter venture out into the veld, even with a rifle.

'My daughter is going hunting, Moosa. Tell Zingeli to bring his spears, he may well have need of them.'

## -4-

'By high sun,' Jim was adamant, 'I want her back here.'

Again, Moosa listened and passed Jim's instructions to Zingeli.

'Zingeli understands, Mister Jim. They will be back when the sun stands at its highest place above the forest. Do not worry, Mister Jim. Zingeli will keep our Missy Kathleen away from all things harmful.'

Kathleen frowned at her father.

'Do you not think that now is the time for you to stop treating me like a child, father – otherwise, how will I learn?' Reluctantly, Jim suppressed his angst.

'You're happy with the Winchester?'

'Like I had it all my life,' Kathleen grinned and slid the rifle from her shoulder, 'lever down, lever up. Aim and pull the trigger.'

'Slow on the trigger or you'll pull the shot; and pick up your spent casings, we cannot afford for you to leave them behind.'

'Aim, fire and pick up the casings,' the laughter was there in her eyes, 'you already told me, father – more than a dozen times.'

She shouldered the Winchester and with her back to her father, rolled her eyes at Zingeli.

'*Hola madoda*, lead on!' she told the Zulu, 'before my father trades you for a wet nurse.' She pointed downstream, to where islands of waist-high grass broke up the forest.

Jim climbed back onto the wagon box and with a father's paranoia he watched them make their way between the trees. Zingeli led, not willing to risk Kathleen walking in front; her father's wrath, if she were hurt would descend upon him, heavier than the weight of an old disgruntled lion.

Every thicket, every overhanging branch and rocky enclave he scrutinised for snakes, the threat of jackal or the warning rustle of wild pig from their foraging in deep undergrowth. He picked out animal spoor where the ground was still soft and to each new recognition, with purpose, he attached the animal's Zulu name, along with definitive pronunciation for Kathleen to learn from.

With a keen eye, Kathleen learned the peculiarities of each and every set of spoor and with her natural grasp of the *IsiZulu* language, for the most part she spoke as adroitly as her tutor. Expertly she curled her tongue about the nuances of each word and took pleasure from her prowess.

'*Umgankla*. The great bull Kudu!' Kathleen expounded, and with her hands and arms, animatedly she described the twisted horns and striped flanks of this pony-sized antelope. Then the *Impofu*, the eland – grey and great and ghost-like, striding through lakes of winter mists, short-horned and regally endowed about the throat with a soft and silken dewlap.

For one more hour they followed the river. Zingeli taught and Kathleen learned and listened intently. When the sun had climbed through the sky's first quarter the pair turned westwards, along the beginnings of a wide arc that would take them back towards the wagon. It was then that Kathleen witnessed a change come over Zingeli.

Increasing the pace to a slow jog, Zingeli wove between the forest trees and at the same speed, Kathleen followed. As silently as the way allowed she mimicked his every footfall and within that first half-mile, she learned the art of aligning her run face-on into the wind. Constantly, though only the slightest of zephyrs, the air moved from north to south, coming at them head-on so that by sense of smell alone, all creatures to the fore would remain ignorant of their approach.

Zingeli concentrated all his tracking skills on smaller spoor and purposely he ignored the deeper, wider prints of the unmanageable, heavier antelope. On the leeward side of a small hill, he went down on one knee, close to the edge of a quiet stream. With the raising of his hand he gestured to Kathleen.

'What do you see?' he asked her and drew her attention to a pattern of indentations in the soil. 'Look closely,' he spoke with his fingers and through the use of hand signals and each other's limited command of both languages, they managed to communicate.

'The spoor of a small antelope,' Kathleen hazarded, and

delightedly, Zingeli nodded his head.

'*Inkonka*, the bush buck,' he told her, 'and what of these?' Again, he pointed out the spoor. These were bigger; twice the size of the first, but he saw in her face only bewilderment. '*Inkonkoni*, the wildebeest,' he explained for her and then his expression hardened.

Set close to where the bank had been broken away, a single cloven indentation stood out clearly, driven deeply into the soft earth by the sheer weight of its maker; ringed by broken ground it was as though the creature had struggled unduly with its climbing out from the stream. Across its spread, the spoor would easily measure the width of Zingeli's outstretched hand. He picked out sounds from the almost silence, and though he were still some distance out from their source, to a hunter's ears the murmurings were instantly recognizable.

'Walk carefully,' he warned Kathleen, and cupped the palm of his hand to his mouth. Kathleen nodded her head; the sounds she could hear were faint; too far away for her to put a name to, but now, like Zingeli she had sensed the danger. What was once flat and open parkland was now the narrow, thicket-strewn valley. At the edge of a long clearing Zingeli crouched down and from within a redoubt of thick shadow he gestured to Kathleen for her to come alongside him. The air was thick with the stench of putrefaction and in the openness of that blue sky a score of Griffon vultures were already spilling air from their wing feathers.

For three days the buffalo calf stood close-in to its mother's side, refusing to stray from the great beast's shadow, for its frame was gaunt, wasted even, the loss perpetuated by an unnatural disinterest for filling its belly with rich, nutritious milk. Through nervous eyes it watched the forest for movement and in those same eyes there showed a strong malaise, a prodigy of that fatal infection; virulent micro-organisms that had lodged and multiplied ten thousandfold, deep inside the animal's brain.

A slight shift in the wind or some otherwise small noise was enough to trigger irrepressible moments of violent panic, and the urge to quench a terrible thirst was now the fire inside its throat. Instinctively, through a halo of bright froth, the calf reached upwards with its tongue to probe the open wounds on its muzzle, each one of them ripe with virulent, yellow pus where the jackal's teeth had cut to the bone.

Distressed by her own confusion, the dam swung face-on to her calf; she rasped the wounds with her tongue, but this maternal, atavistic need for her to clean them of filth proved less than pitiful, like that of her offspring, her muzzle now shone with a thick yellow film of that same infested suppuration.

The calf died within that third night's final hour of moonlight; where it fell, the ground itself was slicked with excrement and saliva. Still, the dam stayed and doggedly she guarded the lifeless carcass lying at her feet. For long nights and days without food or water she watched and waited, and though she could not reason why, she could not find the urge to leave.

'She will not let us pass,' Zingeli whispered, 'the buffalo calf lies dead at its mother's feet. A wise man would turn back.'

Kathleen touched his arm. 'Over there. In the trees – something moves.'

A slow wind had gathered up the smell of rampant decay and spread it inside the forest. Where only a few hours earlier, there had been pleasant accord within the wilderness, now there was change, a manifestation, that of malice and torment – silent, sinister shadows.

Driven to the very limits of her comprehension by thirst and the cruel tricking of her own mind, the buffalo gathered together what strength was left to her, the urge to kill became paramount. Her awareness of what was happening had diminished to an almost nothingness; the finality of the disease roused in her the darkest instincts so that she lowered that great bossed head and through dead eyes she looked about her and sought out focus for her rage.

The scavengers halted their run, merely a yard in from the forest's edge. A dozen pairs of eyes stared outwards; a young lactating female, emboldened by hunger, trotted out into the sunlight.

'*Impisi*!' The word spat from Zingeli's lips, 'the hyena will not leave without their bellies filled.'

Unable to tear her eyes away, Kathleen watched the drama unfold; saddened by the buffalo's plight, her instinct to intervene was strong. Zingeli sensed her agitation and stayed her with his eyes.

At first, the hyena appeared as tentative, unsure even – the female kept her distance and at twenty yards out, on slow feet she maintained a wide circle. The stricken buffalo stood transfixed, fated to die alone on that dusty arena. Every step was cleverly orchestrated and inexorably the circle tightened. Froth and yellow scum coated the buffalo's muzzle. Infected saliva, as yellow ropes hung from her mouth and now, the grass about her feet was also thick with it.

'Soon they will strike her down,' Zingeli whispered, and

aware of the sun's high place in the sky he contemplated their loss of headway. The sun had already passed its zenith, but to retrace their steps was not an option; it would be dark, long before they could make it back to the wagon.

# -6-

Jim threw a saddle on the gelding, cinched the girth and slid the powerful Sharps rifle inside its saddle scabbard. Worry lines creased his forehead and through tight lips he shouted instructions to Moosa.

'Get a halter on the packhorse, you're coming with me.' He found the stirrup with the toe of his boot and swung up into the saddle. He checked the contents of his saddlebags for drinking water and the telescope; across his chest he had looped a full bandolier of brass cartridges. Moosa rode barefooted, with nothing more than a rope halter and the horse's gritty mane for balance, light as a spring rabbit he followed his master between the trees.

Jim found an open vantage point from where he could look out over the surrounding area. Through screwed eyelids he traced the river line and from his own experience, pre-empted Zingeli's direction through the wilderness. In the oppressive heat of midday, the air was leaden; the trees, for as far as Jim could see were listless clumps of dark foliage. It was then that Moosa put up his arm and through half closed eyes looked to where a long valley opened itself to fields of yellow grassland.

'Down there, Mister Jim. Something is making movement. You must take out the spy-glass; perhaps it is Zingeli but I am not for certain.'

Jim followed Moosa's lead; he gave his instructions without lowering the telescope.

'Go back to the wagon. Keep the fires burning, right through the night if need be.'

He widened his field of vision and as he did so the line of his jaw hardened.

'If I'm not back by morning, you will know where to find me.'

'You are going down...?'

Jim nodded his head and lowered the telescope. Habitually, he checked his reach for the Sharps rifle.

'Get on back to camp, take care of things; there's nothing you can do here.'

# -7-

In the heat of mid-afternoon, the rabies virus approached a point of total appropriation, and now in their billions the infected cells travelled quickly along the pathways of the beast's peripheral nervous system. The slightest sensing of moisture in the earth or even of that same smell brought by the wind from pools of trapped rainwater was enough to trigger a violent madness and like some terrible, hellish entity the buffalo shook its massive armoured head and drooled incessantly.

The slightest noise was turned upon, hypersensitive to light and movement, the buffalo's confusion turned to blind rage so that spontaneously she cut and slashed at a hundred imagined demons with those yard-wide horns. Her bellowing, now almost incessant was long and thunderous, tormented by the rampant pain inside her head.

From the forest's edge the hyenas watched and crowded together in the shadows, seemingly bemused by the buffalo's uncharacteristic reaction to their being there. Though they had not eaten for several days, direct confrontation with an animal of more than four times their own weight would serve only to decimate their numbers. When their time came, they would recognise the moment and without hesitation they would act upon it.

Jim hit flat ground at a full canter, slack-reined for his horse to pick its own way between the scrub; with each new breath he cursed his lack of foresight, though up to that very moment, neither he nor Zingeli had expected any such encounter with buffalo. The animals' preference was for lower lying land, where the scrub was thick and the heat and mopani forests even thicker.

Kathleen was heavily under-gunned; the Winchester, though quick-firing and powerful enough to kill a hyena, in the hands of any buffalo hunter it was small-bored and pathetically inadequate, the impact of its .44 calibre bullet to the thick hide of a full grown buffalo would stand as little more than careless provocation. However, a single reckless shot would be enough to turn even a sick or wounded buffalo from a state of benignity into a mountainous, unstoppable killer. Forcing these thoughts from his mind, Jim chose his spot; in the shadow of a red-pear he vaulted clear of the saddle, loose-kneed for him to ride the impact and within moments of him hitting the ground he cleared Sharps rifle from its scabbard.

Five hundred yards of broken scrub stood between him and the buffalo. At that distance, sighting the shot through the dust and heat haze would test the limits of all his skills with the Sharps. From the bandolier across his chest he drew out a single, brass cartridge and fed the rifle's breech. There was a chance that on hearing the shot the hyena would scatter; Zingeli would seize the moment and with Kathleen in tow, would clear the narrow break in the hills before the hyena chanced to regroup.

It was then that the entire clan broke from the treeline; their leader had made her choice and with devilish voice encouraged the others; as a single, co-ordinated pack they came out from the shadows and into the sunlight.

## 8

Jim held the shot in check; he needed a full, side-on showing of the buffalo's flank to be sure of a kill. He rested the Sharps against a crook in the tree and with steady fingers flicked up the rifle's rear sight. He watched and waited for the target to stand its ground; a few seconds would be enough. However, the air above the clearing was thick with colour and from his hide beneath the tree, Jim O'Rourke looked on and cursed his luck; where only hours before the soil had been damp and hard-packed, now, harangued by strong sunlight and a sudden influx of hunting carnivores, it threw up clouds of coloured dust, enough to deny him a clear view of the buffalo.

'My father,' Kathleen realised, and careful enough as not to draw attention from the hyena, she stood up from her hiding place, her heart thumping.

When she raised her hand, likewise her father put up his arm and acknowledged her signal. From the way he was leaning against the tree, Kathleen guessed he was readying the Sharps rifle.

As if her quarters were fixed to the ground, constantly the buffalo rotated about the carcass of her offspring. Laced with saliva and from behind that abhorrent mask, she leered at her aggressors, her muzzle thick with yellow froth and infected sputum.

'It is happening,' Zingeli warned, 'be still; move only when I tell you. Wait for your father to kill the buffalo and when you run, do so as if the devil himself is at your heels.'

The largest of the males broke ranks and turned inwards, coming from behind, it exploited the buffalo's growing confusion and, unwilling to risk injury, went straight for the dead calf. However, without warning, manifested by the latter stages of the disease, the first convulsions drove the dam backwards onto her haunches; with her head thrown high the spasms became more violent and she bellowed pitifully. The pack, startled by the suddenness of the seizures, held off from the killing.

Jim lowered the Sharps and for confirmation of Kathleen's safe whereabouts, again he focused the telescope. A small wind had come upon the clearing from the north-west, it hurried the dust away and as if by magic the haze fell open, it was then that Jim was made aware of an unforeseen, more prominent danger.

In line with Kathleen and Zingeli and no more than sixty yards to their rear, with the unhurried gait of reticent hunters, three lionesses bunched in close together; all were young adults, lithe and willowy – barely a year on from losing their cub spots. Drawn to the melee by smell and squabbling hyena, they were as yet still unaware of any human presence. On silent, padded feet, head and shoulders above the grass they moved line abreast and went down towards the clearing.

Kathleen saw the buffalo go down and she could not help herself. Oblivious to the added threat she broke from cover, concerned only with her avoiding the attention of the hyena she ran within those first few yards of treeline, however, separated from Zingeli, she was now the lone objective and covered only a distance of fifty yards before she was seen.

Dressed in khaki shirt and breeches, her colouring was close to that of a fleeting antelope and, eager for fresh chase, the lions locked on to her. Slowly at first they mimicked her speed, in and out of the trees and then back inside a sea of waist-high grass. There was no urgency to their following; their quarry was slow-footed and clumsy and with that deliberate, half-hearted intent of a cat gaming the mouse, they appeared as if to prolong the chase. Smooth as rocking horses, as golden-coloured wraiths they seemed to float above the earth.

Jim saw the lions pick up on the sudden movement,

Kathleen now the running hare, the lions the closing lurchers. She ran with the Winchester held across her chest and even at that distance, Jim sensed her panic. He lowered his sights from five to four hundred yards and with his weight balanced against the tree he lifted the rifle's butt to his shoulder. He scanned for a target, but the lions were vague outlines, only intermittently did their heads stand out clearly from above the yellow grass. It was then that Zingeli appeared from nowhere, perpendicular to Kathleen's line of flight. Again, Jim found his shot blocked out for fear of hitting either Kathleen or Zingeli.

'*Gijima*! Run to your father!' Zingeli shouted after her; he had seen the lions and without regard for his own life settled himself between the hunters and the hunted. With his spear levelled at waist height, he prepared to stand his ground.

Out of the three, two swung to a halt less than thirty yards from Zingeli. However, as if he were little more than a mound of earth, the swiftest and boldest lioness flew past him, her focus locked unerringly to Kathleen. It was at that very moment that Kathleen dared to look back over her shoulder, the Winchester, though cocked and ready to fire was now the impotent curse, willing her to turn and face her assailant, but her legs refused to respond. She glanced sideways and sensed rather than saw the nearness of the lioness, coming in fast and low to the ground; quick gold rippling through the grass. In her heart, Kathleen cried out for her father to shoot, but the strength had gone from her legs, and it was then Jim saw her fall, her right foot snagged by a rock or tangled fast by coils of wild snake bean.

Kathleen hit the ground and the air was driven out from her lungs. The cat was coming at her head-on; from where she had fallen and from her looking upwards, at that lower angle the full effect of what was happening was now a product of her worst, most terrifying nightmare.

Haloed in sunlight, the cat's great head filled the sky;

sand flew from her paws and already those hooked yellow claws were fully bared, but it was the eyes upon which Kathleen now focused. However, robbed of choice, Jim fully committed to the shot and squeezed the trigger. In that still air, he prayed for the bullet to hold its line, a foot too low and it would be Kathleen who suffered the full force of the strike, an inch too high and the attempt would be worthless.

The bullet went in through the lioness' open jaws and without any restriction to its speed, destroyed the uppermost pair of vertebrae before exiting a pad of thick muscle at the base of her neck. Kathleen shielded her face from the charge, but the lioness had already died on her feet and as a lifeless bundle rolled sideways into long grass. Spooked by the gunfire, her siblings spun away inside the forest.

Zingeli came at a full run; without waiting for Kathleen to speak, he threw aside his spear and with hurried eyes searched her limbs for bite marks. Jim wheeled his horse alongside and jumped down from the saddle.

'Are you hurt?'

Kathleen shook her head; with trembling fingers she checked between her ribs for the give of broken bone. Jim helped her upright and on shaky legs she picked up the Winchester. Less than a yard from her feet, fully outstretched, the lioness appeared as if it were merely asleep in the sunlight, but the wound in its neck and those quiet eyes were already filling with greenbottle flies. Kathleen turned away and only through supreme effort did she prevent herself from retching; neither the sunlight on her back nor any reasoning could halt her shivering.

## 9

Sunrise found the river well below that last day's level of flooding and without concern, Zingeli led the oxen down into water that was now, little more than knee-deep. Kathleen rode alongside her father, her ribs strapped with linen bandage to protect the bruising against her sudden, habitual twisting in the saddle. Moosa coaxed the oxen forwards and with supple arms he put out the whip to its full length and took delight from giving it voice, and though it hissed and crackled like far off gunfire, the act was empty of malice.

From the riverbed, to where the flood waters had failed to reach, the oxen hauled the wagon up and over rafts of cut saplings, and through gaps in the trees, Jim caught a first glimpse of canvas tents scattered across the hillside. Within that next hour, at the beginnings of a secluded valley he shouted out for Zingeli to bring the wagon about.

He kneed his horse close-in to Kathleen's and his smile was infectious.

'The Black Hills all over again, only this time, hopefully, there will be no Lakota Indians for us to contend with.'

'Just miners, father and plenty of them – the place is full-on swarmed with diggers.' Kathleen stood high in the stirrups; the sight of other people she found to be comforting, but at the same time, their being there unsettled her; the diggings were already akin to an ants' nest. From the beginnings of a small creek at the valley head, almost to where it joined the bigger river, the ground to either side bristled with claim pegs. Crude, lean-to timber shacks and faded canvas tents dotted the hillside and where a narrow, gravel track ran through the middle of them, here were the first, rudimentary makings of mud-brick buildings, roofed with sheets of corrugated iron.

Those belonging to the more progressive had been given a lick of lime wash paint and in the sunlight, stood out brightly from the veld. Wagons, left where their owners first outspanned were heavily overgrown with creeper vines. The oxen, either traded straight from the yoke, or were butchered and sold at the roadside; fresh meat straight off the hoof.

'So what now,' Kathleen looked to Jim for guidance, 'do we go on down there?'

Jim shook his head. 'You wait here. Tell Zingeli and Moosa to outspan the oxen and get a fire going,' he dismounted and handed the reins to Kathleen, with uncertain eyes he looked to the nearest building, 'just stay put; give me an hour to find out what we're up against.'

*

Jim followed a network of well-trodden paths, forced to watch his step where diggers had defecated and not bothered to shovel their filth beneath the ground. The Sharps rifle he carried with him and jealously he guarded it, for the heavy calibre buffalo gun he knew would bring him more attention than he bargained for. Like any other goldfield, miners who were down and out on their luck would stop at nothing in order to bankroll their passage back home; by its own merit, sold on, the Sharps would pay a digger's way, at least to as far as the Cape.

Through an open doorway, Jim perused the rudiments of a trade counter; made up of planks stripped from a trek wagon, they had been hurriedly nailed together and to the rear of the improvised store, shelves made from that same rough wood had been fixed between two natural timber roof supports. The roof itself, where time and weather had eaten the metal away allowed in rods of bright sunlight.

Though the store had been roughly cobbled together, the keeper had stacked his goods in orderly rows; candles and matches, salt and tobacco and with his hands splayed against the countertop, the trader watched and waited for Jim to speak first.

'I'm new here,' Jim spoke out, his voice overly loud.

'I can tell. Too much meat on your bones; not many men can afford the luxury, at least not out here on Pilgrim's Creek'

The storekeeper straightened up, leaned with his left hand to the countertop and extended his right to Jim.

'McLeod – Gareth to my friends.'

'O'Rourke.' Jim accepted the hand. 'Jim to you; Ireland raised, but left her for America nigh on twenty years ago.'

McLeod's eyes rolled skyward.

'Another Yankee Doodle. Few more of your countrymen further up the creek, come on over from the Mac Mac diggings ten miles east of here. Good men, keep to their own kind, though; hard lot, same as the Australians, quick with their fists but just as quick to reach down the bottle when the fighting's done with.'

He came from behind his counter and stood in the doorway. He pointed upstream and singled out a covey of faded tents surrounded by gravel heaps.

'If it's good advice or a fight you're after, they'll be the ones to oblige. Follow the creek – take you right to them and be sure to watch your mouth – cocky bastards, even take to running up their Stars and Bars Confederate flag when they hit good gold.'

'Who should I ask for?'

'Bo Furguson. Big fellow – black hair blue eyes, big like a brick-built shithouse and hands like busted shovels, if you follow my meaning.'

'Then I shall heed your advice.' Jim smiled at storekeeper and looked past him. 'Your candles and matches – how much?'

'Depends on how many you want.'

'Six of each, depending on your prices,' Jim countered.

McLeod made a quick calculation.

'Seeing as you're new out here, four shillings the lot.'

Jim looked incredulous, for the price had leapt three times above his expectations. 'What about foodstuff? Mealie meal and meat?'

The storekeeper shook his head. It was always the same; through the space of that last week he had told the story a hundred times.

'Finished, my friend, and you'll not see the likes of it again until the smouse traveller brings his wagon in from Lydenburg.'

'When will that be?'

'End of the month – a week today.'

With reluctance, Jim paid over the odds for the goods and with lighter pockets, he followed the creek upstream to where tons of excavated rock and gravel had been sluiced and then discarded. Haphazardly, the waste had been heaped some twenty yards in from the river bank. Several canvas tents, pitched close-in to either side of the creek stood as sentinels. Ten feet below bank level, four men bent their backs to an exposed, underlying gravel bed; all but one man worked stripped to the waist, all were hard-muscled and easily, they hefted the pick, the steel prising bar and the shovel. All four sensed Jim being there and in unison they straightened up. The biggest, heavily built and taller than the rest looked at Jim through lion's eyes, he spat a sodden cheroot from between his lips.

'If it's broken bones you're looking for, mister, step on down, otherwise best for you to keep on going.'

'McLeod – the storekeeper,' Jim looked at him square-on, 'said this is where I might find a Bo Furguson?'

'And if the man were here, what would you want with him?'

'Nothing he wouldn't take to.'

'We'll be the judge of that, mister.' All four men dropped their tools and climbed out from the gravel bed. All were

110

within an inch of the same height, though bigger boned than Jim. One man, head and shoulders above the others, dressed in calico breeches and buttoned shirt towered a full five inches over Jim O'Rourke.

'I'm Furguson. An hour ago – saw you on the way in – recognised the saddle. A McClellan cavalry; you buy it fair and square back home or thieve it off of some dead Yankee's horse?'

'Fair and square,' Jim countered, 'Dakota, Sioux country. Plenty of gold but more trouble than I could live with. Came over via the Port of London – September time.'

Furguson nodded his head and without looking down, slapped his son's inquisitive hand away from Jim's rifle.

'Buffalo gun...?'

'Sharps .50 calibre,' Jim concurred, 'keeps me in meat.'

He swung the conversation back to the reason for his being there.

'The track for Peach Tree diggings...? I'd thank you to give me directions and I'll be on my way.'

Furguson's eyes narrowed and like before, his voice hardened.

'What're your interests in Peach Tree Creek? The digging belongs to the Dutchman, van Reenen.'

'That's as it was,' said Jim, 'van Reenen passed all mining rights to his property over to me.'

'How'd we know there's any truth in what you're saying? Jumping another man's claim will get you dead. The man happens to be a friend of mine, so best you come up with proof of what you're saying, mister, or get on back the way you came before my blood gets all riled up.'

Jim reached inside his breast pocket for van Reenen's letter of legal transfer; rain had dulled the ink, but the writing was still legible. He offered the letter to Furguson, but the burly southerner shied clear.

'Read it for me – eyesight ain't much good anymore and stick to what's important, none of the Dutchman's church talk, the man was God-crazy.'

Jim read aloud, enough for them all to hear and then, like some dutiful preacher reaching the end of his sermon, he re-folded the letter and buttoned it away.

'I'll stand good for any unpaid wages, that's if van Reenen's boys are still around these parts.'

'One of them works for me, reckoned on no one coming back. The others are still out there, but your setting foot on Peach Tree Creek will not go down well with the Kelly brothers. They took up legal rights to the claims, six months after van Reenen left. Stand more'n a good chance of getting yourself a beating, or worse.'

He wiped both hands on his breeches and extended one to Jim.

'Bo Furguson. My apologies for the bad start; every man between here and the Mac Mac diggings has hungry eyes for my claim.'

Jim accepted the hand. 'Jim O'Rourke.'

Furguson's skin was heavily calloused and though he tempered his grip, the strength in his fingers was that of a powerful man. Jim followed him between the gravel heaps, the tent, badly faded had living space enough for two men. Proven by many storms the inside was dry and orderly. Narrow, improvised cots had been pushed against opposite sides and between them, put together as an integral part of the central support, a roughly shaped table and low stools made up all of what were Bo Furguson's furnishings. Only one other item, a battered tin trunk showed from beneath one of the beds. Furguson dragged it into the open, partially lifted the lid and reached out a full bottle of brandy.

'Van Reenen was a good man, one of the first out here; him, Alec Patterson and George Lilley. Patterson was the first prospector to find gold in the creek, came over from the Mac Mac diggings with his sluice, picks and shovels and everything he owned piled on a wheelbarrow.' He swilled out a pair of glass tumblers with clean water, set them down on the table and pulled up a stool across from

Jim O'Rourke. 'Then Lilley and van Reenen stumbled across rich pickings across the way in Peach Tree Creek; opened up a stretch of rich rubble, bottom of a waterfall, kind of worked their claims side by side until van Reenen started hearing voices.' Furguson shook his head and looked skywards. 'Convinced himself that the Almighty was talking to him; left his claim with hardly a word to anybody – just up and disappeared.' He unscrewed the cap from the bottle and poured both glasses full to the brim.

'And he never came back...?' Jim guessed.

Furguson shook his head. 'Never saw van Reenen again. Told his kaffirs to look after the diggings, left them with a month's pay and a hundredweight bag of mealie meal, some old clothes, boots, two donkeys and his store of picks and shovels.' Furguson clamped a fresh cigar between his teeth and dragged a Vesta across the tent pole. He inhaled deeply and chased the smoke down with a mouthful of raw spirit.

'So where did you meet him?'

'Natal,' Jim told him, 'ministers the Dutch Reformed Church in Pietermaritzburg; the man has little time for anything else.'

Furguson went on. 'George Lilley carried on sluicing not far from here, just above our boundary line; did well for himself. Made enough to go back home and buy that little farm all of us dream over.'

'He left Pilgrim's Creek?'

Furguson nodded his head. 'Not long after finding the Lilly Nugget – topped a hundred and ninety ounces, that's more'n five hundred pounds worth of raw gold for one day's work.'

'Five hundred, a hell of a sum; more than most men earn in three years.'

Furguson smiled at the expression of incredulity on Jim's face.

'Happens all the time, most say nothing; like van Reenen and George Lilley, they vanish before the jackals hear of what they've found and come scavenging.'

'What about you?'

Furguson shrugged his shoulders.

'I've had my moments.' He reached inside his breeches pocket for a small glass-stoppered bottle and passed it over the table to Jim. 'An average day's takings; mostly small nuggets and fines – three ounces, give or take a pennyweight or two. Ten hours of sweat, blood and blisters are what you're looking at there, mister.'

Even before Jim took hold of the bottle, his own insatiable obsession for mining gold came awake.

'Then there's these little beauties,' Furguson went on and opened the neck of his shirt collar.

Strung at regular intervals to a crude rawhide thong, a necklace of gold nuggets hung like weighty yellow beads, all of them punched through with a sharpened steel for the making of their eyelets.

'These I don't sell.' Furguson grinned at him through the smoke. 'To get your hands on them you'll have to kill me. My old man always made sure he had the price of his passage back home.' He held up the largest of the ten for Jim to scrutinise. 'If things go wrong, this one on its own will cover the cost of my ticket out of here. God willing, it will never come to that.'

The smallest was the size of an English half penny, but four times its thickness. The largest of the ten, like overripe fruit shed from the branches of the wild plum, was gnarled and misshapen, though more beautiful than anything Jim had ever seen. Through a natural, unusually high silver content, the nugget's colouring showed up more as a lighter shade of yellow; *kind of blonde*, Furguson insisted, rather than that lustrous, red-raw colour of gold Jim had taken from Dakota's rushing mountain streams.

'Big ones like these are hard won,' Furguson elaborated. He buttoned them back inside his shirt, drained his glass and was forced to wait for the heat in his throat to ease before he could speak. 'The boulders, Jim, that's where you find them; underneath the bastard boulders, rocks big as donkey carts and quick to crush any fool stupid enough not to watch his step.'

He poured their glasses full and re-lit his cigar. His eyes misted over.

'No noise; quieter'n a mouse from out of a grain bag. No warning. Holds a man flat up against the gravel; that's when the water gets you. Take your choice – crushed or drowned, comes down to the same thing, I guess. Graveyard's full of fools and there's room for plenty more. As long as there's gold in the creek, men will die, Jim. Men will die and that's a certainty.'

Furguson studied the man sitting across from him. Like his own, the newcomer's face was burned dark from too many long days in harsh sun.

'You know how to sluice, then?'

Jim nodded his head. 'Ten years. Not saying that I know all there is to. Different gravel, different part of the world, but what I don't know, I'll soon learn.'

'That you will,' smiled Furguson, 'or you'll be running for home before the rains are finished; poor as a church mouse and sickened through to the soul from your going without.'

# -10-

'How much food do we have left?' Jim looked to his daughter for answers. Kathleen watched her pot of water come to the boil.

'Mealie meal, enough for two to three weeks. The meat's all but finished; two more servings after today. Can't say I'm sorry neither. More salt than pork and from the smell of it, more suited to feeding crows than people.' Carefully, she fed the water with maize meal and stirred it till it thickened. Finally, as a folded mountain of stiff porridge it hissed and steamed for it to be taken off from the fire. With her cloth doubled over to protect her fingers, she lifted the pot clear of the heat.

'This Bo Furguson, Pa? How long has been here?'

'A long time,' Jim told her, 'came on over from the Mac Mac diggings. Followed up on a rumour and pegged himself a prime piece of the creek before the rush started.'

'What do we do about van Reenen's claim? Looks like we might have come all this way for nothing?'

'First thing tomorrow,' Jim reassured her quickly, 'we pay the Kelly brothers a visit. There's no going back; too much sweat and too many miles for us to give up now. By rights, that piece of ground on Peach Tree Creek is ours, the Kelly brothers will have to pack up their gear and move on.'

'There may well be trouble. They won't just walk away from six months work, don't see them paying any attention to a letter written by someone who is no longer here.'

Kathleen was right, the claim had been left unguarded for near on six months, from what Bo Furguson had told him, if need be, the Kelly brothers might well put up a fight to keep control of Peach Tree Creek.

'One way or the other, we have to find out,' Jim told her. He crouched in close to the fire and watched its flickering colours parade their fantasies for him. From out of red hot valleys and swirling mists of woodsmoke, his thoughts, regrets and aspirations rolled as sombre waves over sullen embers. From above the forest, moonlight slinked between the trees and to the front, beyond where Zingeli had cleared the ground for their temporary camp, the thousand lighted lamps of Pilgrim's Creek were yellow stars on the hillside. He closed his eyes, the uncertainty of what he had brought them to was now the leaden weight inside his stomach; like melting ice from between his fingers, van Reenen's gifted eldorado was slipping further and further away.

*

The moon was barely visible, by a hair's small breadth, perilously it clung to the very edge of the western horizon, and then it slid away and disappeared. To the east the sun rose up, big and fat and was as always, that softer dawn yellow. Jim watched it colour the sky and habitually he reached down from the saddle and with his fingertips, felt for the familiarity of his rifle.

'I should come with you,' Zingeli spoke slowly, for the American's grasp of the Zulu tongue was still in its infancy.

'You will follow only if I call you to do so, or if you hear a shot,' Jim countered. 'Alone, they will not see me as a threat. Perhaps they will heed the sense in what I say.'

Jim left Zingeli where the stream from Peach Tree Creek tumbled into the Blyde; a narrow, well-worn track snaked between the trees and from some several hundred yards inside the forest, Jim picked up on men's voices filtering back to him. Where the track ran close to the stream, prospect trenches had been cut at right angles to the flow of water, and along the banks, on both sides, the now familiar piles of gravel and river stones were dark islands standing out above the undergrowth.

The forest opened, though only slightly and it was then that Jim made out the scarred and battered heart of the diggings; three, thirty foot sluice boxes diverted water away from the main stream. At the head of each box a native labourer shovelled in fresh gravel from a heap alongside him and with each new shovel the water ran thick and deeply tainted with slurry.

Jim urged his horse towards a cleared area hung with Tilley lamps, here inside the thick forest the sunlight

117

struggled to reach the darkness. A pool of dull yellow light stretched from the centre of the clearing and at its periphery, two bearded men hunched their shoulders over a rickety, deal table, their heads down, hands busy, eyes focused entirely on whatever it was they gave their attentions to.

'Hello the camp!' Jim shouted over the sound of rushing water and the reaction to his voice was immediate.

Both men came out from their chairs as if a poisonous snake had been thrown between them; both were armed and like besieged soldiers came towards the stranger with their rifles pointed up at his chest.

'What do you want with us, mister?'

Jim lifted his hands away from his sides.

'Just talk; no harm intended. You have my word on it.'

'Get down from your horse.' Grey-haired and matted with filth, the older of the two stepped in closer. 'Keep your hands away from that pistol, mate or I'll see you in hell – quick as a bear up a gum tree.'

Jim climbed down off his horse.

'Easy on the trigger or you'll have a dozen more men up from my camp on the river; all of them armed.'

He nodded his head to the younger, less fired up of the Australians.

'Jim O'Rourke. Up from Natal, got here yesterday.'

'Pat Kelly,' his eyes flicked sideways, 'him with more whiskers than me, my older brother, Ethan. What do you want from us?'

Jim handed across van Reenen's note of legal transfer. 'Looks like there's been some sort of confusion over who owns the claim you're working.'

Pat Kelly read the letter and passed it to his brother.

'Says our digging belongs to this here stranger, Ethan...? What do we say to that, mate?'

'I say we shoot the claim-jumping bastard and bury him under the waterfall. We took this claim, fair and square, mister. The ground was abandoned; everyone around

118

these parts knows it.' He glanced sideways in the direction of the nearest sluice. 'Big black fella, the one with the hat, worked for van Reenen; talk to him, he'll tell you what happened.'

'He speaks English?'

'That he does. Reckon he'll tell you how he damn near starved to death waiting for his boss to come on back. Wasn't for me and my brother, the bastard would have turned up his toes.'

Jim led his horse between the gravel heaps and closed to within a few yards of the sluice head. At first, the black labourer avoided eye contact and turned his back on the stranger.

'You worked for van Reenen?' Jim attempted.

'Perhaps. Perhaps not. Why do you ask me, white man?' He turned around and leant on his shovel. His skin gleamed with sweat. Though shorter than Jim, the continuous hard labour of shifting gravel onto the sluice head had ripped his torso of any fat.

'The man spoke well of you.'

'It is easy for a man to talk, but words buy little food for my children. The Boer walked away and left us only with little hope of him coming back. Like the flame from a wasting candle, hope dies and you are left alone with the darkness.'

'What is your name?'

'*Inkunzi*, like the wild pig at a time of little food, always I dig inside the earth, but there is little enough to find. We dig where the earth is empty.' He lowered his voice and moved closer to where Jim was standing. The brothers were back at the sorting table; watching, listening, but at that distance were unable to make good their efforts. 'No gold, no pay. The men you have spoken with are fools, just piece-piece of the yellow metal, none of what they find bigger than a grain of river sand.'

'For how long has it been like this?'

'Many weeks, both are cursed with the gold sickness;

119

they make us dig for nothing and like the gold, the money for one month's labour is small – more than once, our wages have been passed over.' His eyes narrowed and the smile that Jim had hoped for was suddenly there in his eyes. 'The gold is close, white man, but only *Inkunzi* knows of its hiding place. Take the claim from them and if I cannot show you where to dig out gold from the earth, then I give you my word, I will work for you until the rains are finished – without pay.'

'What of the others?' Jim asked him, 'will they join you and work for a man they have not seen before?'

The labourer nodded and looked about him.

'They do as I say, but first you must take the claim. A small price will be needed, but if your purse is strong and you are man enough for the task, by nightfall the brothers will be gone.'

With his voice lowered almost to that of the rushing water, he hefted the shovel and continued loading gravel into the sluice box. From the corner of his eye he looked to Jim. The spark of hope flickered, caught and then burned brightly.

'Do this and I will show you enough gold to please the hearts of a hundred men. Be as the fox or the eagle, watch with open eyes and choose your words carefully.'

Inkunzi bowed his head, aware that the brothers were watching.

'Help us, white man. Our stomachs are empty. Our children lie awake at night; they wait for death to step inside the doorway.'

He glanced across the clearing, wary of suspicion; quickly he directed Jim's attentions to the older of the two Australians.

'The one with many whiskers – be wary of the jackal.'

Pat Kelly expelled a stream of brown tobacco juice straight to the heart of the fire; red heat burned off the spittle as bright steam and then fell quiet. Working a piece of raw charcoal over the table's bare planking, the Australian drew out the creek's direction of flow and then, to the makeshift drawing, quickly he added the approximate, legitimate boundaries of the Peach Tree gold claims.

'Three claims, each of them fifty yards by fifty yards, standard legal size for a gold claim.' He looked over his shoulder to where the most north-westerly of the corner beacons stood in plain view. 'From the base of the hill, back along the ridge and across the creek, all the beacons are in good order.'

'If I were to part with money,' said Jim, 'it would be more for a place to store equipment and provide living space for my men.' He paused for a long moment, purposely allowing the uncertainty to hang there. 'If the gold is good, why would you sell? The word on Pilgrim's Creek is that your diggings here are all but worked out.'

'Then the men you spoke to were bastard liars!' Ethan Kelly flared up and stood upright to the table. 'Coming down on us with your bullshit bad luck stories won't get you anything but trouble, mister.'

Ethan's fingers were bone-white, clamped like dogs' jaws to the edge of the table. Inside his head there argued the many voices of the obsessive; most were those of the paranoid gold hunter, and from the corners of his mouth, like weeping fat from an over-filled griddle, spittle dribbled down inside his whiskers.

'The gold's still there and plenty of it, Yankee. The price stands – five hundred pounds and not a penny under.'

'Then we're wasting each other's time,' said Jim and stood up from the table. 'I've heard there are plenty men looking for a buyer; other side of the mountain – the Mac Mac diggings.' He nodded his head to Pat Kelly. 'If I find there's nothing else, maybe we'll talk again. But my offer will stand at two hundred pounds – damn near all I've got.'

He turned to where he had tethered his horse and it was then he heard the guarded metallic click of a weapon being cocked for firing.

Jim turned on his heels and within that same moment his right hand came up from his breeches belt, the Colt was already fully cocked before it reached the level of his eyeline. At that distance, Jim knew that within an inch of the target the heavy .44 bullet would wreak total devastation; like a fist through wet snow Ethan Kelly's brain would be pulped and flushed from his skull in a fraction of a single second.

'Put down the rifle, Ethan or die where you stand.'

Pat Kelly sidestepped the table and ripped the gun from his brother's hands; he flung it onto the table.

'You bloody old fool, Ethan. We're taking the man up on his offer. Two hundred pounds and the little we have put aside is enough to see us home with money in our pocket. Miss our chance to leave this cesspit and I swear the pair of us will die here.'

Jim lowered the Colt and eased the hammer back down.

'So how do we stand? Do we shake hands or do I walk away and spend my money somewhere else?' He waited for their answer.

Pat Kelly nodded his head; he sank back into his chair.

'When can you pay us?' The fight had gone out of them; all the malice and the fury had drained from Ethan's voice.

'Soon as the claim has been reregistered in my name,' Jim promised. 'Two hundred pounds in exchange for the new licence; shouldn't take you more'n a couple of days, but you leave the claim before nightfall. Once you're off there'll be no coming back, save for you to hand over the new deed of ownership and for you to collect your money and any bits and pieces left lying around, but only when

I'm satisfied the deal is all sewed up and legal.'

Pat Kelly extended his right hand to Jim.

'All we need from here is our personals.' He looked towards a rickety shack set to the edge of the treeline. 'Tin box, blankets and boots – pick them up in a couple of days.'

Jim accepted the hand. 'Two days from tomorrow then – bring me what's due and the money's yours, you have my word on it.'

The brothers wasted little time in saddling up. Ethan Kelly drew his horse alongside and with a change of heart gratefully, he tipped his hat to the American.

'Two days, you said?'

'That's all the time you need,' Jim enforced and watched the Australians ride on out from the clearing.

# -12-

For the first one hundred yards the track to Peach Tree Creek was more than wide enough to take the wagon, but with vindictive fingers the forest tightened her grip and closed in, so that only a narrow space was left, barely enough for two grown men walking shoulder to shoulder.

Jim enlisted Inkunzi and four others, all of them except for one man had worked for van Reenen, and for the first time in many months they chattered like monkeys and their spirits soared. Zingeli worked alongside them with the long axe and the bowsaw and quickly the track widened. Bigger and stronger than all the others, he was a natural leader. Like a man obsessed with winning the prize, Zingeli wielded his axe and as the unstoppable, rolling boulder, he cut and slashed a way for the oxen and wagon to pass through.

When the light began to fade, Zingeli led the oxen out to

grass, but close-in to the wagon for fear of lion and wild dog. He built fires and from the river's edge, Kathleen and Moosa gathered in wild spinach and then just as eagerly, Moosa took his gun deep inside the reed beds and within that last hour of daylight, with his smooth bore flintlock loaded with bird shot, brought down two, plump Egyptian Geese from a skein of more than fifty. In exchange for a share of mealie meal, Kathleen accepted a goose from Zingeli and within that same hour the smell of it roasting over a low fire flooded her mouth with saliva.

'What if the place is mined out, Pa...? Two hundred pounds is a hefty piece of what we have left.'

'It isn't. The gold is far from finished, and on the Zulu's word it's waiting there for the taking. Nothing will convince me otherwise.'

'How would Inkunzi know? Why didn't he tell the Kelly brothers?'

Jim turned the goose on its makeshift spit; fat dripped, splattered and sucked out flames from the embers.

'Why would he? The Kelly brothers would have given him nothing in return, short of more work and no pay for his trouble.' He looked around as if the brothers might be listening in. 'Seen it before, back in the Black Hills before you were born. Couple of old prospectors working the creeks for placer gold; stayed upwards of a week with them, drank too much and swapped too many stories.' He smiled at the recollections. 'Found an old riverbed; turned out the river had changed course, blocked off years back by a massive landslide. Water managed a way through again, but a hundred yards east of its old course. The old timers opened up the bottom of an old, dried out waterfall; went down thirty feet before they hit the glory hole.'

'Glory hole...?'

Jim nodded his head.

'Twenty feet of rich gravel lying against the bedrock; took out more gold in a month than they did in those last two years. Mined it clean and the last I heard was they left for California with their winnings and a couple of young whores in tow.'

He leaned over the fire and riddled new life from the embers.

'Inkunzi showed me where the hillside has been scarred through by fast-moving water. Reckon on a hundred foot drop from the top of the ridge. Never been touched, plenty of hard work before we reach bedrock, mind. I'd say twenty, maybe thirty feet of overburden.'

Kathleen felt the re-awakening of old excitement; seeing that first, yellow flash of gold in the pan was always to her, the momentary breath-stealer, the mere sight of raw gold she found fascinating, more so than McKinnon's diamonds she kept buttoned away in her shirt pocket.

They ate straight from the fire; the meat was dark and gamey, but a welcome change from salted pork, the skin had crisped to a deep, golden brown.

'Soon as the Kelly brothers bring in their deed of transfer, then we start,' Jim expounded and in anticipation of what was there, looked over his shoulder in the direction of the old waterfall, 'I reckon on one month's hard labour and we'll be through the old riverbed and into pay dirt.'

# -13-

Zingeli built a kraal for the cattle with strong poles cut from the forest, and he laced it with thorn to keep out lion and other opportunistic carnivores. Now, the wagon, left beneath the trees stood on silent, immobile wheels and for one last time, Zingeli outspanned his oxen. The whip also was left silent, stored away beneath the wagon; for a while at least, there would be no further need of it.

The Kelly brothers had come and gone, the selling price of two hundred pounds equally shared and fastened away inside their saddlebags; already the brothers were thirty miles out from Pilgrim's Creek, well on the road to Lourenço Marques and with any luck, the chance of a berth aboard the earliest ship outward-bound for Australia.

Through Inkunzi's guidance, Jim put his men to work ridding the area of debris; discarded mining equipment was cleared away, the ground made ready for deep excavation. He paced out the distance between the live stream and the abandoned watercourse, and he took into account the gradient needed for him to divert the water and the optimum place for him to position his sluice boxes. Only a shallow indentation in the ground gave any clue as to the whereabouts of the ancient stream bed and with excitement driving his legs, he followed it upwards to where a thousand years before, from the high ridge, rich gravel-carrying waters had thundered down to the valley floor.

The cliff was streaked with bird excrement and in places, tiny rivulets of bright water clung to the rock face. Kathleen stood alongside her father and with an astute mind she sifted through his theorising.

'Enough rubble to fill a dozen wagons, father...? That's a lot of ground. Either we find what we're looking for or wind up penniless and with our fingers worked to the bone for nothing.'

Jim nodded his head. 'Twice that, I would say, but move it we will, my sweetheart. Any gold carried over the waterfall will have worked its way between the boulders; we have to clear the overburden, all the way down to bedrock.'

He rested his arm about her shoulders. In that small length of time, from their leaving America, Kathleen had grown taller by a good two inches and that coltish, slender shape of the young girl was now the fully flowered figure of a young woman.

'First thing,' Jim mused, 'we need a place other than the wagon to keep the rain off.'

For the next ten days Jim put the bulk of his labour force to building adequate shelter for himself and Kathleen. For the roof, he took the canvas from the wagon tent and drew it tight across a timber frame to keep off the heat as well as the rain. On Moosa's advice they covered the canvas with long reeds cut and carried from the banks of the Blyde. Kathleen insisted on the cookhouse being kept separate from the main structure, so that smoke from the fire would not find its way inside their living space. Whilst Jim complied, behind the makeshift dwelling, Zingeli turned and readied the ground for Kathleen's kitchen garden and within a space of three weeks the seed she had brought with her from the Sutherlands' had struck and thrived, encouraged to a carpet of strong seedlings by the warmth and humidity of their surroundings. The soil was jet black and thick with natural composts, and from the clearing away of trees and undergrowth the sunlight spilled through as a warm lake upon Kathleen's soon to be fecund garden.

With those same river reeds, Zingeli fabricated funnel-shaped fish traps and where the Blyde narrowed he found a place to wedge them between the rocks; held below the surface and with their funnelled mouths to the oncoming current they soon proved more than their worth. By each new evening, the traps were quarter filled with small tilapia and scores of trembling, silver minnows.

Jim, for a generous part of each day would spend his time fossicking the base of the defunct waterfall for signs of mineralised quartzite. Inkunzi barred away the bigger rocks for him and here, forced into crevices were pockets of fine gravel. It was from these crevices that Jim filled his prospecting pan and having carried it back to the stream, squatted against his heels and spun the metal pan below the surface. Gradually, the slurry cleared until only a handful of gravel remained. Jim tipped out the coarser pieces, but where he had hoped to find a glittering tail of yellow gold, only chips of grey quartz and sparkling black sand reflected the sunlight.

'Nothing yet, we have to go deeper,' Jim told Inkunzi.

'It will take many days,' the Zulu reminded, 'waiting will not be easy, a woman does not give birth to her first child without a fight. The gold is there, *Nkosi*, but like the virgin bride, slowly and with great cunning she must be coaxed to the sleeping mat.' He looked at Jim and grinned. 'There is much for us to do before we have earned the right to look upon this beauty – first our hands must bleed.'

# -14-

With the camp cleared of the Kelly's discarded belongings and with the forest cut back for another twenty yards in all directions, an air of expectant optimism fell upon the workers; eagerly, with filled bellies and good voice they took to each new morning. In unison they swung the pick and cut away the earth with their spades, and slowly the ground along the length of the ancient stream bed fell open to the daylight. Boulders, some the weight of twenty men were levered out from their sockets and to those which proved too much for all his men to shift, Zingeli put to task the strongest of his oxen. With trek chains and brute force the powerful beasts took up the strain and with steel bars the men levered and cursed the one ton rocks up and out from the diggings. Through all of this, tirelessly, Kathleen put together the rudiments of a home. Sometimes, often even, she wished she was back in Natal; here in the wilderness there was a strange emptiness, a hollow feeling of impermanence.

From outside the tiny cottage, voices disturbed her moment and like leaves caught by a sudden wind, her memories scattered.

Kathleen brushed aside a makeshift hessian curtain and stepped through the doorway, from that chance angle of sunlight, her face took on that soft, transpicuous glow of the haloed angel.

Bo Furguson's eldest son slid from the saddle. He raised his hand, shielding his eyes against the sun for him to see her better. Kathleen held out her hand and she smiled demurely.

'Kathleen,' she introduced, and to the seventeen year old lad she was the sudden manifestation of all his manly dreams. 'Kathleen O'Rourke,' her voice came over him as a whisper from the deep forest, 'we're not long out from America.'

'I know... I mean if you'll pardon me saying so, Miss.' He accepted the handshake, but gentled his grip on her fingers. 'My father told me to bring this to you, on account of you not knowing it was there – I mean at the store – Mister McLeod said it came in today with the victual wagon from Lydenburg.'

Jim stood back and let Kathleen take charge of the situation. The letter had been folded over with a separate sheet of paper and sealed along its outer flap with candle wax. The edges were scuffed and water stained, but across the face of it the writing still appeared as bold and legible, unmistakably that of a girl – tightly formed, painstakingly held to the horizontal, though written succinctly, without flair or vanity.

'Lucky it got here, Miss Kathleen, could well have ended up chucked on the fire.'

'What's your name?' Kathleen asked, aware of the power she wielded over him.

'Thomas, Miss. Tom Furguson.' Unlike Kathleen's his voice broke and warbled, fleshed with uncertainty. 'I work for my father – across the hill on Pilgrim's Creek.'

'The person who brought the letter?' She reminded Tom of the reason for him being there. 'Would there be any money owed for him bringing it from Lydenburg?'

Tom shook his head. 'Not a penny, Miss. Him coming all this way he would have done anyway, letter or no letter.'

His eyes, like hers were that dark emerald green of an ocean swell; his face, big-boned, burned brown by months of hard work in open sunlight. Conversely, his hair was that deep, blue-black of an unlit night sky; thick and barely curled, like a cat to a warm cushion it nestled down inside his collar. His build was well formed and though in years he was still to know that final shift from boy to man, already his chest and shoulders were tightly bulked beneath his shirt.

'My thanks to your father,' said Kathleen, 'the man who brought it? Has he departed for Lydenburg?'

Tom shook his head and swung up into the saddle.

'Day after tomorrow, Miss. Camped behind old McLeod's store he is, won't leave before his wagon is emptied of produce. Mealie meal, tobacco, soap and the likes, you and your Pa should get on down there 'fore it's all spoken for.'

'Thank you, Tom,' she held him with her eyes, 'I will make sure of it.'

The boy tipped his hat and turned his horse through a tight circle, making it arch its neck as it did so. He smiled down at Kathleen.

'Been a pleasure to meet you, Miss Kathleen, should you come on down to the diggings at Pilgrim's, I'll be watching for you. If ever you need a strong arm and extra pair of hands be sure you ask for Thomas Furguson.'

Kathleen watched him ride out from the camp and when he had disappeared from sight she went back inside the cottage; with trembling fingers she prised away the wax seal from her letter and lifted the paper flap. Determined to savour each and every word she read aloud, but kept her voice to little more than a whisper.

*My dearest Kathleen, father insists that my letter stands little chance of reaching you and if the truth were known, already it has been discarded and lies abandoned to the wilderness. Perhaps some lonely traveller might find it and draw comfort from my writing. However, even if that is so, then at least I have kept my word and have endeavoured to find of you your whereabouts.*

*Forever has come and gone since I last saw you and on the day of your leaving I felt sure my heart would break in two, neither the pain nor my yearning to be with you has lessened, nor will it ever.*

*Father often speaks of your time with us, and Elizabeth, dearest darling Elizabeth, she, I think is worse than all of us and has asked that you well remember our times together, outside in the gardens. So, my dearest, dearest friend, if you are reading this letter, then you must believe me when I say that one day, I will find you.*

*I live each day in the hope of hearing some word of your keeping and know that if there is at all a chance, you will find a way for your letters to reach me. The Dominee, Meneer van Reenen, has assured me that from time to time, wagons and men return from the north. Every day I shall ride the three miles to and from the market square in 'maritzburg, perhaps, if luck is with me, word of your distant endeavours will find me. I pray I do not ride too long in vain.*

*Think of me with each and every sunrise.*
*My heart is with you,*
*Charlotte.*


Kathleen read, re-read and then read again, with unwavering interest she devoured the letter's contents as though she were afraid the words might disappear as a puff of smoke. Feelings emerged from between the lines, those which had endured and followed her through six hundred miles of raw wilderness, this was more than just a letter, more than just words, it was a pouring out of some deep affection, the love of one for another – a commitment of truth that during Kathleen's time in Natal had drawn the pair together.

Outside, Jim O'Rourke waited for Kathleen to finish reading her letter. Absentmindedly, he stared up at the cliff face and fancifully he pictured the height of some long passed rainy season, when the stream, then at its fullest spate and laden with gold-bearing gravel would have thundered outwards from the hillside. Spray, where he now stood, as fine mist would have rolled over him and from that constant hammering the stream bed at the base of the waterfall would have been gouged clean and hollowed out, cleared of all but the heaviest of material for as far down as the natural bedrock. If Inkunzi was right, that is where a greater proportion of the gold would have been deposited, eroded from ancient, oxidised reefs higher up on the hillside, this enriched layer of black sand and polished river stones would stand as another untouched glory hole; virgin ground waiting for Jim to open her up.

Kathleen came out from the cottage; she smiled at her father, the way a contented mother would smile at her son; the gap between Pilgrim's Creek and Pietermaritzburg now less daunting, Charlotte's letter had brought hope to the diggings. Again, the glass was half full and though the poignancy of Charlotte's writing had at first saddened her, now her eyes were bright and she walked towards her father with a jaunty spring in her step.

'Cat got the cream?' Jim cocked an eye at his daughter. 'Good news, I guess.'

'Charlotte Sutherland, Pa.' Kathleen avoided his eyes, her cheeks were flushed. 'I miss her so much. Feels like I spoke with her just yesterday.'

Jim shook his head. 'Not sure how the letter got through, mind.'

Kathleen changed the subject.

'We should get on down to McLeod's store; won't take long for the smouse to sell up. A day – two at the most and he'll be gone back to Lydenburg with an empty wagon.'

McLeod's ramshackle store was alive with eager buyers; diggers stood three-deep to the counter and as the shelves emptied so did McLeod's helpers carry in replenishments from the wagon outside. Jim loaded two, one hundred-weight bags of meal to the back of the packhorse, enough to last until the next supply wagon came through from Lydenburg. From the supplies trader himself, Kathleen cajoled more precious bags of ground coffee beans, sugar and salt and along with her other treasures fastened them away inside her saddlebags.

'I am forced to ask a kindness of you, sir.'

Abe Cohen frowned over his spectacles; the frames were small, round and endowed him with an owlish air. His bowler hat had long since lost its shape to the rains and, moulded to that of his head it was now the black dome of some ancient synagogue.

'And what exactly would that kindness be, young lady?' His eyes dropped down to Kathleen's hand. 'A letter, if I am not mistaken.' Those sparkling, owlish eyes turned upwards. 'And you, I take it, were the fortunate recipient of this morning's English two penny envelope?'

'I was, sir and I am indebted to your bringing it from Lydenburg,' she made as if to reach inside her breeches pocket, 'if there is any charge...'

Cohen reached out and took the letter from her.

'No charge; though even now I stand amazed by your belief in this surviving the return journey.' He pondered the address. 'Natal I see? Back to whoever wrote you, I should think?'

'The Surveyor General's household,' Kathleen emphasized the importance of it reaching Pietermaritzburg. 'Wishful thinking I guess, but worth so much to me if it were to get through.'

Cohen shook his head in wonderment.

'Lap of the gods, dear girl.' He tucked the letter away inside his jacket pocket. 'However, give it a chance shall we, and why not?'

'The cartridges...?' Kathleen pointed them out; boxed in twenties, as enticing pyramids they were stacked along the shelf.

'Pricey,' Cohen warned, 'and besides, what would a pretty young girl be doing with .44 Winchester brass jackets?'

Kathleen opened the fold of her coat. The Colt, tucked behind her waistband appeared as big enough to down a buffalo bull with a single shot. Cohen's eyebrows jumped, almost to touch the brim of his bowler hat. The soft hint of Kathleen's femininity was still there, but her expression was sterner now.

'Three packs, sir – your best price.'

'Two shillings and two pence a box.'

'Two shillings square and I'll take an extra two boxes.'

Cohen winced at his whittled profit margin.

'Bird in the hand, you're saying?'

Kathleen nodded her head.

'To your advantage, Mister Cohen.'

'Then why do I feel wrung out?'

Kathleen skirted the Jew's discomfort.

'What about gold?'

Cohen's eyes narrowed, sidestepping established local buyers was to most, abhorrent, but the temptation he found as always, doubly overwhelming. He waved Kathleen closer. Nervously, he looked about for earwiggers.

'Buying, or selling?'

'Twenty three ounces,' Kathleen dropped the bait in front of him, 'two nuggets, fat and pretty as sunrise – pure metal, no quartz.'

Cohen's breathing changed. His cheek twitched, his eyes now those of the furtive starling.

'Keep your voice down, lassie, or you'll have us both run off the diggings.'

He leaned closer. 'Show me, and if what you say is true, old Abe Cohen might see his way clear to taking them off your hands, but at the right price, mind.'

'The cartridges,' Kathleen reminded him, 'two shillings a box, then?'

'For a first option on your gold...?'

'You have my word on it.'

Cohen held out his right hand. 'Then we agree. Two shillings a box, ten shillings the lot, in exchange for a first look at this gold of yours.'

The trader's fingers were deathly cold and bony, the claws of a crow. Kathleen slipped his grip and looked past him for the cartridges.

'Put aside my five boxes, I'll go find your money.'

'And the gold,' he reminded her, 'you have an hour, lassie, no more; quick as you like now.'

Kathleen found her father struggling to balance the load on their packhorse. The smell of hessian and mealie meal wrinkled her nose.

'You still have to settle van Reenen's debt with his workers, father.'

'I haven't forgotten,' Jim promised, 'but the money we have left is spoken for, never reckoned on using it to buy up our own property.'

'Van Reenen's gold?'

'What of it?'

'You have it with you?'

'In my saddlebag.' His eyes narrowed. 'You're up to something, Kathleen O'Rourke. What is it you're after?'

'We need the money. Trust me.'

Jim led his horse side-on to the crowd. He unbuckled his saddlebag and reached inside. Kathleen marvelled at the weight; bigger than her clenched fist, the moleskin bag was tied at the throat with waxed string.

'I'll find you when I'm through,' she promised and using

the crowd for cover made her way past McLeod's store. Quickly she slipped back behind the canvas flap.

'Twenty three ounces,' she handed the moleskin bag to the trader, 'give or take any difference you find with that measuring contraption of yours.'

'Then we shall see just how right you are young lady.'

Cohen dropped the canvas flap behind her and fastened it closed with rope ties.

'Can never be too careful in matters of great sensitivity; never know who might be listening in.'

With a fox's guile he smiled at Kathleen and turned up the flame on his Tilley lamp. Impatiently, he slackened off the drawstring and then placed the bag on the table beside him. Lamplight picked out beads of sweat on his forehead.

'All will be revealed in just a moment, lassie, but first we must prepare our balance – set out our stall, so to speak.'

Carefully, as if the box contained some rare antiquity the trader flicked aside a pair of brass catches; he lifted the rosewood lid and laid it back on its hinges.

'My contraption, as you called it.' Not without affection, he spoke softly and with precise movement lifted from the box, a gold miner's weigh scale.

No bigger than the outstretched span of Cohen's hands, simple in their construction and cast in solid brass, the balanced arms rocked easily about their fulcrum. From the extremity of each arm, suspended on three cords and no more than three inches in diameter, two brass pans waited for Cohen to load one of them with precious metal; the other with brass weights from a smaller, rosewood casket. On a small pre-suspended chain and hook, Cohen hung the scale by its metal ring and then looked to Kathleen for her understanding.

'There now, ready as we'll ever be.' He smiled at her. For luck he rubbed the seats of both pans with his thumbs and in the blinking of an eye replaced his usual spectacles with his more preferred pince-nez. With bated breath, he tipped the contents of the moleskin bag onto the table.

For long moments, Abe Cohen gazed upon the precious metal in wonderment. In places, the gold was brightly polished and silky smooth, the results of obsessive handling. Light from the Tilley lamp caressed the metal, from a cheerful butter-yellow to that darker, iridescent red of the earth's live furnace, stroked by the lamplight now their patina glowed, dark as the devil's own fire.

Cohen selected the smaller of the nuggets, purposely he held off weighing the larger, savouring the anticipation. He looked to Kathleen for any hint of the nugget's weight.

'Earlier, young lady, I recall you mentioning a figure?'

'Ten and thirteen,' Kathleen told him, 'going off hearsay, mind – could be less or more, even.'

'Then we shall pray for the latter,' Cohen mused and reached inside the wooden casket for one of a full, thirty-two ounce set of bullion weights.

'We'll need the heaviest, I should think – along with some of its smaller siblings.'

Again, he smiled at Kathleen's commitment to learning. Like a kestrel from its hovering over an English meadow, every move he made she watched intently.

With great deliberation, Abe Cohen laid out the weights in order of their seniority. Each one of them had been clearly stamped with an exact value.

'Twenty pennyweights to the Troy ounce; twelve ounces and you have yourself a Troy pound.'

He paused to wipe the sweat from his forehead. Beneath the canvas awning the air was thick with heat and the spice of Cohen's trade goods.

'Ten ounces is the one we are after first.' He selected the relevant weight and habitually, polished it clean with his sleeve. He held the weight into the light and as a matter of course checked its uniformity. 'First time in years I'll be using this one – for one nugget, I mean. Not very often do I get the chance, you see?'

Kathleen nodded her head.

'Best we be getting on with it; my Pa will come looking

for me.'

'Then let us not keep him waiting, lassie. Whilst I hold the balance against it tipping over, I'll ask you to place the nugget squarely to the centre part of our vacant pan.'

Cohen positioned the ten ounce weight and nodded his head for Kathleen to do the same with her nugget. Almost, though not quite, the scale balanced itself weight for weight.

'A shade over ten ounces,' Cohen whispered. 'Hold her steady and I'll make up the difference for an exact tally.'

Whilst Kathleen steadied the scales, with a pair of steel tweezers Cohen scurried out several smaller weights from a pull-out tray in the casket's frontage. After the third, comparatively minute weight had been added, the scales trembled undecidedly, but only for a small moment and then, decisively, they found their equilibrium; both pans balanced exactly to the horizontal. Cohen rubbed his hands together, well pleased with the result.

'Ten ounces, three pennyweights to be precise.' He nodded his head to Kathleen and with the pencil from behind his ear scribbled down the exact figure. 'And now, lassie, your *pièce de résistance*, that's French for best of the bunch,' he explained, keen to dispel her confusion, 'the fatter of the two by far I'm sure.'

Again, he rubbed his hands together.

'Lift her out from the pan and in with the next, lassie before I wake up from all of this dreaming.'

The second nugget levelled the scales at thirteen ounces and six pennyweights. With reverence, Abe Cohen lifted the nugget from the scale and held it closer in to the lamp flame; with the eyes of the victorious alchemist, he worshipped the gold.

'Look at the shape, lassie; fashioned by angels or who knows, perhaps even the devil himself. What any man would not give to possess such a beauty.' His eyes swung onto Kathleen. 'Where did you get it? I can tell by the polish that your gold has been well handled. She's a long

138

time out from the ground, lassie?' His eyes narrowed. 'Be honest with me now. How did you come by it?'

'You're saying my father's a thief?' She let her coat fall open; the .44 Colt revolver spoke out for her.

Cohen rolled his eyes skyward and braved his way back from the brink.

'Merely curious, lassie, nuggets the size of these are never easily come by.' He dragged his eyes away from the Colt and placed both nuggets side by side on the table. Again, he took up the pencil and with shaking hands quickly he calculated a buying price, allowing for himself a fair margin of profit.

'Two pounds and ten shillings an ounce, young lady, and you'll find no better price than mine, at least not anywhere else on these goldfields.'

'I'll take it. Less your money for the cartridges.'

Cohen reached inside his jacket pocket. He had pre-empted the amount, the money was already counted out, almost to the shilling.

'Fifty eight pounds we'll call it, less the cost of your purchase.'

He stacked the coins as three uneven piles on the table and then reached behind him for the Winchester cartridges. Kathleen pocketed the money, along with the ammunition.

'When will you come back this way?'

'A month,' said Cohen, 'maybe longer. Never can tell.' He patted his breast pocket. 'I will make sure your letter gets off to a good start from the wagon yard in Lydenburg. Beyond my wishing it God speed, I can promise you little else.'

'God bless you for that,' said Kathleen and held out her hand to him. 'Thank you for your honesty, Mister Cohen. A month from now and I'll be watching for your wagon.'

Cohen nodded his head and accepted the handshake.

'Be careful, lassie. Get on back to your father and give him this.' He slipped a Romeo y Julieta cigar inside her top pocket. 'Goodwill present from old Abe Cohen.'

'Doesn't smoke,' Kathleen told him.

'Then time he started. Now away with you before I up the price on those cartridges you stole from me.'

He turned his back on her and with a sigh like that of an old man, climbed a set of wooden steps for the steel safe at the back of his wagon.

# -16-

Jim paid his men on the same day Kathleen sold van Reenen's gold, and for the next four days neither a single pick nor shovel cut any ground from Peach Tree Creek. With several months of untouched wages, along with Jim's blessing, Inkunzi and the rest of the workforce went out from the diggings and for those with wives and children it was a time of great rejoicing.

On the morning of the fifth day, men with filled bellies and wide smiles were back on site, weighted down with pots and blankets, barefooted they had walked the twenty miles or more over rocky terrain, and with disbelief, Zingeli welcomed back to work those who had returned. With renewed faith, they followed Zingeli back to the trenches, each with a pick and shovel. Before they began, Zingeli spoke and all of them listened

'Now we dig like devils! Our bellies are filled with meat and our hearts with new hope. For one more month I am your father and your mother; for one more month, each morning your eyes will open and look only to the ground. Speak nothing of those you have left behind, for not before the moon is again at its fullest will you reach for the woman beside you.' He looked to his men and waved them down inside the deep trench. 'Go now, be sure to bend your backs as *amadoda*; make certain it is the man and not his woman who has returned to work.'

For thirty days, Zingeli pushed his labourers almost beyond the limit of their endurance, and for thirty nights they slept as dead men, but at the end of each tortuous shift there was always food enough for twenty, and from the fruits of Jim's rifle, their bellies were filled so that they gave thanks for their good fortune.

The day before that next full moon, Jim called a halt to their digging. They crowded together and listened intently, all were eager for the road home; already their women and children would be gathering to places on high ground for that first glimpse of their men traversing the hillsides. Jim O'Rourke cleared his throat and raised his voice above that of the wind.

'For what you have given in hard labour, I return to you as a gift of seven days.' They stayed silent, bewildered by what Jim had said. 'Seven days, amadoda, for your women to heal your limbs and whatever else might take their fancy.'

Some laughed, others stayed silent, and then, with one voice, in unison, they thanked him.

'*Thina bonga wena, Nkosi nkhulu*!'

They stood in line for Jim to pay them their month's wages and to each man he repeated his appreciation. He watched them leave the diggings and within that next minute the camp fell silent as a church graveyard. Zingeli stood up from the fire and beckoned for Jim to follow.

'Now we are alone, there is something I would have you see, Nkosi. Perhaps it is a sign of our being close, but then again, perhaps my eyes have played me false.'

Jim followed him and on makeshift timber ladders they climbed to where the men had left their digging tools propped against the sidewalls.

The trench, now some thirty yards in length and three across, cut as a deep scar between the trees; twenty yards to the south-west of van Reenen's original strike and parallel to Peach Tree Creek.

Deposited over the millennia, layers of different coloured ground showed up as thick bands in the sidewalls, all had been naturally placed, one upon the other and like the coloured layers of a fancy cake were easily identified – varying in composition as well as colour.

The top-most layer was thick with black soils, decomposing forest detritus visible across its full length. Beneath this, the earth appeared as to be more compressed, streaked through with layers of deep maroon and burnt sienna, the colours of rotting oxides natural to the slow, decomposition of mineral-rich quartzite. Deeper still, as a third specific zone, the ground was peppered through with chips of white quartz and as an undulating line it appeared as a curling wave in some turbulent sea, but it was the recently exposed last few inches that had caught Zingeli's attention; tutored by months of deep digging, he had developed an eye for the more unusual.

'Only this morning,' he told Jim, 'Inkunzi showed me this.' With a miner's pick he dug into the sidewall; here the earth was heavily compacted and across the length of its exposure, smooth, water-worn pebbles, some bigger than a man's clenched fist stood out as rounded plums from their matrix of coarse sand and gravel.

Jim felt his breathing quicken; he had witnessed the same phenomenon once before.

'The old riverbed, Zingeli – has to be. No other reason for this being here.' He reached out and gathered up a handful of the loosened gravel. 'Inkunzi was right. The river changed its course.' He discarded the gravel and went forward to where the trench butted up against the cliff face; again, the same elusive gravel was there, though now it showed as a twelve inch thickened seam, upwards from the footwall and along both sides of the trench.

Gouged out by the downwards drum of the ancient waterfall, the ground had been cut through to bedrock, and only the heaviest of materials had stood fair chance of them settling there. Whereas light soils and sand would have been carried away to be discarded further downstream, this heavier, final layer had stuck fast and for thousands of years, though perpetually hammered by fresh run-off, this blanket of mineral rich gravel had constantly been added to. Tumbled dolomite rocks, brassy flecks of iron pyrite and visible copper sulphides sparkled under near vertical sunlight, and in places, veinlets of black iron granules showed where the finer gravels were more tightly layered and heavily compacted.

'How deep will it run to,' Jim thought aloud, 'and will the gold run with it or have we spent our money on chasing a fool's dream.' He nodded his head to Zingeli. 'Bring me the prospecting pan; time for us to square our debt with the devil, let's find out what we have here.'

# -17-

Kathleen joined her father and Zingeli in the trench and quickly her excitement caught up with theirs; from the look on Jim's face, she realised the closeness of their providence. Where the trench was at its lowest point, it was here the rainwater had collected together as a shallow pool; the amount was more than enough for Jim to fill the pan and work its contents.

To Kathleen, the attraction was always the same and unable to tear her eyes away she leaned in closer; fixated by her father's skill she hung on every controlled swirl of the water. No one spoke, and as the amount of gravel diminished so did the tension inside the trench increase. Jim slopped out the last handful of coarse sand and replenished the pan with fresh water. The heavier, mineralised concentrates formed as a dark, but glittering tail around the bottom of the pan; with his little finger, Jim pointed out a single, yellow grain of raw gold.

'Is that it?' Kathleen asked him and the excitement that had only just flamed in her eyes went out.

'We haven't gone down deep enough,' Jim quantified their findings. 'We could still be twenty feet up from bed rock.' He handed the pan to Zingeli. 'When your men come back, we dig until we can dig no further – then we will know.'

Zingeli stretched the stiffness from his limbs and made his way back to the ladder. He would go to the river and check his traps for fish; perhaps even, he might fall asleep on the river bank and dream of home. He needed to rest. On the high hills to the north-west, an infant storm had readied itself, poised to run amongst them; Zingeli's men would be pushing hard to reach the lip of the escarpment before the clouds opened.

Moosa went with him, down to the river. For hours they talked of Zululand.

'We have come a long way,' said Moosa and in a state of semi-sleep leaned back against the warm grass. Until it was time for him to light the lamps and stoke the fires, nothing else would concern him.

'And there is still much for us to do.' Zingeli sat up. The storm was close now. 'We sit in the sun and prattle as old women.'

'And you in riddles, my friend. Calm yourself. We have seven days of doing nothing. Close your eyes and think of the women you left behind in Natal.'

Zingeli seized the Indian boy by the arm and dragged him upright.

'The rain is coming. Come with me, there is urgent work for the both of us. Your dreaming of women can wait for nightfall.'

Arguing would have been pointless. Moosa had long since learned this and like the obedient spaniel, reluctantly he followed Zingeli back to the diggings.

'Climb down,' Zingeli ordered and with his feet herded Moosa onto the first rung of the ladder.

'What about the storm?' Wide-eyed he pleaded with Zingeli for him to change his mind; to the Indian boy, thunder and lightning shared equal footing with charging lions.

'Are you afraid of water?' Zingeli glowered at him.

'What about Mister Jim?' Desperately he sought an excuse for them to take refuge.

'Mister Jim is not here, he will know nothing of your torment.' Zingeli shook the ladder and laughed out loud when Moosa threw his arms around it. 'Go on down, amaNdiya, or like fruit from a tall tree, I will shake you from the ladder and bury you where you fall.'

From the last rung in the ladder, Zingeli hurried Moosa forwards to where the trench butted up against the vertical rock face. Moosa carried a pick and shovel and the grim spectre of hard labour hung over him. However, Zingeli took the pick from him and hefted the tool high above his shoulder.

'When I have loosened the earth, you will use your shovel, amaNdiya, and with a man's strength you will clear away the stone for me to go in deeper.'

Moosa nodded his head and stood back. The pick went up through a wide arc and with bunched shoulders, Zingeli buried it haft-deep into the footwall; with a grunt of satisfaction, he levered hard down on the wooden shaft and prised open the ground. After a dozen more strokes he looked to the boy and nodded his head for him to clear away the broken earth.

Together, they dug vertically, down into the footwall; the compacted gravel came away as manageable lumps and after two hour's labour, Moosa found himself standing only inches short of waist deep inside their excavation.

The rounded river stones were larger now, slippery as eels, each one of them needed to be manhandled out from the pit.

'The rain is on us,' whispered Moosa and bemoaned his fate, he discarded the shovel and stood with his back to

145

the sidewall, eyes shut tight for him to withstand the storm. On the high ridge directly above the creek, lightning stabbed at iron-rich outcrops and the thunder growled so near to the diggings that Moosa, at the point of losing his nerve mewled like a baby. Terrified by the noise, he covered his ears and shielded his face as if a pride of starving lions were ready to leap upon him from the clouds.

Zingeli turned his face to the rain and without fear watched the storm twist and turn; writhing snakes within the heavens. The feeling of hard rain on his skin enlivened him, the water was warm and he opened his mouth to it and drank it down. However, just as quickly as the storm began so did it end, sunlight caught the trees and covered the hills, and in the trench where Moosa had heaped the gravel, light bounced and shimmered, playing cruel tricks with his eyes. At odds with this iridescence, other colours which had been lost beneath the ground for more than a thousand years were now unearthed, bared to the natural light. Most were the muted, brassy hues of pyrites and tiny, leaden crystals of native galena, chips of quartz and malachite, all of these were worthless and quickly Zingeli's eyes learned to disregard them. However, as his eyes adjusted fully, small flowers appeared as if to bloom from out of the gravel – all were the colour of mimosa blossom – butter-yellow, bright as the yellow sunlight that had brought them back to life.

High enough as to not be threatened by the creek when it was in spate and where the ground had already been cleared and levelled, men gathered to unload timber and iron sheeting from a transport contractor's wagons. Jim and Kathleen looked on with interest, for within those few short months of their arrival at the gold diggings, the miners' tented camp had been changed from a place of chaotic squalor to the more orderly beginnings of a mining village.

Thomas Furguson watched their approach, having realised who it was he left his axe embedded in the bole of a half-felled tree, with an urgent spring in his step, he crossed the open ground and tipped his hat to Jim, but the smile was for Kathleen.

'Watched you come up from the river. Rumour has it you folks have run out of good gravel, Mister O'Rourke, sir?'

'The name's Jim,' he corrected the youngster. 'And our gravel's as good as it gets. Where's your old man?' He looked about the build site. 'Is he here about or down on the creek?'

'Back at the creek; cleaning up one of the sluice boxes.'

Jim nodded his head to Kathleen.

'Give me an hour. When you're finished here, wait for me at McLeod's store.' He looked up at the sky and frowned. 'Soon as we get what we came for, we'll head on back.'

Kathleen reined her horse into the shade and leaned with her arms rested across the pommel.

'What're you building?'

'Hotel,' Tom told her, 'dining room, saloon bar and all the trimmings. Be real fancy when it's finished.' He was watching her, but from the corner of his eye; broken shade and sunlight shuffled her hair with different colours. His heartbeat quickened. 'I can show you what's going on, if you like.'

'I'd like that,' said Kathleen and slid down from the saddle. She led her horse on a loose rein, careful to steer her away from the clatter and bang of wagons off-loading.

'This over here,' Tom pointed out an area pegged out with string and wooden stakes, 'front steps and veranda. Bedrooms and the like will be over there – at the back.'

'The money for all of this,' Kathleen put to him, 'someone rich, I guess?'

'Pretty much so,' Tom concurred, 'won't be long before we see more proper houses neither. My old man reckons the place will double in size before next Christmas.' Emboldened by his insight, Tom went on with his tour of the new township. Kathleen followed him and for another three hundred yards, at a dozen places alongside the track, men were clearing space to build on. Lower down, close-in to the creek, scores of sun-bleached canvas tents still cluttered the hillside; each day newcomers were finding their way to the diggings, and on each of those same days others tore down their tents and left; penniless and in a state of total disillusionment. Amongst all of this, a dispassionate storm had whipped up the soil and turned the land surrounding the tents to fields of glutinous mud.

'Another month and we'll have us our own fully paid up claims inspector.' Tom went on. 'Save us going all the way to the Mac Mac diggings.' He pointed further along from where they were standing. 'By that tree – our own claims registration office, no more twenty mile ride for a man to lodge his rights to dig for gold.'

'There should be more trees,' Kathleen pointed out, 'alongside the road, and gardens with flowers.'

'Might well come to that,' Tom said. 'Won't take long before more womenfolk come up from Natal.' He grinned at Kathleen. 'No offence, Miss Kathleen, but marrying age women are pretty much scarce up here on the creek;

nothing like a pretty dress or two to keep a man's spirits lifted.'

Kathleen swung her mind's eye to her foreseeing the future; fancy carts, those with canvas hoods were everywhere, jostling for the room to pass abreast on the street. Cape carts done out in fine leather upholstery and with blinds to keep out the dust; carts like the one she had seen loaded with luggage and a red-faced, Cecil Rhodes. The memory brought out her arms in gooseflesh, he must have changed by now; older looking, a little more bulked out, perhaps. Drifting further amongst her store of memories, she wandered back along that long and arduous journey from Pietermaritzburg; Charlotte would be watching for a letter. The trader Kathleen had entrusted it to would be halfway back to Lydenburg by now. Tom was speaking, but she heard only sounds that were way beyond the moment; those of bees in the Sutherland's garden, Elizabeth's piping intonations, Charlotte's whisperings and covering over it all, the sounds of heavy trek chains and the creak and groan of turning wheels.

'I have to go now.' She swung up into the saddle. 'Might be nice to see you down at our place, just for a change,' she qualified and again, the smile.

'I would like that,' said Tom, disappointed by her sudden need to leave. He watched Kathleen ride out and disappear amongst a gathering of men unloading their wagons.

# -19-

'You missed all the excitement, Jim boy.' Bo Furguson leaned back in his chair, the customary half-smoked cigar clamped between his teeth. 'In front of you; on the table, what do you think?'

Jim let his eyes adjust to the tent's interior. At the centre of Furguson's rickety table, a butter-coloured lump of yellow metal the size of a girl's fist nestled against a half-finished bottle of brandy. Refracted light from the bottle's innards added an almost religious air of solemnity to the setting. What Jim looked down upon was the realisation of every hard-bitten, gold digger's prayer; the interminable fantasy, a dream that purely by chance, had for Bo Furguson, become a reality.

Taken from the creek less than an hour prior to Jim's arrival, the nugget appeared too large, too perfect; as if it were alive it devoured the lamplight and glowed perniciously. At first, Jim was loath to touch it; the feelings it evoked discouraged him from reaching out. The metal, though precious would to some men appear as repulsive, it was now the coveted find – the unattainable woman flicking her skirts in the face of all who gazed in awe at her beauty.

'Pick her up,' Bo encouraged and found the American's disbelief amusing, 'shade over forty-three ounces, Jim. This one's a definite keeper; sure as hell too pretty for any man to part with.'

Astounded by its sheer physical weight, Jim struggled for a firm hold on the nugget.

Jockeyed upwards on a river of molten quartz, disproportionately, the gold in its liquid state had been collected together, cast as an oversized oddity, gnarled and misshapen, and where once this freak of nature was entombed by solid rock, now, wrapped only in lamp light the simple beauty of this precious metal was all but godlike. Those less fortunate would look upon a rarity such as this with resentment as well as longing, for in the eyes of jealous men this was now the devil's coin – many men had died for less.

Not without some regret, Jim returned the nugget.

'What will you do with it?'

'When the day comes, reckon I'll take it back home with me, not altogether sure yet.'

Furguson locked the nugget away inside the tin trunk beneath his bed; he stood up from the table and gestured to Jim to follow him outside, leading him between heaps of discarded gravel and down to where the sluice boxes were positioned at a slight angle to the creek. He relit the cigar stub and flicked the spent match against the crown of a large boulder. At its base, the three-ton lump of dolomite had been shored with thick timber to prevent it rolling out from a deep socket in the bank; the creek itself had been dammed off and its water diverted.

'Always the same,' Bo told him, 'bigger the nugget, bigger the rock that sits on top of it – cursed things are never in with the gravel. That would be too easy.'

He diverted their conversation.

'The Kelly brothers, heard it said that you bought them out?'

'I had no choice,' Jim told him, 'swore they found the claim abandoned; van Reenen forfeited ownership through default, walked off the place without any mentioning of him coming back.'

'And was it worth the money? Every man I have spoken to is convinced the gravels in Peach Tree Creek are all but worked out.'

'They are,' Jim admitted, and like those of a fox his eyes sparkled, 'the Kelly brothers cleaned them out, Bo – all except for the old glory hole.'

'Glory hole?' Furguson frowned at him, 'what in God's sweet name is a glory hole?'

'Thirty yards south-east of the creek,' Jim told him, 'right under their noses; the old riverbed must have been choked off above the waterfall and changed its course.'

'And you found it? You're dead certain it's there?'

'Sure as I'm standing here in front of you. Cut a new trench to where the original waterfall would have come over from the ridge.'

'How deep?'

'Twenty feet and then some. We cut into the old riverbed

yesterday; seen it with my own eyes, Bo.' He looked around him. 'Same as you have here; gravel and boulders, small ones mind, but they're river stones for sure.'

'What about gold?'

Jim shook his head. 'Just a trace, but with shed gold, you know yourself the good stuff will be hard down against the bedrock.'

'Could be there's nothing there – a layer of barren gravel and then what?'

'I leave for Natal,' Jim sobered, 'tail between my legs, blistered hands and long whiskers and nothing else to show for six months hard labour.'

Furguson pulled hard on the cigar and then tossed the spent stub into fast water; caught in the tail-race it bobbed excitedly and then disappeared.

'Got a proposition for you; finish opening up this glory hole of yours and if the gold is where you say it is, then come back and see me. These gravels won't last forever, six months; eighteen at best.'

He looked over his shoulder and shook his head at the rows of human squalor littering the hillside.

'All that you see here will have gone, the one-man shows, the chancers, all of them will have moved on; gravel dumps and worthless holes in the creek are all this place will stand for.' He smiled at Jim's look of perplexity. 'That's when the big boys move in.'

'What're you saying?'

Furguson looked him square in the eyes; too many long days at the sluice boxes had weathered him brown and creased as old boots.

'Behind your claim, on the ridge above the waterfall. I have ten claims already pegged out and registered all legal like. Early this year, we put down three prospect holes and all of them hit the beginnings of reef at ten feet – from one to six feet wide and all three holes showing good gold, twelve to twenty weights right across the strike width.' He paused to let the information sink in. Inside Jim's head the wheels were turning. 'For the right men there's still a wagon-load of gold waiting to be taken out, but it will take money, Jim – and trust.'

'You're propositioning me?'

'Depends,' said Furguson, 'on what you come up with.' He reached out another cigar from his breast pocket, struck a Vesta with his thumb nail and smiled at Jim through the smoke. 'Get back down to Peach Tree Creek and open up that glory hole of yours.' He held out his hand to Jim. 'Find yourself a stake in Pilgrim's deep reef and we'll talk some more.'

# -20-

By the time Jim and Kathleen got back to Peach Tree Creek, only an hour of daylight remained. The suggestions Bo Furguson had pulled from out of the blue were chasing their tails inside Jim's head, but he knew that Bo was right. It was always the way, that first rush of men was endemic; the valley had flooded with dreamers, clouds of gold dust blinding their eyes. The crash would come; sooner or later the river gold would peter out and one by one the diggers would pack up their gear and leave. Only the cleverest and better-heeled would have accumulated the knowledge and the wherewithal to stay behind and expand their fortunes.

Zingeli watched his master ride in and at the camp's centre, Moosa had piled his fire with thick logs so that every inch of bared ground was now brightly lit. Jim sensed an almost carnival-like atmosphere and, glad to be back on home ground his spirits lifted. He slid from the saddle and allowed an over-eager Zingeli take the reins from him.

'You look like a man with a fat virgin hidden beneath his blankets?'

153

Zingeli held up his hand, palm open to the heavens.

'Nkosi, when a man's belly is full, is it not right that he is happy?'

'There was much rain,' Jim went along with the small talk; Zingeli's eyes glittered.

'There was much rain,' he concurred.

'More than enough for three storms,' Jim agreed.

'Perhaps for ten even,' Zingeli bettered, 'not since I was a small boy have I seen this much.'

Unable to restrain himself any longer, Zingeli reached inside his breeches pocket and then, to the full effect of the firelight he opened his hand.

'After the storm, we found these, Nkosi.'

Moosa followed suit, his palm half-filled with that same yellow metal and in the firelight, those big brown eyes were bright as any stars.

'Very many of them, Mister Jim but the storm was most terrifying!'

'Where?' Jim asked them, but with a broken voice, so that he was forced to repeat himself. 'Where did you get them?'

Zingeli handed his findings to Jim; the metal, though it was a hundred small pieces was now a single, warm and leaden weight. Kathleen stood alongside her father and together they stared at the gold; neither one of them could speak.

# III

# The Goldfields, 1873

# -1-

Kathleen O'Rourke shook her feet free of the stirrup irons and from the saddle, looked down upon that riven strip of landscape with mixed feelings. She shivered from the recollections of her first sightings, already that moment had been left a full three years in the past, but it seemed as if perhaps it were only yesterday when she had first set foot on the diggings. Then, no more than three hundred and fifty men were working claims on Pilgrim's Creek, now, more than a thousand desperate diggers burrowed beneath that same stretch of gold-bearing gravel; all but a few were lean and brown as prairie dogs and all were of a same mind.

'Where it all began,' mused Jim O'Rourke, 'warms my blood just watching them.' He struck a Vesta with his thumbnail and touched the flame to the tip of a thick cigar, his hair was streaked through with silver and the creases at his temples were deeper now. 'Gets inside a man's head,' he remarked, unable to look away, 'never leaves you; from that first flash of gold in the pan right up to the day you die.'

By pure strength of will, Jim turned his eyes from the familiar goings on and on a slack rein turned his horse back the way they had come.

'I need a drink,' he told Kathleen, 'see if I can find Bo Furguson; you get on home and get some food on the boil. I'll be back before dark.'

Kathleen took her time reaching the village proper and still those same pangs of nostalgia were there, riding alongside her. Like spring flowers, colourful red-roofed buildings had risen up from out of a canvas-strewn nothingness. Where only a few short years ago there had been row upon row of diggers' tents and smouldering campfires, now, at the central part of the encampment those first tentative roots of human permanence had struck deeply. The gardens Kathleen had once only dreamed about were now cosseted strips, circles and riotous squares along the roadside. She stopped outside of McLeod's General Store and slid from the saddle. Inside, the air was cool and, not unpleasantly, it reeked of soap and tobacco, of lamp oil, dusty diggers and dusty floorboards. The store had doubled in size and McLeod had seen the need for an extensive annexe to accommodate his living on site.

'Thought you'd left town,' McLeod smiled at her and reached across to a small shelf, 'came in this morning with the mail coach from Lydenburg.'

Kathleen's heartbeat quickened. As always, the envelope was water stained and dog-eared, but the languid sweep of the handwritten name was unmistakable. Six months had come and gone since Charlotte's last letter. She suppressed the urge to tear it open and instead, squirreled it away inside her breeches pocket.

'Somebody else was asking over you, didn't recognise him though.'

'His name...?' Kathleen asked him. 'What did he want?'

McLeod shook his head.

'Didn't say; mentioned you by name though, bought himself a bottle of Smoke and then left.'

Intrigued, Kathleen pushed for more information.

'So was he old, young? How does he look?'

'About the same height as your old man; black beard, same colour hair, but his eyes...' Again, McLeod shook his head and looked out through the doorway. 'Black as hell they were and thin as a snake's. Didn't say what he was after and left before I could find out.' He smiled at her and tiny flecks of light jostled his beard. 'Shouldn't worry too much, anything important and the man will be back; good riddance I say, didn't strike me as the friendly sort.'

Kathleen put it behind her and looked up at the shelves, but her power of concentration had been overshadowed by a strange sense of déjà vu.

'Your bread, how old?'

'This morning's,' said McLeod, 'and those cigars your old man's taken a fancy to – came in with that letter of yours.' He pointed them out.

'Best put three boxes aside, Mister McLeod. He can pick them up when it suits, but I'll take me some bread before the bugs get into it.'

McLeod wrapped the bread with brown paper and set it down in front of her.

'Something else about him; maybe it was the fancy waistcoat and the watch chain – good silver, heavy links – bit of a lady's man, I'd say. Just a feeling, mind. Not the type of man you would mess with.'

Without any conscious inclination, Kathleen's reached down for the Colt tucked inside her waistband. She paid for the bread, nodded her thanks to McLeod and left.

Level with the Royal Hotel's frontage, Kathleen cocked an ear to a poor piano rendition of Waltzing Matilda, incoherent singing and men disputing the outcome of some card game. Driven by curiosity she slid from the saddle and looped her reins to the hitching rail. She checked the straps on both saddlebags before climbing the stone steps to the hotel's front veranda.

# -2-

'Don't like you being in here.' Jim O'Rourke gently chastised his daughter and set down the schooner of beer she had insisted on. 'You're sure this is what you want? Lemonade would be more in keeping.'

Kathleen took up the pint glass with both hands. A mirror fixed to the wall behind the bar counter allowed her an angled view of the far side of the room. Women were not welcome. Like the cigar smoke, a cloud of male resentment hung thickly from floor to the ceiling, merely from her being there.

'I'll be nineteen years old next time round, father; no disrespect, but from now on I'll drink whatever I fancy.' Without stopping she drank down the first three fingers of cool beer. Men were watching her and without diffidence she returned their stare. One by one they went back to their cribbage and dominoes and the silence eased off. The barman rinsed his glasses and the piano player picked up from where he had left off, his voice rose up deep and soulful – Kathleen watched and listened. Diggers followed the words, a step or two behind; some just hummed, some leaned back in their chairs and let nostalgia spark off sweet, but painful pictures of home.

In the corner of the room, two men pegged their way along the cribbage board; one sat face-on to Kathleen, the other with hunched shoulders sat with his back to her. Even though she had not yet seen his face, his being there in the same room was enough to flush her skin with gooseflesh.

'The man with his back to us,' she pointed with her eyes and Jim swivelled sideways-on in his chair, 'something about him,' Kathleen added, 'like I've seen him some place before.'

'Don't recollect,' Jim replied, 'not without seeing his

160

face.'

'McLeod said one of the diggers had asked over me. A stranger, he said.'

'Looks like your friend is leaving,' Jim warned, and for a split second, from within the crowd, the stranger stood face-on – his eyes found Kathleen's and then they were gone.

'A glimpse, that's all,' Jim shook his head, 'can't say I recognised the man. You worry too much; put him out of your head.' He drained his glass and stood up. 'The place is filling up, it's going to get rough. Finish your beer, best we get a move on before fists start flying, and there's a storm brewing.'

They rode in silence and quickly the rain overtook them. Kathleen hunched her shoulders at the deluge and from the wide brim of her hat, the water poured as silver rivulets over her horse's withers. Her mind was in turmoil. From behind, a wet wind flailed through her shirt, but she ignored the discomfort. Faces and names jinked through her head, incoherent voices from as far back as her time aboard the *Eudora*, but nothing fitted. Perhaps her father was right, the remoteness of their living on Peach Tree Creek was playing fast and loose with her mind; twisting her conception of reality. She flung the incident aside and caught up with her father.

'Big storm, Pa – reckon the worst is still to come.'

Jim looked up at the sky, like the contents of a witch's cauldron, with malice, it churned as dark satanic mist above the forest; not the slightest hint of sunlight could penetrate the cloud. Between the darker thunderheads, ice cold rivers of pale light bled from higher altitudes, the forerunners of hail squalls and violent thunder.

'We're almost home!' Kathleen shouted over the storm. 'Down there, through the trees; Moosa has put up the lamps to guide us in.'

They off-saddled moments before the hail struck. Moosa

led the horses away, Jim and Kathleen watched from the cottage doorway and within seconds the ground outside turned white with ice; thunder growled and lightning felt its way across the hillside.

Kathleen left her father alone with the storm and in the seclusion of her tiny bed space reached the letter from out of her breeches pocket; she opened the single sheet of paper across her lap. Every word she perused over, head bowed to the candlelight, deaf-eared to the storm outside.

Half way through her reading, Kathleen stood up from her bed and brushed aside the partitioning curtain.

'What day is it...? I mean the date, Pa – the day of the month? What is it?'

'Twenty seventh, girl. Why the excitement?'

'Charlotte,' said Kathleen, 'she may well be close to reaching Pilgrim's Rest.' She waved the letter. 'This was sent more than a month ago; Abe Cohen, the victuals trader comes in from Lydenburg tomorrow, Charlotte may well be with him.'

'Don't get your hopes up, girl. She could still be weeks away from leaving Natal.'

Kathleen shook out the folds from her letter and with an insistent voice read from halfway down.

*...heard from someone freshly arrived back from the north, said there are now regular monthly coach services to the town of Lydenburg. From what you have told me, from there it is not too far to the goldfields at Mac Mac and your own, Pilgrim's Rest. I have reached agreement with father and have settled upon my departing Pietermaritzburg this coming January, first. If my luck and trust in our friendship both hold true, I will be with you before the ending of that same month...*

With shaky fingers, Kathleen re-folded the letter and looked up at her father.

'That's this month. Tomorrow, rain or flood I will be back in Pilgrim's Rest when Cohen brings his wagon in.'

She looked about the smallness of their cottage and her excitement guttered. 'Where will we put her? There's little enough room in here for us to house a rabbit.'

Jim smiled at her. 'Wasn't going to tell you – at least not for a few more days, not before it was properly all done up and shipshape.'

'You have lost me, father, what are you talking about?'

'Nothing too grand. Three bedrooms, one still not finished. Kitchen with its own stove and small pantry; no need for you to cook outside anymore. Garden doesn't amount to much, but in time, who knows, with a little bit of work....'

'You bought old man Barry's place?' Kathleen tumbled to the ruse and her eyes fired up, 'all this time; right there under my nose...?'

'Wasn't easy – passed the place a dozen or more times with you riding alongside me.'

'Behind the Furguson's,' Jim nodded his head and added to her excitement, 'as we speak, the carpenters are finishing off your kitchen shelving.'

'Tomorrow, I want to look inside. Two birds with one stone. My own room.' Now she twittered like a sparrow, 'yours will be the largest, but mine the sunniest.'

She swung away from him and through fanciful eyes gazed outwards from the doorway.

'Flowers and fruit trees – peach trees, we can find them already a foot grown down here near the creek.' She watched a second squall of hail lash that opened space between the trees. 'Three years, father, gone in a flash, but it has all been worth it.'

With soft eyes she looked at her father.

'Charlotte's room will be next to mine. It will be good to have a friend again – I have missed her terribly.'

Thunder, like cannon fire engulfed the valley. Kathleen recalled her own close encounter with disaster; that terrible storm, the collapsing of the wagon track, a deep ravine and

Zingeli's face above her own when he dragged her back from the brink.

'The road is much safer now, Charlotte will be fine,' she convinced herself and pushed aside any remaining threads of negativity, 'Cohen's wagon must, and shall get through.'

Her smile slipped, her eyes narrowed, her thoughts suddenly tempestuous; as hail from against that hard-packed earth her heartbeat bounded. Faces swirled inside her head and then, without reason, as mindful pieces, remnants of some long discarded puzzle fell into place.

'The man McLeod told me about. The man in the hotel bar room, father.'

'What of him?'

'I know who it is,' said Kathleen, 'the beard,' she whispered, 'it could never cover those eyes.' Jim stayed silent. 'Back in Natal,' Kathleen went on, but listlessly, with bitter thoughts she recalled her first encounter with the boatman; the flooded ground in front of her was now the surface of a warm ocean, the hiss of rain through the trees now the dip of long oars shooting a loaded ferry shoreward from the anchored ship *Eudora*.

-3-

Abe Cohen singled out a gap in the trees.

'From that next bend; your first glimpse of Pilgrim's Rest, got herself the makings of a fine little town.' He leaned back against planking he had fixed in place as a makeshift backrest and with up-stretched arms he worked the stiffness out from his shoulders. 'Not many womenfolk, mind, so best you watch your step,' he glanced sideways at his passenger and chuckled softly, 'or the first digger who claps eyes on you will be melting down his latest find for the makings of a wedding ring.'

164

Charlotte Sutherland smiled at the old man's flirty suppositions, she stood up from her place on the wagon box and like the engine of a powerful train, Cohen's span of sixteen lumbering oxen leaned heavily into their yokes; though the morning was still cool, steam rose up from their quarters, the voorloper's lash crackled barely a foot above the lead pair and like a gull avoiding the highest crest of a wave, never once did its tongue alight to ruffle a single hair. Constantly, the voorloper coaxed the thickly muscled wheelers close-in to the safety of the hillside and without any insistence the others followed.

To Abe Cohen, Charlotte Sutherland was now his Viking figurehead, flaxen-haired and long-limbed – looking seaward from the rolling prow of his warring longboat. Those last three years had worked and set the symmetry of her face; cat's eyes, not the emerald green of the witch's familiar, but rather those of the Persian exotic – deep blue, more startling even than any sky ever mirrored by sea and sunlight. Her hair also had changed, darker now, but only slightly. Charlotte had tied it behind with a short ribbon of blue silk, as a tail of fine gold it hung between her shoulders.

'I can make out buildings of sorts.' Charlotte struggled to see through the haze, the urge for her to run ahead of the wagon was almost unbearable. Cohen sensed her excitement.

'Patience lassie, we'll be there before you know it. Your friend knows well enough that old Abe Cohen brings his wagon up from Lydenburg the last Friday of every month. Chances are that your Kathleen O'Rourke will be watching the road in from the drift, even as we speak.'

'Everything seems so close; the tents, the red roofs, even smoke from their fires.'

'Close enough for us to be there within the hour, lassie. Providing that old bitch of a river behaves herself and lets us through. If you'll pardon the foul expression, miss, the

Blyde is less trustworthy than a hungry whore with an eye for an open purse.'

He glanced up at the heavens; men such as him could read the clouds as easy as a child might read a simple book of rhymes. A mere twist in the wind and that angelic blue sky would be gone, banished by devilish thunderheads, but the breeze held steady and for the most, dropped nothing at all. 'No rain,' he mused, 'not until after dark. That will be good.'

Though on that previous day the rain had been heavy, the track remained firm and well banked-up with rock and gravel. To the fore, the river appeared as a quiescent thread of bright silver; Cohen nodded appreciatively, they had time to make the crossing before the next storm. The oxen would be outspanned before high sun. Friday was always a good day for selling and he would make the most of what was left of it. He smiled at the thought, tonight he would stack his sovereigns and count them by candlelight – perhaps a glass or two of good whisky and a game of Brag at the Royal Hotel. Who knows what might transpire before dark? No one, except for perhaps, God Almighty, but then, to Him it did not matter.

'*Phangisa madoda*!' With the back of his sleeve, Cohen wiped the dust from beneath his hatband and shouted encouragement to his voorloper, rousing the boy for him to quicken his speed.

## -4-

From the veranda of McLeod's Store, Kathleen watched Abe Cohen's wagon lumber on up from the drift; two people sat to the wagon box and easily she recognised the squat, familiar shape of the trader, but it was the more lissom figure of the person alongside him who made her pulse race.

'It has to be,' Kathleen wished aloud and strained her eyes for greater detail.

'Why don't you get on down there?' Jim encouraged, 'I'll wait here for you.'

For twenty yards, Kathleen ran beside her horse and then came up Western style into the saddle, and at a gallop, quickly she closed the half-mile gap. Charlotte climbed down from the wagon box just as Kathleen kicked her feet free from the stirrup irons and, lightly as a cat, vaulted to within arm's reach of her friend. For long seconds neither one of them spoke, though the feelings that passed between them were more powerful, more poignant than any spoken word.

'I've missed you,' Charlotte whispered at last, and at the corner of each eye moist starlets appeared as if by magic. Cohen called down from the wagon box.

'I'll be leaving you here, then?'

'God bless you, Mister Cohen, a moment to free my horse, if you would. My bag, for now, I will leave on your wagon.' She stroked her horse's muzzle, slipped the knot on the head collar and looped the redundant tether about the brake lever.

'You're a good inch taller than me,' Kathleen remarked and stood in close to Charlotte for them both to compare. 'Then again, that's no wonder, it has been so long.'

'Too long,' Charlotte insisted. 'These last three years... it was hard, Kathleen. There were times when I thought...'

Kathleen touched a fingertip to Charlotte's lips.

'It is over now, you are here with me and that is all that matters. Nothing can change that.'

So much alike, both women were dressed in breeches, shirt and leather boots; hair tied back from the forehead. They saddled Charlotte's horse and rode ahead of Cohen's wagon, side by side to McLeod's Store. Diggers halted their work and watched them pass. Kathleen made light of the attention.

'They mean you no harm,' she told Charlotte, 'besides a couple of frumpish nurses and a handful of spoken-for wives, you and I are the only eligible women between here and Lydenburg.'

Charlotte kept her eyes to the front.

'Three years is a long time, Kathleen. It must have been difficult, I mean, for you to survive the urge to settle down.' She looked across at Kathleen and laughed. 'No young man in your life? I would not blame you if there were several.'

Kathleen shook her head and smiled at the supposition.

'Could well have been, there's hardly a shortage.' She cocked an eye at Charlotte. 'What about you...? Anyone left behind in Natal?'

'Just my family and Meneer van Reenen; he worries continually over my coming to Pilgrim's Rest, asked to be remembered. All of them miss you.'

Jim O'Rourke came out from McLeod's store, big smile on his face and a fat cigar clamped between his teeth. Surprised, though not unpleasantly, he tipped his hat to Charlotte; the girl had gone, a woman had taken her place.

'Been a long time, Charlotte; all flowered outwards and upwards, I see.'

Charlotte's cheeks flushed 'Nice to see you again, Mister O'Rourke.'

'Jim,' he corrected her, 'leave out the formalities, no more need for that.'

Charlotte nodded her head, grateful of the dispensation.

'Nice to see you, Jim.'

'Likewise. Wasn't sure you would make it; Pilgrim's Rest is a long way out from Natal. I thank God that it's all over. Kathleen has been unbearable, ever since your letter came in.'

'If my letters unsettled you, then I must apologise.'

Jim shook his head.

'No need, just pulling your leg. Good to see you again. Your father, how is he?'

'He's fine,' said Charlotte, 'mother is more or less the same as she was before you left Natal,' she chuckled lightly, 'so long as the flowers bloom and her teapot is topped with gin, all will remain at peace in the Sutherland household.'

'Your sister...?' Kathleen queried, 'almost as tall as you, I should imagine?'

'Elizabeth is as she will always be – my darling, little sister, no matter how tall she grows. Face filled with freckles and a temper to match. Blessed with her grandmother's fire, father says. Spends most of her days in the horse paddock; has little time for anything else.' Charlotte reached inside her jacket and turned to Jim. 'Almost forgot, Meneer van Reenen asked me to give you this.' She handed Jim the envelope. 'Bit of a sorry state, I'm afraid; I struggled to keep the rain from it.'

Jim smiled his thanks to her and pocketed the letter. 'Will read it later, right now there's something I want you both to see.'

Their ride was short-lived; no more than half a mile out from McLeod's Store, Jim led them through a gap in a post and rail fence and caught the attention of a company employee for the horses to be attended to.

The house had been built with walls of Kimberley brick and its roof, covered with corrugated iron glowed ember-red in the sunlight. Jim had ordered in from Lydenburg, pre-cut panes of glass for the windows; two windows for each side of the house and the frames were startling white, in keeping with the walls. On all four sides, the ground had been roughly tilled, the earth itself had been enriched with barrows of forest compost and after that last soaking of warm rain, the areas set aside for produce and flowers were thick with the pleasant, fecund smells of old Africa.

'Your room, Kathleen, is at the back.' Jim led them

through the house. He frowned apologetically to Charlotte. 'Your arrival caught me by surprise, spare room's bare bones furnished; take a month or so for me to get things brought in from Lydenburg.'

'We could share,' Kathleen insisted, 'at least until we're more organised.' She looked at Charlotte and smiled, but with her eyes. 'Unless you disagree, that is?'

'Sharing will be fine,' said Charlotte and she made pretence of looking out through the window to hide the sudden flush of warm blood to her cheeks.

'McLeod's store,' Kathleen remembered, 'I saw it this morning, father. A bed and mattress leaned up in the corner – I reckon on it still being up for sale. We should hurry though or someone else might get there before us.'

'You get on down there,' Jim told her, 'anything else you might find useful, have him send it up. My credit's good.' He smiled at Charlotte. 'Abe Cohen, young lady; go along with Kathleen and turn on that smile of yours before the wolves get to him, see what he has on his wagon and buy what you need on my account; whatever it takes for two young women to fill up this empty house of ours.'

-5-

Gareth McLeod cast an appreciative eye over the crowd. Most of the men were claim owners, drawn away from the creek by rumours of Charlotte's arrival; most were young, and like jackal to that first scent of a kill, they were overly keen to force their way inside the store.

'Been some months now. Good to see you again, Miss Kathleen.' Tom Furguson got in first and tipped his hat to both women. As with Kathleen, those last three years had changed him, where once there had stood a part-grown boy, now there stood a man, a good two inches taller, powerful and thickly set across the chest and shoulders. With his back to the melee, successfully he corralled the root of all the excitement.

'Saw you ride up to your new house, never reckoned on having the O'Rourke's for neighbours. When did you find out?'

'Couple of hours ago,' Kathleen smiled at him, 'a little bit bigger than what I've been used to. The old shack on Peach Tree Creek will be hard to leave though.'

'Memories.' Tom nodded his understanding then turned his smile on Charlotte and held out his hand. 'Haven't been introduced, Miss. Thought I would get in first before this mob behind me starts fighting over the prettiest girls in Pilgrim's Rest.'

Charlotte accepted the hand; powerful and calloused it covered her own. The room fell silent, save for the shuffle of leather boots on floorboards.

'Charlotte Sutherland.' She sensed the sudden quiet and steeled herself. 'Your name, sir? You haven't told me.'

'Tom Furguson; my old man, Bo Furguson works with Kathleen's father; business partners.'

'May I have my hand back, Mister Furguson – you're hurting my arm.'

As if it were coated with fire, Tom released his grip on Charlotte's hand. Someone sniggered and Tom's cheeks coloured; he looked around the store for the source of his embarrassment. However, the crowd quietened and he turned back to Charlotte. Standing awkwardly, the words he looked for were now evasive, lost inside his head. Like some chastened schoolboy he dropped his eyes.

'Best I be getting along then, there's work to be done on the boxes, my old man will be wondering where I've gotten to.'

Charlotte watched him leave, the way he walked, that wide-legged slope of the disgruntled male lion slinking away for thicker cover. She turned back to Kathleen and

171

the look in Kathleen's eyes said it all.

'Dispel those wicked assumptions madam, my interest was merely platonic, that of a dealer in livestock. We have things to buy – a bed for starters.'

For that next hour, Kathleen and Charlotte rummaged their way through every dark space in McLeod's store; delightedly the storekeeper followed on behind, pencil poised and his sheet of paper already three quarters filled with a comprehensive list of Kathleen's purchases.

'All of it to my father's account,' Kathleen piped, and like a child at Christmas time hurried her latest find to the pile on the counter. Charlotte slipped away to search out Cohen's wagon and within that next half hour, haggled fiercely over her own findings, cutting the fretful trader's prices to the bone. Kathleen tracked her down and together, sated by their bargaining, left their purchases to be accounted for and walked back along the gravel track. The red iron roof of the O'Rourke's newly finished house a bright beacon set to a surround of young Jacaranda trees.

'Tom Furguson,' Kathleen recalled the introduction, 'from the way he looked at you I reckon he's taken a shine.'

'He's nice,' Charlotte admitted, 'but not for me; too full of himself. Trouble that one, far too much of the man's man inside of him.'

Kathleen closed the gap between them, she sought out Charlotte's hand; the gesture was honest and open, their fingers linked and with a soft innocence, Charlotte touched her lips to Kathleen's cheek.

## 6

Bo Furguson stood up from his chair; the impromptu meeting of company directors had been hurriedly arranged. Impatiently, he drummed the tabletop with his fingertips and waited for the small gathering of men to come to order. Three men sat with their backs to the function room's single, heavily curtained window; the inter-leading door had been bolted against any interruptions from the public bar. The air was thick with immobile lakes of blue tobacco smoke and the bittersweet taste of intrigue.

'As of September twenty-second, gentlemen and as we already know, the area inclusive of Pilgrim's Rest and the Mac Mac diggings was officially recognised as the country's first and only, producing goldfield.'

Furguson paused and looked at the other men in turn, assuring himself of their complete attention.

'We now have some fifteen hundred diggers working four thousand registered claims in and around Pilgrim's Rest.' Seated to his far right, Major MacDonald, the Gold Commissioner nodded his head, struck a Vesta against the side of his boot and sucked the flame down inside the scarred bowl of his Meerschaum.

Furguson went on. 'Three years ago, save for old Wheelbarrow Patterson, Bill Trafford, George Lilley and perhaps a dozen other hardy souls, there was no one else out here mining gold from the creek.'

Slowed by that last night's heavy debauch, Herbert Rhodes sagged deeper in his chair, he harboured little sympathy for boring rhetoric, always eager to be on his way for nothing held his attention less than the unguent ebb and flow of rudimentary conversation.

'We already know all this, Bo. What's your point? Time is money and God knows, I have little enough of either.'

The remark evoked wry smiles and a simultaneous nodding of heads. However, Bo Furguson maintained his composure; as the dominant company stakeholder, when it came to the swaying of other men's ideas he was better than most.

'The point being, Mister Rhodes, as you will hear shortly, is one of extreme importance to the longevity of all our mining interests in Pilgrim's Rest. However, if you no longer have interest in the company, might I suggest you dispose of your shares and move on.'

He allowed the moment to sink in, then, without rancour he exploded the core reasoning behind his calling together of the extraordinary meeting. With both hands splayed against the tabletop he dropped his bombshell.

'Our very presence in Pilgrim's Rest is under threat, gentlemen.'

'Nonsense,' Herbert Rhodes parried, 'on what grounds do you base these assumptions? Production on all four claims has never been better.'

Furguson breathed deep; Herbert was beginning to irritate him.

'Outside interest in our mining activities around Pilgrim's Rest is growing exponentially and can no longer be ignored.'

As a perfect, tremulous ring, smoke from Furguson's cigar emphasized his point. It hovered chest-high above the table; hanging on the warm air it undulated, tipped sideways-on and then, having changed its shape to that of some portentous ghostly finger, pointed directly at Herbert Rhodes.

'Pilgrim's Rest is no longer the quiet backwater. Word is out; mining men are talking deep reef. Two such persons arrived this morning – ticketed mining engineers. I have it on sound advice that both men are here under instruction.'

'Who's instruction, Bo?' With raised eyebrows, Herbert Rhodes looked to the others for support. 'More like gremlins at the bottom of your garden, man. Who, from out of all this wilderness would have the financial clout to dig for deep reef in Pilgrim's Rest?' With an imperious sweep of his hand he wafted away the smoke from Bo's cigar. In his opinion, Furguson was fighting a personal war with his own paranoia; supposedly of late, every inbound wagon was loaded full with claim jumpers, interloping mining experts and unscrupulous, gold-greedy entrepreneurs.

'Who are we talking about, Bo?' Jim O'Rourke waited tentatively for the answer; though the things which Furguson purported to were suddenly making sense. Whatever ridicule was being bandied about, irrespective of the will of the few, or that even of fifteen hundred small-workers bent on unearthing gold from Pilgrim's Creek, there was always someone bigger, more powerful watching from the wings; those who were waiting for mistress opportunity to beckon from the shadows and already, Jim O'Rourke, like Bo Furguson had sensed her presence. Swallowing the mining rights to the area as a whole would take massive amounts of capital, only a fool would think otherwise. A complete overhaul of the infrastructure would be imperative if the venture were to succeed; access roads and expensive machinery, the importation of skilled surveyors, mining engineers and a ready supply of general labourers, the list was endless. Only one man Jim O'Rourke knew of possessed such capability.

'Cecil Rhodes.' Jim realised and looked directly at the man sat alongside him. 'Your brother has more than what it takes, old boy.' His eyes shot back to Bo Furguson. 'Tell me I'm wrong and I'll keep you in whisky for a month.'

Encouraged by Jim's picking up on the thread, Furguson smiled wryly and nodded his head.

'You obviously know your man, at least there are two of us who are aware of what is happening. Fifty percent of our quorum – more than I expected.'

Herbert Rhodes pushed himself upright. His lethargy disappeared and now his eyes were bright and needle sharp. Protective of his own blood he went on the defensive.

'My brother would have sent word to me. His interests lie in diamonds, not gold.'

Furguson shook his head at the man's pig-headed inability to grasp the inevitable.

'Then I suggest you wake up, Herbert. Your brother sees himself as her Britannic Majesty's imperial garner of all things precious in Africa. The man is becoming unstoppable. What you and I think of today, Cecil John Rhodes has already, months ago, forgotten about.'

Herbert Rhodes shook his head, struggling with the conundrum, he went from face to face looking for answers; realisation had seeped inside the room. Unbeknown to him, his sibling brother was already snapping at their heels.

'So, if what you are saying is true and, accounting for the situation as it stands, where does this leave us?'

'Up the creek without a paddle.' Jim chuckled, openly amused by his own soliloquy. 'Reckon we're pretty short on options, gentlemen. Either we get in before the rush starts, or in a few weeks' time step aside for the better man.'

'That about sums things up,' Bo concurred. 'We extend our claim holdings to the east of Peach Tree Creek.' He looked directly at Jim. 'Link them through to the alluvial diggings below the waterfall.'

'You're talking about the Beta Reef?'

'For starters,' Bo scowled at the enormity of what he was saying, 'then the Theta and her siblings, though all of them are still as yet, unproven, barely touched. If the reef is proved to be payable over the entire strike, then all of our holdings will need one common access route. Without a track of sorts there will be no way of bringing in the ore to a central reduction works.'

'With wagons, I presume?' Jim saw no other option – devoid of a railway, ox-wagons stood as the only method of transporting mined gold-bearing ore to the mill.

'Flatbeds,' Bo agreed, 'outside contractors, but proving the reef must take priority. Winzes – prospect shafts, one every hundred yards along the strike line. We know that the reef is there and near on in to the surface, but in places, I suspect she's lying almost flat – like a blanket under the greenstone. If the reef dips towards the vertical, mining it will be difficult.'

'Hugely expensive.' The Gold Commissioner entered into the discussion. 'Men, pumping equipment, explosives, at least half your gold output will be eaten up in running costs.'

'And that is providing the values warrant any further investment,' Jim reminded them. 'If the values are good, we have one of two choices; either we mine reef or we go only as far as to maintain the prospect holes, collate the values and tonnage, then we sit tight and pray for the competition to buy us out.'

'Water?' Herbert leaned forward, his fickle mood enlivened by the sudden rising up of this new venture. 'How might we shift it?'

'From below,' Jim seized the moment, 'drive an adit into the hillside.' He drew imaginary lines in the air in front of his face. 'Then vertically – a small winze straight up to the main drive footwall. That way, any seepage coming in from the hill will find its own way out.'

Furguson nodded his head.

'We let gravity do the pumping for us, no costs, hardly any maintenance.'

'Less to worry over,' Jim added, 'give us breathing space; at least until our stoping depth comes in close to that of the drainage adit.'

Herbert Rhodes stood up from his chair and on impulse,

drew back the heavy curtain. Outside it was raining, but gently. Mist had formed along the valley and gave the illusion of him looking down on some autumnal Scottish glen. His brother was set to make his move on Pilgrim's Rest, but silently, Herbert swore to fight off any sibling interference. 'Not this time,' he whispered and the window pane in front of his face fogged from his breathing. Whatever was needed to hold his egocentric brother at bay, by force or any other means, without any hesitation, he would use it.

Bo Furguson cleared his throat and spoke for the others.

'We are waiting for your vote, Herbert. Are you in agreement with our going for broke? Do we pool our resources and mine the Beta Reef? Or do we turn a blind eye to what might happen and leave things as they lie? A simple yes or no will suffice.'

Five hundred miles to the south-west, Cecil Rhodes loosened his woollen tie and from the window of a Kimberley bank, he gazed out and across a mile-wide deepening wound in the earth's crust. As if Herbert had sensed him there, he too found comfort in the act of loosening his collar, and reflectively ran his eyes over that yet, evolving patch of butchered ground some one hundred yards below the hotel's frontage. However, in stark comparison, the diggings encompassing Pilgrim's Creek were minimal, for they had hardly scratched below the surface of the earth.

'Most definitely a yes,' he whispered and then turned on his heels and nodded his head to Furguson. 'You may count me in.'

## 7

Kathleen packed her wicker basket with bottled beer from Cohen's wagon, pasties and crusty rolls from the newly opened baking establishment and covered it over with the light patchwork quilt she had stripped from her bed. Booted with soft leather *veldschoen* and dressed in rolled-up breeches and shirts, with their basket filled, Kathleen and Charlotte shared the weight. On plaited wicker arms, between them, like some playful child the basket swung backwards and forwards through the grass in time with their walking. From a high ridge overlooking the Blyde river, Kathleen pointed eastwards to where in part, the hillside had been cleared of trees; arranged geometrically, waist-high wooden pegs supported by stone cairns marked the legal extremities to the company's recently extended rights to mine.

'The beginnings of the Beta Mine,' Kathleen expounded, still breathless from the climb, 'at least, I hope so, or we will all see out our time on the Peach Tree diggings, wondering how long we have before the gravel peters out.'

'What would you do?' Charlotte asked.

Kathleen shook her head and spread the quilt to a patch of level ground.

'Don't know, haven't really thought about it; feels like we've lived here forever.'

She stretched out on the quilt, rolled onto her back and stared up at the sky. A lone eagle spiralled for height, buoyed by thermals of warm air it appeared as if to weave its way amongst pale strands of wispy cloud.

'Look for new diggings I guess; that would be for my Pa to decide, not sure he could do anything else though, hasn't worked for another man for near on twenty years now.'

Charlotte lay alongside her, a stem of sweet grass

between her teeth. The eagle was still there; above it, the cloud had all but disappeared, the remnants were snowy-white and on a slight breeze the sound of heavy, manual labour carried easily to where Kathleen and Charlotte were lying. Metal on rock, metal on metal and out from it all there came that typical, light-hearted banter of contented men at work.

'I love it here,' said Charlotte and without any forethought reached for Kathleen's hand, 'but if ever you leave Pilgrim's Rest, nothing will stop me from leaving with you.'

Kathleen turned her head to the side. Charlotte's eyes were soft with colour, that of the sky and within the blue were tiny flecks of gold radiating outwards from about each iris. Without any warning, as if a storm had suddenly come upon them from the leeward side of the ridge a loud clap of thunder shattered the quiet and the very air about their heads reverberated.

# -8-

Jim O'Rourke found the mining crew's progression pleasing enough; his skill with explosives and drill steels paid him dividends and though the ground was hard won, those first, exploratory attempts at sinking a vertical shaft already displayed more than fair results. As if cut and shaped by God's own hand, the shaft collar, though still shallow, was clean-edged and well fashioned. Under Jim's instruction, the hammer boys had driven their drill steels two feet deep into solid rock, and twice the holes they made were charged with dynamite and then capped with fuse and detonators. Jim lit the fuses himself, entrusting no one else to the task; the new explosives were safer to use than the old black powder, but shipping the dynamite inland by ox-wagon from the Port of Natal made it hellishly expensive, leaving little room for error; every stick had to be made to count. The charges had to be detonated sequentially, or rather than break cleanly, the solid footwall would merely shake off the dust and give up less than half the tonnage expected of it. Jim estimated the Beta Reef to be lying a hundred feet below the surface; his breaking four feet of rock per twelve-hour shift would, after allowing for mishaps, access the upper most part of the reef in fewer than thirty days.

In full view of other workers, a proud Zingeli stood alongside his master and watched intently as Jim carefully inserted the remaining fused detonator cap into a single stick of dynamite and then, using a wooden pole as a ramrod, Jim pushed the final charge down inside the last of sixteen drill holes. With thick clay he plugged off the openings; sixteen lengths of safety fuse, like rats' tails lay against the rock. He checked and counter-checked his work, making doubly sure that the entire face had been charged and primed correctly before ushering Zingeli out from the pit. He nodded his head to the Zulu for a firebrand with which to set the fuses burning.

From a safe distance, they watched that first pale feather of smoke rise up from the shaft head, and from behind a barricade of thick timber they waited for that primary rush of black smoke that would by mere milliseconds, precede the roar of exploding dynamite. Zingeli covered his ears and through the thrill of his own anticipation screwed up his face in readiness for the detonation.

The bang, when it came was sudden and violent. Like an air-burst shell from a military howitzer, the sound was deafening. Zingeli fell to his knees and stayed that way until he was sure the last, devilish piece of rock had hurtled harmlessly overhead; only when Jim touched his shoulder did he stand up and, belatedly, he shook his fist at the smoking scar on the hillside.

'Dynamite!' Kathleen realised and for Charlotte's benefit, pointed out a cloud of poisonous nitrous fumes rising up from the ridge. 'My father's blasting out the beginnings of the first shaft.'

Charlotte composed herself and, not wanting to appear as having been frightened by the explosion, displayed only mild irritation for the ringing in her ears.

'I suppose it is always so loud?'

Kathleen nodded her head.

'Always. At least, for the first twenty feet or so. The company had a wagonload of new explosives shipped from America. New invention – really powerful, throws up rock like lead pellets from a shotgun barrel, and stay upwind of the smoke, too much of it inside your lungs and you'll wind up in the graveyard.'

They drank beer straight from the bottle and from their wrappings of brown paper, the pasties came out moist and slightly warm; still with that fresh from the bakery smell of heaven.

Whilst they ate, activity along the ridge picked up speed. A windlass was rigged directly over the new excavation and with the strength of four powerful men put to the winding handles, the broken rock was loaded into an iron kibble by Jim's lashing crew, then hoisted out and carted away.

The tranquillity of the ridge and that of the valley below had now been changed, forever. Where only a week ago, dik-dik antelope and spiral-horned mountain kudu roamed with impunity, from now on, those same craggy slopes and deep ravines would be flooded with men and mining equipment. The valley would ring with echoed shouts and curses, hammer crews eager to make their bonus; the clamour of bright steel on hard rock and twice daily, that thunderous clap of high explosive charges ripping out lumps of rock the size of two grown men.

'I know of a quieter place,' Kathleen smiled at Charlotte

and stood up from the quilt, 'if we start now we can still be home before sundown; I would dearly like you to see it.'

They repacked the basket with leftovers from the picnic, and now, lightened of their original load they made good time along the hillside. The sun had reached the high point of its travel and not a single cloud had remained behind to sully the sky.

Kathleen kept to a good pace and after leading Charlotte westwards for half an hour, stopped to look down from the crest of a small ravine. Aloes clung as scarlet flames to rocky outcrops and at a lower point, a ribbon of bright water found its way from ledge to ledge, following the gradient to where a guarded, mirror-like pool threw back the sunlight.

'So beautiful,' whispered Charlotte.

'As I promised it would be,' Kathleen smiled and urged her friend forwards and onto the downslope.

The water barely reached up to Kathleen's waist; from that angle of sunlight, her lissom shadow barely darkened the surface of the pool. Naked and unashamed, she turned to face the sandy bank and instead of some shocked expression on Charlotte's face, she saw in her eyes only feelings of quiet elation.

'No snakes, I promise,' Kathleen chuckled softly, 'and I shall look away, if you wish.'

Without replying, Charlotte slipped the buttons on her shirt. Below the open neckline, her skin, untouched by the sun was still unblemished; white as buck quartz freshly broken from the reef. With slow hands she loosened her belt and with the innocence of some religious initiate, cast aside the encumbrance of her clothing.

Though Kathleen had seen her naked before, the event, in Kathleen's mind had until that moment stood as secretive and shadow-like – observed only from a state of semi sleep and through the flickering candlelight of their shared bedroom, but this, this was different.

Charlotte waded out to her; just inches apart, washed by warm sunlight and at the same time, cooled by seepage from the hillside they reached for one another. The act was guiltless, one of purity and each in the other's eyes they were magnificent.

# -9-

Above the silence of the forest, the sibilance of a low-running creek was the only sound to Moosa's ears. The O'Rourkes had gone; the cottage was his, but alongside of it had settled an insidious sense of loneliness, so that Moosa *amaNdiya* prayed aloud for that next day's sunrise to come quickly. With conviction, he attached good reasoning to his predicament.

'Mister Jim has taken up his much improved accommodation in the village, himself and missy Kathleen will be happier there.' He drew back the hessian curtain and scowled at the night; Zingeli would be gone for as long as the night lasted. The storekeeper's fat housekeeper would hold him fast beneath her blankets. 'Like a cow buffalo,' he mused and chuckled at Zingeli's description of the voluptuous lover. He struck a Vesta and lit his bedside candle. The night would pass quickly, now he would sleep, but first he would take a piss outside, in the dark.

He stepped through the doorway and in the light from a three-quarter moon, McKinnon's eyes were as dark holes burned into his face.

'You remember me laddie; the same old Blackie McKinnon who paid you sixpence a day and kicked that little brown Indian arse of yours when you stole from me?'

'A potato,' Moosa croaked, 'it was nothing more than a potato, sahib sir!'

McKinnon tightened his grip on the boy's throat and touched the razor sharp edge of his skinning knife to the soft flesh below his ear.

'Potato or gold sovereign, boy, it matters not. Facts is facts and you stole from me.' He leaned more weight to the knife. 'I might slit your scrawny throat for that; barring crows and vultures, laddie, no one would know what happened to you.'

'Please, sir, I am more than very sorry for taking your potato. Do not kill me, sahib. I will repay you tenfold the price for what you speak of.'

A jewel of living blood bloomed from Moosa's neck; black in the moonlight it broke away from that point of bright steel and wriggled down inside his collar.

'The girl – where is she?'

'Missy Kathleen...?'

McKinnon nodded his head. 'Don't play me for the fool; one last chance.'

'She does not live here anymore sir. They have a new house; much better and bigger than this one. This is Moosa's house now, sahib.'

McKinnon pressed down with the blade and the Indian boy squealed in fear of his life.

'On your mother's grave, boy – where is she?'

'In the village, sahib! She lives in the village with her father and new friend and now please, sahib, I beg of you not to kill me.'

McKinnon eased back on the handle; like those of a starving crow his eyes glittered, his breath the fearsome Kalahari wind on Moosa's face.

'Three years is a long time. Tell me boy, this missy Kathleen of yours, she must be pretty as a picture by now?'

Moosa hesitated. He knew what McKinnon wanted to hear and forced aside his conscience; his life depended on him finding the right words. McKinnon's hands were shaking; a sudden rush of anger and in the blinking of an eye the blade would be through to the back of his neck.

'Always pretty as a flower, sahib. Her friend also is exceptionally beautiful; hair more golden than the sunshine. Always she is wearing shirts that are most thinly manufactured,' Moosa made a lewd cupping motion with both hands, 'very tasty, sahib; not too big and not too small.' He clenched together his fingers as though squeezing out juice from both halves of a cut orange. 'Just perfect, sahib sir. Young and firm, I would say; very much pointing outwards like puppy dogs' noses when the cold wind is blowing.'

McKinnon's breathing quickened; he withdrew the skinning knife and pushed it back behind his belt.

'This house of theirs, where is it?'

'In village, sahib.'

'You told me that,' McKinnon hissed at him, 'where exactly?'

'Past the hotel on the right hand side; big red roof, but will not appear as to be red in this moonlight, perhaps grey, but the walls are very white,' he nodded his head, 'these you will easily see, I am sure of it.'

'You had better be, coolie-boy or I'll be knocking on your door.' His arm shot out and again, Moosa felt the power of those thick fingers encircle his throat. 'Remember now, you haven't seen me. Mention my name to O'Rourke and you will be dead before the next sunrise.'

Moosa's head shook like a ragdoll in the jaws of a terrier, his breathing faltered and at the very point of him passing out, McKinnon released the grip on his throat and let him fall to the ground.

# -10-

Shamed by his own cowardice, Moosa cursed his hesitancy, then, emboldened by a sudden need to put things right, he hunted out his boots from the space beneath his bed, forced them on and with trembling fingers tied off the laces.

'McKinnon is an evil man, I must warn my master of what is going on!' He stared outwards from the cottage doorway, stricken by his inherent phobia for being alone with the darkness, he shivered violently; the horror of what might be out there rushed about him like a cold wind.

With a pounding heart he blew out the small bedside candle, bravely he picked up a lighted Tilley lamp and with his free hand, took up the flintlock; primed and loaded with ball, it comforted him. For one last moment, he watched and listened, and then, with new courage, through gritted teeth he growled at the darkness and went out alone into the night.

# -11-

Blackie McKinnon tethered his horse in deep shade behind the hotel and so as not to be noticed, he walked where the shadows were thickest and where the ground was still soft from that last fall of rain.

The O'Rourke's house, as Moosa had described, was set close-in to the edge of a wooded kopje. It was there, amongst the trees where McKinnon settled down to wait. The breeze was small; mostly the air was still and only occasionally did the sounds from a hammered piano and men's singing reach to him from the hotel. In the holding paddock to the rear of the house, two mares and a thickset packhorse paced the perimeter fence and the moonlight was bright enough for McKinnon to see that Jim O'Rourke's big bay gelding was missing. From a rear window, light from a single lamp beckoned to him from a chink in the curtains.

Save for a small towel about her shoulders, Kathleen stood naked before the bedroom mirror.

'Sometimes I think that I look like a boy.'

'Then you are silly as well as blind,' Charlotte countered and crossed the room to stand directly behind her. With gentle hands she massaged the base of Kathleen's neck. 'More like a swan.' Leaning forward, she touched her lips to Kathleen's ear and felt her tremble. 'Definitely a swan, nothing else could match what I learned of you this afternoon.' Charlotte drew the towel from Kathleen's shoulders and let it fall to the floor. Her own breathing was quick with excitement; locked inside the confines of the mirror, Kathleen's figure was portrayed as perfect, erotically enhanced even.

Kathleen closed her eyes and willingly she gave herself up to Charlotte's wonderment; the touch of fingertips became a first falling of spring rain upon her face and that warm flood of Charlotte's breathing was now her sunlight. From every subtle movement there exploded feelings of sheer ecstasy, visions of laughter and happiness, and like butterflies alighting to that first opening of young flowers, euphorically her eyelids fluttered.

# -12-

Moosa took the hotel steps two at a time and on reaching the top, abandoned his lamp to the veranda; with the flintlock clasped to his chest he blundered in through the open doorway. The proprietor wheeled from behind the reception counter and cut him off before he made it through to the bar. He caught Moosa by the scruff of his neck and held him wriggling like an eel whilst he relieved him of the weapon.

'Not so fast my little brown friend – no guns and no trouble-making coolies in my bar.' He shook him with the fervour of a terrier and pinned him up against the wall. 'Your intentions boy and quick as you like.'

The boy's eyes were wide with fear and when he spoke the words blubbered out as a torrent of broken English.

'Mister Jim! It is of great importance that I speak with him. A matter of life or death, mister manager sir!'

The proprietor saw the honest terror in Moosa's eyes and grudgingly, he set him down.

'Wait here, boy whilst I find him for you.' He glowered at him. 'Best you be telling the truth now or I'll put the toe of my boot, lace-deep to that scrawny arse of yours.'

'Every word of it! On my grandmother's grave I will swear on what I have told you.'

The proprietor left him in the foyer and within that same minute was back with Jim O'Rourke in tow. Jim took hold of the boy's arm and led him out onto the veranda.

'What has happened, Moosa?' Jim pumped him for answers. 'Has there been an accident? A fire? Someone killed? Spit it out boy, why are you here?'

'From Natal, Mister Jim.' Moosa fought to compose himself, but unsuccessfully. His entire frame was shaking violently. 'The boarding house where you stayed with missy Kathleen...?'

'What of it?'

'The woman, sahib, her husband...'

'You speak in riddles, boy – what are you saying?'

'Moosa is saying that the man who was her husband in Natal is at this very moment here in Pilgrim's Rest.'

Forgotten images sprang to life in Jim's head. The stranger Kathleen had told him about; it all made sense. The pieces were fitting together.

'McKinnon?'

Moosa nodded. 'The very one, Mister Jim. He came to my house only a few small hours ago.'

'What was he after?' Jim's voice growled between his teeth. Moosa shrank away from replying and looked over his shoulder; silently he prayed for redemption.

'He said that if I told you of his presence he would kill me, sahib.' He turned back to Jim. 'Missy Kathleen, sahib, I fear it is she whom McKinnon has displayed his interest for.'

'Why would he do that?' He pushed Moosa towards the door. 'What else did he tell you?'

'He put his knife to my throat.' Moosa pointed out the small nick from McKinnon's knife. 'I had no choice in what I was saying, Mister Jim. On my grandmother's grave I had no choice.'

'What else did he say?'

Again, Moosa started to shake; fear of repercussion choked his voice to a whisper.

'Your house, Mister Jim – McKinnon said he would feed my body to the crows if I did not tell him where it was.'

Created by the moon, from the overhanging eaves, a generous strip of deep shadow covered the full length of the rear wall, it blackened the ground and neatly laid out rows of young shrubs. It was from within this darkness that McKinnon watched and listened. Crouched like a waiting leopard he cocked his head for sound, but everything was still; only his eyes moved.

From his nearness to the open window every spoken word was picked up on, the urgent sibilance of women's breathing left nothing to his imagination, but it was a glimpse beyond that curtain which had pushed his mind far beyond the bounds of normal rationality.

Lifting upwards onto one knee, McKinnon adjusted his line of sight until, through that narrow gap in the curtains, the bedroom as a whole was visible. His eyes bulged, for Kathleen and Charlotte were both of them already lost to that magical, unreal world of their love making.

There was softness, young flesh and pale skin; the whiteness of it all gently subdued by lamplight. What others might interpret as something strange or perverse even, was to McKinnon the rejuvenation of some powerful opiate. Every sound that filtered outwards from the room, like the addict demanding more of his senses, McKinnon drew them in so that he trembled under the awakening of a hundred unsated, sexual fantasies.

'I could never live without you, Kathleen,' Charlotte whispered over the urgency of their touching, 'since our very first meeting, I have thought about you every hour of every day.'

McKinnon, like the wolf drawn to an oestrus-tainted wind moved on all fours towards the rear doorway; his heart pounded and, as had happened many times before, inside his head there clamoured the incessant demands of the perverse alter ego.

In the warm comfort of each other's arms, they lay together, faces upturned to the eaves; a flat, five-legged house spider limped its way through that upwards wash of lamplight, tethered by its own shadow it disappeared behind a wooden roof beam. In the quiet of their after-passion, Charlotte spoke softly.

'No one must ever know, your father would never forgive me.'

'Reckon he would shoot the pair of us,' Kathleen smiled at the truism, she traced the line of Charlotte's breasts with her fingertips, 'not that I would care, my love. The time we have already spent together would more than cover the cost.'

Kathleen tilted her head for a glance of the night beyond the curtains, the shadows were longer now.

'We had best be getting dressed, my father will be home soon.'

Charlotte rolled clear of the bed and with an artful swirl of her gown she covered her nakedness. Without fussing, she pulled on a pair of soft *veldschoen*, left the house through the back door and went out into the warm night. There was no need for a lamp for the moon was bright enough; a silver hole in the firmament and gathered about it were a thousand silver stars. Something had put the horses on edge and she calmed them with her whispering.

'Easy now, quieten down my darlings you're spooking at shadows – there's nothing to be afraid of.'

Making no sound, McKinnon came up on her from behind and like the first constrictive coil of a powerful snake, his arm looped about her throat.

'Quiet as a lamb now, girlie or yer lady friend won't recognise the bits I leave behind for her.'

Charlotte froze against the paddock fence and reflexively her hands locked hard to McKinnon's forearm. His skin carried with it the scent of old smoke; his breathing hot on her neck and soured with drink. McKinnon pressed the tip of his knife to the pliant flesh beneath her rib cage.

'One word, lassie – one single word, cry out to your friend inside the house and I'll spill your innards quick as a flash.' He released the pressure on Charlotte's throat, but at the same time, brought more pressure to bear on the knife handle. 'You keep still now – give me what I'm after and I'll be gone before you know it.'

A terrible, numbing fear settled as eagle's claws to Charlotte's shoulders; McKinnon's ragged breathing, now the beat of that same raptor's wings against her neck. A cluster of bright stars glowed as if on fire and desperate for whatever strength she could muster, Charlotte focused all of her awareness upon them.

'Turn around and I'll kill you – scream for help and I swear by all that's holy I will gut you like a fish.'

Slowly, McKinnon withdrew his hand from her face; from a split in Charlotte's lower lip the salt taste of fresh blood flooded her mouth with saliva. McKinnon found the silk belt to the front of her gown and then the bow.

'Stand still for me my pretty and do as I tell you. Nod your head if you're hearing me right.'

In mortal fear for her life, Charlotte forced herself to comply. From behind, McKinnon kicked her feet wider apart. He leaned in closer and pressed his full beard hard up to Charlotte's cheek.

'Let me guess, lassie; you being one for the ladies wouldn't know what it is that's coming to you?' His left hand slipped inside her gown and with careless fingers, he found the sensitive tip of her breast. Charlotte flinched from McKinnon's sudden perverse invasion and full-blown gooseflesh rustled beneath her gown. Spurred on by his depravity, McKinnon moved his hand and he reached downwards for his belt. With thick fingers he slipped the post on the brass buckle and let his breeches fall to behind his knees.

Charlotte closed her eyes, all hope of her breaking free abandoned her and resolutely, she turned her thoughts to anything that might keep her mind from running amok. For her to try and fight him would prove fatal, for in McKinnon, she had realised a strength she could never cope with.

McKinnon spat on his fingers and greased himself, but so great was his arousal that on his first attempt the beast which filled his hand floundered and slipped away between her legs. He cursed the loss and again, like a stallion committed to finding the mare, he thrust his quarters forwards and upwards.

The pain was a pouring of hot oil to her insides. With her teeth clenched, Charlotte closed her eyes and sunk her nails deep into the wet bark.

'There! Yes, right there my little beauty!' With one arm locked about Charlotte's waist, McKinnon threw back his head and drove his thickened flesh full length into her.

# -14-

Jim ran with his rifle held at the trail; Moosa ran alongside him, his ancient flintlock still primed and loaded with heavy ball. Here, the trees were dark; shadows came alive and more than once, Jim stopped dead in his tracks, delayed by imagined movements. However, through a gap in the trees he caught the faintest glimmering of light from Kathleen's bedroom window and he reached out to warn the boy.

'Watch your step,' he whispered over the sound of Moosa's breathing, 'we're close now. If McKinnon's already here, he will be watching for us. Stay within the shadows.'

'He is here, Mister Jim; I feel it. We must hurry.

McKinnon knows that his time will not be a long one.'

With rifles held at the high port, again, they used those dark shadows to cover their approach; once inside the garden, shrubs and terraced contours concealed their movements, it was then, that a single thunderous report from a Colt revolver crashed in on their ears.

'I swear on my own life, my next shot will not be so forgiving, McKinnon.' Kathleen's warning cut through the moonlight; less than ten yards out from the paddock fence, she squared her stance, re-cocked the weapon and settled her sights to a dark crease in McKinnon's forehead. 'I will not tell you again – let her go or I will kill you.'

'Easy on with that trigger finger, girlie; kill me and you'll step up to those pearly gates alongside o' me, the law will hang you for sure and that's the truth of it.'

He swivelled sideways-on to Kathleen, with one hand he cinched his breeches belt and drew Charlotte's limp form across his chest, holding her there as a shield. It was then Kathleen saw the knife.

Caught by the breeze, Charlotte's gown fell open; she was blackened with virgin blood from the juncture of her legs to her navel. Kathleen's aim faltered, her shocked realisation of what had happened was the distraction McKinnon had hoped for.

'Back off and lower that pistol o' yours, or on your head I'll bleed your precious bitch 'til she's empty.'

'Let her go.' Driven by quiet rage, Kathleen tightened her grip on the Colt.

'When I reach the trees,' McKinnon growled, 'then I'll leave her be, not before.' He started backwards, managing Charlotte's weight as if she were nothing more than a child. Step for step, Kathleen paced McKinnon to where the moonlight ended and the dark forest began.

# -15-

Before Kathleen had chance to react, McKinnon, like some satanic will-o'-the-wisp had spirited away inside the forest; within that same minute, Jim O'Rourke came up through the moonlight. Kathleen fastened the cord on Charlotte's gown and gently she held her head within the cradle of her hands. Jim crouched down alongside them.

'How bad is it?'

'How bad does it have to get, Pa? She's alive, which is more than I will say for McKinnon when I find him.'

'Can you walk?' he touched Charlotte's hand; her skin felt cold. Charlotte nodded her head, raised herself onto one elbow and gestured to Kathleen.

'I need you to help me inside.' Though unsteady on her feet, with Kathleen's arm for support she made her way towards the back door.

'My desk,' Jim called after Kathleen, 'right hand drawer – bottle of brandy. Strong coffee and plenty of sugar, make sure she drinks it.' He beckoned to Moosa. 'You stay here. On your life, no one gets in.'

Wide-eyed and sentry-like, Moosa positioned himself close-in to the door, his rifle at full cock; every fibre of his being trembled with anticipation.

'No one shall get past me, Mister Jim. Not even the devil himself, sahib, sir or I will shoot him back to hell!'

As fast as he dared and with the moon to his right shoulder Jim cut southwards through the forest; to Blackie McKinnon, speed would be paramount, other than what he could carry on horseback everything else would be left behind. He would be making his way back to wherever he had tethered his horse – somewhere close.

'Behind the hotel,' Jim thought on the run, 'has to be there – then south, across the Blyde and down to Lydenburg before word gets out.'

He reached the hotel and quickly he searched the grounds for a saddled horse, but apart from his own and pair of rangy mules the hitching rail was empty. However, the mules were edgy, wide-eyed they watched him. Within those last few minutes something had spooked them.

Hidden by shadows, Jim waited for his breathing to steady. A mile to his front, the Blyde River ran slow but powerful, silver in the moonlight, feeding off yesterday's run-off. To the north-west, heavy clouds were already building above the hills; there would be more rain that night.

'The drift,' Jim realised, 'he has to cross tonight before the storm breaks.'

He rode his horse at a slow trot, keeping to soft ground at the side of the track so as to muffle the gelding's footfalls; another hour and the storm would be over the Blyde.

\*

McKinnon rode the mare belly-deep through the river, on reaching the far bank he knee-haltered his horse and left it well hidden amongst the trees. Light from the moon was close to disappearing and he was glad of it, soon it would be pitch black and when he slid down into the water, the Blyde, still strong closed in around him. Crouched low in the water only his head stood clear of the surface. To hold his balance, McKinnon was forced to lean sideways-on to the flow, overhead and eastwards from the storm's edge the sky was clear, filled with stars; a single white-faced owl flew beneath them. His horse whickered; barely audible, but the slight warning was enough to put McKinnon on his guard.

'Come on down, O'Rourke, I know you're there,' he whispered under his breath. 'That's twice now that girl o' yours has cost old Blackie more than a pretty penny.' His hand went up to his cheek; the wound still bled and burned like fire at the touch of his fingertips. Half an inch to the right and Kathleen's bullet would have shattered his jaw.

Again the mare whickered; with her ears pricked, even at fifty yards distant she had sensed the presence of another horse. However, McKinnon focused solely on the track where it dipped at a steep, downwards angle for the drift. Within those next few minutes the silhouette of a horse and rider seeped from out of the shadows.

Twenty yards to Jim O'Rourke's front, the Blyde hissed its way past tall river reeds; to his right hand, but as yet still far away, the first rumblings of a new storm blackened an already darkened sky. The breeze had dropped and the warm smell of damp soil had settled there amongst the trees; thousands of winged termites rose as a single cloud through those final minutes of moonlight.

Jim reined his horse from the roadside and slid from the saddle and in the lessening light quickly he tethered the gelding to an overhang of small branches. Silently, he moved forwards, ears straining for sound, the Winchester repeater armed and ready to fire.

# -16-

Just as dark clouds overwhelmed the moon, McKinnon picked up a faint reflected glimmer of light from Jim's rifle. He was closer than McKinnon realised and within a foot of the drift, Jim squatted down to watch and listen.

McKinnon shuddered from the cold, the chill had worked its way inside his bones, but he ignored the discomfort and now, under cover of overhanging reeds he edged himself to within a yard of Jim O'Rourke's feet.

The only light was that of the stars, the only sounds those of a river hurrying onwards between the reed beds and in the distance, that faint drum of angry water where the river had found the rocky throat of some narrow ravine. Low in the water, like the hunting crocodile, McKinnon moved forwards, the upper part of his face now all that showed above the water line. Inside his head, voices urged him on, sinister condemnations for the girl with the gun, for the pain she had left him with and for the man who had come after him and now stood close enough for him to touch.

It came at Jim O'Rourke with the speed of a striking snake, driven upwards by the full force of McKinnon's powerful shoulders. The blade found the jugular notch at the high point of the sternum, splitting the larynx and windpipe before slicing on through to where a mesh of carotid arteries nestled in tight to the base of the skull. A fine spray of living blood covered McKinnon's face and chest; he turned his head to the side and waited for his victim's failing heart to stop beating.

'There you go, Jim boy – all about done now, evens up the score a bit I'd say.'

McKinnon stepped out from the water and knelt alongside the body, with his left hand to Jim's forehead he lunged backwards and drew out the knife. Arterial blood followed the blade, black as tar in the darkness. He reached behind and rinsed the knife in the river and then wiped it dry with the front of Jim's shirt.

'More's the pity that girl o' yours wasn't with you, O'Rourke, but the bitch will keep. A year or ten even, doesn't matter Jim boy, doesn't matter a tinker's fuck.'

He straightened up and then realised his opportunity. Quickly he rifled through Jim's pockets.

'Will you lookie-here, Jim boy; not much use to you, is it now, you being dead 'n all.'

He ripped the chain from its fastening on Jim's breast

pocket; the links were cast in thick silver and at one end, McKinnon was quick to recognise the misshapen weight of precious metal. Joined to the chain by a single, silver link, a nugget the size of the first joint of his thumb hung as a dead weight from between his fingers.

# -17-

Zingeli was first to reach the drift; in amongst the grass, Jim's body was almost indiscernible – dragged away from the track, purely through chance it was laid out flat – face up to the new sunlight. Jim's horse had slipped its tether and from where it stood, on seeing Zingeli it whickered softly.

'Wait here.' Zingeli lifted his hand to Moosa and with his spear at the ready, silently he skirted the killing ground for spoor, but there was little or no sign; McKinnon's tracks had been obliterated by that last night's storm.

Left bloodless by the rain the wound in Jim's throat was now a slender, blackened line and his eyes were closed, his facial muscles relaxed as though he had merely fallen asleep in the sunlight.

Zingeli crouched alongside the corpse and through some inexplicable need to know, he touched Jim's face with his fingertips. The flesh was cold and clammy; just dead meat. The man Zingeli had known was gone, flown to a secret place inside the spirit world. He raised his hand and beckoned to Moosa.

'Stay here with Mister Jim. Do not leave him alone or the birds will have his eyes out.'

Unable to speak, Moosa slumped down in the sunlight, rifle across his knees, the reality of what had happened now there alongside him, like some deathly chill it seeped up through the ground and robbed the sun of its warmth.

The years he had shared with the O'Rourke family were left at a loss. Along with his aspirations, pleasant memories like frightened birds were fleeing his life; some had already gone, stolen by death. Sickened by his failure to prevent the killing, Moosa drew on what little strength was left to him and sent the worthless flintlock rifle cartwheeling into the Blyde.

# -18-

Hand in hand, Kathleen and Charlotte climbed the ridge and looked down on what men now called the valley of gold. They climbed without speaking, shoulders touching and with a gentle linking of fingers which had become their mark, though for neither one of them the gesture did little enough to ease their pain. Kathleen knew that fate had forged a rift between them; McKinnon had been the hammer, Pilgrim's Rest the anvil upon which both her father and her lover had simultaneously and most cruelly been struck from her life.

'Remember this moment,' she told Charlotte, 'the view is always best when the sun is at its highest.'

From its start at the valley head, Pilgrim's Creek lay as a broken thread between the gravel heaps, where Jim had first outspanned their wagon so long ago, that same stretch of land had been torn up and swallowed by the river diggings. From amongst groves of jacaranda, roofs stood out as squares of bright red iron to limewashed walls and between them all, clumps of gaily coloured petunias imbued the town with a fictitious air of well-being. To their left hand, the wagon drift on the Blyde was only faintly visible, shielded from remorseful scrutiny by clumps of tall trees.

'How much time do we have?' Kathleen asked, her voice

unsteady.

'An hour at best.' Charlotte replied. 'Cohen's wagon leaves at noon. I have to be on it or be forced into making the journey alone.' She looked directly at Kathleen. 'If there was some other way – any way at all, my sweet, in a heartbeat I would take it.'

'I know,' Kathleen said, and struggled to cope; from the well behind her eyes her emotions were more than ready to spill out, 'your journey home – how long will it take?'

'If my luck holds...? Three weeks, four at the most.' She reached for Kathleen's hand, gentling the act with soft fingers. 'So much hurt has come from my being here, if only...'

With a quick turn of her head Kathleen contained the guilt, pressing her lips to Charlotte's.

'The blame is not yours – I should have killed McKinnon when I first had the chance.' Her eyes narrowed; that soft light had gone from them, in its place, the first dark flames of some terrible hatred had already taken hold.

'Your mind is set then?' Charlotte realised, her voice now little more than a whisper.

Kathleen nodded her head and with empty eyes looked down upon the rooftops; McLeod's store and Cohen's wagon bustled with excitement, restless oxen, already inspanned were eager for the open road.

'As soon as my father's interests in the company have been properly wound up; this coming month I hope. I could not stay in Pilgrim's Rest a moment longer.'

'Zingeli and Moosa,' Charlotte reminded, 'what will become of them?'

'Moosa starts work at McLeod's store this coming Monday. I will miss him terribly, but it's what he needs – store work will suit his temperament.' She stood up from the grass. 'Only Zingeli will be coming with me, the rest will keep their jobs; the company has given their word on it.'

'Let me come with you,' Charlotte pleaded, but Kathleen shook her head and smiled at the impossibility.

'It would not work, the mere distraction of you being there would put both our lives at risk. I have already lost my father to McKinnon, losing you also would destroy me completely.'

It was then that Charlotte understood, any attempt at changing Kathleen's mind would fall on deaf ears; what had gone had gone, what lay ahead had already been determined, there could be no going back.

'Then I shall wait for you, for however long it takes, it will not matter.'

Charlotte held out her hand for Kathleen to help her up. 'McKinnon is long gone; you might never find him. More's the point, your life will be at risk if you do so.'

Kathleen smiled at the warning, but nothing, not even Charlotte's pleading would change her mind. The very core of her existence was now indelibly linked to finding her father's killer.

'West,' said Kathleen, 'McKinnon is heading west. That's where he has gone, Charlotte – I'm sure of it.'

From her breast pocket, Kathleen drew out a tiny carousel of silver chain. Mounted with precious stones, as bright eyes, in the high sun of almost midday, all three diamonds glowed portentously.

'Diamonds are all that McKinnon spoke of; finding them is all that he cares about. The Vaal River is where he is at, Charlotte. He was there before. Other than Port Natal and Pilgrim's Rest, the diamond fields are all he knows. I swear on my father's precious memory that is where I will find him,' she looked westwards, 'and when I do, this time I will kill him.'

The walk to Cohen's wagon passed all too quickly, that of condemned men being led away for execution, and within the half-hour, Charlotte had been summoned to take her place on the wagon box.

'Be sure to write,' she held her composure, but inwardly a thousand regrets were gnawing at her insides. 'Once you have settled, but no later. I will ride every day to the market square; promise me Kathleen.'

'As soon as I can,' said Kathleen and reached across the gap between them. 'There will be a next time for us, Charlotte, I know it.'

The lash went out, and with the hissing sound of an overzealous wind it reached for the foremost oxen; as if brought back from a deep sleep the animals raised their heads and eagerly they shook the slack from out of their chains and with bright eyes looked to the road. The voorloper took his place at the front and on Cohen's slight nod of the head, coaxed the oxen into a slow walk for the drift.

With a heavy heart, Kathleen rode alongside Cohen's wagon; Zingeli followed at a small distance and then, as the wagon pulled away he drew level with Kathleen's mount. Kathleen slid from the saddle, they walked abreast, but only for as far as the river.

'We must go now, Zingeli, there is much for us to do, though I would not blame you if your plans were otherwise. The people you left behind in Natal; they would welcome your return. If that is where your heart lies, then I would not begrudge you going back to them.'

With solidarity, Zingeli shook off the chance to follow Cohen's wagon, and without any hesitation, he turned his back on the drift; there was a purpose to his step and without diffidence he lengthened his stride. The shadow he cast was small for the sun was at its highest point; in his right hand the assegais he carried were once again his closest allies, and his yearning for wide horizons was great, for the soles of his bared feet burned for the feel of a new road.

On splayed elbows, Bo Furguson leaned as a tired man against the tabletop. Directly opposite, Kathleen O'Rourke sat with her arms folded, her face expressionless, for the more obvious signs of her pain had been forcefully hidden away.

Herbert Rhodes watched her carefully, but like his colleague, found no outward signs of her morbidity, nor that of any obvious regret for the violent passing of her father. However, Herbert knew that both these sentiments were there, sleeping perhaps, marking time and like those of a man condemned to face the gallows for a crime he knew nothing of, one day, when it so suited her and with a fury sent from hell itself, she would explode.

Furguson sighed heavily and rocked back in his chair; as was the norm, his half-spent cigar thickened the air with blue smoke. With slow fingers he picked up a folded sheet of paper and passed it across the table to Kathleen.

'Your letter of credit from the Standard Bank in Lydenburg.' He waited for Kathleen's eyes to find the writing before going on with his explanation. 'One thousand pounds, Kathleen; the sum we agreed to. My colleague, Mister Herbert Rhodes will see to any necessary paperwork and on your acceptance, all rights to your father's share of the company will be relinquished *ad infinitum*.'

'That means, forever,' Herbert added, 'there can be no going back.'

Kathleen ran her finger over the content.

'The last line... signature of guarantor?'

Herbert cleared his throat. The entire, discomforting affair had unnerved him. Eyes like Kathleen's he had seen before; those of a man to whom the losing of his own life meant little or nothing at all.

'My brother's signature; it will stand as our final codicil to the agreement. Without it, the funds will not be released.'

Bo Furguson interjected. 'Cecil Rhodes will be watching for your arrival in Kimberley. I believe the two of you are already acquainted?'

'A long time ago,' said Kathleen. Eager to leave the room she nodded her head compliantly. 'Your paperwork; let's get this over with.'

'You are sure of what this means?' Furguson reminded her of the implications. 'There will be no turning back. You will leave Pilgrim's Rest within a week of signature and will be disallowed the involvement with any other mining venture within a ten mile radius of our company holdings; for a minimum period of two years.'

'I understand.' Kathleen told him. 'What made you think I would choose Kimberley?'

Furguson smiled at the question. 'Call it intuition. The hotel bar – men talk. Not a lot goes unnoticed. Your interest in Kimberley is yours to do with as you see fit. Your reasons for going there, or otherwise, are not for me to pass judgement on.'

Kathleen buttoned the letter of credit inside her breast pocket. The first, faint tingling of apprehension moved alongside her. All that her father had worked for would soon be gone, all that she had become, and in its entirety, what little she owned would ride out with her; the O'Rourke family would be remembered in name only, at least by a few, or perhaps by none at all; it did not matter.

'I will leave in the morning; first light. Whatever chattels I leave behind have already been promised to one of my father's employees, namely the Indian boy, Moosa.' She looked at Herbert Rhodes. 'Please ensure that he is in receipt of them. The registration of my father's rights to Peach Tree Creek has already been annulled and a deed of transfer citing your company as sole owner has been lodged with the government mining commissioner.' She held out her hand. 'Your pen please, Mister Furguson.'

Bo Furguson marvelled at the change in her; her astute, businesslike mannerisms, even her voice was different, only those who knew her would pick up on that slightest hint of her American accent. Her eyes, though still as green were devoid of any feeling; reptilian almost. He handed over his pen and watched Kathleen put her signature to the document.

'Will you be leaving alone?' Bo asked her; as a father himself his concern for Kathleen's welfare was obvious.

'Zingeli will be coming with me. I want for no one else, Mister Furguson; nor do I have any specific needs for a man in my life.'

Kathleen laid the pen down and pushed the completed document to the centre of the table.

'Would that be all you require of me?'

'That's it. Nothing more,' Furguson told her. Kathleen stood up from her chair and nodded her head to the men sitting opposite.

'Then I'll be on my way. Thank you for your consideration.'

Furguson followed her outside. From the hotel veranda, in the moonlight a thousand opened workings showed as a scourging pox upon the face of Pilgrim's Creek.

'Changed just a little since you first got here,' he rested his hand on Kathleen's shoulder, 'your father was a good man, Kathleen; if you have need for anything, our door will always be open to you.'

'One day I will come back,' she promised, 'but only when I am ready and on my terms.' She turned her head and kissed him lightly on the cheek. 'Not for a long time though, Kimberley holds a lot in store for me, Bo, hopefully some of it is good.'

# -20-

In those hesitant moments of false dawn the headstones were barely discernible, but soon, from above the horizon there appeared that smallest inkling of first colour. Kathleen sat with her back to a tree and watched the sun come up; it was then the enormity of what had happened fell upon her, ravenous and wolf-like it gnawed at her heart, a tangible wave of grief and anger and in that tumultuous moment, thoughts of joining her father were never far away. She cried without weeping; no sound, just silent tears. Where they had buried her father, the place had been set aside and marked with low walls, his grave a mound of turned earth; red earth, for red was the colour of the diggings, the colour of old blood, the colour of old Africa. Bouquets of wild flowers had withered and died; one still lived, a simple posy of pretty white daisies picked from the banks of Peach Tree Creek; gathered in last night's moonlight they still had their freshness, but soon the sun would rise and like the pain in Kathleen's heart it would scorch that freshness from out of them.

Zingeli looked to Kathleen's horse, today they would go away and far into the wilderness. Across his back, tied with leather thongs was the sum of all his wealth, but to the Zulu, now was not the time for counting cattle, nor were there children for his women to mind, for all these things were far inside the future.

From the topmost branches of a lone acacia, high up on the ridge, a go-away bird's human-like rebuke broke the silence; the bird demanded solitude and insistently it urged for Kathleen to abandon the graveside, for her to leave behind that quiet setting on the hill. To Kathleen, the bird's raucous clatter became her pointer, the sign she had been waiting for. Knowing what had to be done she left her place by the tree and for one last time, with her hands pressed against the soft earth she whispered her final words of remorse.

'It should have been different, Pa,' the words choked in her throat and she waited for the pain to ease, 'I have to go now. Stay with me, father – I cannot do this alone.'

Zingeli steadied her horse, Kathleen swung up into the saddle and unwittingly she stroked the walnut stock of her Sharps rifle; without looking back she followed a path that would for one last time, take her down into the valley of gold.

The Blyde would be running full; bank to bank, but to Kathleen O'Rourke such a hindrance would stand for little.

# IV

Kimberley, 1873

# -1-

Whenever the way ahead was obscured by forest or high ground, Kathleen took out a brass compass from the pouch on her belt, and with regularity checked the true alignment of their march towards the south-west. Silently, she thanked Bo Furguson for the gift; without the compass and the rudiments of a pencilled map from Herbert Rhodes, the journey she had undertaken would not have been possible. *Take fresh readings whenever you lose sight of your last marker,* Bo had warned her, *irrespective of the distance lying between you and your nearest horizon.*

They made fewer than ten miles on that first day, for the terrain was ruggedly steep and in many places thickly wooded, but on the night of the third, flickering light from the town of Lydenburg stood out clearly from the darkness. The thought of a soft bed and shelter tempted her, but Kathleen saw folly in her going down amongst the settlers and instead rolled herself in her blanket. With her father's revolver close to her side, she settled in next to the fire. For long moments she gazed upwards, baring her soul to the heavens, and in that clear sky the stars were bright and in her mind's eye those last three years flowed as a river, then tiredness came over her and not even her sadness nor the hard, unevenness of the ground were enough to keep her from sleep.

Every day, Kathleen maintained her trust in the compass needle and never once did she veer off course; arrow straight they crossed the hills, and when a thirty mile ridge of white quartz rose up in front they crossed that also, with a cold wind urging them onwards. Where the ground dropped naturally to its lowest point, marshland shone with sour grass and strings of shallow pools, rocky crags and tumbling waterfalls that gave this lonely, barren tract of land its name *Witwatersrand* – The Ridge of White Waters.

During those final one hundred miles, Kathleen was forced to cross the Vaal River, and on the advice of a Boer contract hunter, turned south-eastward for what had once been the farm *Vooruitzicht*. 'The DeBeers brothers are long gone,' he had told Kathleen, their farm had been hurriedly swept aside by the voracious march of colonial diamond hunters.

For three more days, Kathleen held her line of march and on the afternoon of the fourth day, with the sun at her right shoulder she happened upon a sight so grotesquely overwhelming that what little spirit she had left, threatened to desert her.

Across a broken horizon, men of a dozen different countries had covered the earth with canvas tents, not a single yard of ground was spared, only space enough for a man to walk between them had been left. Though still some distance out, Kathleen caught the glint of steel shovels being put to diamond-bearing ores of rotting Kimberlite, ground that had been forced from those unholy depths of the earth's mantle a billion years before any living creature had first stepped foot upon the continental shield of Africa. Sometimes, the raw clatter of metal on metal and the bass, hollow sound of a thousand picks being buried haft deep in friable rock carried up to her – then above it all, there echoed the sharp crack from a digger's pistol, for already the shanty-like bars and whorehouses were half-filled with human detritus from the diamond field's New Rush.

Kathleen drew in the lapels of her jacket then lowered the brim of her hat to fend off a listless July wind; she tasted dust from the workings and with it came the heartache of a thousand desperate souls who were still, at that late hour, burrowing insect-like into that foreboding outer rim of the Great Karoo. Strengthening her resolve, she urged her horse into a slow walk and within that next hour closed to within plain sight of miners working the eastern periphery of the diggings. As agreed upon, Zingeli stayed back. To guard against any white men's suppositions he would make his own way in, and when the time was right, his instincts would lead him to her.

'Got us a newcomer,' the cry went up, and a dozen wind-burned diggers leant on their shovels and watched the rider come down from the skyline. A raw-boned Scot took advantage of the lull; he struck a Vesta with his thumbnail then sucked the flame down inside the blackened bowl of his pipe.

'Rides like a Yankee cattle man – the fool's come all the way out here to find himself some easy money.'

'You're guessing, man. Too far out to tell, more like a Natal sod-buster out on his uppers.'

Jock Forrest hawked a mixture of dust and phlegm from his throat. Ripped of excess fat from his time behind the pick and shovel, in that cold wind, his chest and gut were lined across with sinew and hard muscle – the bark of a Scottish oak.

'So put your money to mine, Doherty. That's if you have the nerve for it.'

'The Queen's sovereign,' Doherty blurted – an amount he could least afford. Through the twitching eyes of a gullible fool he watched the faces around him cloud with disbelief.

'I accept.' Forrest snapped up the wager. 'Have your money ready, Irishman. I feel the need for a drink coming

215

on at the Digger's Rest.'

Twenty years in the company of hunters and prospectors had tutored his eye for a good horse and more often than not, the origins of its master. The way a man would sit to the saddle, be it with the old country's schooling for a short rein and a straight back, or that deep and easy long-legged reach for the stirrups favoured by Boer hunters and frontiersmen. Now, the excitement of his commitment to Doherty's wager nipped at the back of his neck; like a hardened prize fighter he growled through clenched teeth, eager for the fresh opponent to step inside the ring.

'Best dig out that sovereign, Doherty.' He held out his hand, still with his eyes on the newcomer; the eyes of a leopard – cunning and cold as the wind that whipped about his bare shoulders.

'May as well hand over your money now and be done with it. Look at the saddle, Irishman... and the rifle, got to be a Winchester .44-40.'

Doherty shook his head. To him, the Scot's assumptions were inconclusive, but through the failings of his own uncertainty he felt the weight of that single gold sovereign spirit away from his pocket.

'Don't stand for nothing,' Doherty countered, though instinctively his fingers curled about the coin, 'could have bought the lot off some freebooter down in Natal.'

'Then we will find out soon enough,' Forrest replied and went forward to where he guessed the rider would pass between the gravel heaps.

Kathleen kept her eyes to the front. For a full mile to either hand, scores of men worked bared to the waist, some with little more than strips of ruined cloth about the juncture of their legs. With their backs turned into the wind, obsessed by what they might chance upon, they ignored the cold and like so many ants fought their way beneath the ground. The diggers themselves afforded Kathleen little more than a cursory glance, less even by those who crowded vulture-like to the sizing screens and sorting tables, for they were the alpha wolves and would fight to the death to protect their stake in the diggings. Interlopers, as she had already experienced, would be made less than welcome here.

Overshadowing this hostility, Kathleen sensed another, far more powerful presence, the aura of desperation; that same spectral bird of prey had followed her here from the goldfields, and now it hovered falcon-like above this other manmade wasteland. For upwards of a thousand men it fostered only fear and rampant avarice, nurturing those who could not find the will to leave for fear that a follower-on with that first turn of his shovel might well unearth the perfect, priceless stone.

Jock Forrest raised his arm. Kathleen tightened her hold on the reins and instinctively reached inside the folds of her jacket. It was then the Scot caught sight of the Colt's intricately carved, walnut grip.

'No need for violence mister, just curious to know where you're from.'

Kathleen withdrew her hand. She took advantage of the subterfuge and, instead of speaking, with gloved fingers lifted her neckerchief even higher about the bridge of her nose. Now, only her eyes showed and even they were engulfed by shadow.

Jock moved in closer and habitually, leaned his weight against the shovel.

'Some say you're American – I would say they're right; judging from the way you sit that fancy saddle o' yours?'

'Bankrupt farmer boy!' Doherty shouted over the conversation – his confidence rekindled, 'already told you that Scotchman. Ask the man where he hails from – sure to the memory of my own sweet mother it will be your money that gets us drunk tonight.' He looked around him for support. 'What do you say lads, looks to me as though the digging's got herself a busted cotton grower?' But no one laughed. Their eyes were on the newcomer. Something about the rider had already forewarned them;

with their mouths shut, they watched and listened. Wary of loose remarks they followed Jock's lead and waited for the stranger to speak.

'So who would be right mister?' The Scot smiled, and the crow's feet from those leopard's eyes cut all the way back to his hairline. 'Yours truly, Jock Forrest; or my simple Irish friend back there on his dung heap?'

Kathleen felt her patience slipping, she was eager to reach the town before dark; somewhere to sleep, soap and towel and a deep tub of hot water.

Unable to keep his mouth shut, Doherty goaded Kathleen for a reply.

'Swallowed your tongue, mister?'

Kathleen shunned the remark and touched her heels to the gelding's flanks. However, freed from the wager by the uncertainty, the Irishman loosed his grip on the sovereign. Fuelled with fresh bravado, he stood his ground as the rider swung in close. His eyes found the Sharps buffalo gun.

'Big rifle, mister...?' He sniggered. 'Where did you find it – bit too much gun for a sod buster, boyo?'

Kathleen let her jacket fall open, showing the Colt was warning enough; Doherty's bravado withered and slack-mouthed he backed away. Without speaking, Kathleen kneed her horse into a slow walk between the gravel heaps to where the ground opened up and a half-mile wide hole loomed in front of her. She gazed down into the abomination, fixated by all that lay before her. Slowly, the pit bottom came into focus and the tiny creatures that crawled inside of it were not as they had first appeared; not as insects, but as grown men.

'Obviously your first time out here on the diggings – it shows. The proverbial sore thumb, old chap.'

Kathleen swivelled in the saddle. She held her silence and the man carried on with the tirade.

'You're on private ground, my friend. Almost every inch of what you see is spoken for.'

Kathleen stared at him; every bone in her body ached, muscles in her back trembled from exhaustion, three weeks in the saddle had left her with little sufferance for this cocky windburned, overdressed overseer. However, other men had locked on to the disturbance and already they had abandoning their workplace; like pack animals drawn to the trapped rabbit they closed in on the altercation.

'Best you get on out of here whilst you still have the chance, my friend; there are others here who might not be so tolerant of your trespassing.'

Kathleen left him there and without diffidence she ignored the abuse that followed her away from the pit edge. Now the ground inclined – a stretch of unturned scrubland led her to where the diggings ended and the town began. The wind dropped and mercifully the dust settled and as if a definitive line had been struck in the sand, permanent wood and brick buildings stood up as a solid wall in front of her. People crowded the rutted street and a brass band struck up with God Save the Queen; in the blinking of an eye, Kathleen was sucked in and carried along by the revelry.

-2-

The proprietor demanded the price of a week's board in advance of Kathleen being given the key to room twenty-three. When he entered her details into the guesthouse register, habitually, the corners of his mouth worked up and down in time with his pen.

'A last minute cancelation,' he delighted in showing her, 'the place is filled to bursting for another week at least.' He glanced up from his writing. 'Bad timing; the town is awash with dignitaries and government toffs. Yesterday we were the New Rush and now, all of a sudden, the Kimberley Mine.' He rolled his eyes to the ceiling. 'It would appear we have no choice; take it or leave it, we are the freshly risen, brightest star in the crown of British imperialism; Victoria's most grandiose inception to her colonial Africa.' With a foppish shake of the head, he flicked a lock of hair away from his eyes. 'Enough to drive a person mad. All change as from this morning, and no doubt the events of July fifth, 1873 will cost us all a pretty penny.'

'New Rush?' Kathleen looked at him for an answer.

'The very place you have come to, deary; name of our town, or was. Every digger within a hundred miles rushed for a stake in the new diggings, left their claims on the Vaal River as quick as the devil himself were after them. Prior to that, Colesberg Kopje we were known as and as of now, the Kimberley Mine, town, whatever. After Lord fancy pants bloody Kimberley, Secretary of State for the Colonies.'

'Explains the brass band and all the flag waving,' Katherine realised and refocused on her immediate needs, 'more importantly, I need a bath.'

'Tub of hot water is extra or should you prefer, threepenny bit cold baths are available at the rear of the George Hotel; Colorado Baths, I believe the establishment is called.' Again, his eyes went up to the ceiling. 'Personally, wouldn't be caught within half a mile of the place. God knows what you might catch.'

'The hot water?' Kathleen asked him,' how long before you send it up to my room?'

'I'll have the maid stoke up the fire. Give it half an hour. What about soap?'

Kathleen gave in to the extras. 'How much?'

'Chuck it in for free; just a shilling for the hot water.'

'What about something to eat?'

'Beef sandwiches and whatever cook has in mind for pud of the day – or take your chances at the Queens Hotel along the street. Pricey, though.'

'My horse?' she reminded him.

'Already taken care of. Stables are out the back; down the corridor, last door on the right and across the courtyard. No discharging of firearms on the premises, see that you lock them in your room. Stepping out with a rifle in your hand may well get you an early entrance to our cemetery.'

'One more thing, Mister...?'

'Watkins, Christopher Charles at your service.' Titillated by her enquiring after his name, a smile blossomed. 'What would that be?'

'A barber...? Where can I find one?'

Watkins waved his pen at the front door.

'Across the street, can't miss him.' His eyebrows lifted as though on strings. Without rancour he vetted the state of Kathleen's hair. 'A gentleman's hairdresser, mind; ladies usually prefer something a little more gentile, a little more haute coiffure, rather than basin-cut-Billy's across the road.'

'The barber across the street will do just fine.'

'Your personals...?' Watkins reminded, 'Besides the stuff you're carrying?'

Kathleen smiled at the manager's bewilderment.

'What you see is all that I have – besides my horse and whatever's tied to him, that's it, nothing else.' She laid out the Sharps rifle and Winchester carbine on the counter in front of her.

Watkins cleared his throat. He had noted the Colt and visibly, his head wobbled.

'The place you have come from – some kind of battlefield?'

Kathleen closed the front of her jacket and for the first time in many weeks managed a small chuckle.

'You could call it that. Pilgrim's Rest; home to a bunch of crazy river diggers a few hundred miles north-east of here.'

'Heard about them, rough types I can well imagine. What

made you leave?'

'Personal reasons.' She changed the subject. It would be a long time before she was ready to dip back into the real reasons for her being here. However, like herself, Watkins was hungry for news. They traded stories and in exchange for a small measure of flattery, Kathleen learned a lot.

'What about this place? Plenty of building going on; looks to me as though this town has been around forever.'

'Feels like it damn well has been.' Grateful of the chance to gossip, Watkins swivelled side-on to the counter and leaned on one elbow, more than eager for virgin conversation. 'The place never changes; miners, drunks, fugitives and diamonds, nothing else in this tip of a town to talk about.' He smiled at Kathleen. 'What about you? Anyone here in Kimberley we both might know?'

For a moment, Kathleen held back, but curiosity got the better of her.

'Friend of mine. Haven't seen nor heard from him in near on three years.'

'A name, sweetheart; give me a name.' With small, glittering eyes Watkins watched and waited.

'Rhodes,' Kathleen capitulated, 'Cecil Rhodes.'

The proprietor's reaction was immediate.

'Start at the top why don't you. Powerful man your Mister Rhodes, not many others out there on the diggings hold a candle to him.' He lowered his voice as if some unseen informer were listening in. 'Wealthiest man in town and free as a bird, if you get my meaning. No women in his life. Good scrub and a haircut and you could well strike lucky.'

Watkins was enjoying his hold on their small talk, as an informant, the proprietor was worth his weight in gold; Kathleen listened compliantly, encouraging him with recollections of her own time in Africa.

'The both of us came over on the same ship – three years ago.'

Like a child in its mother's thrall, Watkins hung on every

word. From the docking of the ship *Eudora*, to Kathleen's journeying north by ox-wagon, to her extracting gold from living streams and abandoned riverbeds around Pilgrim's Rest, the more sensitive happenings she left alone. The pain was still too close to the surface; as a furtive shadow it was always there, eager for the chance to show itself.

'What about family?'

Kathleen shook her head and looked sideways to the window.

'Don't have any,' she told him, 'guess I'm the only one left.'

Twice, Christopher sent the maid to Kathleen's room with pails of water, still steaming hot from the kitchen boiler, and twice Kathleen's enamelled tub was emptied and refilled before she was satisfied the smell of dust and horse had left her. Wrapped in a large towel she waited for the maid to leave before standing naked in front of the wardrobe mirror. Easily, she traced the line of her ribs with her fingertips, for the journey from Pilgrim's Rest to the diamond fields had stripped her clean of even the slightest excess. From the high point of her sternum to her hairline, the skin had been burned brown, burned to the colour of old leather by all those days of her riding directly into the heat of full sun. Her forearms were of the same deep colour so that fine hairs along their length showed as copper strands when touched upon by incoming late sunlight. However, where her body had been protected from the elements, here her skin glowed pink, the after effects of her languishing in the tub.

Her clothes had been washed and then hurriedly dried by the kitchen fire; the creases ironed out. In a matter of one hour Kathleen had been transformed – no more the nondescript, long distance rider she was now, though boyish in her attire, very attractive. The muscles in her forearms were overly defined, too obvious as to shout aloud of her hidden femininity, but sleek as those of a leopard at its time of full adolescence. In all, to Kathleen

O'Rourke the image she saw in the mirror gave weight to her poise and her confidence soared. She rolled up her shirt sleeves, high enough to expose the strength in those arms and, still with her eyes on the mirror drew back her hair, bunching as much as she could manage within the grip of her clenched fists.

'Short,' she instructed her reflection, 'or perhaps all of it, I have not decided.'

Quickly, she pulled on her boots, driven by the urgency of her decision. Christopher said that the barber across the street sometimes worked till late if his flow of clientele remained steady.

Locking the door behind her, Kathleen shrugged on her jacket, turned up her collar, descended the stairs to the front door and stepped into a street shrouded in last light. Another half hour and it would be pitch black, however, the weight of her father's pistol inside her jacket stood as protection enough; she had equal footing with any man out there on the street. She found the barber's door ajar and pushed it back on its hinges. Immediately, the bull voice of a razor-waving giant stopped her dead in the doorway.

'Too late – shop's closed. Come back tomorrow morning at eight.'

'Can't wait for tomorrow. I'll pay you double your going rate. Watkins from over the road said you might well fit me in.'

'Watkins is a bloody nuisance.'

Three lamps splashed the room with yellow light. With his long broom, the barber pushed a pile of multi-coloured snippings into the corner. He dropped the broom alongside the hair and growled his irritation at the latecomer.

'Five bob – take it or leave it. At this late hour I'll not be soothing my temper or blunting my precious scissors for anything less.' His own hair was wild with curls; copper-coloured, the same as Kathleen's. Broad across the shoulders and thick about the waist, he appeared as more suited to the wrestling ring than the barber's shop.

Kathleen reached inside her breeches pocket. She counted out the exact amount and stacked the coins on the window sill.

'What do I call you?'

'Same as you would have called my father – Patrick William McCrery. Paddy to my friends, Mister McCrery to you sir, until I get to know you.'

With her collar turned down, the light got into Kathleen's hair; lustrous and long it fell to her shoulders. McCrery folded his arms in front of his chest; amusement danced in his eyes.

'Be damned if you're not a woman and an Irish one at that; tell me I'm wrong and I'll cut your hair for nothing, lassie.'

'My money's as good as any.' Kathleen shot back at him. 'Yes or no? I'm short on time, nothing fancy, just the same all over – an inch up from bare skin is all I'm looking for.'

'Sit down.' McCrery repositioned his leather barber's chair and cleared a lock of hair from the seat with a flick of his fingers. He warmed to her. 'Why so short?'

'No particular reason,' Kathleen lied, 'less trouble.' Long hair would attract attention, an attribute she did not want. She slumped into the chair and saw her reflection fill the wall mirror in front of her. Her hair shone, lit by the lamplight and for a brief moment she doubted her decision. 'Short as you please, Mister McCrery, before I change my mind.'

McCrery covered her neck and shoulders with a square of clean linen and then moved in behind her chair; his scissors, sharp and silver in the lamplight hovered rapier-like above her head and already his fingers were moving, eager to work the blades.

'You are sure of this?' One last time he questioned her reflection.

'Sure as I'll ever be,' said Kathleen and nodded her head

for him to begin.

With her eyes shut, Kathleen talked as McCrery worked; hair flurried as auburn snow about her feet.

'Got here this afternoon,' she told him, 'booked into Watkins' place for a week, but I'll be looking for somewhere more permanent and less heavy on my pocket.'

'The Queens Hotel takes lodgers,' McCrery told her, 'ask for Lizzie Jardine and tell her I sent you. May well be full up, but there's usually a trader or two short of paying his way. Without next month's rent in advance they don't last long at the Queens.'

'Looking for an old friend of mine; Cecil Rhodes...?' Momentarily, the scissors stopped.

'Rhodes is a hard man to pin down, the man's never still. Could be down at the Queens or on his way to the Cape – take your pick.' The scissors restarted; he lopped away the last thick tress from Kathleen's scalp and let it fall to the floor.

What was left of Kathleen's hair he trimmed to an inch proud of her scalp.

'All done, any closer and we'll be down to the bone. Good as you'll get for a hundred miles.' With a cupped hand he ruffled the stubble, the remains of what was once, a beautiful head of auburn hair. 'Don't forget, tell Lizzie I sent you; nothing goes on around these parts without her knowing about it.'

He pocketed the money; her mentioning Cecil Rhodes had piqued his curiosity.

'Rhodes, where do you know him from?'

'Natal,' she told him, 'three years ago – shared the same ship. Worked with his brother on the gold diggings north-east of Lydenburg.'

'Herbert isn't one to settle anywhere for long,' McCrery mused, 'ask anyone who knows him; his own worst enemy. Too busy chasing dreams for him to make a fist of anything.'

Kathleen stood up from the chair; where once there had been a woman's face in the mirror, now, as if by magic there had appeared to her the likeness of a young though pretty man. She cocked an eye at the image and, with a sardonic smile on its lips the new likeness instantly acknowledged her appreciation.

'Guess I'll be needing a new hat.' She smiled at McCrery and outstretched her hand to him.

McCrery accepted the handshake. 'To your left, down the street as far as the corner. Rawston's Store, always open till late; everything you need.'

He walked her to the door; now it was dark outside. Matches flared and Tilley lamps wove as fireflies through the blackness. Kathleen shrugged her shoulders against the cold, in July, once the sun had set over Kimberley, any warmth it had left behind was quickly bled away by cloudless, night skies.

# -3-

Kathleen paid the storekeeper the exact amount, plus an extra shilling for his assistant to drop her purchases off at the boarding house.

'I'll thank you to leave them with Mister Watkins at the desk.'

Rawston smiled, the sale had been a good one, all top shelf, right down to tins of hard to come by embrocation and spare laces for the boots.

'Apart from the hat,' Kathleen corrected herself, 'I'll take that with me.' Like her old drover's hat, it was wide-brimmed and at the angle she preferred, it concealed her eyes.

'Anything else that might take your fancy?' Rawston scrutinised her stature and though her voice was undoubtedly that of a woman, her arms, bared to the elbows were heavy set and he envied her the definition. Kathleen shook her head.

'Just directions. The Queens Hotel, how do I find it?'

'Top of the street; double storey place with a fancy balcony, you can't miss it.'

It took less than ten minutes for Kathleen to find Lizzie Jardine's hotel. The upper balcony was guarded by fancy, waist-high wrought iron panels and from the hotel's innards, piano music and men's ribald laughter poured out into the street. She went inside, the hotel foyer was half-filled with diggers and in the far wall, a set of ornate double doors were fastened back to allow access to the bar-room.

'Either you're lost or looking for someone.' The voice came out from behind a small, wooden counter top; behind it were the rudiments of a busy reception office. 'Picked a bad night for whatever it is you're after, sweetheart, the rooms are all filled up.'

'The proprietor,' Kathleen took off her hat, 'I'm looking for her.'

'And you've found her.' Lizzie Jardine ducked from behind the counter. 'You're new to Kimberley; sticks out like pearl in a coolie's ear. What is it you're after?'

'McCrery, the barber, said you might well help me out with a room; long term and I'll pay in advance.'

'As sure as little apples, friend, if I were to take your money it would not be in arrears. Where are you from?'

'A long way north-east of here – place called Pilgrim's Rest.'

Lizzie nodded her head. 'Heard of it; new goldfield, supposedly.'

Kathleen liked her manner. Lizzie Jardine, though slightly frayed at the edges saw life for what it was. Swept away from her forehead and tied at the back with a bow of black silk, her hair was neat and sun-coloured, bleached blonde by too many years in Africa; too many years away

228

from the cloud-filled skies of her native Scotland. In with the gold, strands of bright silver glittered in time with her movements, all of it enhanced by the foyer's central chandelier.

Without diffidence, Lizzie Jardine studied the youthful characteristics of Kathleen's face. Her own, though camouflaged with rouge and powder showed off creases at the temples, and below the eyes, where again time had puckered the skin, first lines openly betrayed her age. An inch shorter than Kathleen, with her fists balled into her sides, Lizzie Jardine stood close-in to the newcomer, her waist tightly belted and waspish, but a heavily laden bosom and buxom rear made up for any shortfall.

'You're an attractive young woman; the truth now, why the pretence? When I first clapped eyes on you, could have sworn you were a man. Why the cropped hair? You running from someone?'

Kathleen shook her head.

'Other way round; looking for a friend, an old acquaintance, but it can wait.'

Without any hesitation, Lizzie took hold of Kathleen's arm and led her into the office. She pointed to a chair.

'Proposition for you, might well benefit the both of us, but I'm sticking my neck out, mind. Don't know you from a bar of blue soap.'

Her eyes softened. She retrieved her half-finished cigarette from a tray on the counter; ecstatically she filled her lungs with smoke.

'I'll get straight to it; I want you to work for me.'

Kathleen opened her mouth to protest but with alacrity, Lizzie threw up her hand to silence her.

'Hear me out before you make your decision.'

Kathleen settled back in her chair; she had nothing to lose, whatever the final choice might be it was hers to make.

'Go on, but if it involves men for my money the answer's no.'

'Two nights a week, no hanky-panky for your money – I swear on my husband's grave.'

Kathleen twisted in her seat. It was all too easy.

'What's the catch?'

'No catch. I know what I like and as the saying goes, I like what I see.'

She crossed to a roll-top desk and rattled back the frontage. The insides were cluttered with opened letters and office bric-a-brac.

'Need someone like you to work behind my saloon bar; keep the gents smiling and their glasses filled.' She paused momentarily, reached out a bottle, poured a tumbler quarter full with London dry gin and drank it down in one. The fumes made her eyes water, but her voice remained clear. 'You'll be free to help yourself from the shelves, but aside from what the punters leave behind for you, there won't be any wages.'

Again, Lizzie Jardine paused to assess the choice she was making; with amusement lighting her eyes she watched the set of Kathleen's face for those first contrite signs of outright refusal. She saw none, Kathleen's expression remained unchanged.

'However, not all is as it seems; in place of any wages, you will get your room for free within my hotel, including meals, hot water and whatever else – within reason that is.' She left the empty glass on the desk. 'Two nights work in return for full board and lodgings; what do you say?'

'Because I look like a man…?'

Lizzie smiled at the expected assumption. Kathleen was quick witted and mentally alert, exactly what she was looking for.

'Because you're young and beautiful and the short hair won't be a problem. Besides, from what I see, you're strong enough to look after yourself, been known to get a little bit rowdy back there in the bar room, 'specially on Saturday nights when the place fills up with big-spending, hard-headed diamond diggers.'

'Already paid a week in advance for a room at Watkins' guesthouse?'

'Then tell him you have to move on and I will re-reimburse you for any losses.' She picked up a lighted Tilley lamp, dropped the cigarette in a sand bucket and beckoned to Kathleen for her to follow. 'Think about it. Meantime, come take a look at what you would be missing out on if you decide on turning me down.'

The room, big and airy was set to the hotel's south-east corner; two windows, fitted to the street facing wall would both of them, catch their fair share of any morning sunlight.

'Goose feather mattress,' Lizzie expounded, 'big enough for you and anyone who takes your fancy. No one permanent, mind.'

She placed the lamp on a small table and flopped down on the bed.

'Wardrobes, two of them, three sets of drawers and your own, private water closet – through that door,' she pointed it out, 'towels, linen, everything in and laundered weekly; no extra cost.' She swung her legs sideways off the bed. 'And my *pièce de résistance* – stay with me for the next six months and I'll cut you in for a share of the takings, three percent of everything you take over the bar – back paid all the way to day one.'

Kathleen crossed to the window and looked down into the street. Though it was dark, she sensed the life out there in the night; noises filtered up to her, matches flared, red-eyed cigars glowed and dimmed as their smokers found a way between the buildings. The heartbeat of a fledgling city was there, right in front of her, every whisper of information ebbed and flowed through the hotel doors; her own excitement quickened. Everything she needed to know, every face, smile and sideways glance was down there in the hotel's smoke-filled bar. She pondered over the offer, but only for a moment.

'Sounds too good to be real; still waiting for the catch.'

231

'Already told you, there isn't one. Believe me, girl, every penny you get from me you will have earned a hundred times over. Never said it would be easy, but you're tough enough to cope and I know an honest face when I see one.'

She watched and waited long enough for Kathleen to make up her mind.

'So what do you say? Throw your hat in the ring with old Lizzie Jardine, or scuttle off back to Watkins' hole in the wall and pretend we never met.'

'What about decent clothes, and my hair – didn't figure on being offered hotel work?'

'Leave all that to Lizzie Jardine,' she held out her hand, 'welcome to the Queens Hotel; busiest, roughest, but dare I say it, friendliest watering hole as you'll find anywhere in this wreck of a Kimberley town.'

## -4-

Kathleen slept out her first Kimberley night at the guesthouse and for the first time in weeks, she woke to the comfort of a real bed. However, though he was outwardly disappointed by Kathleen's imminent departure, Christopher Watkins well understood her need to move on, the offer of work at the Queens was a gift from heaven; work unrelated to mining diamonds was hard to come by and along with free accommodation, opportunities such as the one Kathleen had told him about were few and far between.

'I'll have your things sent round to the Queens,' he promised, 'shouldn't prove too difficult to re-let the room.' He reached for the cash box, but Kathleen stopped him. 'No need; keep the money, but if things go wrong, the chance of my moving back in would be much appreciated.'

Christopher's face lit up. 'Mind you don't forget now. Any time you need a bed you know where to come.'

'And any time you need a drink and a measure of good gossip, the same applies.'

'Best looking bar lady in Kimberley.'

Kathleen leaned across the reception counter and dropped a kiss on Christopher's cheek.

'Nicest man I know,' she parried. Christopher's eyes starred with moisture.

'Helping you onto the ladder has been a privilege; now please leave before you upset me completely. Soon as you're settled, I'll drop in at the Queens.' He turned his back on her and made pretence of sorting through some paperwork. He heard the door close, only then did he turn around.

Invigorated by the excitement of her new commitment, Kathleen shouldered her rifles and with a spring in her step strode out along Stockdale Street; her horse had already been stabled and well-tended to by the Queens' own livery yard. Early sunlight streamed in over Kimberley and through a gap in that last line of wood and iron buildings, Kathleen caught a brief, second glimpse of those already infamous diamond diggings.

'Just a few minutes,' she promised herself and from her original route detoured her way through to that ragged frill of denuded ground.

Less than a hundred yards of littered veld stood between Kathleen and a scene that was looked upon by most as one of total devastation. Dubbed, The Big Hole by mining men as far away as Australia and the Americas, the ground to Kathleen's front had been mercilessly ripped through by a thousand desperate men, some had already made their fortunes, whereas others not so lucky were forced to sell up all they owned for the price of a fare back home. As some grotesque patchwork quilt, the diggings stretched a mile across from where she was standing. With ever deepening, thirty by thirty feet claims and sheer-sided man-made cliffs, the opencast mine now covered a bed of ruined earth that would not, even through the passing of another thousand years find the will to heal itself. Awestruck, and in part frightened by the enormity of what she gazed upon, Kathleen turned her back on the world's greatest diamond mine.

Lizzie Jardine was waiting for her. Attired in leather boots, loose fitting calico breeches and billowing cotton shirt, rather than the proprietor of Kimberley's biggest hotel, she appeared to Kathleen as the epitome of the ship's master. Her hair, draped about her right shoulder was a single whisk of plaited gold and where it ended, the usual ribbon of black silk held it securely. She stood with her hands clasped to either side of that svelte waistline and below that mass of corn-coloured hair the smile was genuinely warm and welcoming; the winsome look of a female buccaneer.

'Was afraid you might have changed your mind; been stood out here in the doorway for the past half hour.'

Kathleen shook her head.

'Gave you my word. Once I make my decision there's little chance of my turning back.'

Lizzie lifted the Sharps rifle from Kathleen's shoulder.

'My late husband had one of these beauties; wouldn't let anyone near it. Up against his marriage vows, the Sharps would have won hands down.' She turned for the stairs and Kathleen followed, the Yellow Boy Winchester held at the trail.

Within those last few hours, Kathleen's room had been polished, cleaned and dusted from floor to ceiling, furniture rearranged, some of the older pieces thrown out and generously replaced with new.

'Decided on different curtaining,' Lizzie said, 'the others were dowdy, not bright enough.' She stepped in front of the nearest window and with her arms outstretched, mentally she encompassed the room as a whole. 'So what do you think?'

'Pretty as a picture,' Kathleen remarked and without any contrivance thrilled at the homeliness of her room.

Lizzie crossed to where Kathleen leaned against the window ledge.

'Saddle's been stored in the livery yard, along with the rest of your things. Just one small request before I leave you alone to settle in,' she pointed to Kathleen's waistband, 'the gun you're carrying...?'

Kathleen opened her jacket. 'It was my father's,' she defended, 'don't go anywhere without it.'

'No need for it in here,' Lizzie assured her, 'I know my clientele are pretty much down to earth sorts, but wouldn't take kindly to being served by some gun toting, woman gold miner. Better a smile than a bullet, sells more liquor.'

'Old habits take some shaking off,' Kathleen explained, 'too many bad experiences, I guess.'

'My cellar man, Joe Walsh is always to hand if there's trouble.' The tension eased. 'Believe me sweetheart, he's more of a deterrent than any pistol. However, just to be on the safe side – under the counter – twelve bore double, loaded but not cocked. Last resort mind, no dead punters for your aunt Lizzie to clear up after throwing-out time.'

She folded her arms beneath her bosom and the look in her eyes turned motherly.

'How old are you, girl? The truth mind – no lies.'

'Why would it matter?'

'Matters to me, but you're right I shouldn't have asked.' Lizzie shook her head at the folly and backed off. 'Forget I said that – none of my damned business.'

'Nineteen,' said Kathleen, 'just turned. My folks are dead – both of them.'

Lizzie stopped herself from reaching out.

'I'm sorry, Kathleen. Didn't intend on opening up old wounds.' The smile resurrected. 'Come take a look from your balcony, best view in Kimberley.'

The doors opened outwards and folded back against the

outer wall. Both women stepped outside and the birthing pangs of a freshly christened town rushed up to them; sounds and smells and stronger, more prevalent than all of them together were those coming in from the diamond diggings.

'That noise?' Kathleen looked to Lizzie for answers.

'The pit edge,' said Lizzie, 'dry pulley-blocks; no grease. Steel on steel – without grease they squeal like stuck pigs. The diggers' rope-and-pulley system for bringing up fresh-dug ground from the pit bottom.'

Yellow dust hung as an immovable cloud above the diggings.

'If the wind comes up from the south-east, which it will and soon enough, make sure your windows and balcony doors are closed or you will be ankle deep in yellow dust before you know it. Kimberley gets more than its fair share of dust storms; wind springs up from nowhere. Yellow dust when it's dry, red mud when the rains set in.'

Looking out across the rooftops, Kathleen recognised little if any semblance of order across the entirety of the diggings; where the diggers' will to mine was long established, their insatiable lust for precious stones had dropped the level of many registered mining claims to sometimes a hundred feet below that of those adjoining, and on makeshift ladders, hampered by blinding dust squalls, desperate men were climbing hand over hand into holes that measured no wider across than a Cornish cottage living room.

'When it rains?' Kathleen queried, and Lizzie's eyes narrowed.

'Turns this place into a living hell,' she hissed, and, through closed eyes drew from a willing store of bitter memories, easily she recalled the turmoil brought by every rainy season. 'Red mud, everywhere you look, from one week to the next everyone and everything is red. Dogs, wagons, horses, men; nothing escapes being covered in the damned stuff.' She paused as if to steady herself. 'Then there's the cave-ins. Eight men, all at once, buried alive under a hundred yards of broken earth.' She gestured with her hands, emulating the sudden, sideways rush of a lethal slip of ground. Her mind's eye, unable to close off the horror, re-enacted the carnage of that unforgettable day, where it happened, deep down towards the centre of the pit. 'Came out from the pit edge like a red snake; no warning, all of them dead. Twisted up like rag dolls they were. Saw them laid out – down there in the street. Every open part of their body rammed full with mud. No blood – never any blood, no place left open enough for it to come out.'

Her eyes opened. She turned away from the street and with the look of a woman recently bereft of her husband, shook her head at the misfortune.

'Stays like that until the rains have finished – then the dry comes back and right on cue the dust you're looking at now floats up thick and yellow from that cursed hole in the ground.'

Kathleen watched it move, loathsome, but strangely pretty; primrose-yellow, and as some mindful entity it clung to the diggings, content to hang above them. It churned and spiralled inwards and upwards, a malignant yellow cloud beneath that blue, Colesberg sky. As if it were alive and through the purposeful spreading of its diaphanous shroud it would slowly poison most of those who toiled beneath it.

'They suffer all of this?' Kathleen mused at man's stupidity.

Ruefully, Lizzie smiled at the truth and nodded her head.

'All for a few shiny stones, you will see enough of it tomorrow night; once the booze takes a hold of their ego, though I suppose without them none of us would be here, save for a handful of Boer farmers.'

'The Boers...?' Kathleen broadened their conversation. 'Get the feeling they don't much welcome us being here?'

'They don't. Can't say I blame them either. Everywhere

they go we follow along behind. Look upon us British as some sort of hell-sent plague. All the Boers want is to be left alone. They're farmers through choice and a pious sort by nature – put their trust in God Almighty, in their rifles, the rain when it's needed and an open road to the north. Preferably one that leads their wagons as far away from *uitlanders* as the Almighty will allow.' She shook her head and smiled wryly. 'Reckon they're a yard or so closer to the truth than us *rooineks*.'

'*Rooineks*...?'

'Rednecks', Lizzie explained. 'That's what they call us. New settlers straight from gentle-weathered old Blighty and quick as a flash burned up bright red from too much sun; at least for the first few months.'

Kathleen glanced over her shoulder at her reflection in the glass door panel; inside the neck of her shirt the skin was leather-brown and she was grateful for it.

'Any Boers working in the diggings?'

'Just a few,' said Lizzie, 'most don't last for long – not down there in the pit. They look to the openness of the wilderness – that's just how they are, God-fearing and true only to their own kind. Hard as nails and smile little. Like the others, you'll get to know them – if they'll let you. Honest people with the loneliness of the veld and a commitment to God burned right through to the backs of their eyes. Most of them make their living hunting meat for the diggers; everything within fifty miles of Kimberley has been shot out. Firewood as well; stripped clean. Never-ending demand for meat and kindling, cold as hell out there on the flatlands when that wintering bitch of a *guti* wind whips in over the ridge.'

'*Guti*?'

'Fine rain,' Lizzie explained, 'cold, wet drizzle, lassie – weeks of it – like a hag's old bony fingers, feels its way inside your shirt and if given the chance she'll chill you through to the soul.'

She looked out above the rooftops, towards a thousand

miles of barren landscape where it stretched as an arid, shimmering line beyond the diggings.

'Out there, without firewood and shelter, down-and-outs die a miserable death from the cold and no one's the wiser; at least not before the crows find them.'

'And what about you?' Kathleen asked. 'Before Kimberley, where were you?'

Lizzie's eyes brightened, most of the memories she had amassed on the river diggings were good ones.

'Built me a hotel and general store near the diggers' camp at Klein Kebi, close-in to the Pniel diggings; stone's throw over the river from Klipdrift on the banks of the Vaal, some fifty miles west of where we're standing.' She turned nostalgic and at the same time, remorseful of her move to Kimberley. 'Might not have been as filled up with diamonds as Fleetwood Rawstorne's New Rush, but the times were better – easier on the mind than this godless, piss-ridden hole in the ground.'

She shook off her dissatisfaction and not without some effort, re-established the beginnings of a new smile.

'My next move will be back home, lassie. Back to bonnie Scotland, a land of gentle rain and hills so purple with heather your eyes will ache from the pleasure of watching the sun go down.' Her eyes clouded. 'But not yet, a few more years to go before Lizzie Jardine has gotten together her wherewithal to make it back across the water.'

Kathleen didn't hear her, from amongst the crowd a familiar face looked up to her balcony, his hand raised to catch her eye.

'Down there Lizzie, my Zulu servant, Zingeli.'

Lizzie saw him also. 'Followed you all the way from Pilgrim's Rest, I suppose?'

'Yard for yard,' Kathleen said.

'Then get him off the street before the diggers commandeer this Zingeli Zulu of yours and put him to work in the diggings. Take him round to the livery yard and tell him to wait for me.'

'You'll give him work?'

Lizzie nodded her head. 'Nothing fancy mind; stable boy, five bob a week, free lodgings with the other hands and as long as he proves his worth, two pairs of work breeches, a blanket and as much as he can eat.'

# -5-

Kathleen handed Zingeli a single gold sovereign, she avoided his eyes – the work was beneath him, skipping out twenty stables she saw as demeaning. However, readily, Zingeli accepted his job as a livery yard stable boy – it was a start and as a newcomer to the diamond town of Kimberley there was much for him to learn.

'You are both my mother and my father,' he spoke softly to Kathleen, 'from our first meeting, without anything in return, as did your father, you cared for me – for that and a thousand other things, I thank you.'

'It is but a small matter,' Kathleen held off from the sentiment, 'the work is that of a boy, but be warned, Zingeli, the time will come again for the pair of us to work like ten men. A month from now, perhaps two even, but no longer.'

'I will be ready, those who work here tell me the food is good and the job is easy; the days will pass quickly, a month of this woman's work and Zingeli will be ready to take up the pick and the long bar. Stay well, *Ndabezitha*, when the time is right, send word and Zingeli will find you.'

## 6

'Two more minutes and I'll be forced to open the doors, lassie.' Lizzie Jardine grinned at Kathleen and did her best to make small of what was waiting for them.

Outside the saloon bar's double doors, men crowded twenty deep and like shoaling fish, pressed in close to the entrance. Faces jostled for open space and through the glass panelled doors managed to commandeer the view for only a few seconds before being thrust aside by others more determined.

'Saturday nights?' Kathleen queried. 'Are they always like this?'

Lizzie shook her head; the night was well set to be a record breaker. Her fingers fondled the cash box drawer.

'Word's got out about my taking you on. Best get behind the bar and barricade yourself in, sweetheart, I don't think we can hold them off for much longer.'

Kathleen ducked through an opening in the bar's frontage; some sixty feet long and fashioned from old mahogany, it covered the entire width of the room. Across the bulk of that rear wall, four equally spaced shelves had been bracketed on to the brickwork and all of them were loaded full with glasses, boxed cigars and strong liquor, contracted in by high-costing hauliers from as far afield as Cape Town. At the centre and again, secured to a backing of whitewashed wall, a string of wide, leaded mirrors threw back light from high chandeliers and across the room as a whole, fresh sawdust had been scattered liberally in anticipation of the night's spillage. A score of heavily varnished round tables and low-backed wooden chairs added an air of American western style saloons to the Queens Hotel, heavy brass spittoons shone like the foot rail, close-in to the bar. It was then Kathleen remembered herself as a child, peering in past batwing doors for a glimpse of raucous, dance hall decadence. However, though the Queens fell short of sporting a dozen, high-kicking burlesque girls, the atmosphere inside the room had been cleverly primed. A new piano and raised stage with its gaudy, gold-tasselled, red velvet drapes added fresh enticement to the room. At the back of the stage, hidden by more velvet curtaining, a doorway gave access to the hotel's more covert accommodation; for those with ready money and in need of those little extras, a digger could leave and return to the bar without being noticed.

Central to the room and positioned as a triangular redoubt, three crown and anchor tables waited as hungry lions, eager for those first tempted to the waterhole; along with a black iron spiral staircase and small balustrade, the picture was complete. The room, to every working digger in Kimberley was with regard to their Saturday nights, the treasured bolt hole, a place where hard-bitten mining men could spend their gains and for those next few hours, leave their demons to their own ends down inside the pit.

With less than a minute to spare before the doors were flung open, Kathleen appraised her reflection in the mirror. Her hair, though drastically shortened, rather than distract the onlooker from her femininity, projected the elfin sweetness of her youth, but her employer, through the experience of her years spent cajoling drunken diggers of their cash, had dressed Kathleen in a calf length skirt of dark brocade and topped it with a blouse of soft silk; stunningly white, close-fitted but not too drawn across the pertness of her breasts – virgin snow and to those ignorant of her past, was as yet, fresh and unsullied, still untrodden. Confident of her being there, she took in one, last deep breath and then turned face-on to the double doors.

Lizzie nodded to her cellar man for him to slip the bolts on both doors, then, with a brusque stride made her way back to the bar.

'Here they come, girl – keep your temperament warm-hearted and the bell ringing on your cash drawer, we run right on through to twelve midnight. Joe will keep an eye on things and help you find your feet. Any trouble, give him the nod.'

'What about you?'

Lizzie ducked behind the counter.

'I'll be right here with you; at least until you get to grips with controlling this herd of Cape Buffalo.' She turned to the shelves. 'Don't forget, the measure prices are on the bottles. Beer's two shillings a glass and Joe will change the barrels for you and keep the shelves filled. Any complaints – send the buggers over to me.'

'A favour, Lizzie; if anyone asks, I arrived here from the Cape, not the goldfields; you being the only person who knows any different.'

'The Cape?' Lizzie nodded her head to Kathleen's small deception. 'Not for me to ask why, one day you can tell me all about it. Now watch your front girl, grit your teeth and don't feel bad about taking money from men with money to burn.'

Like surf to some rocky shoreline, the first human wave broke four-deep against the bar. Within a space of ten minutes the air was filled with brandy fumes, tobacco smoke and hard language; already emptied, a dozen brandy bottles had been disposed of beneath the counter. Diggers jostled one another for Kathleen's attention; a smile, a single line of conversation was for most of them, enough. However, some men spoke with their eyes and lewd suggestive smiles, but Kathleen quickly brushed them off and without any outward display of malice learned to overlook them. Overall, though loud and boisterous, the majority were easily placated. Temporarily freed from a prison of high, dirt walls they had come to the Queens solely to forget; embittered creations of mistrust and self-imposed solitude, borne of that terrible life in the deep diggings. Hard-muscled and bad-tempered, starved of female company they clamoured to ease the shortfall, eagerly they drank down their beer for an excuse to summon Kathleen over for her to refill their glasses. Conversation centred around thoughts of going home, or that next big find. Diamonds, women, and the wherewithal to get back home – nothing else featured.

'You're new to these parts, seems to me you don't belong here, miss. Too pretty by a digger's mile to work behind a bar, at least not amongst the likes of this rabble.'

The miner raised his eyes and judged the contents of the top shelf, at the same time he pushed a brace of golden guineas across the counter. Hard labour had criss-crossed his fingertips with crack-lines; the knuckle bones were deformed and thickly gristled over, to him, the afflictions were nothing more than an act of God, by-products of his working a claim in the pit.

'House brandy, sweetheart; choose me down a bottle of clear spirit and a good cigar, what's left of the money is yours to keep.'

Kathleen reached down a bottle of Cape Smoke; she placed it on the counter and scooped up the coins. The digger cursed under his breath and pushed it back at her.

'I said clear spirit, girlie, not Smoke; keep that gut rot for the kaffir trade and your down and outs.'

Lizzie wheeled in next to Kathleen and in the blinking of an eye the Smoke was whisked away and substituted with a bottle more suited to Bradshaw's preference.

'She's new here, Thomas Bradshaw. Give the girl a chance.' She smiled encouragingly and draped a motherly arm about Kathleen's shoulder. 'Be wary of what the gentlemen ask for, darling. Give them Smoke if they want it, but for our more discerning gents like Thomas here, good quality grape brandy at twice the price and no arguing.'

The digger relaxed, his eyes went back to Kathleen.

'White Lightning, girl, *Witblits* the Boers call it; distilled from good grapes, pure as rainwater, comes with a mother of all headaches, helps a man forget but leaves him with his eyesight intact and a steady hand when he takes a piss.'

His smile softened and he winked an eye at Kathleen. 'No desire to piss on my boots or be blinded by the Smoke, sweetheart. Thomas Bradshaw may be old, but he still likes to piss straight and watch the sun come up.'

Lizzie rounded on him, chastising him playfully.

'Watch that tongue of yours, Thomas Bradshaw. Some men prefer their Cape Smoke, more of a kick, they tell me – more the strong man's drink.'

With a mischievous glint his eyes, Bradshaw fended off the reprimand.

'Then your strongman friends are more than welcome to it, Lizzie Jardine. Short of using it for cleaning my boots I never touch the stuff.'

Kathleen was intrigued.

'What's the difference? Why're you so full on against Cape Smoke?'

Bradshaw pulled the cork on the *Witblits*, sniffed the contents and poured a thick-blown shot glass full to the brim.

'Nothing short of the real McCoy, lassie; mother's milk.' He grinned at Kathleen and downed the spirit in a single gulp. 'Now a light for my cigar, if you would be so kind as to do the honours, girlie.'

Kathleen held the Vesta for him. He leaned across for the flame and before she could withdraw, the digger's hand closed vice-like about her wrist.

At first, Kathleen resisted, but the strength of his grip was totally overpowering, and though he intended her no harm, Thomas Bradshaw held her as if she were no bigger in build than a fledgling English sparrow. The force behind his arm frightened her – that of a man twice his size. Hands that without any effort and within the smallest of moments could beat her senseless.

'You ask what's wrong with Cape Smoke?' He trickled smoke from his nostrils. 'I'll tell you girl. Mixed from the devil's own venom and grape dregs, it is; leftover skins and stalks along with a goodly measure of black rum and black powder. Doubles the strength and may well blow a man's head clean off at the shoulders if he falls asleep too close-in to the fire.' He thrust the tip of his cigar inside the flame, his eyelids thin strips, but the glint was still there. 'Kill a man in less than a year, lassie; but it's cheap, see. Double the drink for less than half the price of the good stuff.'

Slowly, he released the pressure on Kathleen's wrist. His mouth twitched at the corners and those lion's eyes glowed in the candlelight – indomitably, they were still fixed to Kathleen's.

'Remember what I tell you, lassie and leave the cursed stuff well alone.' He let go of her arm. 'Now watch carefully and old Thomas Bradshaw will show you something that will more than bring the sparkle back to those pretty green eyes of yours.'

He clamped the cigar between his teeth to free up both his hands.

'This morning – round about an hour before midday,' he reached inside his jacket pocket, his focus still with Kathleen, 'next to each other – a nest of the beauties, swear on my own mother's sweet memory they were put there by an angel; special like, for Thomas Bradshaw to come upon before these other claim rats smelled an inkling.'

With beggared fingernails he loosened the drawstring from about the neck of a moleskin purse.

'Aside from yours truly, you're the first on God's earth to witness my good fortune. Cast those lovely, emerald eyes of yours over the makings of Thomas Bradshaw's passage back home to mother England; first class along with the toffs, no twenty quid bunk-up with the other unfortunates down in steerage for me, lassie.'

Kathleen made pretence of cleaning the counter top, but she was unable to tear her eyes from the open neck of that silken, moleskin purse.

The largest of the three was of a size comparable to that

of a pullet's egg, but what the others lacked in magnitude they made up for in shape and sheen. To Kathleen, the fire of a hundred stars appeared as if to be compressed and locked inside of them, and though none would tip the scales at less than three carats, with the back of his hand, Bradshaw brushed the smaller stones aside, disregarding their beauty in favour of their queen. With undisputed radiance, triumphantly she sat resplendent to a pool of oily light.

'Pick her up, lassie, feel what it's like to hold a purse of twenty thousand guineas in the palm of your hand.'

Kathleen grasped the stone between her thumb and forefinger. She held it to the light, slightly above the level of her eyes; some men shook their heads in wonder, whilst others cursed its finder's luck, for they themselves had dug within a single yard of it.

'Tell me what you feel, girl. What would any man give to possess such a stone?'

'Anything that was asked of him,' Kathleen replied and meant every word, though hardly loud enough for him to hear; unable to tear her eyes from the gem.

'Look around you,' he smiled at the mental furore the diamond had caused, 'they slaver like starving dogs at a butcher's window, but not one of them has the wherewithal to buy me out.'

He turned his back on Kathleen and raised himself up on the brass foot rail. The diggers sensed what was coming and jostled one another for better placing.

'Come now gentlemen,' he raised his arms and the crowd stilled, 'afford old Thomas Bradshaw a hearing – who amongst the lot of you will offer me a fair, but wholesome price for my queen of the Kimberley diggings?'

'What do you say it's worth, Bradshaw?'

Bradshaw sourced the perpetrator and looked down on him.

'More than your useless life, Rabinovich; been too long inside the pit to allow a crooked kopje-walloper such as yourself to cheat me out of this one.'

Rabinovich bridled at the name attributed to his trade by every diamond digger in Kimberley. Kopje-wallopers were tolerated on the grounds of them being permanently to hand on the diggings – self-styled diamond buyers. The majority, hardened opportunists and were for the most part, of little, financial clout. All that a man needed to enter the diamond trade was a small shack to stand as business premises, a set of scales, jeweller's glass and the will of a starving wolf to close a deal in favour of himself, the buyer. Experience, if he lived that long would come only through luck and dogged perseverance.

With the stone already weighed, Thomas Bradshaw, with his jeweller's glass had found it less than slightly sullied; apart from a single pale, featherlike inclusion, it lacked those feared, value slashing, dark imperfections that would in the blinking of a buyer's eye, cut the stone's value by half.

The colour would stand as fine white, and at its weight of over one hundred and four carats, the gem, if the buyer's mood was right and his purse full, could well fetch the goodly sum of twenty thousand pounds; a fortune, and a quarter as much again if he were to take the uncut jewel to the offices of the Caffyn Brothers in Cape Town.

'Just as I expected,' Bradshaw smirked at their lassitude, 'anything upwards of ten carats and immediately you all fall short.' His focus went back to Rabinovich. 'What about you, smouse? Though I will wager a gold guinea to your penny piece you do not, nor will you ever find enough to buy a stone like this.'

Rabinovich visibly shrank. Though he was disadvantaged by distance, from what he had already seen he knew that financially, the gem was far outside his reach. However, not wanting to be ridiculed in front of his regular clientele, he spoke out.

'Without weighing and my assessing the quality of your find it would be impossible for me to say...'

'Then I will say it for you,' Bradshaw reached behind and lifted the stone from between Kathleen's fingers, 'one single inclusion and the smallest one at that; next to bugger all, gentlemen.' He rotated the diamond in the candlelight. 'None better, Rabinovich; nothing between here and the Vaal diggings can match such a stone.'

Amused by the Jew's feeble excuses he drew out the moment and then, loud enough for every man in the room to hear, he gave the smouse his final chance to purchase the treasure.

'At one hundred and four carats twenty three points, Rabinovich; without a doubt, this is finest diamond you are ever likely to see; twenty thousand pounds cash or promissory note of credit from the Standard Bank of Kimberley.' He twirled the gem beneath the overhead chandelier so that like some distant star it pulsed with coloured lights. 'Come now Rabinovich, dig deep my little wizened friend, or has old Thomas Bradshaw for once in his life, found you lacking?'

Avidly, Lizzie Jardine watched the goings on, a wry smile on her face.

'He hasn't got it, Thomas; none of them have. Now get down off your high horse and let the people spend what money they have across my bar.'

Kathleen looked about the room and like her employer, realised the power wielded over them by Bradshaw's find. It was then she heard the voice of a man she knew, but a man she hardly recognised, three full years had passed since their last meeting.

'Twenty thousand pounds is a lot of money, Thomas Bradshaw. More than most would earn in a dozen lifetimes.' Slouched in a chair by the doorway, the latecomer swivelled face-on to the crowd. 'If what you are saying is true, we should discuss your price.'

Every last digger stayed silent, as penned lambs they shuffled uneasily, intimidated by their own impotence, for a lion had come amongst them. Bradshaw steeled himself and one at a time, returned the diamonds to his moleskin purse.

'My word on it, sir. The back room if your interest is full-blooded. I have with me a set of scales and a glass; I would be more than pleased for you to bear me out.'

Cecil Rhodes stood up from his chair; everyone in the room knew, or had at least heard of him. The financial reputation of this mussy-haired entrepreneur in breeches, crumpled jacket and riding boots had long since caught the attentions of Kimberley's elite. Others envied him, jealous of the young man's drive they tried their utmost to emulate his panache and quick eye for business, though for the greater part, unsuccessfully; ordinary men found the task of setting their mark by him, impossible.

'Bring me your stones, Bradshaw along with your bottle and your cigar. My time is precious; hopefully it will not be wasted.'

He nodded his head to Lizzie Jardine.

'Something to chase down the dust, my dear. Would I be right in saying the room we spoke of has been made available?'

'Open, cleaned and if you'll give me a moment I will organise some refreshments.'

Rhodes crossed to the bar and like the opening up of a biblical sea, the crowd parted for him, submissive greetings from men in awe of their icon rolled out behind him; dust in the wake of the pack leader.

'Here's your chance, young lady.' Lizzie cocked her head at Kathleen. 'I'll thank you to do the honours.'

'What do I take him?'

'Just tea and your sweetest smile my lovely; that's all the man needs. No booze for Kimberley's Cecil Rhodes, not until the sun is well beyond the yard arm.'

## 7

'Great Scott! Kathleen O'Rourke.' Rhodes came out of his chair with alacrity and took the tray from her. 'By God you've changed.' He abandoned the tray to the table, straightened up and embraced Kathleen within the circle of his arms. 'My brother sent word through from Pilgrim's Rest a while back; said you were on the way.' His smile faltered but the rippling, falsetto voice did not and the questions flurried. 'Often thought about you, but your father?' He shook his head. 'I can hardly imagine how you must feel. What can I say? Such a terrible experience – how are you coping?'

'Barely,' Kathleen admitted and as had happened on that fateful day of their first meeting, could not prevent herself from marvelling over the colour of Rhodes' eyes. 'I take each day as it comes – some are harder than others, but I will get through it.'

'Splendid mindset, never expected anything less.' He released his hold on her and pulled out a chair from between himself and Thomas Bradshaw. 'Sit down, my friend. As your estranged travelling companion I deserve at least five minutes of your time.' Though pleasant, his tone was insistent. 'Your intended interests here in Kimberley my dearest, dearest Kathleen. God it's so good to see you again. From the beginning, if you would be so kind. I want to know everything. Three years is an awfully long time. Your friends, the Sutherlands, Elizabeth and Charlotte, do you still communicate?'

Kathleen sat down. Rhodes' purposeful geniality had touched her deeply so that for the first time in many weeks she was able to relax her guard. Bradshaw looked on in silence, his suffering some delay to his business dealings with Rhodes was of little concern to him. He prepared himself for a long wait, poured himself a measure of White

Lightning, drew on his cigar and watched the goings on with amused interest. Rhodes leaned forwards and without diffidence studied the angelic face before him.

'Still pretty as a picture, but why might I ask, have you cut off your hair? Seeing you as a young man in women's clothes somewhat perturbs me.'

'Short hair suits my purpose,' Kathleen defended her decision, 'less troublesome; easier for me to hold off the locals if I kind of look like a man,' she smiled at Bradshaw, 'present company not included in that.'

Unable to resist, Rhodes reached out and with soft fingers caressed her cheek. The act was one of innocent adoration, that of a master sculptor obsessed with touching the silken face of some marble statuette. From that time of their first meeting aboard the *Eudora*, Rhodes had looked upon their crossing of ways as fateful, orchestrated by whatever spiritual forces watched for them to come ashore; him the ailing, seventeen year old, Kathleen the vibrant young settler woman from Dakota.

'The time has passed so quickly,' Rhodes mused, 'some of it good, some no doubt, we could both do without.' He shook off the nostalgia and with shared understanding, smiled softly at Kathleen. 'We must both refrain from looking back for the experience of what might have been; your plans, Kathleen, if you would be so kind as to tell me what they are.'

'My father's business interests in Pilgrim's Rest.' She came straight to the point. 'A letter of credit from the Standard Bank in Lydenburg was drawn up by the company as full and final settlement.'

'So they have bought out your father's share in a mining venture?'

Kathleen nodded her head. 'But I need your signature; only you can stand as guarantor of my having reached Kimberley and that the transfer of company money is legitimate.'

'Consider it done; this coming Monday at precisely two

o'clock. Meet me in the foyer of the Standard Bank and I shall cajole our respected, Mister Paterson into witnessing my standing as your guarantor.' His eyes sparkled; it was then that Kathleen realised the influence he wielded over all matters of local importance. She remembered that pale-skinned youth stepping ashore in Natal; how much he had changed. Three years in Africa had burned away the puppy fat and hardened off those once flaccid arms indicative of his genteel upbringing, those work-shy pampered features of a mother-nurtured son had disappeared. Since her first meeting with Cecil Rhodes on the deck of the *Eudora*, the boy had gone, Rhodes, the man had stepped into his shoes.

'Problem solved,' he assured her and reached for his tea, like that of an irresolute wind his mood swung north to south. 'We will talk again, my dearest Kathleen. Mister Bradshaw here has been more than patient, there are matters of some importance in need of my immediate attention.'

He stood up from the table and without further explanation, took a gentle but firm hold on Kathleen's elbow and steered her towards the door; time he was short of and because of that fact, his own patience was prone to sudden bouts of deferral. If he were given access to twice the hours, for him, that extra time could never stand as to be enough. Every hour of every day was to Cecil Rhodes a thousand times more precious than all the diamonds ever found in that deepening hole of the Kimberley diggings.

Kathleen closed the door behind her and drew across the heavy velvet curtain. She followed the short passageway back to the main hall and quickly her ears were filled with diggers' revelry. The crown-and-anchor tables were already crowded out, diggers cursed the dice for spiteful flurries of poor results; those lucky enough to win cheered their good fortune with loud voices, snatched up their winnings and without second thoughts, elbowed their way back through the crowd for a place at the bar.

In the privacy of the conference room, Cecil Rhodes disguised his interest and with stoic expression looked to the job at hand. Bradshaw placed the gem in front of him, in that meagre glow of thirty candles, short of natural light the diamond's carbon heart was barely beating. Rhodes picked up the jeweller's glass and expertly he appraised the stone for faults, clarity and purity of colour.

'There is no doubt, Thomas – you have found yourself a sizeable fortune. However, were it not for one almost invisible transverse inclusion the gem would have, by its own right stood as an example of near perfection.' He lowered the jeweller's loupe and fixed the man sitting across from him with a hawkish stare. 'A pity, my friend. Nothing, nor any man alive is ever found to be totally devoid of shortcomings. No matter how hard we seek out that unattainable phenomena, perfection will always remain an arm's length beyond our reach.'

His focus went back to the stone.

'You quoted a weight of one hundred and four carats?'

'There's the scale,' Bradshaw pointed out the apparatus, 'see for yourself.'

'No need, Thomas. No need. You know me too well; play me for a fool at your own peril, my friend. Some men have tried – all of them failed.'

Rhodes held the diamond at different angles to the candlelight; he surmised his own delights, mentally witnessing at least three separate stones cut to suit the whims and wants of London's wealthier socialites. How gaily they would sparkle, how, once subjected to the magic of the polisher's wheel and the right light, would those glittering stones double, perhaps even treble the investment of his buying price.

'The colour I would fix as Top Cape; to be more precise, a subtle shade of pale yellow. Less valuable than some, though nevertheless a worthy find.'

'I agree to that,' Bradshaw nodded compliantly, 'and the inclusion you mentioned, though inoffensive, is again, true enough.'

Rhodes went on; Bradshaw's resolve was steadfastly and very cleverly being worn down. Every man had an in-road, a weakness waiting to be found out, and when the time was right, more often than not, that weakness might be exploited by the stronger of the two adversaries.

'After the initial cutting, one would be left with three, four or perhaps five manageable pieces with which to work. The possibility of a single, facetted stone would therefore be out of the question the inclusion would not allow it. No cutter of sound reputation would promise the vendor anything other than several smaller pieces.'

Rhodes replaced the diamond on the table, mimicking the benign act of the mildly interested buyer. Bradshaw twisted in his seat. Unwittingly he was losing his grip on the transaction; that first, insidious whiff of doubt, had within those last few seconds joined him at the table.

'How much?'

'Your aforementioned sum was that of twenty thousand pounds, Thomas,' Rhodes shook his head, 'that amount I could never hope to match, there would be little or nothing left in it for me. Had there been no fault within the stone,' he shrugged his shoulders, 'I would, without any further discussion have by fair means or foul got together your asking price.'

Bradshaw leaned across the table, his expression wolfish, though the flicker of uncertainty was undoubtedly there, embedded in his eyes.

'Eighteen thousand – not a penny less.'

Without the slightest reaction, Rhodes ignored the adjusted price.

'I have seen your claim, Thomas. Three months, six at the outside and your kaffirs will be bending their steel against solid ground. Blue ground, Thomas, that's what they are calling it and harder than a whore's heart. The easily accessible softer oxides are coming to an end, some of our more adventurous diggers have already bottomed out. Whether or not there is anything at all beyond where the diamond-bearing gravel meets the underlying hard rock formation has already raised goodly amounts of wild speculation.'

Rhodes added hot water to the teapot and without averting his eyes from Bradshaw's, mashed the contents enough for him to secure a second cup.

'I have seen it with my own eyes, my friend. Without powder and drill, a man will do little more than scratch its surface. To most, the cost of such an endeavour would consume more than a month's total worth in diamonds. Men would starve themselves to the brink, surrounded ironically, by the greatest fortune the world has ever seen.'

He added milk and sugar, stirred the mix with a silver spoon and with the cup poised just inches from his lips, cocked an almost fatherly eye at Bradshaw.

'Imagine, Thomas, what it will be like in the pit with upwards of a thousand desperate men fighting for space to mine whilst blowing each other to hell.'

He allowed the reality of what he said sink in. When Bradshaw lowered his eyes, Cecil Rhodes, like an adder pre-empting the final intent of its prey, manoeuvred his thoughts into place, mentally homing in for the kill.

# -8-

'So, in the end, how much did you come away with?' Kathleen stared at Bradshaw for an answer. 'The full twenty thousand – or as I foretold, Kimberley's up and coming colossus beat you down to half of that amount?'

Bradshaw looked up from his glass. The brandy bottle was less than a quarter filled from the bottom.

'Watch that tongue of yours, girlie; why should you give a shit?' A finger of ash broke from the end of his cigar and pooled against the counter top. His words slurred, hemmed in by clenched teeth, but his eyes were bright, alert and all-seeing; the eyes of a dangerous, rested man.

'Suit yourself,' Kathleen cut back at him, 'sorry I showed concern.' She went to turn away, but Bradshaw called her back.

'Bought me out he did.' He filled his glass to the brim and pushed aside the empty bottle. 'Lock, stock and barrel, lassie. Even my kaffir labourers; promised to double their pay if they stayed on for him once I've gone.' He drew in smoke from what seemed to Kathleen to be little more than a tiny ember at the corner of his mouth, then spat the cigar stub into the palm his hand before grinding it out with his bare fingers. 'Bastard made me feel like he was doing me a favour; either way, can't say I'm sorry. What's done is done and old Thomas Bradshaw here will soon be rid of this God forsaken pox hole – forever.'

He pointed at the top shelf. 'Reach me down another cigar and a bottle of *Witblits*, sweetheart and I'll tell you a story or two about our Cecil bloody Rhodes back there.' He winked an eye at Kathleen. 'Not many people knows what old Thomas Bradshaw knows, make your toes curl. The very first day he stepped foot on the diggings, I was there; three years ago if memory serves.' His eyes clouded. 'Three years ago, my little red-haired darlin'; feels like nothing less than a day and a lifetime.'

Kathleen took down the full bottle and counted out the cost from a pile of coins in Bradshaw's hand; the cigar she pushed between his lips and struck a Vesta for him. She fixed the face in front of hers with her own hard stare.

'I need you to take me down inside the pit. I want to see what it's like; where the diamonds come from.' Her eyes were dead level with Bradshaw's. 'Will you do this for me? Show me what goes on down there, I need to know.'

'Why would any woman want to go down in that hellhole?' He frowned at her through a mist of cigar smoke. 'You have no need for it.' He shook his head. 'I'll not be party to you getting hurt, lassie. Stay away from the pit. The answer is no.'

'Then I will find me someone who will – or I will go alone.'

Bradshaw's cigar pointed directly at Kathleen's face, the barrel of a loaded gun.

'You have no rights to the diggings. Get caught on another man's claim and all hell will break loose; especially when they find out the trespasser is a woman.' His eyes narrowed, warning her to give up on the foolhardiness of the idea. 'You will never get out of there, lassie; at least, not in the same fettle as when you went in.'

'I'll take my chances,' she countered and as an act of bold defiance folded her arms across her chest. 'Mining is how my family's always made a living; nothing new to me about holes in the ground, mister. The men, if they are as bad as you say, I will handle in my own way.' She scowled through the smoke and relentlessly those green, almond eyes glowered back at him. 'If you had known my father, reckon you would think better of me.'

Bradshaw picked up the unopened bottle of Cape brandy, this shorn-headed young woman from Pilgrim's Rest had rocked him back on his heels. He gathered his wits, straightened up from the bar and then balanced his weight evenly for the walk to the hotel's open doors; a woman, half his weight and reaching up no further than his own chest had worked her way beneath his skin.

'Six o'clock tomorrow morning,' he told her, 'outside in the street, that is if your mind is still made up.' A wry smile broke over his face and he acknowledged defeat with a slight nod of his head. 'Cover your face as best you can, can't risk you being recognised. Strong boots and get yourself a hat and jacket; a jacket heavy enough to keep out the cold and thick enough to hide those perky little titties of yours.'

## 9

July's final dawn came in cold and clear over Kimberley. Just as the horizon coloured so did the temperature plummet enough to turn the breath in front of Kathleen's face brittle-grey with frost steam. She drew down the brim of her hat, a habit she had brought with her from the goldfields and with her collar fully raised about her ears, she shrugged down deep inside the warmth of her drover's jacket.

Kathleen looked out over the diggings; positioned further back from the mined out ground the sifting cradles were still and empty, the area about the sorting tables, most of it deserted. A thousand windlasses stood idle and about the entire rim of the pit, emptied of gravel, leather kibbles rocked impotently on their guides, for today was Sunday, and by rule of local law on that seventh day, no man could demand the right to mine his claim.

Bradshaw stood alongside her, aware of the spell this vast wound in the earth's crust had already woven over the landscape, and like the strands of some giant web, ropes of twisted hide, or for the more progressive, those of spun steel descended into the very darkest corners of the abyss. He struck a Vesta against the iron tub of an abandoned cocopan and his hand shook when he lit that first cigar of the day.

'Easy on the loud noises, lassie, you are dealing with a sick man this morning.'

Kathleen grinned at Bradshaw's new timidity.

'After a full bottle of White Lightning, old man, more's the wonder you're still alive.' She looked down upon the waking vista before her, the only living things inside the pit were flocks of red-winged starlings; wheeling through the quiet, the tips of their primary flight feathers appeared as blood-orange when caught in those earliest rays of sunlight. Their peculiar whistle-like calls echoed back from the void.

'You still want to do this?' Bradshaw pleaded with his eyes for Kathleen to change her mind, 'nothing down there, save for dust, worn out shovels and old piss.'

'And diamonds,' Kathleen reminded, 'I need to see for myself where they come from.'

Bradshaw gave up on the argument; irritated by his own display of conformity he tugged down the brim of his hat and at a slow pace, started forwards.

'You do what I tell you, girlie, one mistake on the ladder and I'll be forced to leave what's left of you for the crows to pick over.'

To Kathleen O'Rourke, the pit edge was more terrifying than any other place she had ever come upon. Moving in close to where Bradshaw had rigged his hoisting tackle and tipping chute, she stood just short of the edge and it was with much trepidation that she forced herself to take a firm hold on the topmost part of a wooden access ladder, and then dared to look down.

The entire pit was a ragged chequer board of mining claims, each claim jealously measured off by its owner to fit the legal size of thirty one by thirty one feet square. Few were of the same depth as those adjoining, some were already more than a hundred feet into that yellow, diamond-bearing layer of guarded earth.

'Claim number, 339.' Bradshaw explained the layout. 'Got her for a song before word got back to Cape Town and every jack-the-lad fit enough to walk or ride a horse came down on the New Rush like locusts on a pumpkin field.' He raised his arm and singled out the northernmost edge of the diggings. 'Claims along the central, north south lines are the richest,' his eyes sparkled and he grinned at Kathleen, his aching head already part forgotten. 'My own, number 339 is slap bang in the middle, right there on the southern edge. Easier to work, straight down to the digging shelf; your Mister Rhodes has bought himself a winner, that is, until he comes up against the hard stuff.'

'Hard stuff?' Kathleen looked to him for an explanation.

Bradshaw shook his head and smiled without turning his eyes from the pit.

'Blue ground, sweetheart – hard as hell's iron, or so I've been told. Some diggers reckon on having seen it; patches of blue limestone in the lowest parts of the sidewall.' Once again he shook his head at the rumour. 'Who can tell; ten to one it's still a mile down, or more's the chance of it not being there at all.'

The sun climbed higher; sunlight washed the western wall and after each new minute it angled deeper. Instinctively, Bradshaw ran his eyes over the sidewall and with silent invocation thanked his personal gods for his recent flood of good fortune. Gratefully, he took comfort from seeing those streaks of yellow ground; the colour of far hills washed in winter sunlight. The blue ground Rhodes had warned him of was there also, and though still hidden, he could sense it, close enough to the surface for his skin to crawl with trepidation.

'Or maybe she's closer than we think. A day, a month, a year even; apart from the devil himself, who can tell?' He hawked phlegm from his throat and spat it over the edge. 'First hint of the diggings bottoming out and every man in the pit will sell up and run for the home like ferreted rabbits.'

Bradshaw took lead place at the ladder head, out of habit, fearlessly he swung his weight over the edge and onto the first rung.

'Follow me down,' he told Kathleen, 'stay close, one step at a time and keep your eyes on the sidewall; don't look down, lassie. Whatever else you do, never look down.'

As soon as Bradshaw's hat disappeared below the edge, Kathleen took a hold on the ladder. With her foot dangling mid-air she reached out with it for that first rung and though the ladder was well secured, like a waking snake still it convulsed, tormented by the extra weight.

Kathleen felt every tremor, every slightest fractional give in the wooden structure and she feared each one of them. Bradshaw slowed his own descent and with a steady voice encouraged her down inside the pit.

'Almost half way there, lassie; nice and easy, now, take your time.'

The terror evoked by her first stepping onto the ladder began to ease, unexpectedly her breathing quietened, as though after each new rung her fear was being left further and further behind. She allowed herself a sideways glance and found she was no longer intimidated by the openness of the sheer pit face. Below her, Bradshaw's head was less than a yard clear of her boots.

'Shake the lead out, old man or we'll be climbing in the dark.'

'Or lying dead on the pit bottom with a broken neck, girlie; watch that impatience of yours and careful when you step off the ladder, ten yards square is all the ground you have before another thirty feet to the bottom. Stay in close to the sidewall and no noise; the Diggers' Committee would not take kindly to us being down here without their saying so.'

Bradshaw picked up the pace and within the confines of that minute, both climbers stood together on the digging platform.

Kathleen looked around her; columns of yellow ground rose up vertically from the pit bottom. As if by some subterranean force each one of them, though at a different rate appeared to be pushing skywards. The blue sky above her head was a precious, coveted window. It was a sight most men took for granted, but to those who were forced to work below, it was a lake of precious air. However, come tomorrow's afternoon, that same joyful firmament would be choked with yellow dust; the sun blanked out by towering, ochre-coloured thunderheads.

Her senses settled and adjusted to her surroundings, it was then she became aware of the pungent scent of human excrement, and as the temperature increased, so did the strength of those smells rise with it.

Bradshaw saw her grimace. 'Warned you – not a pleasant place to spend your Sunday mornings, not when two thousand men have been confined to this hellhole for nigh on three years now.' He chuckled at the look on Kathleen's face. 'No place to be when the sun sits full-on overhead. Biggest shithole in the world, if you'll pardon my swearing.'

Kathleen shook off the discomfort and knelt on one knee; she scooped up a handful of gravel and studied its composition. Oxidised over the millennia, the decomposed matrix was a rich tawny yellow in colour and, locked inside the softer oxide were splinters of pyrope garnet and olivine, both were natural indicators as to the close proximity of precious stones. She selected one of the more colourful pieces and rubbed it free of yellow dust. Though it was tiny, by its own right, like some shard of stained glass, the garnet glowed blood red between her fingertips.

'Worthless,' Bradshaw mused and smiled at the disappointment in Kathleen's eyes, 'garnets, lassie; find them by the buckets-full alongside the sorting tables.'

Kathleen stood up, dusted her hands against her breeches and for a second time the enormity of the diggings came over her; the vastness of that man-made pit and the absolute smallness of her standing there inside of it.

'The beginning – what was it like. How would any man know there were diamonds so deep down inside the earth?'

Bradshaw spat away the stub of his cigar.

'No one did, came upon this place by chance, lassie,' he leaned against the sidewall, 'owes its very existence to one man.'

His eyes clouded and he reached out a second cigar from his shirt pocket. How many times had he heard the story

263

told, and more to the point, how many times had he told the story to others.

'That July month of seventy-one; all hell broke loose when a man rode into the river diggings and like the idiot that he was, screamed out *New Rush*.'

'Fleetwood Rawstorne.' Kathleen recalled the name. Many times she had heard the story bandied about the Queens bar.

'The very one, lassie. Down and out digger, bedded down at Gilfillan's camp; pitched his tent below an old Camel Thorn. Story goes that his cook boy found three diamonds in the sand and handed them over.' He looked upwards, into that blue expanse hovering over the pit. 'All gone, best part is, Rawstorne came away with damn near nothing to show for his efforts, pegged his claim that same night; like a fool he squared off his ground in the moonlight.'

'But in the wrong place,' Kathleen mused.

'Within ten yards of the main pipe, men alongside him pulled out a fortune. Compared to them, old Rawstorne found sweet bugger all. For the some of us, filling our boots with diamonds was never meant to be.'

Kathleen pocketed the garnet; it was her first find in the Kimberley diggings and though in essence it was worth nothing, to her, it was the beginning of her empire.

'Now, I understand,' she told him, and quietly, without reserve she accepted the reasoning behind men's obsession with their mining the pit; from that first boiling up of diamond-bearing magma to that present time of her standing on the ledge, there, beneath her feet, for more than a million years had lain the makings of untold wealth. For as long as men knew it was there, they would without second thoughts suffer any hardship, trade a portion of their lifetime as fair exchange for the chance to possess a single glittering stone.

She looked to Bradshaw and nodded her head.

'We can go now. I have seen enough.'

264

## 10

Outwardly, the Standard Bank of Kimberley would appear to the casual onlooker as a single-storeyed, wooden fronted building of meagre consequence, however once inside, Kathleen was put at ease by an atmosphere of pleasantry and financial order. Arched windows let in the sunlight, but the lower part of each glass panel had been partially blanked out with a coating of paint, thereby deterring any unwanted, prying eyes from meddling inside. Burgundy coloured carpet whispered against the soles of Kathleen's boots.

'Bang on time, young lady!' Rhodes waved her from the foyer, 'come on through, everything has been made ready for you.'

Kathleen followed him into the manager's office and accepted a seat nearest to the window. The walls were wood-panelled and with exactitude, hung at regular measured intervals, were various artists' impressions of Kimberley's earliest development; strikingly outstanding, expertly sketched in black ink and pencil, glassed and then framed with ornately gilded plaster. Kathleen admired them openly, one sketch in particular caught her attention.

'You like that one?' Rhodes had been quick to pick up on her interest, he commented on the artist's prowess. 'Powerfully portrayed, if a little contrite and simplistic. Would have suited a lighter frame, but of course, being a man of limited artistic flair my opinion must stand for little.'

He stepped up to the wall and with his hands clasped behind his back, allowed his eyes to rummage A.B. Ellis' almost childlike impression of the diamond diggings. The ticking of the office clock added a sense of poignancy to his scrutiny.

'Desperate times, Kathleen. Insects tearing up the

ground. Hope and fear; both are indomitably linked. Just one more day in the pit, that is all it will take and all their wildest dreams may well be realised.' He turned on his heels and faced her. 'Or so they all believed. Those are the grandiose expectations of each and every one of them, myself included.' His eyes glowed, blue as the open sky beyond the window. 'However, only a handful of men will find their eldorado. As for the rest,' he shrugged his shoulders, 'thousands will abandon their dreams to the darkness of the deep diggings and then disappear – beggared and stony broke, back along that rutted road that first brought them to their nemesis.'

Rhodes came back to his place at the desk and nodded his head to the manager.

'Enough of my sentimentality, Mister Paterson, time is short and we are both of us busy men. Let us get on with it.'

He gestured to Kathleen, his mannerism now brusque and businesslike.

'The letter of credit from my associates in Pilgrim's Rest, do you have it?'

Kathleen reached it out from her shirt pocket and handed it to Rhodes. He scanned the contents and took less than a minute to realise its authenticity.

'My brother, Bertie? When you last saw him, how was he?'

'Appeared to be in good health,' said Kathleen, 'with regards to his standing with the company, I cannot say. I had very little involvement with his dealings.'

'Still drinking?'

Kathleen nodded her head.

'As if there were no tomorrow, but that is not for me to pass judgement on. We all have our failings.'

Rhodes signed the credit note with a flurry, as if the amount stated were a mere handful of petty cash. In the eyes of most men, the amount would hold its own against a matching up to three year's earnings.

'You will bank your thousand pounds here with our Mister Paterson, of course?'

Again, Kathleen nodded her head to Rhodes' terms; she had no choice, Paterson's was the only reputable bank in Kimberley. To Rhodes, the bank was a window, an access point to financial transactions around the diggings, large or otherwise. The movement of capital was a reliable measure of Kimberley's business fluctuations, to which, through their subtle manipulation, Paterson had become his personal barometer.

'Why did you opt for Kimberley?' Rhodes pushed the letter of credit across to the manager, but without shifting his interest from Kathleen. 'Why not Natal? You could have made your way back to Pietermaritzburg; the Sutherlands would have welcomed your return with open arms, I'm sure of it.'

'No particular reason,' Kathleen lied, 'barring that Kimberley's a mining town and mining folk are all that I know.' She smiled affably. 'Guess this is where I fit in best.'

Rhodes nodded his head. Up to that moment he had fallen short of fathoming Kathleen's intentions, the failing irritated him intensely.

'There are plenty of opportunities here for those of sound judgement, Kathleen. General merchandising, a small hotel or eatery, whatever might take your fancy? However, take my advice as soundly meant and gladly given when I recommend your staying well clear of any involvement with the diggings. The odd stone as a fancy bauble or investment, yes, I will grant you that, but not as some permanent means of putting bread on the table.' He shook his head at the implications. 'Bringing out diamonds from that cursed hole in the ground is looked upon by most as a pastime reserved solely for the insane; a thousand times more difficult than sluicing free gold from any stream bed – aggravated no less by the physical exacerbations of your being a woman.'

He smiled at her, but the act was placatory and a noticeable flicker of resentment leapt the gap between them. The remark had struck a nerve and Rhodes was quick to consolidate, skilfully he held the moment together.

'I sincerely hope we are in agreement, Kathleen – your mining days are over, in Kimberley at least, or have I missed something?'

Kathleen twisted in her seat. Friendship had been pushed aside, this was the hardened, fully fledged Cecil Rhodes with whom she was dealing; he was tearing holes in her armour, as easily as the wind would tear that cursed yellow dust from out of the diggings. Her will to compete with him on an even footing was being cleverly whittled away; already he had taken control of her monies, whatever else she stood for was inexorably being stripped from the bone. Cecil Rhodes had expertly anticipated her every intention and still, those piercing eyes held her spellbound. A further tell-tale flicker of Kathleen's aggravation confirmed his suspicions and like the kestrel for the tiny bird he fell upon the moment.

'Well I'll be damned,' his eyes lit up, 'Bradshaw – the man at the Queens,' Rhodes rocked back in his chair, hands clasped behind his head, 'the look in your eyes when you held the diamond – I should have seen it coming.'

For a long moment, Rhodes stared at her and though the look was empty of malice, still, Kathleen felt her innermost secrets flounder under his plundering.

Invigorated by his findings, Rhodes leaned across his waxed redoubt and pressed her for more information. With his fingers hooked talon-like to the table edge, triumphantly he towered in front of her.

'What has he told you? Tell me that I am wrong, Kathleen. Or has our Mister Bradshaw seeded errant thoughts inside that head of yours?'

He slumped back in his chair; the excitement of his discovery had left him short of breath.

'Mining diamonds is a thrilling if dangerous game, Kathleen, I will grant you that, unfortunately for the pair of us the need for adventure has hooked its claws in all too deeply. I see about you a resurgence of your father's adventurous spirit; mining the ground for whatever treasure, be it gold or diamonds, the substance is of little consequence. Our satisfaction is achieved, not through the possessing of some precious commodity, but rather the act of hunting it down.' He paused momentarily, allowing the credence of what he was saying to strike home. 'The search for that which is lost, my friend, the will to cross the finishing line ahead of the pack; whatever the race, whatever the prize, to win is the reason for our being here; it is an addiction, the very opiate on which we thrive.'

Kathleen held steady, from their dealings of that past half hour she had been forced to sharpen her business acumen, rather than indulge herself with moody innuendo. She gathered her thoughts and spoke with authority; the insidious beat of the office clock gave weight to her determination.

'Why is it, that my being a woman bars me from taking an interest in the diggings?'

Rhodes' expression hardened; as he had already realised, Kathleen had changed. Those last three years had produced in her the makings of a powerful adversary. Openly, he bridled at the thought of desperate women flooding into Kimberley to toil alongside ruthless diggers at the pit bottom. Allowing it to happen would, to some of those thousand hard-bitten men stand as easy pickings upon which to sate their most perverse fantasies.

'At your peril, Kathleen. Whatever your reasoning, as a woman you would last little more than a month. Alone, you would be at the mercy of a thousand dehumanised ruffians and illegal diamond dealers.' He paused again, to let the warning sink in. 'Away from the pit, as a buyer, you would at best be safe, at least physically. However, financially you would be at the mercy of every predatory kopje-walloper within a hundred miles of Kimberley; a desperate breed of self-taught scoundrels, some who would not hesitate for a single minute before clearing your pockets of anything worthwhile.'

He leaned forward on his elbows, his eyes glowed, his stare leonine.

'You would do well to remember my influence down in the pit, Kathleen. Change is coming. To most men the cost of maintaining a claim is becoming more of a burden than a would-be bonanza. Men are digging deeper by the hour; access roads spanning the diggings are in many cases, verging on their own destruction.' Rhodes continued to add prominence to the uncertainty of her folly. 'Every week, diggers' stagings are collapsing; those who work below are sometimes buried alive, without warning and in the mere blinking of an eye.'

He rubbed the palms of both hands across one another, simulating the sudden, silent sheering away of loosened earth.

'Widow Maker, the name given to each treacherous fall of ground. No sound, no warning; a hundred tons of broken staging. Within seconds, men, mules and weeks of precious time are dashed against the pit bottom.' Kathleen's expression remained unchanged.

'I am no weakling, Rhodes, I feel you have pre-judged me; for the most part, unfairly.'

'But judged you well, Kathleen O'Rourke. We are not too unlike, you and I. Your father's interests, his needs, the need to seek out treasure is now with you, a legacy of dangerous, backbreaking toil has followed you here from Pilgrim's Rest. Watch it carefully, my friend or I will be laying flowers upon your grave in Kimberley cemetery.'

'Cemeteries are for the aged and the foolhardy,' Kathleen countered and then changed the leaning of their conversation. 'Thomas Bradshaw sold you his claim; number 339, south side of the pit.'

Rhodes was taken aback by her reference to his latest

acquisition.

'What of it? Bradshaw was paid well for his trouble; he can find no reason for complaint.' He frowned at her and then, glancing sideways, shook his head at Paterson. 'The man is a drunk and a blabbermouth, what else did he tell you?'

'Nothing untoward, you have my word on it.'

'So, tell me, Kathleen, why this sudden interest in Thomas Bradshaw?'

For a fleeting moment, Kathleen was tempted to back off, unsure of her getting the result she was after, then she redoubled her efforts and steeled herself for the full journey.

'I was with him yesterday – at the diggings.'

The room fell silent; like a gathering of thunderheads, Rhodes' face darkened.

'He should have known better.'

'He did nothing wrong – an hour at the outside was all that I asked of him.'

'The Digger's Committee... had we found him there, without any hesitation, Bradshaw would have been drummed out of town and yourself along with him. It is forbidden for any man or woman to access their claim on a Sunday. I would have withheld payment from him until the matter was settled.'

Kathleen bit her tongue, antagonising Cecil Rhodes would offer little in the way of support for her grandiose expectations. What she was about to ask of him would draw them both towards the furthest, tenuous limits of their friendship.

'Then I am to blame, not Thomas Bradshaw,' she insisted, 'I asked for him to take me down inside the pit.'

Rhodes' eyebrows jumped skywards. Again, his face darkened, deep red, deeper still about the jowls, almost the colour of the office carpet beneath his feet.

'And he acquiesced?'

Kathleen nodded her head. 'I needed to see the diggings

271

first hand, not just from the pit edge, there would be little gained without my climbing down to the stagings.'

Again, Rhodes clasped his hands behind his head and rocked back in his chair. The frown had disappeared, replaced by a firm smile, partly in awe and not without a deepening sense of respect. Kathleen had accomplished what many men could never aspire to. Through common fear, most would turn their backs on a chance to work a claim inside the pit. The sheer drop and rickety ladder-ways would prove too much for them. His eyes took back their sparkle; inspired by Kathleen's courage, he felt a resurgence of his own, first experience on the ladder. He was there again, eighteen years old, frightened, but excited by the prospects of what he might find; balanced above that void, his feelings were those of boundless excitement and simultaneously, those of abject terror. Beyond all his wildest expectations he had had found himself ensnared, mesmerised in fact by that terrible gaping hole in the earth.

'You climbed inside the pit?'

Without rancour she matched his smile.

'The ladder was well secured, if a little bit shaky at the point of halfway down.'

'A little bit shaky be damned. As in one wrong move and you would fall to your doom, more like.' He swivelled in his seat. 'What do you say, Paterson? Would you take your chances on those ladders?'

Paterson shook his head at Kathleen and reflexively, re-seated his spectacles.

'People who would climb the pit ladders of their own free will deserve the security of an asylum.'

Kathleen smiled at the remark before turning her full attention back to Cecil Rhodes.

'Your advice and your help, I need them both, but I must speak with you in private.'

'You have me at a disadvantage, madam. You know more about my latest acquisition than me.' He nodded his head to the manager. 'Give us few minutes alone,

Paterson.'

They remained silent and waited for Paterson to close the door behind him.

'What do you want from me, Kathleen?'

'First, you will give me your word that you will not dismiss what I ask of you as presumptuous or in any way out of hand.'

'Very well, as a friend I will hear you out, though I can promise you nothing.'

'And I ask for nothing that will not benefit the both of us.'

Rhodes folded his arms across his chest, his expression warm but non-committal.

'Go on, Kathleen, get on with it; drop your keg of powder right in my lap.'

The venture she had planned was less than a week old and had on more than one occasion denied her a full night's sleep. Even now, still in their infancy, her ideas were merely tiny sparks flying willy-nilly above some open camp fire. However, without Rhodes' concurrence, all her plans would fall apart and turn to nothing, those tiny sparks would die on the breeze – wild and fanciful, all would be blown away, gone forever.

'The claim you bought from Bradshaw.'

'What, exactly are you suggesting?'

Kathleen held up her hand, stifling his impatience.

'Bear with me. Hear me out; whatever you decide, I will stand by that ruling.'

She took a deep breath and then added to what she had started.

'Three years ago, at the Sutherland's house, shortly before my father and I left for Pilgrim's Rest, Charlotte's younger sister, Elizabeth?'

'I remember her well,' Rhodes smiled fondly at the recollection, 'bouncy girl with a face full of freckles.'

'Outside the house, you sat with her on the veranda steps?'

273

'Watching a column of ants dismember a moth, I think it was.'

Kathleen nodded her head, the images were still vivid. A garden filled with colour, little Elizabeth, saddened by the immensity of so many people leaving. Kathleen and Charlotte had unintentionally been party to the conversation, hidden from plain view by a wall of flowering cannas.

*No matter how small or frail we might appear to others, it is our strength of will that matters.* She quoted Rhodes' words verbatim.

'What you said to Elizabeth has since that moment stood as my personal yard stick; I will never forget it.'

'Spur of the moment invention,' Rhodes confessed, 'A natural flair for twisting matters to suit my own ends; nevertheless, one that is worthy of remembrance. One could do worse.'

Rhodes shook himself free of those balmy, sunlit days he spent with the Sutherlands.

'Where is all of this leading, Kathleen?'

'Bradshaw's claim.'

'You have already brought it to my attention, what of it?'

'Half my money – a full five hundred pounds for a quarter share in claim number 339 and I include my labour and that of my servant; no recompense, the both of us for nothing.'

The colour drained from Rhodes' cheeks. He was tempted to dismiss the rhetoric as it being that of the delusional lunatic. However, he calmed himself and endeavoured to see beyond his cynicism.

'After what I have told you, Kathleen, still, you would put yourself at the mercy of the pit?'

'The pit holds no fear for me, Rhodes. Like my father, I have little interest in anything else; working the ground for gold or diamonds is what I do best, it is where I belong.'

'Your father, Kathleen, God rest his soul, if he were here with us in this very room, how would he react to this conversation? What would he say if I were to grant his daughter free access to the most dangerous cesspit on the entire continent of Africa?'

He stood up from the table and crossed to the window; with his hands braced to the windowsill he raised up on the balls of his feet for him to see beyond the painted, lower part of the glass. Rhodes let his eyes drift slowly over the panorama, never once had he tired of scrutinising that scarred and barren landscape, for it was amongst this desolation that he was able to find the insight he needed; his measure of what was happening out there on the diggings. Only the shape of it had changed, and where mankind had ripped great holes in the earth, this change was irreversible. The original, Colesberg Kopje had gone; now, like some discarded Emmental cheese, the red earth was riddled through with prospect holes and open pits. Heaped about the sorting tables were mounting piles of treated gravel, ready for contract transport men to take away with their donkey carts to dump wherever they saw fit. Only the very edge of the main pit was visible to him and like so many ants about an open bowl of sugar, frantic workers scurried between the gravel hillocks, manned their tipping platforms in readiness for those next, fully-laden tubs of ore to come up from below. The gem-bearing gravel would be tipped onto the ore chutes, and then the emptied tubs sent spinning back along their endless wires for refilling at the pit bottom. Beyond the diggings, a wilderness of ragged tents crowded almost far enough as to reach the town's limits; were there three, four or even five thousand human souls living out there? He did not know, the figures had long since eluded him.

'I was eighteen years just turned when I landed here. New Rush, they had named it. One beggared prospector and his native cook-boy can be thanked for all of this.'

He turned on his heels and smiled at Kathleen, his eyes heavy, ringed with fatigue and his battle with a slowly failing heart.

'How does The Almighty make His choice as to by whom, and as of which particular moment the world's greatest treasure house is to be uncovered?'

'By chance,' said Kathleen, 'nothing more – and a chance, Rhodes, is all I will ask of you.'

Cecil Rhodes reached out his hand to the auburn-haired woman in front of him, his expression was one of bemusement, that of a man who had at that very moment wagered his life's savings against the uncertainty of his latest venture. However, what he had seen in Kathleen's eyes was enough; that same determined look was there, reminiscent of the man he himself had become.

'You have your wish, Kathleen O'Rourke. By whatever devilish means, you have achieved what most would only dare to dream of. Now leave me in peace before you beggar me completely, go back to the Queens and ready yourself for a place in hell. I'll have our Mister Paterson draw up the necessary paperwork.'

He led Kathleen towards the door, his hand on her shoulder.

'Be mindful of our arrangement; your five hundred pounds will secure for you a one quarter share in what we shall, from this moment onwards and for the sake of our mutual convenience, refer to as Bradshaw's Diggings.' He turned the handle and held the door for her. 'Should you be tempted to sell, option to purchase will in the first instance rest with yours truly. Only for as long as you yourself work the staging will I allow a woman personal ingress to the Kimberley diggings. Though as yet, I still have to convince the committee as a whole that my intentions are sound.'

He leaned over and with gentle lips placed a kiss on Kathleen's cheek.

'In the event of your demise, through accidental fall of ground or otherwise, your share of the claim will be absorbed by my estate, though heaven forbid, I pray that will never happen.'

Outside the bank the heat was oppressive, the sun had reached its high spot in the sky and to avoid the discomfort, Rhodes stepped back inside the entrance to the foyer and mopped his forehead with a plain, linen handkerchief.

'I will be in touch, my friend. Warn that Zulu of yours to exchange his spear for the pick and shovel and stand at the ready – as soon as we are up and running, Bradshaw's Diggings will be expected to turn a handsome profit; diamonds by the bucketful,' his eyes glittered, 'like peeled grapes on our sorting table.'

# -11-

From Paterson's office window, Rhodes followed Kathleen's progress along the street, watching the bob and tilt of her hat until it fell from view behind a lumbering ox-cart.

'So, what do you think, Paterson? Bad move on my part, or have I found myself an affable business partner?'

'Not for me to pass comment, Rhodes, though I am inclined to say, personal friendship and business make for poor bedfellows. No doubt all will be revealed once the young lady has, for a day or two, been subjected to the horrors of the pit.'

'You make it sound as though this whole affair is my fault?'

Paterson shook his head.

'Opinions are the product of their maker. The girl has guts, Rhodes, I'll give her that.' He made pretence of fussing his desk drawer for better order. 'Perhaps you would be well advised to put the word out; inform some of the more trustworthy diggers that Kimberley's first woman miner is about to take her place alongside them?'

'Was thinking exactly that,' said Rhodes, 'a wary eye for any untoward developments; a surreptitious insight to her safety, though I suspect Kathleen is gutsy enough to manage her own wellbeing.'

He thrust a clenched fist out in front of him.

'Her arms, Paterson! The muscle in those forearms – hard as rope I would say. When she shook my hand I swear I heard my bones crackle!'

Paterson chuckled at the analogy. The recollection raised up a sudden rush of gooseflesh from inside of his shirt.

'Strong woman, Rhodes. Undoubtedly, some will find themselves attracted by the fact.'

Rhodes detected the change in him.

'But you were not?' From the corner of his eye he watched for a reaction before tormenting him further, quietly he gauged Paterson's interest in Kathleen. 'You surprise me, old boy; for someone as handsome as yourself I thought the attraction would prove to be irresistible?'

Paterson shook his head and smiled at the banter. Control and power were to him, far greater attractions than the capricious wiles of some pretty girl. He changed tack and swung the focal point of their conversation back to the disadvantages of Kathleen working in the pit.

'If she cannot cope – if the woman flounders, what then?'

'A month,' Rhodes measured, 'I see myself as a reasonable man. If Kathleen breaks, I will return her five hundred pounds and take back the quarter share.' He flopped down into his chair and swung his legs across the corner of the desk. 'Something tells me that will not happen, old boy. The lass is made of sterner stuff, she will see this through or die trying. Mark my words, Paterson, the mining fraternity is about to suffer a rude awakening. A virulent state of deep mistrust is rife amongst the diggers, their working alongside our fresh-faced Kathleen O'Rourke will only serve to aggravate those fears. Their superstition will undoubtedly do me some good; their foolhardiness will strengthen my status amongst the diggings' most prominent entrepreneurs.' He leaned back and smiled his contentment at the galvanised iron roof. 'The makings of my empire, old boy; the first seeds of discontent have taken hold. A grandiose harvest awaits. Only the bravest of the brave, Paterson, men who dare to push aside the boundaries of some lesser expectation – these are the men who will reap the ultimate prize.'

Paterson appeared as to be confused by Rhodes' correlation.

'By what reasoning? On the basis of your partnership with one, single-minded woman, what difference would that make to the diggings?'

'None at all old boy, only to the diggers themselves. Seeing a woman at work on the stagings may well be the straw which breaks their proverbial camel's back.'

He glanced at the office clock; the act was reflexive, that of a man whose mind was simultaneously in touch with a dozen different thoughts.

'Superstition, my friend. A woman at the helm of a man o' war or digging out ground from the stagings, makes no difference; red rag to the maddened bull. The introduction of women in what up to now has been a male dominated environment will be severely contested, old chap. One woman amongst a thousand men will appear to many as the first feminine foot in the door, the dropping of our guard to that fateful harbinger, mistress bad luck. Those on the verge will throw in the towel and sell for a song.'

'To you, I suppose?'

'To me indeed, Paterson,' Rhodes nodded his head, shunned the clock and flipped the lid on his watch, 'to me indeed, who else do you know might have the nerve for all of this,' he snapped the lid closed. Time for my walk along the pit edge, then a leisurely beer or two at the Queens. Follow me down when you've shut up shop and I'll stand you a drink.'

'Dinner at your place...?'

Rhodes feigned disinterest and though hardly noticeable, the natural colouring about his cheeks darkened.

'Of course, old boy. Karoo lamb, garden peas and roast potatoes. You can bring the wine if you like, couple of bottles of best Cape red should do us nicely.'

Rhodes stood up and reached down his hat from its peg near the door. The brim was indelibly stained, that familiar colour of old rust from a constant mating of sweat to red, airborne dust. He put on the Homburg and slackened his tie, then rolled his shirt sleeves to just above the elbow.

'Should be down at the Queens for six o'clock, Paterson; a cigar and our usual tipple or two and then back to my place.' With raised eyebrows and the faintest hint of a smile, he glanced sideways at Paterson. 'Lashings of mint sauce, hey?'

'Goes without saying, Rhodes.'

'Lamb with mint sauce it is then. Six o'clock, Paterson – don't be late.' Rhodes started for the door, shrugged on his crumpled Norfolk jacket and adjusted the brim of his hat to cope with the harsh sunlight.

Outside the wood and iron building, like the contents of a potter's kiln, everything had been baked dry; the ground, the shade between the buildings and if it moved, even the air itself appeared as listless, loath to manage its way above that shimmering vista of wasted earth. Though tempted to take a direct route to the Queens Hotel, Rhodes held his line for the diggings and within those next ten minutes found himself staring down from the edge of claim 339, down inside the scorched innards of the pit.

Forced from the deep diggings, on thickening pillars of heated air, yellow dust and the stench of sweat from a thousand unwashed diggers floated over him; grit coated his teeth and fastened itself to the moisture at the corners of his eyes. The paradox upon which he now gazed still confounded him; that of abject poverty and, at the same time, of immense wealth.

'You're later than usual, Mister Rhodes. I'm afraid word is out over your buying up old man Bradshaw's stake in the diggings.'

'Matters not, Wilson. When the devil drives, my friend... The opportunity presented itself, forgoing the option to purchase Bradshaw's digging could well have cost me dearly.' He wiped a line of new sweat from the fleshy crease below his chin and looked around him. 'The black fellows – the labourers, what have you done with them?'

'Sent them off before the other diggers could commandeer them; back to the labour compound, told them to wait there.'

'How many?'

'Eight in all. Four Zulus, all Natal boys and four Shangaans from Portuguese territory.'

'Their wages, what did you tell them?'

'Doubled, Mister Rhodes, as you instructed.'

Rhodes nodded his head. 'Good man, get word to them; a week today, I want them here at sunup – well rested and cold sober.' He looked about him. 'What of the sorting tables and the rest of Bradshaw's mining paraphernalia?'

'All accounted for. I have made my own list and cross referenced the items with those on Bradshaw's deed of transfer. The numbers tally and everything appears to be in working order.'

'Then we are ready to start mining, Wilson. Bradshaw's claim did not come cheaply, hence our desperate need for more funding. Three months at the very outside and I will expect the books to be well balanced.'

Rhodes paused momentarily and then, with only the slightest lascivious gleam in his eye, 'someone else will be joining our little venture, Wilson. Please bear in mind this person is a fully entitled shareholder and will thereby exercise the right to a full, predetermined split of all the diamonds brought up from Bradshaw's claim.'

Wilson frowned at the spur of the moment revelation.

'Do I know him?'

Rhodes smiled at the assumption.

'I think not, however, I will expect your full co-operation; I will not tolerate any untoward remarks or hindrances. The newcomer will be of equal standing alongside the rest of us.'

Deliberately, Rhodes swung his attentions back to the pit. From a mental picture he had of its layout, he pinpointed some of the claims he had already bought; fifteen out of a total complement of five hundred, a mere handful, though to most men, owning the rights to that much diamond-bearing ground stood as sweet providence to a vast unearthly fortune. Any money accrued from his latest acquisition of Bradshaw's prime mining lease at the edge of the pit would add greater credibility to his position within the Diggers' Committee. However, time, that ever strident taskmaster was running out. Whatever geological assumptions were being bandied about, through his many discussions with Kimberley's mining elite, Rhodes had come to the conclusion that nature's compliant bonanza would eventually end. The weathered yellow gravels inside the diamond pit were not going to last forever, for the softer, easily accessible upper zones of any enriched earth always petered out. The very nature of the ore body would mutate from that of friable ground to a solid wall of resilient, iron-hard sulphides. Through experience gained by years of hard rock mining, only a few, having been labelled for years as naysayers, would, through the strength of their convictions stand head and shoulders above the thousands. What lay below that plug of friable yellow earth, these men had hazarded well, a feared column of blue-grey rock was waiting there, in situ, a billion tons of blue ground descending untold miles, deep inside the earth's mantle.

Lizzie Jardine poured herself a small measure of Gordon's gin and sipped it down through clenched teeth. Her eyelids puckered and squeezed closed.

'Good old mother's ruin. God only knows how much I needed that!' She opened her eyes and smiled at her reflection. Kathleen stood alongside her and they conversed via the bar room mirror.

'So what do you think?'

'About your investment in the pit...?' Lizzie folded her arms beneath her bosom and shrugged her shoulders. Her blouse was fresh on and like a drift of snow to the curves of some Scottish hillside, stood out starkly against the dimly lit interior. 'The mother in me says, stay the hell out of there, the twenty year old is jumping up and down like some hungry cat for a fattened budgerigar.'

Kathleen couldn't help smiling.

'Never had a mother who cared that much before.'

'Get used to it. You're stuck with me, sweetheart. I suppose your mind's made up then?'

'Too late in the day for me to turn back now,' Kathleen acknowledged, 'a large part of what I had put away is now invested in Bradshaw's old claim.'

'From Rhodes?'

Kathleen nodded her head.

'Half of every penny I own; the bank is drawing up the paperwork.'

'How much?'

'Cannot say – part of our agreement, not as much as you might think.'

'What about your work here at the Queens?'

'That will stay as it is, nothing has changed,' Kathleen promised, 'my Friday and Saturday nights are both of them yours, the rest I spend in the pit, up to my neck in dirt and hopefully, clutching a cap full of diamonds.'

'You'll be labelled up as a lunatic – no woman in her right mind would risk digging dirt in the pit.' She refilled her glass; the room was crowding up, tonight's takings would be good, she had made sure of it.

'Someone I would like you to meet.' She raised her arm and with an open hand beckoned for that someone's attention. 'My latest addition to the hotel's repertoire, so be nice. Don't go frightening her off with that black-as-hell glare of yours.'

Kathleen guessed the woman's age as to be somewhere around thirty-five; well-blessed in the bosom department, if a little plump about the waist, but her eyes, they were still bright and blue and like wetted sapphires they glittered rapaciously. Matching Kathleen's height to the quarter inch, the newcomer stepped in front of her.

'Trixi-Marie, you must be Kathleen?'

'I am.'

Kathleen was unsure of which way to drive their small talk, already the conversation came over as brittle and, through her own doing, guarded, if not somewhat stand-offish. However, for the sake of keeping the peace she brought back her smile and applied greater effort to encouraging a more convivial atmosphere. She was aware of Lizzie Jardine earwigging from the far corner of the bar.

'Where are you from?'

'London. Been out here for just over a year. Worked my passage over from Southampton on some dilapidated steam ship; believe me when I say that I ran my little legs off, washed dishes and peeled spuds the whole way over. What about you?'

Kathleen restrained a sudden urge for her to turn around and walk away. She trusted no one. Trixi-Marie was not the sort of woman who would tight rein her ego, at the slightest encouragement her mouth would be allowed run unchecked, anything she heard would be eagerly passed on and in the blinking of an eye. The diggers would milk her dry, in less than a week every man in Kimberley town would know her shoe size. Word of Jim O'Rourke's daughter's arrival in Kimberley would, if not controlled, soon filter back along the grapevine; rumours and second hand talk would spread through the diggings like wildfire.

'Ireland,' she told her, purposely covering up the truth of her American birthright, 'three years ago.'

'You must have family back home in Ireland?'

Kathleen shook her head and the smile faded, quickly she swung their point of conversation back to Trixi-Marie.

'All gone, I'm the last. There's no one else. What about yourself?'

Trixi's eyes flickered.

'Left all that behind in London; both parents are long dead and that bastard ex-husband of mine played me dirty, threw me out for his other woman.' She looked about her and like some threatened cobra, arrowed a jet of hot spittle at the nearest spittoon. Those sapphire eyes reflected the venomous depths of her hatred. 'Some tight-fannied, socialite strumpet from the West End; slack knickers and fat purse, I hope he catches the pox and his cock rots off.' Again her spittle found the spittoon. She shrugged her shoulders and shook her head. Her voice softened. 'I try my damndest to put it behind me, but it's not so easy.'

Kathleen's first negative impression of Trixi-Marie tempered; like herself, the woman had taken a beating and similarly, she was being kept alive purely by unsated needs for retribution.

'The boss said you were a singer?'

Trixi nodded her head; her features softened and the smile reappeared.

'Singing was the easy part. Members only place down Regent Street – a so-called gentleman's watering hole where they could hide from their wives and grope my rear without fear of their infidelity being dragged out into the open.' Her eyes took on sparkle and she chuckled at the afterthought. 'Good money, though and more often than not the old farts hardly ever lasted more than a couple of minutes before running out of puff.'

The room was filling up; diggers crowded the bar and jostled for attention. Lizzie Jardine looked back over her shoulder for assistance.

'We had best get over there,' Kathleen realised, 'time for us to earn a crust or two.' She reached for Trixi's hand. 'You'll do just fine. Keep the buggers smiling and their glasses filled. The prices are on the bottles, follow my lead and shout out loud and clear if you have any problems.'

Trixi checked her face in the mirror, wetted her lips with the tip of her tongue and with her strawberry-coloured pout repaired, pointed her heaving breasts at the nearest group of diggers, like the twin barrels of some great gun.

'What will it be gents!'

'Quart of your best beer, lassie,' the miner pushed his schooner across and, fixated by the enormity of Trixi's bosom, he stared like a boy at a loaded sweet shop window, 'and whatever your price for an hour alone with those two fat pups o' yours.'

Trixi slapped his hand away.

'And what would your darling wife say, you coming home minus a hard earned sovereign or two?'

'No wife, girlie just me and the dog. What's yer name?'

'Trixi-Marie to my friends.'

'I'll be your friend, Trixi-Marie.' Like those of an old bloodhound, his eyes drooped. 'What does it cost, sweetheart, for us to be friends for half a night?'

She shook her head, but her smile said otherwise.

'I'm new here, mister. Give old Trixi a day or two to settle in and then we'll talk.'

By eight o'clock the street outside the Queens Hotel was pitch black, inside, candlelight thrown by three crystal chandeliers added its usual regal atmosphere to the true commonality of the saloon bar. The room heaved and overspilled with men eager to part with their money, beer slopped onto the floor, cigars were ground underfoot, dice rattled against the crown and anchor tables and from her raised dais behind the bar, Lizzie Jardine looked on and smiled sweetly. Already the takings were good, twice she had emptied the cash drawer and twice she had topped up the big iron safe with fresh piles of gold coin.

Trixi leaned against the bar counter; supported by her forearms her bosom rode up high and firm and to men across the bar they were the very essence of their dreaming.

'Lizzie said you can sing?'

Trixi's eyes glowed; the digger was drunk, like some slavering dog for a yard of butcher's tripe he lusted over her breasts.

'What if I can?'

The digger's head wobbled, his eyes rolled; the head of a china doll, loosened by too much beer.

'How much for Pretty Sally, or Yellow Rose?'

She looked to Lizzie Jardine for her approval and like a hawk from its high perch, Lizzie dropped from her dais.

'That's what I'm paying you for, sweetheart. Break their blackened hearts and empty their pockets with that sugary voice of yours,' she pointed to the cash drawer, 'half in the till, half in your purse.' She leaned in close enough for Trixi to catch the gist of her whisper. 'Equal partners, deary; straight down the middle, whether you sing on your feet at the piano or flat on your back upstairs in your room, makes no difference, a straight split will make it easier for the both of us.' Her smile was that of a vixen, hungry for the chicken coop. 'And don't you forget, my sweet Trixi-Marie, your dear old aunt Lizzie will be watching.'

'Give me twenty minutes,' Trixi chimed sweetly and blew a sultry kiss to a growing pool of admirers. The way had been thrown open, a year at the most and she would be taking the coach southwards to that far though fair, most fecund Cape, her account at the Standard Bank stuffed full with diggers' money.

Kathleen glanced up at the bar clock, Trixi-Marie had been gone a full quarter hour before the diggers' mood changed, rumours of the hotel's new busty entertainer ripped from man to man. Like wild dogs to the beleaguered wildebeest they closed in; voices which only seconds earlier appeared as raucous and overpowering, were now subdued.

Lizzie took her stance alongside Kathleen, her eyes on the east wall with its redoubt of red velvet. From behind the heavy drapes, a nervous pianist's first familiarisation with his keyboard filtered through to the bar. Every man in the room fell silent, and the eyes of young and old were now inexorably fixed to slight, tentative tremblings in those scarlet curtains.

With a sibilant rush of velvet and gold brocade, the curtains slid open, and in the light from a single lamp, adorned in scarlet silk and glittering paste set in silver, Trixi-Marie, like some languorous cat leaned to the side of a patched-up concert piano.

Like her dress, Trixi's lips were matched to that same deep scarlet, her hair, black as a storm sky had been gathered purposely about her cheeks, giving her that lax, laid-back look of the young, available debutante. The piano player tapped a single middle C and nodded his head.

'For all you lonely diggers, to every one of you, a song from your sweethearts.' Trixi's voice purred amongst the miners and every last one of them stepped willingly under her thrall. The pianist re-seated his spectacles before striking up his rendition of George Cooper's, *Somebody's Coming To See Me Tonight.*

Trixi-Marie sashayed those few short yards to the very edge of the stage. She played the crowd, and with her legs parted and mountainous breasts thrust out for best effect, skilfully she entranced every single digger in the room.

Like a slow but powerful wave awakening from the quiet of neap tide the crowd surged forwards, those at the front were forced to brace their feet against the five feet tall wooden frontage for fear of being crushed. As her voice soared to a livelier tempo, so did the mood inside the room catch fire.

'Give us *The Yellow Rose of Texas*, or *Sweet Eveline*,' girlie – for all us Yankees stuck out here in this God forsaken dust bowl!'

The Yankee held a sovereign at arm's length above his head, and then, on a whim, flicked the gold coin high above the podium; in the lamplight the precious metal winked as it spun and with deft hands, Trixi plucked it from the air. Without breaking the mood, she leaned out from the stage edge, at the same time gesturing to the digger for him to move in closer.

'Yellow Rose it is my lovely,' she called on down to him and just inches from his face her breasts were rising crescent moons above the bodice of her dress, 'and just for you my darlin', sweet as ever I can.'

# -13-

'Two bob's worth of your best beer, sweetheart, that's all I've got.' The stranger pushed his bowler hat to the back of his head; his hair was thick with sweat and grime from the open road. Kathleen reached down a glass from the shelf behind her and filled it with beer.

'You're new in Kimberley?'

'New as this morning's catch offloaded at Billingsgate market.' He saw her frown and to clear the confusion, quickly he explained his place of embarkation. 'London, darlin' – grew up in Whitechapel, son of a ragman and poor as a church mouse.' He emptied half the glass and waggled a corrective finger. 'No, I stand in error, poorer than that even – a church mouse has a goodly covering of fur to keep him warm, whereas all that I have are my threadbare jacket, shirt and breeches, worn out boots and a well-battered bowler hat.' His smile was that of an East End jack-the-lad. 'And my spectacles,' he prodded them into place with his forefinger, 'couldn't have made the trip without them; all the way up from the Cape, walked every, stony, night-frozen, spiteful yard of it.'

Kathleen took to him. His eyes, though they sparked full with fanciful stories were bright and honest as silver threepenny bits.

'You walked from Cape Town?'

'Couldn't afford the price of a seat. The Dutchman let me walk alongside his cart though and did odd jobs for him in return for food and water. Too much extra weight for his oxen, he insisted, so I walked it. For three months I slept every night underneath his wagon with his mangy, flea-ridden dog, the cold, the dust and the scorpions.'

He emptied his glass, belched his belly clear of trapped wind and roused a beseeching smile for Kathleen.

'God that was good. Don't suppose you will open a slate for me? Square with you as soon as I find the wherewithal to pay you back?'

Kathleen shook her head and chuckled at the folly of her dishing out credit to total strangers.

'More than my life is worth, mister.' She retrieved the empty glass and refilled it with cool beer. 'I'll stand any man a drink, but I won't lend him a guinea.' She slid the filled glass in front of him. 'My father told me that; must have worked, never been owed a penny and never lost me a friend through lending money.'

'I'll remember that. Good yardstick by any man's book. You still haven't told me your name?'

'Kathleen, Kathleen O'Rourke. What's yours?'

He grinned at her. 'My first Kimberley business venture – trade you my name for the price of a smoke?'

She nodded to Lizzie Jardine, her intention to foot the bill and then lifted a box of the hotel's cheapest cigars from off the shelf. She struck and held a Vesta for him.

'Your name then, and whatever it is you're after in Kimberley?'

'You're a sweetheart.' He pulled on the cigar. 'My friends call me Barney.'

'Barney?'

'Barnato, Barney Barnato, an easier to remember version of Barnet Isaacs. My brother, Harry came out here in seventy-one.'

'A digger?'

'Don't know; don't even know if he's still here in Kimberley. If he isn't, I'm up the creek without a paddle; more to the point, I'll be without a place to stay.'

'Wait here,' Kathleen told him, 'maybe I can find out.' She moved to the other end of the counter and searched the crowd for a familiar face; two minutes later and she was back with the newcomer.

'If it's the same Harry Isaacs I've just been told about, then you're in luck.'

Barney's face lit up.

'What did they tell you? Did Harry strike it big in the diggings?'

Kathleen shook her head and gentled him down to earth.

'No diamonds – a share in some hotel or other, but I hear he's alright.'

Barney's excitement fizzled; he hadn't seen Harry for three long years and cursed himself for not making firmer commitment to his reaching Kimberley sooner. However, though his mind was firmly set on finding his brother, his optimism struggled to stay afloat upon a rising tide of depressing probabilities, more importantly, after all this time he prayed that Harry would still be glad to see him. His eyes found Trixi-Marie, she had diggers queuing up six deep for a chance whiff of her perfume. Every digger in the first two rows was shouting for her to sing their song. Money showered the podium floorboards, Barney Barnato was quick to pick up on an opportunity and he winked an eye at Kathleen.

'Tell your boss I can sing, juggle, anything she wants for a small cut of the takings up there on the stage.'

Lizzie Jardine cut into the conversation.

'The girl's doing well enough on her own, Mister Barnato. I'll thank you to leave her be. If it's work you're after, come see me in the morning.' She went back to watching Trixi-Marie; the diggers loved her and her store of popular songs seemed endless. By the end of that night the till would be well sweetened with her cut from Trixi's takings.

'What are you going to do?' Kathleen asked him.

'Find somewhere to kip. Harry can wait till the morning.' Again, he caught Lizzie Jardine's eye and with upturned palms, implored her.

'For a plate of food and a shake down, wash your glasses and keep the counter clean as new – more if need be.' His persuasive skills were absolute; his smile bright as the chandelier above his head. Lizzie stood up from her stool and craned her neck.

'There's your chance for you to earn your night's keep – the drunk on the stage, get him off before he costs me money.'

'It will be to my pleasure Ma'am. Would you prefer him physically dispatched or should I try a more genteel approach?'

'Whatever suits, just get him off my stage.'

Barney tipped his hat to her and again, winked at Kathleen.

'Fill up my glass and guard it for me, sweetheart. Thirsty work awaits – I could be a while.'

Trixi kept the show alive, there was too much money lying around on the floor for her to abandon her place on the platform. However, like some persistent bloodhound the drunk dogged her every movement and on faltering legs he followed her around the stage. Barney vaulted onto the platform and reached Trixi-Marie just as the drunk caught up with her. He touched the man's shoulder and stepped backwards, out of range of his fists.

'Leave the girl alone, friend. Time for you to get on home.'

Though fat-gutted, the digger stood broad as a horse across the shoulders and a good four inches taller than Barney; he looked about him for the source of the annoyance. Lively as a fox terrier, Barney ducked past him and flashed a smile at Trixi-Marie.

'Five bob, sweetheart and I'll take him off your hands.'

Trixi nodded her head and kept well out of harm's way. At the back of the stage, the pianist kept the music flowing, but like a rabbit about to bolt for cover his eyes were locked to the developing fracas. The crowd bayed for the drunk to be taken off.

'Ten if you're quick enough!' Trixi mouthed between her lines.

'For ten bob I'll brawl with the devil himself, my little flower!'

Like an aggravated bear, the drunk turned on his heels and with both arms outstretched, lumbered forwards. His beard thick and black and about his mouth those curls still glistened with peach *mampoer*. From the far side of the room, Cecil Rhodes followed the developing altercation with amused interest.

'Five pounds says the cockney puts the giant flat on his backside.' He grinned at Paterson. 'Well then? Are you in on the bet or do you lack the nerve, old boy?'

'Gambling on brawling drunks holds little attraction for me, Rhodes.' He sensed Rhodes' disappointment and quickly changed his tune. 'However, for the sake of friendly competition, I shall, from a state of some duress dispute your prediction; your friend up there in the bowler hat is half the weight of his adversary. Therefore, based purely upon the laws of probability, I will raise the stakes by a further five pounds.'

'Ten pounds it is then.' Gleefully, Rhodes rubbed his

hands together. 'And cash money, Paterson, none of those rubbish banker's promissory notes on the outcome of this one.'

Barney saw movement out of the corner of his eye and swung side-on to his attacker with his fists up and balled like hammers. Every punch the drunk threw, though backed by the weight of powerful shoulders, was mistimed – slow and cumbersome. He was the stumbling colossus, Barney the agile will-o'-the-wisp that danced light as a feather about the drunk's feet. He was untouchable, the twirling meerkat watching for an opening, probing with his left, lightning fast and always on target, a scorpion's lethal sting to the flaccid underbelly of his adversary.

With vociferous ecstasy, the crowd roared its appreciation; Rhodes came out from his chair, awed by what he was seeing. It was at that precise moment that Barney Barnato realised his worth.

'Watch him move, Paterson.' Rhodes emulated the fighter's prowess. 'Professional, I would say. Dig out that pair of crisp fivers, man, you are about to lose your money.'

Barney was enjoying the attention; every man in the room was behind him, so that he purposely squeezed out extra mileage from the altercation. There was money to be made and already his reputation as a fighter had taken root.

'He's ready enough to take him Paterson, your man is finished, old chap – almost down on his knees!'

Barney steadied himself for the *coup de grâce*; the digger managed one more windmilling slog at Barney's head, but the target jinked away and the blow found only an empty space in the air. The clip, when it came was just behind the digger's ear, high on the upper line of his jaw and in full view of the crowd.

The spectacle, for one brief moment appeared as if to be sketched on canvas. To every man in the room, in their mind's eye there was a halting of the clock; the marrying of the cockney's fist to the digger's jaw had become the breathtaking, final seconds of a dream. Barney, with all the force of the attack now expended, spun himself clear of the toppling drunk and watched him hit the floor.

'Bravo, sir!' Rhodes applauded the performance and fought his way through the crowd. 'The bar!' he shouted to Barney, 'get yourself over here, man.'

The crowd opened up, men at the bar made way for him and on stage, Trixi-Marie waved her arms to Lizzie Jardine for the unconscious drunk to be carted away.

'Whatever our friend here is drinking,' Rhodes instructed Kathleen, 'and a good cigar, lassie.' He extended his right hand. 'Cecil Rhodes. What's yours man, your name, what is it?'

'Barnato,' he grinned, 'preceded by Barney, wayward son of Isaac and Leah Isaacs of London's East End.'

'By God he was spot on! Described you to a T, we have been expecting you. Your brother Harry sings your praises at the smallest of opportunities.' Rhodes peeled the wrapper from the sweet-smelling Julieta and jammed it firmly between Barney's teeth. 'Where are your lodgings?'

'I have none. Came in with the Dutchman, Vermeulen's wagon this morning. Was hoping Harry would be here to meet me.'

Rhodes shook his head.

'Harry's away until the middle of next week. How're you fixed for funds?'

'Poorly, used up every penny.'

Lizzie Jardine picked up on the conversation and stepped forward.

'You're good with your fists, young man.' She frowned a warning at Rhodes, willing him to restrain himself from a usual pre-empting of her thoughts. 'I have a proposition for you.'

Rhodes knew what was coming; the fight had stirred up more than just Lizzie's business acumen. The wheels of his own mind were already fully turned, but he held his tongue. The Queens was his bolt hole and upsetting its proprietor would do him no good. Silently, he assessed Lizzie Jardine's canny exploitation of the situation. She was direct and to the point.

'What I saw tonight suggests you might well have fought professionally?'

'Since the age of fourteen.'

'Once a week,' she went on, a soft purr overlaid her voice and with glittering eyes she laid out a plan that would suit them both. 'Saturday nights only. One fight unless otherwise agreed to for twenty percent of the purse – what do you say?'

'Forty,' Barney grinned back at her, 'forty percent and lodgings here at the Queens will get you Barney Barnato; bare-knuckle entertainer, singer, juggler, whatever might take your fancy.'

In the background, Trixi-Marie was crooning her way through the final bars of *When You and I Were Young, Maggie*. Now the crowd was silent and every listening man inside the Queens Hotel was tearfully enraptured by Trixi-Marie's sweet, angelic voice.

Lizzie gave in to him, a sixty-forty split was more than she had hoped for; loath for the opportunity to slip from her grasp she held out her right hand to him.

'Then we have an agreement, Mister Barnato; your forty percent to my sixty and a room for you here at the Queens.'

Barney grasped her hand, firmly, so that the muscles along his forearm bunched together like elvers fighting the fisherman's trap. He felt her shiver and caught that first, slight fluttering of her eyelashes. Lizzie felt it also, and for the first time in ten years the tips of her breasts stood hard and dark to the inside of her blouse.

# -14-

Rhodes threw his hat across the room, pushed a lighted cigarette between his teeth and dragged his favourite chair out onto a small veranda, and though it was dark, from memory he was able to put together a clear, unrestricted image of the diggings. Paterson brought their drinks and like Rhodes, settled for a blanket and seat on the covered veranda. Already, that fast African onset of night had lowered the ambient temperature and because of it, they would not stay long outside; July nights were cold, cold as any English winter. The lamplight wavered, but it was enough to cover the steps and the shrivelled remnants of what was once a small but fecund garden. Rhodes blew the ash from his cigarette and settled back in his chair with a glass of Paterson's hard won Constantia red.

'I saw the change in her eyes, Paterson, the woman is besotted. A toothsome smile and one, bare-armed handshake with Barnet Isaacs Barnato and Lizzie Jardine was batting her lids like the proverbial, lovesick bovine.'

'Your imagination knows no bounds, Rhodes. Lizzie Jardine must be ten years his senior, at least.'

'I know what I saw Paterson; one wrong move and our young Barnato will be biting off more than he can chew. Our Lizzie will gobble him up – piecemeal.' He waved the thought away. 'But to hell with all of that, it matters not what either one of them will or will not do, what does matter, is how we predict the future of the Kimberley diamond diggings.' He filled his mouth with wine and followed it down with smoke from his cigarette. 'So, what do you think, Paterson? Which way will the monkey jump?'

'You refer to the pit bottoming out?'

Rhodes nodded his head. 'Rock as hard as pick steel. The rumour is rife, my friend, every digger with a vested interest in the pit lives each day in mortal fear of hitting the blue.' Rhodes stood up from his chair and crossed to the veranda railing; beyond, though no more than two hundred yards from where he was standing, the very edge of the diggings descended sheer-sided down inside that darkened hole in the earth. All around, for as far as Rhodes could see, the night was speckled with lamplight; fires, built some ways back from the rim showed where the diggers were putting together a meal from whatever food they could muster.

'How long will it all last, Paterson? A year, five perhaps? How long can a thousand desperate souls exist in a place such as this, or will this devil of a pit surprise us all and see men here for another hundred years?'

'Your female prodigy.' Paterson diverted their conversation.

'Kathleen...? What of her?'

'You mentioned her starting this coming week.'

'Her first day in hell, Paterson, it will not be easy for her.' He emptied his glass and set it down on the veranda railing. 'However, I am still convinced the lass will make a firm fist of things.'

He shook his head at the slight though nagging uncertainty of a woman taking up work on the stagings.

'The dreaded pit, Paterson; I could bring you a dozen men, myself included, who would sooner throw in their lot with the devil himself, or stand shoulder to shoulder with a half dozen meagrely armed men against the entire Zulu army. Now that, I would commit to, rather than face the perils of that stinking hole in the ground on a daily basis.'

'I thought you loved the place?'

Without averting his gaze from the dark, Rhodes moved to within reach of Paterson and laid his hand on his shoulder.

'I do, my gentle-mannered friend, I do, but only from the safety of its upper edge.' From the corner of his eye, Rhodes studied the features of the man alongside him.

298

'You're looking tired, old chap. We could both do with an early night – can I tempt you into staying over, or would you rather I walk you back as far as the market square?'

Paterson offered Rhodes his empty glass, his face already flushed from that first measure of strong wine. Like his voice, his eyes were soft and on his lips there had settled the first inklings of a wry smile.

'Pour the drinks if you will, Rhodes. Time to move, must be the chill out here bringing me out in goose bumps.'

'Then another bottle it is old boy, let us go inside, Paterson, I had my servant put in a fire before he left.'

# -15-

The last man left the Queens Hotel at just turned two o'clock, less than three hours before sunrise. Barney Barnato seated himself on Kathleen's sofa and from between his finger and thumb there dangled a silver fob; fixed to its train of silver links were three small diamonds, set upon by lamplight. Mesmerised by the sight of these precious stones he knew then, just which way the hand of fate would lead him.

'How many millions more like these are waiting to be dug out from their nests in the pit?' He examined each one of them in turn. 'How did you come by them?'

'In exchange for a man's life,' Kathleen told him and she felt a sudden, overwhelming urge for her to burden the cockney with her secrets. 'Three years ago. Look upon the diamonds as a down payment on my letting him live.'

'Dare I ask why?'

Kathleen shrugged her shoulders.

'The man was drunk, he made a mistake – one that would cost him dearly.'

Barney turned his attention back to the diamonds, but

the story had already dug in its claws; the bitterness in Kathleen's voice was palpable.

'From the look on your face, it would appear you will not be forgiving him any time soon?' Without averting his eyes from the stones, he sensed the hatred rising about him; Kathleen's voice was thick with it.

'That will never happen,' Kathleen assured him, 'the stones you hold in your hand belonged to the same man who killed my father.'

As if the diamonds had turned white hot, Barney abandoned them to the table.

'As God is my witness, Kathleen, I had no idea.'

'How would you? I take no offense from your asking.'

She crossed the room and peered out through the window, into the darkness. Along the street only a few late lamps showed as properly trimmed and still burning brightly.

'That's why I'm here in Kimberley, Barney, not for gain.' She turned to face him and besides her sadness he saw in her a terrible need for retribution. Her eyes looked through him. 'Out there on the diggings, I have sensed him.'

'Then you should expose him, sweetheart. Dish the swine his just desserts.'

'Wouldn't do any good, no one would believe me. I have no proof of what he did.' She shook her head. 'No my friend, no one else must know of what I am telling you. Little by little, I will destroy him.' Her eyes were those of the watching raptor. 'A month perhaps, a year even. His money, even his soul, Barney, I will have it all. Anything and everything I will take from him and leave him wanting, and when he least expects it, when the man inside the man has gone I will strike him down and leave his body for the crows to pick over.'

'Does this poor, unsuspecting son of the devil have a name?'

'Do I have your word on you saying nothing?'

Barney nodded his head to her.

'I swear on my family name. What you tell me will go no further than this room.'

Kathleen's expression darkened; through a break in the wall of her loathing she forced her lips to speak the killer's name.

'McKinnon,' she whispered, 'Blackie McKinnon, a name I will spit on for every waking moment of my life.'

'A Scot...?'

Kathleen nodded her head.

'Tall man, black beard. Dead eyes, Barney; as long as I live I will never forget them. His interests lie only with diamonds and the bedevilment of every woman he claps eyes on.'

'Then I must watch for him; a needle in the haystack, but find the man I will, this much I can promise you.'

Kathleen pulled up a chair opposite Barnato and as quickly as it had risen up, her anger crawled back inside its lair and let her be, the wall had been re-sealed, she was again, safe inside her room at the Queens. She pocketed the fob and with it hidden from view, magically, her temperament softened.

'The reasons for your travelling all the way from London? Diamonds, I should guess? A guinea says I'm right.'

Barney relaxed, her demons had fled the room.

'Haven't got a guinea to lose, but yes, you are correct, sweetheart. The lure of Kimberley diamonds is the very reason for me being here. London was buzzing with stories of Africa's New Rush – diamonds at every turn of the digger's spade.' He cocked a sceptical eye and grinned at the fantasy. 'Not much truth in that, I know, but apart from hope, I expect little else.'

Barney settled back on the sofa, time was something he had plenty of.

'What about yourself? Besides you're clearing the slate of this McKinnon fellow and working for Lizzie Jardine?'

'The same.'

'Diamonds...?'

Kathleen smiled at the cockney's shocked expression.

'Look upon my interest as a way for me to get closer to McKinnon, but I see you do not agree?'

'You're a woman,' Barney interjected, 'diamonds and women have always complemented one another.'

'But not through digging them out from the ground?' Quickly, she added to his confusion. 'Then what would you say to my owning a share in a diamond claim?'

'Part ownership in a diamond claim,' the revelation astounded him, 'how in God's sweet name did you manage that?'

'The claim, as a whole, belongs to Rhodes. I bought interest in the venture to the value of one quarter share; minor shareholder, working partner, call it what you may. I committed also to my working the sorting table as well as the staging.'

'Staging...? You forget that I'm new here.'

'Inside the pit.' Kathleen shed more light on what she was getting into. 'The claim itself is merely a square of ground no bigger than this room. The gravel is mined, loaded into leather buckets and hauled to the surface for sorting.'

'And why would he need an outsider for that?'

'He doesn't,' Kathleen admitted, 'we have known each other a fair few years, I need to learn how things work in the diggings and he has agreed to give me that chance. Hopefully, I will recover my investment and make myself a few pounds along the way. In return, Rhodes gets himself an extra pair of hands and an honest eye on his labour force.'

Barney leaned on the table, now totally intrigued by what he had learned.

'A couple of months here at the Queens and I'll have my start. Between bouncing the drunks for Trixi-Marie and a purse or two from the boxing ring, I will accumulate enough loot to secure my first diamond.'

'Then I have something else which might well be of interest you,' Kathleen told him and stood up from the table. She crossed the room, lifted a small cedar wood box from the mantle above the fireplace and then returned with it to her chair.

The box was no bigger than her hand, it was softly hued, the lid was deeply finger-worn, ghost-grey along its leading edge. Carefully, with the respect of the connoisseur for some precious collectable, Kathleen drew back the lid and with finger and thumb she reached inside. She withdrew the object of her attention and held it at an optimum angle for it to catch the lamplight.

'So, what do think, Mister Barnato?'

Barney, who at that very moment had struck a Vesta against the sole of his boot, stayed the lighted match an inch short of his cigarette.

'Your fingers,' Kathleen warned him.

'Is that what I think it is?'

She chuckled at the unplumbed depths of his naïveté. A deep hush fell over the room. Kathleen placed the stone on the table in front of him.

'Three carat, blue-white; perfect octahedral with no inclusions.'

Barney blew out the Vesta and removed the unlighted cigarette from between his lips.

'Might I pick it up?'

'Help yourself.' Kathleen encouraged.

With some trepidation, Barney manoeuvred the diamond onto the palm of his hand; a wonderful aura was cast upon his skin, and though it lacked the fire refracted by the cut and polished gem, still the carbon crystal was an entity of intractable beauty.

'It was a gift,' said Kathleen, 'from Thomas Bradshaw, Rhodes bought him out, the claim I will be working on was his. To help me on my way, he said, or do with it as I see fit.'

Barney looked at her and smiled wryly, he had been in Kimberley for less than one whole day and in that short time, already he had been left wide-eyed.

'Your best guess Barney, how much would you say it is worth?'

Turning the stone on its axis he searched for some clue as to what he should say, but found himself wanting.

'The little I do know comes straight from books, I wouldn't know where to begin,' he admitted and with some embarrassment, returned the stone to the table.

'You will soon learn,' Kathleen promised him, 'talk to the diggers, the old hands, men with grey whiskers and slow smiles. Saturday nights at the bar, for a glass of beer and friendly face they will tell you anything you want to know.' She turned the diamond over with her fingertip. 'Diamonds are measured by weight, lack of imperfections and quality of colour.' Barney nodded his head and though he had gone without sleep, still his eyes were attentive.

'Most will have suffered inclusions,' Kathleen continued, 'small discolorations, oxides, the leftovers from other diamonds trapped inside the stone.'

For that next hour, Kathleen talked and the cockney listened, every word, one more pointer to the treasure he was looking for and like a sponge to a pool of spilled water, he absorbed it all.

Just as the first inklings of dawn broke over Kimberley, Kathleen, for one last time examined the precious stone before sliding it over the table to Barney.

'Take it, the stone is yours,' she told him, 'but there is good reason behind me giving it to you.'

Barney shook his head and leaned back, distancing himself from the diamond. Outside, the sky was slowly turning pearl-pink. Crows were out from their roost, he could hear them squabbling for discarded titbits in the alleyways.

'I cannot accept. Bradshaw meant for you to put it to good use; for your benefit, not mine.'

She reached over and pushed the diamond closer to him.

'Take it,' her eyes sparkled, 'it will provide the start you are looking for, but on condition that when you are well established, you will pay back the price you get for it, plus interest.'

# -16-

With Kathleen standing alongside him, Barney Barnato nonchalantly flicked a smear of yellow dust from his brand new bowler hat, seated his spectacles firmly to the bridge of his nose and then, from a small pocket in the lining of his worsted waistcoat, drew out Kathleen's three carat diamond. With contrived aplomb, Barney placed the crystal on the counter, directly in front of the buyer. From a hole in the corrugated iron roof, at a slight angle, a solitary shaft of sunlight, like some divine benediction fell upon the gem.

'Seventy quid and the stone is yours, sir. Damn near colourless, no inclusions, weighs in at three carats, give or take a point or two – half a gram of pure perfection.' He rattled off the facts, exactly as Kathleen had told him. The Romeo y Julieta cigar between his teeth and the jeweller's loupe about his neck added credence to his play acting.

The buyer raised his eyes to meet Barnato's.

'Your name, sir, I do not recall our having met?'

Barney extended his right hand. On his fourth finger, the onyx inlayed ring with its gold menorah motif caught at the sunlight.

'Barnet Isaac, to my parents, Barney Barnato to my friends and business associates.'

The buyer accepted the hand. He glimpsed the ring and the fine lines of mistrust lifted from his brow.

'Libernurski,' he nodded his head to Barnato. Like the

stones that he dealt in, his eyes sparkled. 'You are not long out from England, yes?'

'Less than a month,' Barney corrupted the truth of his time in Kimberley, 'still getting used to the dust, the fleas and the flies.'

'And there are, unfortunately, plenty of those, Mister Barnato.' He turned his attention back to the stone and with a jeweller's glass pressed to his eye, grasped the gem firmly between the metal jaws of his tweezers. With a surgeon's eyes he delved inside the crystal for him to probe amongst its innermost secrets.

Kathleen felt her heartbeat quicken. In the silence of that small shack, her three carat diamond now floated in that half-world, a place of uncertainty, a waiting place between acceptance and obscurity. The credibility of both stone and the man were, without diffidence, being put to the balance.

Libernurski took his time examining the eight-sided crystal for any discolorations, using that same shaft of sunlight to illuminate its innards. An error of judgement, a poor assessment would cost him dearly, but the diamond was spectacular and would in turn sell at double the seller's asking price to Mosanthal of Port Elizabeth. Without any doubt, the stone would grade as Fine White, Top Wesselton.

'Your assessment is quite in order, Mister Barnato, not a single inclusion and fortunately, the colour leans more towards white than yellow.' He dropped the loupe against his chest. 'Not quite colourless, but nevertheless a fine example and as close to perfection as I have seen in months.' He turned sideways-on to the counter; with practiced fingers and a midwife's care for a newborn child he lifted the precious stone across to his scales.

'A hair over three carats. However,' He peered over the top of his spectacles, 'I find your asking price a little weighty. My parting with seventy pounds would leave me with little, or even no margin for profit.'

'Your best then...?' Barney stared at the buyer, the smile he had walked in with now gone from his face.

Libernurski held his nerve. 'Sixty pounds, my friend and by David's holy Star I swear that is my fairest price.'

'Sixty five and we shake hands,' Barney went for the throat, 'not a penny less, my Jewish friend, or by that same star I will take my business elsewhere.'

# -17-

For Barney Barnato, at that precise moment there was no brighter place on God's own earth than the Kimberley diamond diggings. Even the sulphurous looking clouds of dust had about them, a promissory, gay sparkle, enhanced by late sunlight and the urge for him to hunt down his first, profitable transaction. Like a ferret for the entrance to the rabbit's warren, he nosed his way between the gravel heaps, pausing to watch and listen, and even the smallest threads of information were eagerly gathered up and stored away. Kathleen walked with him, remonstrating his actions should he come across as too much the pushy entrepreneur, cajoling him with her optimism when his spirits floundered, or the task he had set seemed doomed to failure, falling further from his grasp with each new rebuff.

'You try too hard,' Kathleen highlighted his weaknesses, 'ease back a little on the big smiles and vigorous handshakes. Win their trust and the sales will come.'

'My patience has worn thin, sweetheart. My debut as a Kimberley kopje-walloper has so far turned up nothing more than sore feet. One more attempt and then to hell with this rat hole; it's back to the Queens for a quart of Lizzie Jardine's best beer.'

He scanned the diggings and as luck would have it,

caught sight of a man stood to the sorting table, head down, and perusing his find like a hawk inspecting a fresh kill.

'There's our man!' Barney gestured to Kathleen for her to follow on and like parched francolin for the last dregs of some desert pool they homed in on the digger.

The Afrikaner was big-boned, whiskered down to the insides of his collar; with a black bear's growl in his throat he turned face-on to the strangers.

'What are you after, *meneren*? You have no business here.'

Barney smiled up at the giant, tempted to walk away he forced his feet to stay where they were.

'The Queens Hotel, Friday night,' for a brief moment he held back, recognition flickered behind his eyelids and it was then his terrier attitude got the better of him, 'the singer, Trixi-Marie, was it not you on the stage with her?'

Like Goliath from out of the Valley of Elah, mountainous and broad-shouldered the Boer stepped forward; fingers wrapped to the wooden shaft of his digger's pick. His eyes, clear and sharp were flecked through with gold; the pupils cut from the devil's coal and then burned to twinkling cinders by those very same fires of hell.

'So, *engelsman*! It was you who struck me down on the floor.'

'An honest blow, Dutchman and you were pissed drunk; had I chosen to, you would still be lying in the infirmary.' Kathleen prodded Barney's shoulder, she had seen the anger flare up in the Boer's eyes.

'We should go now. The both of us are short in the leg and it's a fair run back to the Queens.'

'Not so fast, sweetheart, my Boer friend here has just found himself a diamond and is in need of an honest buyer.' He nodded his head to the digger. 'Well, Dutchman, today is your lucky day, you have found one.'

'Rather than sell the stone to you, *engelsman*, I will give it to my kaffirs for free.'

'Then you use your brains as poorly as you do your fists, Dutchman. Five pound notes are what they say they are, nothing more, nothing less. Where I come from a man is not judged by his birthright, rather the reputation of his word.' Barney drew out a silver cigarette case and sprung the lid. He held out the case and the sweet aroma of Turkish tobacco flew the gap between them. Barney saw the Boer's nostrils flare. 'Where money and women are concerned meneer, there are no friends, but friendship is not what I am after, all I ask is a fair and honest chance to win your findings.'

The Afrikaner closed to within a foot of the digging's newest diamond buyer; with thick fingers he levered out a cigarette from the silver case and ran the length of it between his upper lip and the base of his nose.

'Tobacco is of little use without a light, *engelsman*.'

Barney struck a Vesta and held up the flame for him.

'*Magtig*, that is good smoke; not since they threw me out from the hotel have I found the time to buy tobacco.'

With smoke still billowing out from his nostrils, he waved his hand for Barney to follow.

'Bring your money and your eye glass Englishman, let us find out just how honest the three of you are.'

They followed the Boer to where he had strung a canvas sail above his living space, the camp was littered with rusted metal and rusted memories and as the night drew in, the fires and lamps of other desperate men bloomed as yellow, lonesome flowers from amongst the gravel heaps.

'Sit where you can,' he told them and shouted for his servant to boil up a kettle of fresh water. Behind the sorting table, everything the Boer owned was there; yellowed and half rotted, the failing canvas tent would be lucky to see out another rainy season. Barney left his opened cigarette case at the centre of a rickety table and gestured to the Afrikaner for him to help himself.

Kathleen twisted sideways on her stool; the Afrikaner was staring at her, his eyes were black slits set between a

309

beard and hooded eyebrows, those of the canny horse dealer. On the diggings, unmarried women stood for little more than a night's distraction.

'Your face,' he told Kathleen, 'I do not forget a face. I know you, somewhere else I have seen you before.'

'At the Queens,' Kathleen reminded him, 'you bought your bottle from me.'

'Not at the Queens,' he shook his head, 'long time before that.' A look, a sideways glance, a flash of auburn hair in the sunlight. One piece at a time, it all came back to him. His expression softened. 'Your hair was long then, not short like that of a boy, and you rode my horse bare feet,' he drew out the mystery, 'your father how goes it with him? The Sharps rifle, does he still have it?'

Kathleen strained her eyes in the half-light, and then pointed to his face, their recollections mixed and the mood settled. His belly laugh, when it came, was that deep, rumbling voice of running surf.

'Your whiskers Meneer Jooster, they were not so big back then.'

The Boer stemmed the tide of his amusement and leaned across the table, eager for a glance inside of Kathleen's last three years.

'Your father – how is he?'

Kathleen lowered her eyes, her smile faltered, but then quickly she rallied. The pain, though still alive inside her chest was not so strong this time.

'My father is no longer with me, Meneer Jooster.'

The Afrikaner reached out and covered her hand.

'Forgive me, but I did not know.'

Kathleen managed a smile.

'Pilgrim's Rest. On the hillside above Pilgrim's Creek. That's where I left him, he can see the diggings from there, he would have liked that.'

'He was a good man.'

Kathleen nodded her head and then changed the direction of their conversation, for still she lacked the inner strength to talk for long about her loss.

'What about you? What made you leave Natal for Kimberley? From what I remember, your business was good. Horses, guns, there was nothing you did not sell, meneer?'

'The call was too strong,' he told her, 'every day I see men with the smell of God's wilderness stuck in their throat, but like a good husband I looked the other way and to keep my woman happy, I work my fingers to the bone breaking horses and mending carts.' He shook his head and chuckled over the memory. 'Until one day, my friend, I could take it no longer. It was then I said to my wife's brother for him to look after the business and I tell my wife that Hendrik Stephanus Jooster is going into the wilderness to make his peace with God,' he winked an eye at Kathleen, 'and if his luck holds true, perhaps he will find a few diamonds to ease the burden of his living like a baboon in this shithole of a diamond pit.'

Jooster's servant set three enamel mugs upon the table; a muslin bag filled with coffee grounds hung on a looped string inside the kettle. Without asking, Jooster sugared all three mugs and poured them almost full to the brim with steaming coffee. Barney held his mug with both hands and through the steam he watched and listened to the Afrikaner's reminiscing. Only when the light had faded and the cigarette case was at a point of half empty, did the Boer look to Barney with different eyes.

'You are wanting to see the stones, my friend? There is more than one.'

Barney came awake, his interest fluttered to life.

'Without a doubt, meneer, but I am ill-prepared, I do not have a scale with me.'

'Just an honest smile and your fancy cigarettes?' His eyes shone, enhanced by the firelight. 'No matter, I have my own.' He looked to his servant. 'The scales, Johannes and the stones. Bring them out, perhaps we can make some money, and If God is good to us, for this next month we sleep with full bellies.'

For a full half-hour, Barney measured, re-measured and recorded the weight of all three diamonds. Two were unevenly shaped, by some spiteful roll of the dice they had been spewed from the earth's bowels as roughly formed, created hurriedly, haphazardly even, and were both of them maliciously shot through with feathers of pale yellow. Put to an expert eye the gems could well be looked upon as poor offspring – the runts of an elite Kimberley litter. However, the third, Barney likened to the one he had traded to Libernurski; it was a stone so perfect that even in that small light from Jooster's fire it glowed as a single, two carat drop of God's sweet rain.

Barney set the stone down alongside its poorer siblings and like the morning star, from amongst a firmament filled with minor celestial lights, the beauty of its creation overpowered them both.

'The smaller stone weighs in at a half, the other slightly larger of the two, at three quarters of one carat.'

Jooster nodded his head in agreement; poker-faced he leaned forward, his forearms thick as boiler logs stacked on the table.

'How much, *engelsman*? Pray to God your answer does not offend me.'

Twelve pounds and ten shillings, Meneer Jooster, for the pair. If the colour had been better... as much as double that.'

The price was left hanging in the air, and then, like an old dog ready to nap in the shade, Jooster sighed, shook his leonine head and smiled at Kathleen.

'Your friend drives a hard bargain, but his price is fair; perhaps a shilling or two below what I had hoped for.' He shrugged his shoulders and separated the two inferior stones from their pile of three and pushed them across the table to Barney. 'Now your money *engelsman*, and for the other stone I will fight like the devil himself before I agree to your price.'

312

Barney paid him and then spirited the two lesser stones away inside his jacket pocket. From what he had learned, he would make nothing more than a pound profit on each stone. However, his dealings with Jooster had progressed amicably and he knew that in the future there would be more. The money he had just parted with, he looked upon as good investment, as encouragement – a down payment on some bigger fish, the proverbial sprat. Whether he had enough knowledge and business acumen to emerge from the next hour financially unscathed, still remained to be seen.

'First you take a *dop* with Hendrik Jooster, *engelsman*; then for one more time we talk money.'

Again Jooster helped himself from the open cigarette case and with bare fingers juggled a live coal from the edge of the fire, rolling the ember around the leathery palm of his hand before touching it to the cigarette. His servant ducked from under the sail, left a two thirds full bottle of Cape Smoke on the table and then, without speaking, like a wraith to deep forest disappeared back inside the shadows.

Jooster swung his attention to Kathleen.

'For six months I have lived like a pig in this hole in the ground, and every one of those days I have prayed to God Almighty for him to guide my hand; for just one time and then I will leave this *verdonder* place and go back to Natal. I leave it to those who will cut each other's throats to possess a piece of sour earth no bigger than my kaffir's kitchen.'

Jooster refilled two of the three enamel mugs to the half way mark, the remaining space he filled with Cape Smoke; Kathleen's, he filled to the brim with coffee alone.

'When the bottle is empty,' he told her, 'yours will be the eyes that lead our friend back to wherever he sees as fit enough to spend the night – if he is still able enough to walk. Stay awake, my *meisie* and watch a pair of grown men haggle as children over a stone no bigger than my smallest fingernail.'

Kathleen settled her elbows to the tabletop. The stone, she knew, would be hard won; the fight would be spirited. Indomitably, the battle for this beautiful two carat gem might well be carried deep into the early hours.

Jooster filled his mouth with smoke and coffee; Barney did the same and like running flames over dry grass, the potent spirit seared the lining of his throat.

'So, let us begin *engelsman*; give the stone your best price for Hendrik Jooster to pour his scorn on.'

Through slitted eyelids he watched Barney wrestle with his conscience. The stone's worth, Jooster already had a fair idea of, but to achieve what he was after would involve a full day's journeying to a buyer on the Pniel river diggings and the inevitable loss of a day's production from the pit.

From behind a thickening cloud of cigarette smoke, each man watched the other and in the place of gold coin and playing cards, a single perfect diamond, no bigger than a kernel of yellow maize demanded fully of their concentration.

'Never have you seen a stone more beautiful, *engelsman*,' Jooster rolled the diamond over with his fingertip, so that it dropped a pool of soft colours wherever it came to rest, 'she is small, yes, but her skin is smooth, clear, her eyes bright as the very stars above your head; the perfect shape and if she were indeed a woman, no amount of money would ever be enough.'

Barney played him down, the Afrikaner was well schooled. He went in with a price; an amount that he knew was markedly lower than the one he would eventually be forced into paying.

'Twenty pounds – ten pounds a carat. A fair enough price in any man's book, what do you say?'

Jooster's eyes narrowed and slowly, like a wolf watching the rabbit, his lips parted and from within that veil of flickering firelight, the Boer's teeth appeared as bone white and needle sharp.

'You insult me, *engelsman*,' he growled at the man seated opposite, 'perhaps the diamond is already where it belongs.' He reached across for the stone but Barney blocked the attempt.

'Thirty. Fifteen pounds for each carat.'

Jooster sat back on his stool. The night was all around them, only a thin vermilion smear remained above the western edge of the diggings. The Boer's hand went back to the bottle. Both mugs were again filled to within an inch of the brim and then topped off with sweet, steaming coffee.

With mute interest, Kathleen followed the goings on. From opposite sides of the rickety table, two men projected the full force of their will, one upon the other, each determined to gain the upper hand, for both were totally besotted with that small, enticing crystal of pure carbon.

Jooster lit another cigarette from the stub of the last and then ground the smouldering remains to nothing more than a black smear between his thumb and forefinger. He raised his eyes from the diamond and smiled sardonically at the newcomer.

'Have you ever been down inside the pit, *engelsman*?'

'In the mine itself?' Barney shook his head. 'Not yet, meneer, but I hope to soon.'

'Eighty-nine steps on the ladder to reach my staging.' Jooster let the statement hang; never for the slightest of moments did his eyes leave Barney's. 'Eighty-nine steps, *engelsman*, to a place where only at midday can the sun reach all the way down to the bottom. Not rats nor crows even; other than desperate men, no other living creature goes of their own accord to the bottom of that cursed pit.'

Barney drained his mug and pushed it over the table to Jooster for a refill. The mixture had warmed him through, though what mental strength he had left was running like fine sand from between his fingers.

315

'Perhaps, I could go with you – down in the pit. There's a lot for me to see, Dutchman. I could learn first-hand just how hard it is to find a stone such as the one you now torment me with.'

Jooster threw back his head and laughed.

'I like you, Meneer Barnato.'

He nodded his head, grasped both empty mugs with his left hand and extended his right to Barney.

'Twenty pounds for my princess and she is yours for as long as God allows.'

With relief, Barney accepted the hand; exhaustion had painted a blue line beneath each eye.

'Then twenty pounds it is. Now be a gentleman and pour us both a drink and then I must indebt myself to the lady here for her to see me safely home.'

# -18-

A note had been left at the desk, in the zealous care of the hotel's eagle-eyed night watchman; thin as a coolie rickshaw boy, the rangy Zulu stepped from the shadows and grinned at Kathleen.

'Madam said for me to give you this, Miss Kathleen. I have not forgotten.' He tipped his head to her. 'If it pleases, now I will light the stairs lamp for you.'

'Thank you Mathew.' She smiled her thanks to him and watched him light the candle for him to find his way upstairs to the landing. She unfolded the note and angled the written page to pick up light from a single, guttering lamp.

'It concerns you, Barney.' She handed him the sheet of paper. Barney held the note to the light and read aloud.

'Moved you to a bigger room. Knock on my door for the key.' He looked at Kathleen. 'Lizzie's door...? Where will I find it?'

'End of the corridor – last door on the left, number seventeen.' She turned for the stairs and with her foot on the bottom step she paused and called back to him. 'We will talk again in the morning,' her smile spread, 'watch your step Barnato; beware the lonely widow. Your rescue of Trixi-Marie from Hendrik Jooster put a merry twinkle in the old girl's eye. Reckon she's after you.'

'Your imagination is running amok, Katie my love,' theatrically he tipped his hat to her, 'not that I would blame the wench. Where else at this time of night might she find a man more dashing, more virile, more infested with dust and vermin from Jooster's mining camp than yours truly?'

Kathleen shook her head, the cockney was in a state of effervescence. Lively as a strutting Bantam cock he turned on his heels and made for Lizzie's door. Kathleen heard him knock, just once; then, subdued voices, the subtle click of the latch and a few seconds later, as she well expected, that final sound of a dead-lock bolt being slammed home echoed back to her from along the dark corridor.

# -19-

Barney Barnato plundered his plate of its soft fried eggs and bacon. He ate in silence and, like a man denied of a week's rations, devoured the food in a matter of minutes.

'The best I've had since leaving home.'

He belched into a linen napkin, dropped it alongside his plate and then smiled across the breakfast table at Kathleen.

'I know what you're thinking, Kathleen O'Rourke,' he wagged his forefinger, 'but I am the innocent party here;

believe me when I say that, armed only with my very best intentions did I venture close-in to the spider's web. My knocking on Lizzie's door was in itself the act of a tired, very slightly drunk, though innocent young man.'

Artfully, he steered Kathleen away from his dalliance.

'This claim you bought...?'

'A quarter share,' she corrected him, 'what of it?'

'Presumably, you will soon be starting work in the pit?'

'This coming week, unless Rhodes has a change of heart and he reneges on our agreement.'

Barney shook his head.

'He wouldn't do that, too upstanding. His reputation would take a tumble. Lizzie told me just how much clout he wields with the Diggers' Committee.' He winked an eye at her. 'Give me a year, two at the most and your friendly Jewish, learner kopje-walloper will also be up there with the best of them.'

Kathleen was impressed. 'You have obviously done your homework.'

'Lizzie is a good teacher.' Barney chanced and avoided her eyes. He made pretence of slowly refilling his coffee cup. 'Anything worth knowing and our darling employer has it stashed away inside that blonde head of hers,' he tapped the side of his head, 'and as a spin-off from what happened last night, my dearest most innocent friend, your uncle Barney knows exactly how to get at it.'

'This Saturday night,' Kathleen reminded him.

'I know, I know – time for me to earn an honest crust, I haven't forgotten.' He balled his fist in front of his face, all four knuckles were scarred – the gnarled, exposed roots of some ancient vine, only his thumb showed any sign of normality. 'Has to be a good one, Katie my love. Lose my first fight and my stay at The Queens will be less than short-lived.'

'People are already talking about it,' Kathleen went on, 'the Vaal river lot, they'll all be there. Like foxhounds they will be baying for your blood.'

318

'Then you and I will make some money out of man's raging thirst for morbid entertainment. Same as back in London, rather than spend their hard-earned cash on necessities, drunks will gamble away their last shilling on the outcome of a good bare knuckle fight.' He lit a cigarette and smiled through the smoke. 'Liquor, women and a good fight – the bloodier the better. If that's what the diggers want, then that's what the devils will get.'

He blew a perfect smoke ring and watched it rise on a cushion of warm air.

'I have a proposition for you.' He allowed the words to sink in before going on. With impassionate eyes, Kathleen waited for the punchline.

'Firstly,' he began, 'on the basis of your helping me up from the gutter, might I suggest the combining of our talents, a mutual partnership.'

He grinned at her, in a way that a wild dog would encourage its young to snap off a rabbit's head.

'Kopje-wallopers...?' Kathleen bridled.

Barney rolled his eyes to the ceiling.

'I thought more along the lines of upper class intermediaries.'

Kathleen shook her head.

'Won't have the time. Save for Saturdays and Sundays I'll be down in the pit.'

Barney leaned with his elbows against the table. Kathleen needed the hot spark of ambition put back in her eyes. He spoke slowly, accentuating his ideas.

'You are the miner, I, Barney Barnato will be your commodity manager, your business intermediary.'

'You will buy directly from me?'

Barney nodded his head. The more he brought the pieces together, the more, in Kathleen's eyes, it all fell apart.

'You will be entitled to one whole quarter of whatever comes out from claim 339.' He smiled at her, encouraging Kathleen's belief in what he was saying. 'A quarter share in production, everything taken care of. Even after taking into consideration labour costs and other running expenses the power you will have at your fingertips will be limitless.'

'Then why would I need you?' Now her eyes, like Barney's, glowed inventively. Her own entrepreneurial juices had started to flow. 'Why would I give up any of what I find when already I would have it all?'

Barney had pre-empted her negativity.

'Because most of the top buyers will be Jewish, Kathleen and you are not, a simple fact, nothing personal. Flash the old school tie in the right places, or in my case,' he tapped the side of his nose and smiled, 'the Isaac family business appendage.'

'Rhodes might well insist on paying my quarter share in cash,' Kathleen pointed out, 'or how would he decide on which stones he would be willing to part with?'

Barney pondered over every possibility, but the problem Kathleen had brought to mind refused to go away. He still had a lot to learn and reluctantly he accepted the fact. Rhodes would more than likely refuse to relinquish control of one quarter of all the diamonds taken from claim 339. With respect to buying and selling the stones, Cecil Rhodes and Kathleen O'Rourke were streets ahead of him. However, to Barney Barnato the business road was only open to those who followed it without any deviation, buying or selling diamonds from the Kimberley diggings, or bric-a-brac down London's Petticoat lane, the process of sale or acquirement was always the same; right approach, right time, right amount of ready cash and things would start to happen.

'Then we will change tack.' His acceptance of Kathleen's point of view was hard to swallow, but she was right. 'I will negotiate directly with the man himself.'

Kathleen shook her head and smiled.

'You haven't got a clue, Barnato. Rhodes would never entertain the idea; the man would swallow you whole. He deals in thousands, tens of thousands even, your meddling in his affairs will bring you nothing but trouble.' Now it was Kathleen's turn to put forward an idea. 'Go back to the beginning, learn your trade, put up your little shack and fly the flag of England from its roof. Become the diggers' number one, kopje-walloper, someone they can trust. Walk the diggings and befriend the men who know what it's like to work the skin from their hands and lose their fat to the pit. Offer advice when you can and take it on the chin when you lose a diamond to some wilier, better man.'

For a third time she refilled their cups with coffee and momentarily looked back over the passage of that last month. Whatever insights she had accumulated came from those who knew, from the likes of Thomas Bradshaw, Cecil Rhodes, Hendrik Jooster and droves of talkative drunks at Lizzie's bar. Her accrued knowledge of the pit and the selling-on of its diamonds was, to Kathleen O'Rourke, a treasure house of information.

'Build on your winnings by doing what you do best,' she bunched her fist and held the weapon in front of Barney's face, 'the money you make in the ring will set you on the road.'

'So where do I go from here?'

'You find yourself the best available site on the diggings,' Kathleen replied, 'and a man good enough with a hammer and saw to build your first premises. Your winnings this coming Saturday will see to the fixtures and fittings; couple of chairs, table, weigh scales and whatever else you will need for Barney Isaacs Barnato to trade as a respected diamond merchant.'

## 20

'The place is filling up too quickly. Another few minutes and we'll be forced to close the doors or risk a free-for-all.' Lizzie Jardine signalled to her man on the door; her hotel was bursting at the seams, the saloon bar and main hall thrummed with excitement. Diggers packed in three deep to the bar, but like before, their eyes were on that heavy, red velvet curtain where it hung from its rail on the east wall, for every man within fifty miles of Kimberley town had heard about the fight.

Kathleen and Trixi-Marie kept the money flowing, poured drinks, lit cigars and took bets on the outcome of the bout. Lizzie scribbled off betting slips – even money – no limit to the amount wagered. The till bell pinged and the cash drawer filled and Lizzie Jardine licked her lips in anticipation of that full night's takings; tonight would be a good night.

'The opposition, where is he from?' Kathleen asked. Her eyes flicked over the curtain, there was movement there, and voices, however, noise from around the bar all but covered them over. Like Kathleen, Lizzie Jardine could not restrain herself, mesmerised by what might be going on behind the curtain.

'The Pniel diggings on the Vaal, some of his digger friends are bringing him in on the late coach.' Lizzie glanced over her shoulder at the bar clock. 'Chances are they will be along soon enough and mark my words young lady, like their champion, their bets will be big.' She shook her head at Kathleen and smiled thinly. 'I hope your Jewish friend is as good as he says or we'll all three of us end up stripped clean and lynched from the hotel's chandeliers.'

'There's always the back door,' Kathleen chuckled and pushed another bottle of White Lightning across the bar.

'Got yourself an admirer, girl,' Lizzie pointed with her eyes, 'up against the wall; been watching you for near on ten minutes – black beard and slouch hat.'

Kathleen saw him, but only for a second and then he was gone, away inside the crowd. Uncertainty fluttered inside her head; could have been anybody, someone she knew or then again, perhaps not. Either way it did not matter, there were too many distractions for her to concentrate on finding that face again.

Lizzie turned to Trixi-Marie and tapped her on the shoulder.

'We need a curtain raiser, girl. Get that buxom body and nightingale voice of yours up on the stage before they tear the place apart. Wear something sparkly and not too modest; give the buggers a glimpse of Kimberley paradise.' She steered Trixi away from the counter. 'Fifteen minutes to doll up and I want you up there.' She leaned over and planted a kiss on Trixi's forehead. 'Reduce this mob to eating out of your hand and I'll pay you double for the night and as much champagne as that sweet little belly of yours can hold.'

'Plus my usual fifty percent...?'

'That as well,' Lizzie smarted, 'better you get a move on, time to knock 'em dead sweetheart before they lose what patience they have left and rip my curtains down.'

Lizzie stood in for Trixi-Marie at the bar and kept the beer flowing. The main outer doors were closed; wall to wall the room was shored full with mining men, their clamouring for entertainment now incessant. To Lizzie Jardine it seemed as though an eternity had passed before the velvet curtains whispered back from centre stage.

'What do you big spending Kimberley gents want?' Trixi's voice ripped as a velvet tide above the melee and in an instant the clamouring faded to nothing. Save for the furtive rustle of boots to a sawdust-scattered floor and the clink of glasses, there was no other noise. However, every man in the room craned his neck for a clear view of the

Queens Hotel's latest temptress.

With both arms outstretched and palms upturned to the heavens, through her insightful act of supplication, Trixi-Marie drew them out from their stupor.

'Cat got your tongues! I asked you what you want, gentlemen. Or are those tongues of yours slack and soft as your trouser fronts?'

Like shoaling fish in thrall to powerful ocean currents, more than a hundred diggers were mesmerised by what they were seeing and hearing and within those same few seconds, one by one the comments started to fly.

'What does it take for you to slip the knot on your bodice, sweetheart!'

Trixi took no offense from the innuendo and instead, singled out the source of the ribaldry. Her voice remained that sultry Karoo breeze, stirred from deep summer, but now her eyes glittered provocatively, bombarded by light from three crystal chandeliers they sought out her adversary.

'You aren't strong enough mister. It'll take a man on a wild horse, not some boy fresh out from school.'

The diggers erupted and it was then that the first gold coin clattered onto the stage.

From the metal steamer trunk in her room, Trixi had rummaged out a black, lace-front bodice and scarlet taffeta bustle skirt – at her throat she had fastened a ribbon of black velvet, and her high-heeled black leather boots were tightly laced from knee to ankle. To her rear, the pleats had been freed from their bustle and fell as a foot-long taffeta train for it to whisper over the floor, though at the front, Trixi had purposely raised the skirt to just an inch below the level of her knee. As a titillating finishing touch, she had chosen a pair of fingerless wristlets; cut from burgundy velvet and edged with French lace they accentuated the slenderness of her hands. However, elegant couture was a far cry from what the diggers were after.

324

Trixi gestured to the man watching from his place at the piano, warning him to stand at the ready and then, for the benefit of her audience, she turned her face in line with the nearest chandelier. The act was purposeful and cleverly orchestrated. Gathering in that strength of light thrown down by those fifty candles, she allowed it to flood her hair with spangles and fill her eyes with starlight. The action of tilting her head stroked the shadow from her sternum, and now her breasts showed up as pale, unblemished crescent moons where they part protruded, swelling provocatively above the laced front of her bodice.

Every man in the room was filled with wanton admiration, enraptured by the night's manifestation of their ultimate fantasy, for standing alone on the stage was this lustrous, beautiful woman, scantily robed in scarlet taffeta and black velvet. Like Karoo grass under warm sun, her hair reflected the candlelight, and in exchange, to those who ogled it, she gave them back the soft gleam of spun gold.

'Give us Maggie for starters, sweetheart!' Others picked up on the familiarity of the title and even before the opening notes were punched from the piano, grown men steeled themselves against the melancholy they knew would come over them.

Trixi-Marie nodded her head to the piano player and on his animated count of three, the voice of the diggers' adopted angel floated down from the stage; as a mellifluous opium breeze it moved amongst them.

Lizzie Jardine, like the men across the counter from her, lifted her head and stepped back from what she was doing. Save for Trixi's voice, the piano and the ticking of the bar clock there was nothing else for her hearing to compete with.

Not until the beginnings of the third verse did anyone move, and rather than usual bawdy outbursts, it was the sound of money striking the podium floorboards that stirred the atmosphere.

## 21

Cecil Rhodes opened a chink in the velvet curtains and peered down at the crowd. Behind him, manila rope and supported wooden poles had been used to fashion a makeshift boxing ring, Rhodes had ensured that the proper measurements were adhered to and that the poles were scrubbed and sanded down to ward off unnecessary injury. The stage had been cleared of all its fancy frippery and made ready for the fight, and on the other side of the heavy curtains, where once there were a hundred diggers, now, like a settling plague of winged locusts there was well in excess of a hundred more.

'Where in God's name are they all coming from?'

'Through the stable yard,' said Kathleen, 'in through the scullery door before we knew what the devils were up to.'

Rhodes released the curtains and turned to Barney Barnato.

'You are sure about going through with this?'

'And how would any man judge as to what he is sure of and what he is not, Rhodes?' He grinned at the allusion. 'Sure of winning? Or sure of getting my face pushed round to the back of my head, whatever lady luck has in store for me. If I lose,' He shrugged his shoulders, 'come visit me at the infirmary and bring a bottle of brandy with you; not grapes, I detest grapes.'

Rhodes chuckled at his humour.

'Ten more minutes,' Kathleen warned them and looked about her for any sign of Barney's opponent. 'If he doesn't show by nine o'clock,' she clicked her fingers, 'he will lose by default.' She turned to Barney and made sure the strips of cloth he asked to be tied around his wrists were still tight. 'You're in this right up to your neck, Barnato. Reckon you should have stuck to juggling beer bottles on stage with Trixi-Marie, that and keeping Lizzie happy.'

Barney could not stop himself from smiling, stripped to the waist, he epitomised the long-haul street fighter. The six hundred mile walk from the Cape to the Kimberley diggings had left him lean and hungry looking. His body, though slim, was hard set with muscle; wiry as a desert fox he was more than ready for a fight.

'Fighting for a living I find to be a lot less hazardous, my sweet.' Gingerly, he felt for the scratch marks left by Lizzie's finger nails; they were still oozing lymph and stung with the rawness of fresh, acid burns when he touched them, 'fighting a lioness even more so; her claws, I would imagine are a lot shorter than her ladyship's.'

A roar of approval went up from beyond the curtains. Kathleen re-opened the peep hole and peered through at the gallery. As if a million pairs of eyes were looking back at her, she baulked under the scrutiny.

'Damn it, he's here – just coming in through the front door.'

'What's he like?' Barney needed the measure of his opponent. He jumped up from his seat, climbed between the ropes and took over Kathleen's place at the curtain.

'Big as a bloody ox! Half my weight again, I would stake a guinea on it.'

Kathleen exploited the folly of his fighting for money.

'No one else but yourself to blame for this. You could always make a run for it and I'll tell them your wife pitched up unannounced and dragged you back to the marital bed in London.'

'Let me see him,' Rhodes brushed between them and put his eye to the hole. 'Well, well, Barnato. Today you have drawn the short straw my friend. Seen this chap before, the Dutchman is well known for his underhanded fighting techniques. Keep his hands away from your neck, or I will be footing the bill for your plot in our Kimberley Cemetery.' He stood back and with commiserations gently patted Barney on the shoulder. Like Kathleen, Rhodes could not resist the opportunity for him to play the comedian. 'That is old boy, if we find anything left of you for us to bury.'

Rhodes re-lit his cigar and as a momentary distraction from the inevitable, watched the smoke fasten itself to the velvet curtaining.

'Who will stand as your second to this debacle?'

'I will,' Kathleen announced and stared objectively at Rhodes. 'I know as much about bare knuckle fighting as is needed, and besides, he's kind of short-changed in the friend department; there is no one else.'

Rhodes smiled at her commitment to helping the stranger; Kathleen O'Rourke was ready to bare her soul to the mob. Unequivocally, her borderline feminist ideals would be flown in the face of upwards of two hundred drunken diggers.

Drawn to both the Jew and the American by their strength of camaraderie and his own empathy for the underdog, Rhodes prayed for a favourable outcome. What was happening now, neither one of them could ever have foreseen. Whether or not anything commendable would be left for them on fate's doorstep would be realised within that next half-hour.

The crowd roared for the curtains to move and like wild animals they sniffed the smoke-laden air for blood. Rhodes nodded his head to Kathleen.

'Neither one of you has to go through with this.'

Barney grinned at him.

'A full belly or my quick demise in the ring; either way, we will know soon enough.' He flexed his fingers and instinctively balanced he weight to the balls of his feet. 'Open the curtains, Rhodes and to hell with the consequences, let's get this over with.'

Rhodes flipped the lid on his watch – the hands showed exactly nine o'clock.

## 22

Barney stood with his back to a corner ring-post, his arms rested along the topmost ropes. Kathleen leaned at his shoulder, towel draped around her neck and through her best endeavours did her utmost to bolster his confidence.

'He's big,' she admitted, 'but not that big.'

'Then swap places with me, woman. God gave this big ape shovels instead of hands.'

Less than two yards from the ring, a solid redoubt of human faces looked to the referee, urging him to strike his bell. Like a sea at neap tide, the mob as a whole rolled and troughed, waiting for the onset; each man forced hard up against the next, pushed forwards to a point where men in the front rows were hardly able to move. In the ring, opposite Barney, a bare-chested gorilla of man in breeches and mining boots tested the strength of his grip on the ropes, but his eyes were on Barney. One blow to Englishman's head with the flat of his hand and it would all be over; a purse of forty pounds, his for the taking.

'Gentlemen!' The referee raised his hands. Lizzie's cellar man had been persuaded to take on the mantle of adjudicator, himself a powerful figure, with a temper to match.

'Sure as damn it there aren't any ladies down here so ring the god-damned bell, Walsh or I'll climb up there and fight the Boer myself!'

Joe Walsh acknowledged the crowd and then turned to face both contestants.

'You know the rules – a round ends when either one of you is downed by a punch or a throw, half a minute's rest then back on the scratch line.' He moved to centre stage and with the toe of his shoe indicated the chalk line. 'If you cannot find the strength to come to scratch, you will be declared the loser.'

Walsh scowled at the Afrikaner; rumours of his flaunting the rules were rife.

'On penalty of disqualification, Meneer Vermeulen, there will be no biting, gouging or scratching with the fingernails; nor will head butting your opponent or striking him whilst down be tolerated. Any one of these will be deemed as a foul and the offender will forfeit the match.'

He crossed the ring and stood directly in front of Vermeulen and though some two inches less in height, his eyes were filled with foreboding; that of the Bodmin executioner at the point of his throwing the dead-fall lever. With his back to the crowd, purposely, Joe lowered his voice.

'I know of your reputation, Vermeulen, bear in mind, meneer that you are not beyond the rule of law. This is not some no-holds-barred event expected of your Pniel diggings. Keep your hands away from Barnato's throat or I will put my pistol to your head and not even for one second will I hesitate before pulling the trigger.'

# -23-

Those last few seconds before the referee sounded his bell were, to Barney Barnato, the shortest moments of his life. His consummate mastering of an East End upbringing was about to be tested to the full; every trick in Barney's book of artful irregularities would be needed if he were to survive this fight. Pound for pound, the odds were stacked in favour of the Boer. The power in his right arm alone was enough; when he clenched his fist, the long muscles inside his forearm flexed and jumped as heavily laden pit ropes.

'Watch that right arm of his,' Kathleen warned, 'run him to ground, he's too heavy in the gut for him to go the distance. Stay out of reach. Try to match his strength and Vermeulen will finish you.'

'Like a bantam cock with a fattened turkey,' Barney concurred and with a final, lopsided grin handed his spectacles and bowler hat over to his second. Whatever the outcome, the run-up to it would be arduous, perhaps even life threatening; his seeing that next day's sunrise was by no means guaranteed.

Barney stretched his back to the ropes and steeled himself mentally for the rigours of a long fight. He glanced over his shoulder; the room was filled to the gunnels with diamond miners. The same miners who, after this fight, would recognise him either as their champion, or wash their hands of the nondescript, pretentious smouse from Blighty. On or off the diggings, if he lost, few would acknowledge his aspirations to rise up through the ranks from lowly, learner kopje-walloper, to that of the reputable diamond buyer; his life as a credible dealer would be over before his first solo foray onto the Kimberley diggings had chance to find a footing.

The bell clamoured and Walsh called them into scratch.

'You will fight till either one of you is knocked down or concedes the match honourably to his opponent.' He waved them either side of the scratch line and like dogs bred to die in the pit, they squared up.

'*Ek slaan jou lekker dood, engelsman*; I will beat you to death,' Vermeulen growled at Barney, and had the cockney not been quick on his feet, his head would have at that very moment been rolling out from under the ropes.

A roar went up from the gallery. There was money on both men, a lot of it. Lizzie Jardine's cash drawer had been emptied four times and the money locked away in the steel safe at her feet. On a shelf below the counter top, Lizzie's fingers found the stock of a twelve bore Winchester double; loaded with buckshot, the weapon's presence gave her comfort, though it was the sight of Barney Barnato stripped to the waist that now gripped her full attention.

She trembled at her recollection of his first night at the Queens and her breathing caught; unwittingly, she pressed herself hard up to the corner of the drawer. From where she was standing, her view of the makeshift boxing ring was open and though some forty pounds the lighter of the two, in Lizzie's eyes, Barney's presence completely overshadowed that of the Pniel giant. She was forced to incline her head for her to catch Barney's terse rebuff of the Boer's intimidation.

'Then you had better try harder, Dutchman. Are you slow like this for your wife in the bedroom?'

A fist the size of a tsamma melon hissed just inches from Barney's chin, and whilst the uppercut still travelled towards the chandelier, Barney drove his own, bony knuckles deep into Vermeulen's soft flesh, an inch below the Boer's ribs. Like a boulder shocked loose from the mountainside, Vermeulen rolled sideways-on to his attacker and grunted like an angered wild pig when he stumbled against the ropes. Barney increased the consequence of his gamesmanship.

'That's what she told me, Boer; pretty girl, I remember her well.'

Vermeulen gathered himself and now, enraged by the Englishman's goading, like a Zulu in thrall of the turning battle his eyes misted over; there was nothing, nor any hidden depths he would not descend to in order to destroy his adversary. Brought on more by rage than physical exertion, the Boer's face had darkened to a deep, ember red as far down as his throat, and as though he were caught in the spray from a tumbling waterfall his chest and forehead glistened with perspiration.

'You're leaking sweat, Vermeulen,' Barney took advantage of his weakness, 'and your face is the colour of a baboon's backside in full season; maybe your heart is not so good anymore.' He lured the Boer into lumbering after him; purposely, he increased the speed of his footwork and spun round the ring like some lively will-o'-the-wisp.

'Maybe we should get the doctor in to check your staying power, it's obvious to every man in Kimberley that you lie on your back and let your wife do all the work.'

'*Ja engelsman*, save your breath for when I catch up with you. Stand and fight like a man, why do you dance about like a rat on a stove plate.'

Barney danced the Boer into a lather, jabbing at Vermeulen's gut and sternum with his left, feigning an all-out attack with his right, but always withdrawing to a safe distance before another of the Boer's round-house thunderbolts slogged a hole in the air, so close to Barney's head that the wind from it ruffled his hair.

Kathleen watched their every move and concentrated her efforts on picking up on the Boer's propensity, for as a young girl in her native Dakota, from her hiding place on the roof of a local saloon, she had watched many fights turn bloody. Sometimes for hours on end, wild, relentless men beat each other to a pulp – mostly over a woman, or the lesser trouble, bad debt. However, every fighter developed his own unique ways with which to confound his opponent. The pretence of losing concentration, feigning disorientation or loss of footing – all of these ploys were carefully orchestrated and would, on many occasion draw in the ignorant contender, more often than not to his swift demise. It was then that Barney appeared to slip on the wooden flooring and went down onto one knee. Vermeulen moved in for the quick kill but the referee warned him off.

'The man is down, Vermeulen; one knee and one hand on the floor so let him be. You both have thirty seconds to rest and eight more to get back on the line.'

Barney found his feet and went back to his corner, he winked an eye at Kathleen and took a swig of water from the bottle she held to his lips.

'He's strong, the man is going to take some beating, sweetheart, pray for the ape to run out of steam.'

Kathleen made pretence of towelling Barney's shoulders,

her face close-in to his.

'Watch his face. Every time he goes for that shovel hook, he closes his left eye.'

'You're sure of that?'

'Sure as I'll ever be. I've been watching him – left eye closes, then comes the hook.'

Barney nodded his head and winked again.

'I'll turn on the speed for five more minutes and then we'll have the bastard. Well spotted. Time to pick up our money and get out of here, his breath is the by-product of an opened grave.'

The bell sounded; both men returned to the line and squared up. Again, Barney goaded the Afrikaner, but this time with a wild rolling of his eyes and a purposeful, high pitched girly voice; his smile now fey and thin-lipped, that of the lunatic inmate too soon released from Bedlam's pox hospital.

'Fancy another early swing at my head, deary,' he tapped himself on the chin, 'but this time I'll be ready for you.' His voice lowered. 'And leave off eating dogs, meneer, your mouth stinks a hundred times worse than the rotting corpse of a Whitechapel whore.'

Vermeulen came over the scratch line, fists flailing and his face redder than seeds from the African lucky bean. In his eyes there burned a dark malevolent storm, the madness of a hundred raging men. To Barney Barnato, his opponent was now the bolting cart horse, eyes rolled back in their sockets, nostrils flared and expelling fire – only a bullet would stop him now. Even Walsh, the referee, was loath to stand in Vermeulen's way. Barney realised his mistake and instead of attempting to down the giant, stepped to the side and flicked the Boer's ankle with the toe of his boot. Like a roped, rodeo heifer, Vermeulen crashed to the floorboards a yard from Kathleen's feet, and as if the stage were now in a state of being demolished, men in the first two rows reared back for fear of being crushed. Like the hum from a disturbed hive, anger rose up to both contestants from out of the crowd.

'On your feet Vermeulen! I backed a fiver on your winning, the Jew is half your size!'

'Finish him, Barnato! My money's on you for the win, run the bastard Dutchman into the ground!'

Miraculously, before the referee had the chance to declare the round complete, Vermeulen took hold of the ropes and dragged himself upright, but instead of returning to his corner he was now the tall ship turning broadside on for a fresh line of attack. Swinging away from the ropes and with blood-reddened eyes, he bore down upon the Jew.

The image perceived from four yards distant was to Barney Barnato in denial of any human form, for the wide expanse of Vermeulen's outstretched arms was now the terrible armoured boss of the enraged bull buffalo – the crenulated battering ram, and above the roar and curse of the crowd, like that of the beast itself, the deep drum of Vermeulen's bellowing was thick with malice, blackened with rage.

'Get out of his way!' Kathleen shouted a warning. It was then that Barney turned face-on to the full force of Vermeulen's charge.

The Boer was now the solid wall of water and nothing in its path would escape; everything would be swept away. Barney balanced his weight evenly to the balls of his feet and as a final act of desperation leaned into the attack; he would make sure of at least one last, full-blown hammer blow for the Boer to remember him by.

With the full weight of his body stacked behind his fist, Barney powered himself forwards, ready to take the Boer head-on, mid-stride, mid-ring.

The crowd fell silent and collectively held its breath for there was not a man amongst them who would have dared go head-to-head with the burly Afrikaner. It was then that Vermeulen's left eye blinked shut so that intuitively, Barney rolled his weight out of line with the shovel hook

335

he knew must follow. When the two men came together the chandelier above their heads shuddered on its fastenings.

Mere inches to the left of Vermeulen's sternum, his ribcage absorbed the full force of the collision so that a single, living rib sheered cleanly off from its anchorage. Vermeulen's momentum was enough for the fractured rib to be turned inwards and the razor edge plunged deep inside the Boer's already, diseased heart. Barney spun off sideways into the ropes, but with the air driven out from his lungs, he was unable to defend himself; he waited for the Afrikaner to turn on him, fists raised for that final *coup de grâce*.

However, Vermeulen went down on his knees, arms loose at his sides, a bewildered expression came over his face and those dark eyes that stared at Kathleen were already sightless. Outwardly, there was no sign of any injury, but for those next few seconds, from his ruptured heart, the blood pumped hard and hot inside the chest cavity.

Kathleen saw him flounder. She sensed the severity of the injury and was half way between the ropes just as Vermeulen's limp body slumped forwards onto the wooden flooring.

'Someone get a doctor up here on the stage!' Frantically she searched for a pulse. Vermeulen's eyes fluttered and in that moment of his dying were crystal-bright as the chandelier above his head.

With impotent regret, Kathleen looked up at the referee and shook her head.

'This man is dead, sir, there is no heartbeat.'

Vermeulen's corpse was stretchered out from the main hall and in a small annexe storeroom was laid out full length to a makeshift bed of oak tables. The doctor completed his examination of the deceased, filled out the necessary declaration and handed the completed death certificate to Lizzie Jardine. He avoided her eyes, her ten pound note already folded away inside his jacket pocket.

'Heart failure. A day, a month, would have happened sooner rather than later, the man was obviously on the verge of a massive seizure.' He packed away his paraphernalia and snapped the catch on his leather valise. 'I'm sure you will agree, the strain induced by the fighting would have been enough to turn the scales.' He tipped his hat to Lizzie. 'I'll have someone round to pick him up. What about burying the man?'

Lizzie shook her head.

'I will see to the cost, it's the least I can do for the poor soul.'

The doctor turned his attentions to Barney.

'Easy on with that wrist of yours, young man. Keep it bandaged for a week to ten days, or at least until the swelling goes down completely, and no heavy lifting.'

Barney nodded his head. 'How much do I owe for the treatment?'

'Nothing at all,' Lizzie interrupted, 'you were working for me when it happened; the hotel will cover the cost of your injury.'

'Once again I am indebted to your kindness, madam.' His eyes flared, the suggestiveness of the attention flustered her; her cheeks coloured to a soft pink and then to a deeper, almost bright red where the blush had spread to her throat. Realising that others might well be listening, she steered her interests back to squaring the bill.

'Thank you doctor, please have your invoice delivered here to the hotel, to me personally.'

Lizzie waited for the doctor to leave and then closed the door. With a wry smile she turned the key and waved the death certificate under Barney's nose.

'The strain on his heart, Mister Barnato?' she chuckled softly and dropped the official cause of death on top of Vermeulen's body. 'Massive seizure?' She shook her head. 'I think not.' She looped both arms around Barney's neck. 'Whisky and an open box of Romeo y Julieta cigars in exchange for your blow by blow account with our friend over there on the table.'

Without waiting for a reply, she drew his head down level with her own and then insistently, she drove her tongue deep inside his mouth. When she pulled away, her eyes were almost closed, from low in her throat her voice was now the soft, bass purr of the partially sated cat.

'Upstairs to my room, Barnato, time for you to work off some of that debt.'

# -25-

Sunlight flooded in through the Standard Bank's windows and though still relatively early on, the temperature inside the manager's office was already inching upwards. Cecil Rhodes stood to his favourite vantage point; from the window, he could watch the goings on between the bank's frontage and the pit edge.

'Convince me otherwise, Mister Barnato. Any astute businessman must certainly look upon your setting up as a dealer in precious stones as an adversary, rather than an asset.' He turned on his heels, hands folded behind his back. 'I can recall from memory a hundred other desperate souls who would jump through hoops for a chance of the same opportunity.' In that light, his eyes were very blue, iridescent even. He smiled thinly, more so with his eyes than with his mouth. 'Would I be right in saying that it was our mutual friend, Kathleen O'Rourke who planted the seed?'

Barney nodded his head; covering over Kathleen's involvement with his affairs would attract more trouble than the subterfuge was worth.

'She told me about her investing a goodly sum in the diggings.'

'Claim 339,' Rhodes smiled at the truth and accepted the fact that within that next week every digger in Kimberley would know of his dealings with Kathleen, 'a one quarter share for as long as she can stomach the degradation of her working the staging on my behalf.'

'The woman shows great courage.'

'More than a lot of men I know,' Rhodes agreed, 'though some would interpret that courage as an obsession, madness even. There are numerous other business opportunities more suited to a woman. Her foregoing them in favour of the diggings somewhat beggars belief, Barnato.' He went back to his place at the window. 'Why would she do it? Why would any other woman you know risk their all inside that stinking pit?' He frowned at the perplexity of his own question. 'No my friend, I believe there is some greater reason for her venturing onto the diggings – something more demanding of her time than a chance to fill her cap with dirt and diamonds.'

'I would rather that you were aware of my intentions from the onset. Finding out through a third party would create a nuisance for the both of us.' Barnato paused, but only momentarily. 'My proposition then – how do you view it?'

'With some interest,' Rhodes admitted, 'though not without concern, Mister Barnato.' Once again, he turned to face the source of the conundrum. 'I accept your willingness to buy diamonds from Miss O'Rourke's part

339

ownership of claim 339. However, I am in business to make money, not only for myself, but for the furtherance of a cause which through present circumstance, at least for now, you would find more fanciful than real.'

'I did not expect to come away from here scot-free, Rhodes. All I ask is that I be given a fair chance to purchase stones from you at a fair price, hopefully with some leeway for a slight profit, nothing more.'

Rhodes warmed to him, the Jew's business aspirations were totally transparent, there was nothing underhanded or sinister about him. Helping Barnato onto that first rung of the kopje-walloper's rickety ladder would provide him with a much needed ally amongst Kimberley's growing army of diamond dealers. If well-heeled men like himself were renowned as the heartbeat of the diggings, then men like Barney Barnato were the barometers of the future; exploratory fingers to that very pulse.

'I will meet you halfway, Barnato. I will grant you part access to whatever diamonds are brought out from claim 339 and at a price as seen by the both of us to be of a fair value. However, you will deal directly and exclusively with me. Any diamonds purchased from the said claim, will be done so only through my own brokerage, that way I am able to keep control of price, numbers purchased and if anything untoward comes to light, I shall be the first to know about it.'

Barney smiled at the success of his venture.

'I am indebted to you, Rhodes.' He extended his hand. 'You will not regret my coming to Kimberley.'

Rhodes accepted the hand. 'Regrets are collected only by fools, Mister Barnato, I see myself as more the collector of grandiose possibilities; rather my commitment to the furtherance of our imperial holdings in Africa than wasting my time with disappointments.' He gestured to Barney for him to retrieve his hat and jacket from the rack near the door.' Walk with me, we still have an hour or two left before Paterson buys me lunch at the Queens.'

Both men stood shoulder to shoulder at the very edge of the pit, for those first few minutes they were mesmerised by the sheer scale of the ruination. Even Rhodes, as a man who had been hardened to it, only through his indomitable strength of will was he able to sweep aside that perverse entrancement of the deep diggings.

'The words have been used a thousand times before, Barnato, but all these men I see at work down there in the ground? I see them as ants, drones, harvesters – call them what you will, but they are so alike, every desperate one of them.'

Still with his eyes locked to the deepest innards of the pit, Barney struggled to draw any sense from out of the chaos, the ground itself was a chequerboard of broken earth; hundreds of square stagings, each one of them in a different state of development and all were no more than ten yards across, hosts to a thousand native diggers and most were covered in shadow, for once the sun had passed its zenith the lowest claims were left abandoned by its light.

'Claim 339,' asked Barney, 'where is it, exactly?'

'You are standing within an arm's length of where it began,' Rhodes told him and pointed out the boundaries. 'Thomas Bradshaw, the previous claim holder took the staging down to a hundred feet below the surface.' He inched his way forwards and with due care peered down from the edge. 'There, directly below us, on that ledge is where your friend, Kathleen O'Rourke will be working; God help her, Barnato. A month from now and either her fortune will be well established, or like skin from her ruined hands her reputation will hang in tatters.'

Barney took a small step forward for him to grasp the topmost section of a wooden ladder. With trepidation, he moved to the pit edge and like Rhodes gazed down into the furthest, darkest limits of the void. His breathing tripped and like some phantom bird of prey his fear of heights soared upwards through the dust to greet him.

'Be careful,' Rhodes warned, 'the topmost section of sidewall is in a constant state of poor order, only a week ago a digger lost his life through doing the same.'

Barney drew back from the precipice, droplets of sweat stood out from his forehead and unlike his experience in the boxing ring, here on the pit edge, fear was still his master. Aware of his own mortality, he sucked in the air and gratefully he revered the hard, friendly ground beneath his feet.

'You say that Kathleen found nerve enough for her to climb down to the staging?'

Rhodes nodded his head.

'Bradshaw told me as much,' he smiled at Barnato, 'quick as a flash, he said, without any hesitation, old boy.'

Comparatively, Rhodes recalled Barney's moment of triumph over the Afrikaner. Now, that same man, who without any thoughts for his own wellbeing, had battled and beaten an opponent of almost twice his own size, looked upon his accomplishment through small eyes. Compared to Kathleen's domination of that makeshift ladder, his victory in the boxing ring appeared to Barney Barnato as to be insignificant. Rhodes picked up on the cockney's latest bête noire and immediately, he understood. Being overshadowed by a woman's determination to descend the deep pit would be difficult for any man to accept.

'It takes time, my friend. You have chanced to look inside another world. Getting to grips with climbing the ladders is something that every new digger and dealer alike must aspire to – or give in to your fear and trade your line of work for something more sedate.'

Rhodes lit up a pair of Turkish cigarettes and handed one to Barney.

'The overly timid should find themselves a more suitable profession, one that lends itself to earning a living above the ground, rather than below.' With purpose, he went on with the warning. 'And believe me, when I say you are far from being the first man ever to shy clear of climbing the ladders. Bigger men than you and I have walked away from their first day's work in the pit. Many of them never come back; those who do, find the courage and the will with which to make their fortunes.' He inhaled deeply, flicked the spent match out into the void and watched it tumble. 'Make up your mind my friend, choose which of the two you will side with – only you can decide. Favour the latter, then might I suggest you come to terms with your fear of high places, or prepare yourself for the discomfiture of being upstaged by our lady friend.'

Barney drew on the cigarette and though only slightly, his fingers trembled, as best he could he forced back his fear of heights and looked out across the abyss.

'A week at the most and I shall have it whipped, Rhodes. Whatever it takes, I will not be beaten by some mere hole in the ground.'

'Splendid attitude,' relief lit up in Rhodes' eyes, 'then I am sure we might well make a go of things. Let us move on.' He turned away from the open workings and encouraged Barney to follow him.

'Here we have it then, the main reason for my bringing you along; have a look at this, something every kopje-walloper worth his salt should be made aware of right from the onset.'

A digger sat with his elbows splayed to a covering of yellow gravel spread across his sorting table, he recognised the authoritative figure of Cecil Rhodes and politely relinquished his seat. The table's only protection from the elements was a broken shadow cast by a sheet of tattered canvas. Without embarrassment, Rhodes sat down and gestured for Barney to stand alongside him. With an outstretching of both his hands, animatedly he

343

encompassed the length and breadth of the miner's workspace.

'Not hard for you to fathom out I would hope; a metal-topped table of sorts, loaded with ground from the sieving cradles.' He looked at Barney and found recognition of what was going on. 'Somewhere amongst this lot, we might, if luck is on the sorter's side, help him find the price of his next meal.' He held out his hand to the claim holder and with a wry smile took charge of the digger's sorting tool. Cut from a thin slat of boxwood, the business end of the scraper had, through endless hours of employment been worn to a thin edge.

'The key to good sorting, Barnato, is achieved only through experience. By their own admission, many a new chum arriving on the diggings has unwittingly indulged himself with costly mistakes,' he grinned at his protégée, 'a degree in mining techniques or the use of explosives will stand you well in many circumstances, but here on the diamond diggings?' With a vigorous shake of the head, he dispelled the myth. 'It is the man with a strong back, a keen eye and the tenacity of an elephant searching out a cupful of water from some desert riverbed who will be most likely to succeed.'

Rhodes leaned over the table, his power of concentration now supreme. With his head bowed close-in to the sieved earth, he focused on the job at hand. Doggedly, he explored the gravel for size, colour and any quirkiness of shape that might give away the whereabouts of even the smallest of precious stones; a mere chip even. With deft fingers and a keen eye, he studied the screened earth for the tiniest pointers; cajoling with his scraper, ready to pounce on any irregularities that, through the passing of his time in Kimberley had been hard learned and were still, deeply embedded within his memory. He knew that the smaller gems might easily be overlooked and discarded within a single careless moment, hiding from the searcher beneath a thin disguise before being swept away with the waste gravel.

Barney held his breath; anticipation strained his senses to the limit. With every flick of that wooden spatula, wide-eyed he urged Rhodes to hand him the chance of making his first legitimate find.

Rhodes sensed his agitation and looked up from the sorting table.

'The look on your face is more intense than that of a starving vulture, Barnato,' he stood up from the table and handed over the scraper. 'I would rather watch than be hounded by your lascivious excitement, see what you can come up with man.'

With the eagerness of a terrier's nose to its first rat hole, Barney swapped places with his mentor. Before him, spread from a small heap at the table head, a thin covering of yellow Kimberlite caught at the light; chips of peridot, jasper and pyrope-rich garnet glittered from amongst the overall blanket of decomposed matrix. At first, it was these bright though worthless indicators which commanded his attention, and for a while longer, Rhodes gave him free rein and looked on with some amusement.

'Ignore the colours. Look for the less obvious. What you are looking for is the slight anomaly, something different – stones which stand out from the dross, different from all the rest, Barnato. Concentrate, man, just like a pair of young hounds your eyes need a goodly amount of training before they are able to find the fox.'

From his pocket, Rhodes took out a small, uncut diamond, a miniscule stone of average quality. He made sure of the claim owner's awareness of what he was doing before dropping the stone on the table in front of Barney.

'Because of a slight yellow discolouration, when cut, this would more than likely be graded as, Top Cape. As it stands, perhaps a fiver, six pounds at best. The same stone, if it were a colourless, Finest White, would be worth three or four times that amount.'

'Depending on the gem's physical imperfections, or lack

of,' Barney expounded and nodded his head. 'I am not totally in the dark, Rhodes, though I have never experienced the excitement of working the sorting table.'

He returned the gem and went back to the task of sorting his pile of gravel; the waste, once condemned was discarded, swept from the table edge with the back of his hand. Rhodes left him to it, in time, in an hour, a day or a month even, depending on the ability of the individual, the eyes and mind would eventually adjust.

For that next hour, Barney managed his way through a second full bucket of gravel brought from the screening cradle. With Rhodes' help, quickly he learned the art of separating and identifying stones of a hundred different colours, exposing them to the sunlight, scraping them out from their cocoon of rotted Kimberlite, perusing their colour and form with interest before discarding them to the ground. However, annoyed by his own failure and just moments away from him giving up on the quest, from that last handful of gravel a small stone, one that was almost symmetrical about its axis, angular and seemingly aloof from the common make-up of the rest, tumbled onto the tabletop.

Both Rhodes and the claim owner restrained themselves from reaching out. Both men held their breath and waited for the cockney to speak first. It did not take long before Barney realised the stone's presence, and though excitement was there in his voice, he spoke quietly, fearing the gem might disappear in a puff of smoke.

'I think we have something, Rhodes.'

With trepidation, Barney separated the stone from amongst a skimming of waste gravel; he rolled it between his thumb and forefinger to rid the stone of its yellow dust coat.

'By all that is holy,' Barney whispered, 'I think I have found my first diamond.' Again, Barney cleaned the stone, using the flap of his shirt tail as a cleaning rag. Seeking out the nearest patch of bright sunlight he held the find head high, close to both onlookers for them to either applaud or condemn his efforts.

It was the size of a green pea; not quite clear, nor was the stone opaque enough for the light to be totally shut out, the crystal's octahedral symmetry was its giveaway. In that sunlight, a fire that through the millennia had remained asleep was suddenly and unpretentiously, brought to life, and from a heart of almost pure carbon, though subdued by the gem's natural uncut state, the colours of some tiny spectrum were thrown outwards at every angle; to his fingers, the texture was one of cold glass slicked by the rain.

'So now you know, old boy.' Rhodes took the stone out from between Barney's fingertips and handed over the find to its rightful owner. 'There you go, my friend. A month's wages for your native labour with some to spare; I would say without any hesitation that our Mister Barnato here has brought you a small measure of good luck.'

The digger's face lit up with warm appreciation and he held out his hand to Barney.

'That you did, sir. The first I've had all week; would have been chewing on grass if it weren't for your breaking up my run of bad luck.' He pumped Barney's arm with increasing fervour. 'You'll forgive my saying so, Mister Barnato, but your fight with Vermeulen, I was there when you dropped the man. What happened to him? Some men reckon you killed him, boxed the bugger to death you did. At least that's what everyone's saying?'

'His heart gave out.' Rhodes was quick to smooth the waters. 'All in the doctor's report, old boy. Nothing sinister, would have happened sooner or later. Vermeulen was already at death's door, our champion here merely turned the knob and helped him over the threshold.'

The digger nodded his head. Satisfied with Rhodes' explanation his eyes went back to Barney Barnato.

'Kopje-walloper and champion bare knuckle boxer all in one?' he held out the diamond to Barney, 'take it, for a fiver she's yours. If you're as fair with your prices as you are good with your fists, then you'll get my business and a lot more from those who know me.'

Rhodes nodded his head and grinned at Barney. The price was more than fair, with enough bargaining leeway left over for Barney to turn a reasonable profit.

'Pay the man, Barnato, before he sobers up and changes his mind.'

Barney drew out a single, five pound note from his wallet and with a twinkle in his eye handed over the money.

'Your name, sir, you haven't told me?'

'Thomas Brown, Tom to my mates.'

'Then Tom it is,' said Barney and along with a fistful of high hopes spirited the gem away inside his jacket pocket.

# -27-

Zingeli had been waiting at the entrance to the hotel's stable block since an hour before sunrise; Kathleen sensed him standing there and called him out from the shadows. With a blanket draped about his shoulders and dressed in woollen breeches, shirt and leather boots, he fought off the early August cold and his smile, like the crescent moon above his head was wide and white. When Kathleen saw it her spirits lifted.

'I see you, Zingeli, son of Mashobane.'

'And I see you also *inkosazana*, why would you have me leave the comfort of my fire if it were not to find the beginnings of a new road?'

Kathleen smiled at the small talk, but it was his way and strangely, the slowness of their meeting comforted her. She drew the sheepskin collar of her jacket tighter about her throat, but in the gap between her collar and drover's hat, the cold still nipped at her ears. Across her shoulders she had slung the same canvas miner's bag that served her needs on the gold diggings, and even now, from off of it, the smell of Pilgrim's Creek rose up to her.

'The road is a short one, but the dangers are many. Go back to sweeping dung from your stables if that is what you are better suited to.'

Zingeli chuckled softly at her goading him.

'As all women do, you learn quickly that your tongue is your spear, were I to let you go alone, your father's spirit would spare me no peace, *inkosazana*.' He shuffled deeper into his blanket and nodded his head to Kathleen. 'Lead on before this cold puts us both inside the ground.'

They went down between the billiard halls and trading stores, dogs barked and a child's sorrowful wailing followed them through to the town's edge. It was here that Kathleen stopped in her tracks and with Zingeli at her side, the pair of them gazed out across the diamond diggings.

'The grave of all graves,' Zingeli mused and not even the sun coming up over that far edge of scarred landscape could hide the truth in what he was seeing.

Kathleen remembered the way she had come with Thomas Bradshaw, she found the wooden uprights for the tipping ramp and looked about her for any sign of Rhodes' men. Zingeli crossed to the ladder head and as every first timer had done before him, through narrowed eyes he followed the ladder's reach for as far down as the shadows would allow him.

'You'll be the new 'un, Mister Rhodes mentioned,' the voice came out from shadows thrown by a flickering camp fire, 'asked me to watch out for you and said for you to wait for him.' The digger stood up from his seat and with his chin, pointed sideways from where he was standing. 'There's coffee on the fire, thought you might be needing some on account of it being so cold like.' He looked past her to Zingeli. 'Tell your labourer to get round the back. My lot are making themselves a brew before climbing the ladders, if he's quick enough, he might get lucky.'

He came forward with his hand outstretched.

'Thomas Brown's the name my mother left me with, Black Country man, three years out from Blighty. Mates call me Tom and I reckon on you fitting that bill, seeing as mine's the claim next door.'

Kathleen accepted the hand; the palm and the inner pads of his fingers were thickly calloused. Thirty years her senior and his arm was still muscular, so that she was forced to try and match the strength of his grip for fear of him crushing her fingers.

'O'Rourke,' she told him and watched the digger's face for those first adverse signs of him seeing her as a woman. Tom smiled at her unease and slowly he eased the power from his fingers.

'No need for you to hide beneath that hat of yours, lassie. Rhodes gave me fair warning of your being a woman; a first name will do me for now, if you don't mind me knowing it.'

'Kathleen,' she told him. Their heights matched.

'Anyone close?' the digger went on. 'You got family...'

'My folks are dead.' She cut in on him. 'One back home in Dakota, my Pa, I buried early-on this year.'

'The goldfields, Rhodes mentioned?'

Kathleen nodded her head. 'Near on to the Blyde River diggings.' She looked about the digger's encampment. 'Rhodes, when will he get here?'

'Any time soon, gets here when he feels like. You'll not be rushing our Mister Rhodes away from a warm fire.' He tapped his chest with flat fingers. 'Cold gets inside of him, struggles to breath he does. Got to watch himself.' He handed Kathleen a battered enamel mug. 'Help yourself from the pot on the fire, got no sugar though. Bloody traders want more than the stuff is worth.'

The coffee was strong, bitter and black as tar, but it held off the cold.

'Yesterday,' Kathleen looked across the fire at Thomas

Brown, 'Barney Barnato told me about you helping him learn some tricks with the sorting table?'

Tom nodded. 'Learned quick he did. Picked me out a fair stone and bought it off me, a fiver he paid. Good as gold, cash on the nail.' His eyes narrowed. 'Friend of yours, this Barnato fellow…?'

'We get on alright.'

'Good with his fists,' Tom shadow boxed in the firelight, 'saw him down at the Queens. Put the Dutchman flat on his arse he did, for a little 'un your Barney friend throws a goodly punch. Quicker than a kick from a wild horse it was.'

'How long have you worked on the diggings?'

The digger tilted his head and looked skywards as if the answer were there, etched into the firmament. With split fingernails he scratched a path through his whiskers and on his picking out the morning star from that waking Colesberg sky, he recalled from memory those first arduous days in the pit.

'Nigh on a year and six months,' he told Kathleen, 'feels like a bloody lifetime, mind.' He turned to the fire and refilled his cup. 'Been some good days, I suppose, round about the time of my first getting here, been some bad bastards as well. Went for three weeks with nothing but mealie porridge – no meat, no tobacco, no coffee. Little enough of bugger all if you'll pardon my saying so.'

'Any good finds?'

Tom shook his head and hawked a ball of phlegm from his throat.

'Plenty of small stuff, just enough for me to keep on looking, puts me some grub on the table and pays the kaffirs' wages; not a lot else, nothing worth chucking your hat in the air for.' His eyes misted over and his lips formed the beginnings of a wry smile. 'Apart from a year ago this past week, now that was something special.'

'Go on, then. What happened?'

Tom dug out the makings of a roll-up from his shirt

pocket and with just his right hand, he rolled the paper full with tobacco. He held the tip to a live ember, then fixed the cigarette between his lips and pulled in the smoke. With his teeth, he tugged in the string draw of his tobacco pouch before sliding it back inside his pocket.

'Rained the hardest I've ever seen that night, just as we were ready for climbing the ladders. Never forget it, drops as big as grapes they were, bouncing off the kaffirs' heads and wriggling down their backs like snakes over wet coal.' His head nodded and his eyes swam full with recollections. 'Black sky, black rain, sweetheart,' he held up his hand, 'thick as these fingers the raindrops was, and then, from what little light the lamp had left in her belly, I saw what I saw.'

'You saw what?'

'A miracle,' he whispered, and by now he was lost inside the magic of his own telling, his face veiled in wonderment. 'Never seen anything like it since, and don't suppose I ever will again.' With every new word his storytelling became even more fantastical. 'Some say I was seeing things that weren't real,' he touched the side of his head, 'makes a man crazy. Spend too much time in that cursed hole and it happens. Maybe they were right, maybe there was nothing there.'

'What did you see?' Kathleen could hold back no longer and prompted his storytelling. 'Tell me Tom – tell me what you saw.'

He pulled on the cigarette and smiled through the smoke, the moment was his.

'A diamond, lassie, big as a baby's fist it was. Came from out of the sidewall and gone before I could get my hand to it. Mud took it.' He shook his head and scowled at the pit edge. 'Still down there somewhere, has to be. Any man turning in a stone as big as that and every digger within a hundred miles would have known about it.'

'How could you be so sure? Could have been quartz or a piece of limestone? You said the light was bad?'

352

Tom shook his head at Kathleen's scepticism; the stone he had seen forced from the pit wall was real enough. For a hundred other nights, he had come awake from his dreaming, yet again with those vindictive storm rains lashing at his tent. Silently, he cursed the stone's hold on his sanity. Trapped so many nights by the thrall of his own nightmares, he had fought to end the torment, only to see the diamond reappear, then slip from his grasp back inside its muddy hiding place; the pretty girl, a quick wave of her hand, the blow of a soft kiss before spitefully she ducked away, back inside the crowd.

'You'll find out soon enough what I'm talking about, lassie; another world down there. Short of being in prison or paradise there is no worse nor better a place. Every turn of your shovel could be the last you will ever need, or that next thump of your pick, the folly that brings a hundred tons of ground crashing down on your head.' He held his thumb and forefinger just inches apart, 'close as that to hell or paradise, lassie – whichever way up the devil's cursed dice chooses to fall.'

Kathleen set her empty cup down next the fire, she knew that from then on there would be times when her own resilience would be tested to the full. However, like Tom's dream, her own fate and that of another were already intertwined, down there in a pit deep enough to swallow the whole of Kimberley town as a single mouthful. Two names threatened to trip from her tongue, but she let loose only one of them.

'Thomas Bradshaw? You must have known him well?'

'That I did, sorry to see him leave, I was. A good man, many were the times when he helped me out.'

'How did he fair?' Kathleen asked, 'I saw his last find, the stone he sold to Rhodes along with everything else.'

Tom's eyes, though spiked with admiration for Bradshaw's success were unable to hide his avarice.

'More than his fair share of good stones. One day alone he pulled out seven diamonds, not one of them less in weight than six carats, made more money from an hour's work than yours truly made in the entire year.' He flicked the stub end of his roll-up at the fire. 'That's the way it goes, lassie, some of us are born to it. Others, the likes of old Tom Brown here, are put on this earth just for the devil to watch them suffer.'

He smiled at Kathleen. Now sated by his storytelling, he relaxed and fell back in with the moment.

'You be careful, lassie, watch yourself down there on the staging and trust nobody. Every man and his dog are in this for the money, nothing else, whether or not his neighbour lives or dies is of no concern to any of them.' He turned side-ways on to the fire and looked out over the diggings, the sun was halfway over the lip, big and warm and orange and already, like an eager flame it licked amongst the gravel heaps.

'Rhodes is here.' For Kathleen's benefit Tom pointed out the barely recognisable figure of a man coming towards them from the western edge of the diggings, jacket slung contemptuously across his right shoulder. Even from a distance, there was no mistaking that familiar urgency. 'From the way he is almost running, I would say the man is pretty much of a mind to dig himself that next bucket of diamonds.'

Both of them stood with their backs to the fire and watched the approaching figure take on better substance, within those next five minutes they heard Rhodes' high pitched voice carry the distance. He cursed the red dust when it billowed up knee-high to cover his leggings, and he cursed the diggers' haphazard dumping of waste gravel when it got in his way. He reached the encampment and slumped into Tom's rickety high-backed chair. Kathleen sat down opposite him and waited for Rhodes' first flurry to begin.

'Coffee, man before I expire. Hot as you like,' he nodded to Tom and reached inside his jacket pocket, 'one packet of sugar, remembered you had run out,' he tossed it over the fire to Tom, 'three spoons and the rest is yours. Full cup my friend or I'll not be making it back across that cursed piece of rubble.' He nodded his head to Kathleen. 'Should have used my horse, thought the walk would do me good. How bloody wrong can a man possibly be?' He pressed the palm of his hand to his chest and growled at the discomfort from his negotiating bad ground and watched Tom stir in his allotted three spoons of brown sugar. Eventually the pain inside his chest subsided and he lit a cigarette in anticipation of the over-sweetened coffee. He smiled at Kathleen.

'You made it then,' with two fingers he spread his moustache and made way for the rim of his mug, his eyes still on Kathleen, 'must admit, at times I had my doubts, and to be honest with you, old girl, can't say I would blame you for packing this in.' He grinned at her, smoke and coffee steam swirled from his moustache.

'I gave you my word,' said Kathleen, 'Tom here has been telling me all about the diggings.'

Rhodes glanced across at Tom Brown.

'The story of your lost treasure, I should hazard. Am I not right, Thomas?' Tom didn't hear him. There was no malice in what Rhodes had said, every man on the Kimberley diggings had at least one good story stashed away for as and when. Kathleen stood up from her chair.

'So, do we have ourselves a labour force?'

Rhodes looked to Tom Brown for answers.

'Any idea where my lot are?'

'Three are already down on the staging, the rest are over there,' he pointed sideways, 'over by the windlass.'

'But no digging as yet?'

Tom shook his head. 'Just as you asked, nothing gets moved until you give 'em the nod.'

'Good man, our own Mister Wilson will be along shortly to take charge of the cradles and sorting table,' he turned back to Kathleen, 'what about your Zulu fellow, or has he already scarpered off back to Natal?'

'He's with me now. Picks, shovels and the like, where do I find them?'

Again, Tom interrupted. 'Already down in the pit.'

'This Zulu fellow of yours,' now Rhodes was talking to Kathleen, 'you will vouch for him, of course?'

'Never missed a day's work, not since my father took him on three years ago.'

'His experiencing the peculiarities of a mining environment...?'

'Gold mining – placer and reef, strong as an ox and quick to learn, wouldn't go down in the pit without him.'

For a moment, Rhodes mulled over what he had heard and then nodded his acceptance of their situation. Within those first few days he would know. Kathleen had no choice but to pull her weight, or after a week at best she would be gone, her failing to control a gang of four black mine workers would unbalance the work routine. In such confined working conditions, organisation and the miners' overall safety was paramount, or there would be accidents, fatalities even. Fatalities brought about down time, production would halt. What was left of the workforce would abandon claim 339 and within that same hour find employment with the other claim holders. Labourers were almost as valuable as the diamonds they searched for, without either one of them, all the mines, from Kimberley to Dutoitspan and then westwards to the Vaal River diggings at Klipdrift and Pniel would grind to a halt. Like any army, it was men with bayonet and rifle who powered the war, and likewise, in the mines, it was the men who wielded the pick and the shovel who drove the diggings ever deeper. Without the black man and his ability to suffer the heat and dust, and his natural contempt for ever present danger, Rhodes knew the game would be over; there would be no more Kimberley. He smiled at Kathleen, the sun was fully up; a fearsome fiery ball bounced from off the horizon. It was time for her to go down inside the pit and the feelings he carried for her were more those of concern for her safety. Voluntarily, Kathleen had placed herself in the path of terrible danger, and hard labour, for up to twelve hours of every day was waiting for her, but there in her eyes he could see there would be no changing of her mindset.

'You are sure of this, Kathleen?'

She nodded her head. 'I am sure, Rhodes,' she told him and matched his smile with her own.

Rhodes acquiesced. 'Then let us get on with it, I will see you onto the ladders.'

# -28-

Zingeli was first to step out from the pit edge, behind him, Kathleen looked down from the ladder head and watched the whites of his eyes disappear inside the semi-dark, for it would take the passing of one more full hour before that low angle of sunlight reached deep enough for it to light inside the abyss.

'Watch the ladder for broken rungs,' Rhodes warned Kathleen, 'and keep your eyes fixed on the sidewall. One hundred and nine steps to the staging, if memory serves.' He reached for Kathleen's arm and gently, with brotherly concern he squeezed her wrist, but in his eyes the worry was all too easy for Kathleen to see.

'I'll be alright, Rhodes, keep the diamonds piling up.' She grinned up at him. 'I expect nothing under fifty carats, or there will be hell to pay when I come out.'

'You don't have to do this.'

'Yes I do,' Kathleen argued, 'how else might I learn?'

Unlike her first time on the ladder, the descent, rather than instil in her a fear of falling was now the powerful exhilarant. Instead of recreating that initial aura of terror, the climb evoked in her, feelings of complete freedom, of excitement even. As her eyes adjusted to the gloom, Kathleen found herself in a world of total openness; she was the eagle, soaring close-in to the cliff face, the updraft of air from the pit bottom, now the wind beneath her wings. Zingeli had almost reached the staging, his voice and those of the other miners, the muted rustlings of an ant's nest, but as Kathleen climbed further into the pit the rustlings became the coherent drum of the Zulu language, and above her, Rhodes' head was now a small, meaningless shape against a strengthening dawn sky.

Zingeli watched her down from the ladder bottom, the others, with dumb expression leaned on their picks, open-mouthed they discussed the folly of their overseer for allowing a white woman to take up a man's place amongst them on the digging platform.

Kathleen turned to face them; she removed her hat and stood within the light from a single, guttering oil lamp. Defiantly, she stood undeterred in the presence of four, work-hardened Zulu miners. She spoke to them in their own tongue.

'My name is Kathleen. Like you, in my heart, there are other places I would rather be and like you, the *amadoda*, I come down inside this devil's hole not for peace, but for a fair chance that I might stand with some respect in the eyes of my father's spirit.'

Kathleen stayed silent and allowed the Zulus time to come to terms with her reasoning, her will to succeed now more resolute. Slowly, the barrier between them crumbled and withered, and though it was a woman who spoke like a man of men's things they saw in her a truth. In turn, each one of them, prompted by Zingeli, stepped towards her and raised his hand, acknowledging the right for her to be there.

'I am *Zimuka*!' From a head-height of more than six feet he looked down at Kathleen, chest almost twice the width of her shoulders and solidly muscled like that of the Cape buffalo. His face was round and black as a vanished moon, his smile now that of a thousand lively stars. 'The fat one,' he chuckled, and then slapped the palms of both hands against the great drum of his belly so that the full strength of his laughter rolled forth as distant thunder.

'Like that of the elephant,' Kathleen laughed, 'more than a week's food would be needed to fill such large a cavern.'

He looked sideways and over his own laughter appraised the man to his right hand.

'The thin one, we call *Thwalambiza*, the praying mantis.' He mimicked the insect's stick-like movements, arms tucked and folded into his belly as if ready to strike out and seize his quarry. The others roared delightedly and nodded their heads in agreement.

'Then I shall call him, *Lambiza*,' Kathleen expounded, 'the shorter name I will find chance to remember.'

She looked to the last man; standing alongside Zingeli he was the smallest of the four, slight as the Kalahari Bushman but hard set and wiry as the *strandloper* desert wolf.

'I can but guess,' she proffered, and through bulbous eyes and little ears he watched and listened intently, pleasured by Kathleen's full-on attention. Reaching only to Kathleen's shoulder, he awakened in her a sense of surreal make believe; eyes too big for his face and with his woollen hat set to a rakish angle, he was to her, an elfin caricature straight from the fanciful tales of Brothers Grimm.

'*Isichwe*!' he said at last, 'the smallest of us all, borne of the dwarf people!' Theatrically, Isichwe spread his arms and commandeered the moment. 'But are not the lion and the leopard as short in the leg as I?' He took to the ladder and like those of a cat his feet whispered over the rungs. Within those next few seconds, Isichwe had reached the halfway mark and then, just as quickly his feet were back on solid ground, his breathing quiet, not laboured nor hurried, but that of a man who only seconds ago had been roused from a deep and restful sleep.

'All day, without rest if need be, I will dig the ground, it was I, Isichwe, who found *Nkosi* Bradshaw's last stone. It was big, very big,' in its absence, animatedly, he sized and shaped the diamond with his thumb and forefinger, 'bigger even than the egg of the *ijuba*, the bush dove, but there were others,' he narrowed his eyes at Kathleen, 'my stone, did he not show you?'

'He showed me,' Kathleen told him, 'the same day he sold his claim in the mine to Mister Rhodes. It was a stone of great beauty.'

'Others, the ones that I see when I sleep, are like this,' he formed a tight ball with his fist, 'as fallen stars they wait beneath the ground for our digging to set them free.' He lowered his voice and now, like the assassin bringing favourable news to his master, he relished his moment of triumph and with ease he switched from his mother tongue to English. 'The white man,' he glanced upwards to the pit edge, 'The man who works alongside you. Did he not tell you?'

Kathleen shook her head. 'You speak in riddles?'

'The last night of last year,' he put it to her, 'when the pit walls ran top to bottom as rivers of mud, *inkosazana*. I was with him, waiting my turn on the ladder.' He pointed out the adjoining staging, a few feet lower than claim 339; Tom Brown's digging platform was no more than three yards out from where Kathleen now stood. 'I saw what he saw, a queen amongst queens. A stone so big that when the storm shot its light inside the pit, the rain itself caught fire.' He willed her to believe, urging with his eyes for Kathleen to grasp the truth in what he was saying.

'He said the mud covered it over before he could reach it?' Kathleen recalled.

Isichwe nodded his head.

'Like fish when the river runs shallow, the diamond buried itself beneath the mud,' he clicked his tongue against the roof of his mouth, 'with my own eyes I watched the cursed stone dance like the fallen star to the white man's fingertips.' He looked up at the sidewall to a point some thirty feet higher than where they were now standing. 'Up there, *inkosazana*.'

'So the story is true? The treasure he spoke of is real?'

'As real as Rhodes' anger when his bucket lies idle for too long.' He grinned at Kathleen and searched out his digging tools from the rubble. He spat on the palms of his hands and hefted the pick. 'It is time for us to work, *inkosazana*, like the king baboon, Rhodes watches from his high place on the hillside.'

# -29-

Once the sun had cleared the horizon, the heat inside the workings quickly rose to nigh on unbearable heights. Only the hardiest of men continued to wield the pick and lift the loading shovel, and by midday, from the full reach of its high arc, mercilessly the sun stood vertically to the diggings. What shade there was, hung thin and curtain-like amongst the stagings, and from off that heated gravel the stench of piss and putrefaction banded together with that of sweat from a thousand wretched souls. From every quarter, dust rose up sulphurous yellow, churning clouds of powdered Kimberlite, big and hot as the hellish sun that nurtured them.

Doggedly, Kathleen worked alongside the Zulu miners, though after a full six hours of hard labour, she was forced by heat and exhaustion to lay the pick aside. Zingeli threw down his loading shovel and went to where she leaned against the pit wall.

'You must climb the ladders, *inkosazana*, no woman, not even yourself can live through a full day's work in the pit.'

Kathleen shook her head and drank down half the remaining contents of her water bottle. Already, her face and forearms were covered in tiny blisters, and the palms of both her hands had been worn raw from the constant demands of the ore skips.

'I will be all right, Zingeli.' She forced a smile and squared her shoulders, but that sudden resurrection of her bravado floundered and fell on deaf ears. 'Just a little more time for me to rest and my strength will return.'

Zingeli stepped up to her and with gentle strength he prised the pick from her fingers.

'You have done enough. Were your father still with us, he would have me shot for allowing your suffering.' He steered her to the ladder bottom and looped the strap of her canvas carry bag across her shoulders. 'Go now. Your eyes are still young; Rhodes will find good use for them at the sorting table.'

# -30-

From her seat at the sorting table, Kathleen had a clear view of the goings on around her so that whenever the opportunity presented itself, she would look out across the diggings, reminded of the real reasons for her being there. Every face that fell within range of her eyesight was scrutinised, checked for those familiarities which she would never forget and was always watching for, she knew that eventually, a chance glimpse would put her onto McKinnon. Somewhere on those very diggings, the same man she had held a gun to was out there and she cursed herself for having forfeited that last lawful chance for her to pull the trigger. Rhodes came up on her unexpectedly and rested his hand on her shoulder; his expectations about to be tempered.

'So what have we found then?'

'As yet, not very much.' Kathleen banished her

phantoms and with a clear mind, handed Rhodes a manila envelope containing the day's findings. Rhodes tipped the stones into the palm of his hand; like the disgruntled bear he growled his dissatisfaction at the collection of small diamonds.

'A few days' wages – nothing more.' He returned the stones to the envelope and dropped it on the sorting table. 'Whilst you were down on the staging, just three claims along from ours, the old Afrikaner, Danie Vermaak, found himself a fine pair of Cape Whites.' He sprung the lid on his cigarette case and with some irritation snatched one out. 'Seven and twelve carats; beautiful examples of what still lies down there,' he lit his cigarette and inhaled, wistfully he gazed out over the pit edge, 'so much more to be found, Kathleen. Our next skip-load of earth, or perhaps, even now as we speak, such a stone could be lying there, waiting for you, barely under the surface of your next handful of gravel spread to the sorting table.' He shook off his own, grandiose expectations and checked the time on his pocket watch.

'Five after five.' He nodded his head to Kathleen. 'We'll call it a day. Shout the men up from the stagings and we must hope for tomorrow's luck to turn up something better.'

He pocketed the envelope and shrugged on his jacket.

'Your friend, Barnato. Will he be fighting again this weekend?'

'Saturday night,' Kathleen confirmed, 'nine o'clock. So far there are three challengers – none of them from further away than the Pniel diggings.'

'Then I shall be there,' he promised, 'perhaps a bout of real excitement will do me some good.' He pulled down the brim of his hat. 'Sometimes I wonder if I would have not been better off following my brother Herbert onto the goldfields rather than spending my time fossicking this cesspit.'

'Reckon you haven't missed much, not a lot there, won't

363

take long before the river diggings are all worked out.'

'Ah yes, of course. The placer deposits your father warned me about; no longevity to be had from sluicing the streams.' The smile was barely noticeable. 'But if there were deep reef of workable size...' Rhodes slapped the dust from his breeches and tipped his hat to Kathleen. 'I'll be away then. Might I suggest a good night's sleep, young lady, after today's ordeal I should say that you need it.'

Kathleen watched him make his way between the gravel heaps, twice he stopped to catch his breath; fifteen minutes it took for him to reach the town's outer limits before disappearing behind a general dealer's store and then onwards past the Digger's Rest drinking establishment. She walked across to the pit edge and shouted down to Zingeli, within those next few minutes all four men were back on surface, all were coated in a thick film of yellow dust and all of them were burned of that last night's excess weight they had taken with them into the deep diggings. Isichwe stacked his pick and shovel alongside those of the others and then crossed to where Kathleen sat at the sorting table.

'I see you, *inkosazana*.' Respectfully, Isichwe lifted his hand, saluting her with open admiration. 'It is good that the day is over, you are the only woman I know of to have suffered time in a place such as this.'

'Little more than half a day,' Kathleen reminded him.

'Other men have suffered much less.'

'Or perhaps these others you speak of are not as thick-skulled.'

'Nor might they have your courage,' Isichwe countered and frowned at the ruined state of Kathleen's hands.

'They will mend,' Kathleen told him, 'A few days and the skin will have hardened.'

'Zingeli spoke of your loss, *inkosazana*. Is that not the true reason for your being here?'

'For everything that happens, there are many reasons, Isichwe. There are many ways, many roads to travel before the answers are found.'

Isichwe nodded his head at this truth.

'Your burden is heavy, *inkosazana*; reasons are the wild dogs of what might have been, only when their bellies are filled with answers will they leave you alone.'

He looked at her through soft eyes, but his lips were hard set when he spoke.

'The man who killed your father...?'

Kathleen's expression hardened.

'What of him?' The sleeping snake inside her belly lifted its head, both eyes slightly open.

'His name. Is it not, McKinnon?' Isichwe proffered.

'Zingeli,' Kathleen realised, 'the pit has loosened his tongue, what else did he tell you?'

'That if I tell others of your grieving he will kill me.'

'If I have not already done so,' Kathleen warned him. 'This McKinnon, tell me what you know of him.'

'For twenty days I worked for him – it was enough.'

'Go on.'

Isichwe hawked up dust he had breathed in from his work on the staging, still unsure of how Kathleen would react to what he was telling her.

'Where the sun is setting,' he pointed to where the periphery of the pit curved away towards the north; Kathleen followed the line of his outstretched arm. However, with the dying sun directly behind the diggings, hidden by a veil of haze and yellow dust, the diggers she made out were mere, ghostlike silhouettes, shadows even, floating silently between the gravel heaps. 'His claim is there, face-on to the rising sun.'

'Describe him to me. McKinnon, what does he look like?'

'*Isilevu mnyama*,' he told her, 'a black beard, thick as a new hive recently swarmed to the rock face.' With the tips of two fingers he touched the soft skin of his lower eyelids. 'The eyes are the same, black as the devil's own and always with a mamba's rage trapped within them.'

365

'How tall does he stand?' Kathleen pushed him further for answers and the Zulu's arm extended full length above the peppercorn dome of his skull.

'Alongside that of Zingeli,' he told her, 'also, the man is strong; those who work for him do so in fear of their lives.'

Kathleen nodded her head, it had to be McKinnon, the description fitted. As before, when chance had brought them together, that same mixture of contempt and grief played as icy fingers about her throat, the temptation for her to go looking for her father's killer was virulent and almost impossible to contain.

'When did you last see him?'

'Last night, I stood in darkness and let him pass without him knowing I was there.'

'Tomorrow,' said Kathleen, 'you can tell me more about this McKinnon. All you can find, I wish to know everything about him; where he sleeps, where he drinks. Everything, Isichwe, but say nothing of this to anyone.' Without drawing attention, Kathleen left a gold sovereign on the sorting table.

'Like the leopard, *inkosazana*, I will watch and listen to the comings and goings of the baboon,' Isichwe promised, and with a magician's sleight of hand spirited the coin away to his breeches pocket.

# -31-

Kathleen allowed Barney Barnato to bathe her hands with a warm solution of salt water before drying them off and dabbing each patch of torn skin with iodine.

'Stings for a while, but has to be done,' Barney spoke matter-of-factly, 'God alone only knows what diseases might well be lurking down there in that pit.'

Kathleen ignored the burn of antiseptic and stared out through her bedroom window. Kimberley was still awake; horses, carts and people milled through the darkness. Each and every day, more fortune seekers flooded in from the Cape and Port Natal, all of them cloaked in that now familiar, optimistic aura of the gullible treasure hunter. Barney finished binding her hands with strips of freshly laundered cotton and then, from his jacket pocket took out a pair of leather riding gloves.

'These you will wear for every minute you spend on the diggings and for as long as it takes for your hands to properly heal.' He dropped them in her lap. 'Every night I will replace the bandages for you; a week should do it, by then the new skin should be well grown.'

'Saturday night,' Kathleen changed the subject, 'are you going ahead with the fight?'

'Bets have already been placed,' said Barney, 'three purses, fifty pounds apiece. Those that don't show will lose their money by default,' he grinned at the possibility, 'so I'm not really bothered if any one of them or all three decide in favour of staying in bed.'

'Rhodes will be there, rest assured he will have a good enough sum riding on the outcome of your winning.'

'Then we must not disappoint him, Rhodes is a valuable ally. I like the man, gets things done.' He smiled at Kathleen and lit a cigarette. 'Not the type to hide behind a tree when his purse is threatened.' He pulled up a chair, close to the window. 'How did the pair of you face up today?'

'We got on well; nothing untoward happened, though production on 339 fell a long way short of spectacular.'

'His first day as new owner, Kathleen, would have been foolish of the man to expect anything more.' He blew a smoke ring and watched it spiral upwards for the open window. 'Even to a newcomer like myself, it is obvious that the lack of hard and fast rules apply just as much to mining diamonds as it does to selling second-hand shoes down London's Petticoat Lane. Finding even a half decent stone of three or four carats is entirely down to pot luck, the length of a man's fingers away from the greatest treasure the world has ever seen,' he held up his hand, fingers outstretched, 'no further than the span of my own hand, Kathleen, that is all that sometimes stands between the extremes of terrible hardship and the surety of immense fortune.'

# -32-

Barney made his way to claim 339 and just an hour after sunrise he reached the pit edge; the first heat of the day was already rousing the dust, sucking it out from the pit, forcing it skywards on young insistent thermals. Two men stood to the tipping ramp, four more to the windlass, but the screening cradles and sorting table were quiet, unattended. Rhodes' man, Wilson, still hadn't made an appearance. Barney questioned the windlass operators.

'*Inkosazana* Kathleen, where is she?'

'*Umgodi*.' Both men looked to the pit and pointed out the ladder head; for the whole of that past hour, Kathleen had been down on the staging. Barney moved to the edge and with nervous hands took a firm hold on the ladder. Directly below, through the dust he made out Kathleen's shape and those of her Zulu labourers. He cursed her foolhardiness as much as he cursed his own fear and then, having summoned every last ounce of courage, swung his weight onto the top most rungs. Kathleen, aware of sudden movement in the ladders, looked upwards.

'Watch your step, Barnato.' His fear of heights was obvious. 'Some of the rungs have rotted through – hold on tight or you may well fall the rest of the way!'

Like a rat to the slippery slates of a church steeple,

Barney inched his way downwards. With his heart still in his mouth he stepped from the last rung and moved away from the open side of the digging platform. He stood with his back hard pressed to the sidewall and with his eyes closed waited for the panic to leave him, for that inward fluttering of birds' wings to abate.

'Only madmen and swallows would do what you are doing, O'Rourke.' He looked around him and took in the vastness of the open workings; as an ant's nest freshly broken open, the earth itself was constantly moving.

'Welcome to hell,' Kathleen grinned at him, 'careful of the edge, there's another thirty foot drop before you reach pit bottom.'

Close to either side of the staging, crowded to earthen platforms, gangs of diggers ripped at the ground and sent their filled buckets spinning skywards. Fixed to an endless system of ropes and steel pulleys were two leather buckets. Those just emptied of gravel reached the bottom just as their filled counterparts were winched to within easy reach of men on the tipping ramps; here the buckets were snared and their contents emptied into wheelbarrows. The noise was incessant; from amongst the bedlam there came the clattering of uncountable picks and shovels and the deep, bass intonations of a thousand Zulu labourers.

> 'Why do we dig the ground, *madoda*!
> For fallen stars *obaba*!
> Are they not the tears of *uNkulukulu*?
> They are the tears of God, *obaba*!'

In unison, the pick heads bit into the earth and then rose again as waves of steel about the diggings. Barney peered into a world that only a few short weeks ago, he could never have imagined existed. The noise swept over him, the air itself was thick with dust and darkened even more by a web of twisted hide, and steel wire ropes. The heat he knew would come soon enough and the mere expectation of its arrival brought out sweat along his hairline. The smell was the worst; that of human excrement, the mixing of piss, sweat and the stench of last night's two shilling whore. He shook his head at Kathleen.

'One month in this rathole and you will be either dead, or insane.'

'I will be neither dead, nor insane,' Kathleen countered and at the same time, with her pencil added the morning's tally to her pocket book. 'No more than you Barnato.'

Barney crouched against the staging and scooped a handful of gravel from the ground at his feet.

'Who would have guessed, just how vast a fortune nature has hidden beneath this little piece of Africa.'

'Save your creative strengths for Saturday night, Barnato. Waxing lyrical doesn't fit your face; beating men to a pulp is more your style.'

Kathleen stood aside for the loaders to work the gravel, within that same minute the leather skip was filled to the brim and she signalled to the man looking down from the high edge for the windlass operators to take up slack from the rope.

'Your hands,' Barney asked of her, 'are they holding up?'

'Better than yesterday, thanks to your nursing skills. Setting my hands alight with iodine must have worked.'

Barney smiled at his purposeful heavy-handedness with the iodine bottle; he avoided a shower of earth from the swinging ore bucket and with a hopeful glance at the ladder hinted for them to climb out.

'You said you had found a suitable site for my office?'

'Western edge of the diggings,' she told him, 'I can spare you twenty minutes, we can take a look.' She gestured for him to follow her onto the ladder. The structure shuddered before the weight of two people settled it to the sidewall. Like before, Barney cursed his phobia and climbed reflexively; with his pulse at a full race, the need for him to reach level ground became paramount.

Kathleen saw him out from the pit; his face was drained

of blood, the colour of Dover chalk.

'You don't look well, Barnato?'

'I have no head for heights. I would fight ten men all at the same time rather than re-negotiate that ladder way.'

He flustered away from the pit edge and with shaking fingers reached out a cigarette from the case in his pocket. He struck a Vesta against the metal frame of a diamond cradle and with the exaggerated needs of two men he sucked down the smoke.

'Never again,' he shook his head, 'not unless my life depended on it would I go down there for a second time.'

He followed Kathleen between the gravel heaps; she led for almost a quarter mile before turning face-on to the western edge of the pit. With the heel of her boot, Kathleen scribed out a rough square in the dust.

'Right here. This is where you would do best to site your office.'

'Why this particular spot?' Barney asked her.

'Look around you,' Kathleen insisted, 'most of these tents belong to men with claims along the south-western edge of the diggings. According to old man Bradshaw and our neighbourly, Thomas Brown back there, more good quality stones have been taken from that section than from anywhere else in the pit.'

'So I snuggle on down between them?'

'Like a pup in a basket,' Kathleen nodded her head and smiled indulgently, 'right alongside them. Living within easy reach of an honest buyer, why would they bother taking their findings any place else.'

She stood with both hands pressed to her hips and stared out across the diggings. Canvas tents were rigged from as near as twenty yards to her front, spreading to more than a mile at either hand, row upon row, or clumped together as small encampments bordering onto the workings. This was the heart of the diggers' far-flung empire. Behind her were the newer, wood and tin built establishments of a more permanent township. Barney's closest rival was a good one hundred yards from where they were standing and from there onwards, the competition increased proportionately; a dozen or more wooden, box-like buyers' shacks stood out head and shoulders above the canvas encampment. Like naval ensigns, as a mark of their honest brokerage, the buyers' flew their national flags enticingly from the rooftops.

'Tomorrow, then, I'll get the joiners in to make a start. A fortnight, three weeks at the outside and Kimberley's latest diamond merchant will be ready to throw open his doors.'

Barney rubbed his hands together in anticipation of what might be.

'A wide open road to that first million, Kathleen my lovely, and no one, not even your Mister Rhodes will stop me.'

Kathleen didn't hear him. Her concentration, like an elusive bird of prey jinked between the diggers' tents, looking to find a face, the swinging of an axe or the careless lifting of a canvas tent flap for its owner to step outside. In front of a dozen different tents, bearded diggers stretched the stiffness from their backs and then, casually, each man opened the front of his corduroy breeches for that first long piss of the day.

'So what do you say, ten pounds for the timber, and the same again for the joiner to build the premises?'

Kathleen agreed with his guesswork.

'Time me for me to get back to work, Barney.' She held up both her hands in front of his face, the gloves were stained and torn through from her digging in the pit. 'I'll see you back at the hotel after dark,' she glanced back over her shoulder and ignored the look of despair on his face, 'and don't forget the iodine and fresh bandages, Barnato, reckon I'll be needing plenty by the time I get home.'

\*

From his vantage point on a gravel heap, a lone digger watched Kathleen make her way back across the diggings. From memory, he recalled a moonlit night far to the north-east of Kimberley and could not help himself from smiling.

# -33-

The sorting table was now the inequitable master of all her concentration. At any moment, the treasure Kathleen sought so avidly, might, for a split second, reveal itself as a mere waxen glimmer. Any unusual stone would catch her eye and clamour for attention. Coupled with its texture, and if fortune had left its eight-sided form unaltered, the uniqueness of its shape would insist on it being lifted out from the dross rather than for it to be ignored and then discarded. However, not all diamonds were that easily recognised – many were unevenly shaped, sheared from larger stones over the millennia and in colour, might range from the brightness of a lightning flash to pale yellow, and even to that of a mud brown or a dull, repellent grey – the mark of the imperfectly crystallized stone.

From the lower, third deck of the sieving cradle, collected from between a screen of medium mesh and another of very fine, more of the selected gravel was brought to the sorting table and carefully tipped at its head. From this select heap of concentrates, with her wooden scraper, Kathleen drew out a small measure of gravel and with the scrutiny of the circling hawk, began her task of carefully picking through it.

'Garnet, olivine and zircon.' Kathleen recognised them all as worthless indicators and brushed them aside with a contemptuous flick of her sorting tool. Zingeli stood to her right shoulder and from his watching her, he learned quickly.

'Here.' He insisted, now impatient for that first find he pointed further back to where that last bucket of sieved ground was still untouched. Kathleen leaned side-on to what she was doing and with the corner of her scraping tool, plucked Zingeli's discovery from the heap.

Isolated from the rest and cleansed of its yellow dust, the stone tumbled from the scraper to the sorting table. To Zingeli, it was now a single drop of white rain, rain so pure of colour that in the brightness of that blue sky, from within that soapy exterior, it appeared to both onlookers as a crystal of chastened sunlight. Without looking up, Kathleen gave instructions to Zingeli.

'Rhodes is over by the winding platform, tell him he is wanted here at the sorting table.'

Kathleen varied the diamond's angle and lie to the metal surface, repeatedly she turned the stone for it to catch the full, unrestricted flow of raw sunlight. Rhodes stepped up from behind her and leaned on the table.

'What have you found?'

'This,' said Kathleen and pushed the stone in front of him. 'Zingeli found it, just a few minutes ago.' Apprehensive, though eager for his evaluation, she watched Rhodes' face for signs of excitement, or at worst, those of rejection. 'So what do you think?'

Rhodes picked up the stone and as a matter of course, held it to the sunlight.

'Was beginning to think I had bought myself a run of bad luck. However, methinks the woman doth prove me wrong.'

From his pocket, he took out a jeweller's loupe and put the lens to his right eye; Kathleen held her breath. Rhodes bettered her experience on the diamond fields by a good two years and she would, in those next few seconds know if the stone was worth anything less than she had anticipated.

The loupe went back inside his pocket, and without

passing comment, from that same pocket he withdrew his Winn's measuring calliper.

'A rough guide, you understand, but better than nothing.' He smiled reassuringly at Kathleen. 'We shall soon have the measure of what your Zulu friend has found for us.'

With steady fingers, Rhodes expanded the calliper's brass jaws, just wide enough for it to encompass the diamond. He read from where the pointer aligned itself to the graduated, curved rule at the opposite end of the gauge.

'Just as I thought, half of one inch in diameter. I would hazard a weight of just above the one gram mark, six to seven carats, give or take,' he looked up at the sky and pondered the measurement, 'going off past dealings I would say five carats cut and readied for mounting.'

Again, through the jeweller's loupe, he delved inside for any signs of missed inclusions, slight imperfections that would either enhance or destroy the stone's desirability. His face lit up.

'Good depth, not too thinly spread. Eighty pounds as it stands and three times as much cut and polished.' He patted Kathleen's shoulder and without fuss, pocketed the diamond. 'Made yourself twenty pounds, young lady. Your first day on the sorting table, bloody well done.'

'What about Zingeli?'

Rhodes appeared confused and shook his head.

'What of him?'

'He found it,' Kathleen reminded him. 'Every man should be acknowledged for his efforts or the next one he finds might well end up in his own pocket.'

Rhodes was quick to agree. IDB, the abbreviated term for Illegal Diamond Buying was well on the increase.

'An extra pound on his pay, a blanket and a pair of new boots, that will do for the man. Let us not forget, Kathleen, your Zingeli is an employee, not a shareholder. Must keep a hold on things or he will be after room and board at the Queens.'

Rhodes lit up a fresh cigarette and watched the smoke

curl upwards through the sunlight.

'We should celebrate. Tonight. A drink at the London Hotel, what do you say?'

'The London Hotel...?' Kathleen shook her head. 'Don't know it.'

'Upper Street,' Rhodes told her. 'Past The Digger's Rest and Honiball's Butchery. Look for the sign on the hotel's frontage and bring your friend along.'

'Barney? He's pushed for cash, Rhodes, the chances are that he will not want to risk the expense.'

'I think you'll find that he will, old girl. Tell the man I will pay for the evening's entertainment and that his brother, Harry will also be there.'

Rhodes smiled at her doubting the attraction.

'So don't you worry about our Mister Barnato, when he finds out that Harry Isaacs is part owner of the London Hotel, he will move heaven and earth to get himself in there.'

# -34-

Rhodes instructed his driver to remove the Cape cart to the hotel's livery yard.

'Have the stableman feed up your horse and bring the bill to me, and something for you, Johnson. Looks as though you could do with a goodly plate of meat and potatoes,' playfully, he jabbed a finger at the soft flesh below the Basuto's ribs, 'you're all bones, man, more meat on a jockey's whip for God's sake.'

Kathleen and Barney watched him from the open doorway. Rhodes saw them and made for the hotel steps.

'Well, what are we waiting for? I sent word ahead for Harry to hold a table for three, so let's get in there. The night is young and through Kathleen's astute running of my sorting table we have, all three of us, the means with which to enjoy it.'

The table was set to the far left corner of the room. Rhodes checked the reservation card for his name, and then, satisfied the table was his, looked about the room for service.

Like some leggy giraffe, an auburn-haired waitress in black bustle and bright red shoes arrowed between the tables. She recognized Cecil Rhodes and with quick eyes picked up on the five pound note part protruding from between his fingers.

'Harry said for me to watch out for you, Mister Rhodes,' with practised politeness she dipped her head to Barney and Kathleen, 'what can I get you? Wine, champagne, whatever's your fancy. Our wagon came in this morning, so we're pretty well-stocked.'

'Bollinger,' Rhodes decided for them, 'has to be cool though. Too damn warm and the stuff froths up like barber's soap on a grandmother's whiskers.'

'One or two bottles...?'

'One to start with and another if we take a liking to your first.'

Barney settled for a schooner of beer; he smiled up at the redhead.

'Harry, my layabout brother... half sober and here on the premises, or out philandering?'

'The gaming room, Mister Barnato,' she pointed out a curtained doorway, 'I shall tell him you're here.'

'No need, I'll tell him myself,' Barney stood up from the table and nodded to Rhodes, 'back in a couple of minutes, hopefully, the sudden appearance of his younger, poorer brother might trigger heart failure.' He winked a jubilant eye at Kathleen, 'don't look so shocked, sweetheart, with Harry out of the way I would legally inherit all of his ill-gotten cash.'

He crossed to the curtain and stepped beyond it. The inter-leading door was slightly ajar. He waited for his eyes to adjust; the room was softly lit with strategically placed candelabra and a single, crystal chandelier. Set to green baize-covered gaming tables, spinning roulette wheels threw back the candlelight; the reds and blacks of the wheels' brightly numbered pockets and the sharp, hypnotic clatter of ivory balls held their punters spellbound. From the nearest table, the final call went out.

'*Faites vos jeux*! Last chance ladies and gents, place your bets.'

The croupiers were French Mulatto, bought and brought from rum traders anchored off the Cape waterfront. Harry Barnato had shipped them up by coach and had personally fitted them well to his own interpretations of the entertainment business. Both girls were slim at the waist and ample enough about the bosom – hidden though barely restrained, their breasts, to every man at the tables were for most of the time the focal points of all interest, more so even than that spiteful, bouncing, ivory ball about to relieve them of their money.

'*Rien ne va plus*! No more bets!'

Barney smiled at the goings on; both girls bubbled over their clientele and under the exaggeration of candlelight and coconut oil their skin matched up with the rich mahogany of the roulette wheel. From where he stood at the doorway, he caught the sweet reek of cheap perfume. Their lips were painted bright red, the whore's ensign, and with their reaching across the table and each purposeful flutter of brown eyelids, both women flaunted themselves as for sale to the highest caller.

'Slutty, but toothsome.' Barney decided and stepped up to where his brother leaned the weight of his gut to the edge of the nearest table.

'Harry old mate, bit fatter than when I saw you off from the Pool of London; from raggy-arsed lad to silk cravat and fancy waistcoat, not bad progress for the son of a Whitechapel ragman.'

Harry Barnato turned on his heels. Slightly older, fatter

and an inch taller, he engulfed his sibling.

'Twenty three red!' The ivory ball fell to its favoured number and the clattering ended.

Harry looked at his brother in total wonderment.

'Was beginning to think you would never make it! How did you find me? And father, how did he take to you catching the steamer for Africa? Been a long time, Barney my lad, when did you get here?'

'Slowly, slowly, Harry.' Barney returned the scrutiny, 'too many questions.' Light-heartedly, he patted Harry's cheek and then looked around him. 'Some of this, I believe is yours then?'

'A half share of every inch. What about you, where are you staying and how many juicy pies have you so far plunged your bony Jewish fingers into?'

'I board at the Queens Hotel, we have an arrangement.'

Harry narrowed his eyes at his brother. 'The widow's palace,' he exuded, 'Lizzie Jardine's come one come all establishment. Good woman, our Lizzie – mother, sister benefactor to half the down-and-outs in Kimberley.'

'I work for my keep, Harry, so cleanse that filthy mind of yours.'

'Doing what?' Harry pushed for answers. 'Taking the hotel's proprietor out for her regular evening canter?'

'You must join us,' Barney ignored the witticism, 'we need to talk.'

'Give me a minute to sort things out.' Harry broke from the conversation and responded to a raised hand from the furthest croupier. From the look on her face, all was not as it should be.

'The gentleman over by the fireplace,' she pointed him out, 'wants me to raise the house limit to thirty pounds.'

Through trained eyes, Harry isolated the contentious punter from a dozen other people.

'The big fellow with the whiskers? What's his name?'

'Wouldn't say,' the croupier told him, 'told me the game of roulette does not require the names of those who win or lose, just for either one of them to part amicably with their money.'

Harry kept his eyes on the punter. He could not recollect having seen him before. At over six feet tall and broad across the shoulders, his mere presence was intimidating enough for Harry to appreciate the feel of the pistol tucked inside his waistband. He approached the man with caution.

'Afraid we can't oblige you, sir. We are a small establishment and only recently have we found our feet. Your winning would force me to bankrupt the table; a thirty-five to one, straight-up bet of thirty pounds would cost me dearly. I cannot take that chance.'

Without speaking, the punter went back to his place at the roulette table. Harry held up five fingers to the croupier and having confirmed his hard ruling of the table's limit, turned his attention back to Barney.

'Happens all the time. A digger turns a stone or two and his usual perception of normality flies out through the window.' He grinned at his brother. 'Not going to happen, not unless you would be willing to cover the bet, little brother.'

Barney shook his head at the amount.

'Stand good for over a thousand pounds? I think not. For most men that would see them fed and housed for a good three years. Conversely, if he were to lose, your gain for a single spin of the wheel would be well worth the torment,' he smiled at Harry, 'though not guaranteed, old chum.'

Both men left the gaming room and pulled up a chair at Rhodes' table. Kathleen appeared relaxed; the champagne had worked its magic. Harry introduced himself and immediately took a shine to the town's only female diamond digger.

'I'm intrigued, young lady. What made you pick out Kimberley? I mean, as your choice of abode rather than Natal, or the Cape even.'

'Purely through chance,' Kathleen lied, 'heard people talking about the diamond-covered streets of the Colesberg diggings.' She shook her head and laughed. 'Got it wrong, I guess. Should have stayed in Natal and snared me a wealthy sod buster.'

'She means, a farmer.' Rhodes explained the vernacular. He stood up from the table and gestured to Kathleen for her to do the same. 'We shall leave the Brothers Grimm to re-acquaint themselves.' He crooked his right arm for Kathleen to take a hold. 'Enough of the serious stuff, young lady, we're here in this dubious den of iniquity to facilitate our having some fun.' He smiled at Harry and now, enlivened by a third flute of champagne, like those of a roguish lad his eyes sparkled. 'Your gaming chips, Harry my friend. Your top mark, how much for one?'

'A pound, Rhodes and conversely, one shilling chips are our smallest denomination.'

'Then ask your young lady at the table to count me out some one hundred of your topmost denomination, nothing less.'

# -35-

Within that last half hour the gaming room filled almost to capacity; three more mulatto beauties were drafted in from their quarters to work the newly opened card tables.

'The game of twenty-one,' for Kathleen's benefit, Rhodes explained the rules and nuances of the card game, 'if what I have been lead to believe is correct, your fellow countrymen have already renamed their version of the game and now refer to it as blackjack; heavily favoured I believe by your Mississippi steamboat gamblers.' He recognised Kathleen's interest and went on with the tutelage. 'Originated in France as *vingt-et-un* and like roulette, as the gambler's welcome plague it has spread throughout the colonies with alacrity; fortunes are won and lost at the turn of a single card.'

The dealer's hands were lightning fast and with a house advantage of one point, were quick to strip the unwary digger of his cash. However, not all the punters were slow-witted miners dressed in corduroys and woollen shirts. The London Hotel attracted well-heeled men in tight-cut suits and ornately tooled dress boots, eager to push back the boundaries of their last night's winnings; men fresh out from Nevada's fabled Comstock Lode with money to pour into Kimberley's, Big Hole. Two of the more prominent claim owners were gambling men from New Orleans and Sacramento; another, a once professional gambler at the Gentry and Crittenden Gambling Saloon of Virginia City was wearing that same benchmark black suit, black boots and white, ruffled shirt, where at its centre there sparkled a three carat, blue-white diamond stickpin. Kathleen, warmed through by champagne could not help herself from staring at the precious jewel. As some flashing all-seeing eye, the diamond glittered and goaded her, so that in her mind she pondered over its origin. Rhodes realised the focus of her interest and moved alongside her.

'Well spotted, girl, you have an eye for a good stone,' he expounded the diamond's attributes, 'near colourless. One from Dutoitspan or the river diggings, or perhaps the other side of the world, who would know, save for the man who found it.' He steered Kathleen towards the roulette tables, the croupier had been forewarned and with the sweet, effusive smile of an angel, stacked the one pound chips as ten, orderly piles in front of Rhodes.

'As you requested, Mister Rhodes, one hundred pounds – perhaps tonight will be your night.'

'Let us hope so.' Rhodes acknowledged the pleasantry and tossed a single, one pound chip to the croupier. Kathleen shuddered at the possibility of their losing more money than some men might struggle to earn in a whole year.

'So what do you fancy?' Rhodes looked at Kathleen, urging her to make her choice.

'*Faites vos jeux.*' The croupier called the table into play and spun the wheel.

'Number thirteen,' Kathleen hazarded and with excited trepidation watched Rhodes cover her chosen number.

'One on the nose it is then, and for interest's sake, we shall place one chip at each of the number's four corners.' He grinned at Kathleen, though he was not a habitual gambler, on occasions he could not resist the very risk of losing it all to one, slowly decaying spin of that whirling wooden wheel.

Kathleen's eyes followed the ivory ball. Purposely put at odds with the rotation of the spinning roulette wheel it clung determinedly to the highest point and then, as momentum left it, the ball began to flounder. Enticed by gravity it abandoned the security of its grooved maple track and collided with the nearest metal deflector. Kathleen's breathing faltered, with each erratic bounce of that ivory ball her heart leapt. It was then that a hand reached out from inside the crowd and placed a bet of five, one pound chips alongside Kathleen's; like the placated serpent, slowly it withdrew.

'No more bets! *Rien ne va plus*!'

Like silence before a storm's first thunder, apart from the sibilance of the spinning wheel there was no other sound.

'*Treize noir*!'

'Thirteen black, Rhodes!' Kathleen bounced with excitement. 'For God sakes pick up the money and run!'

With busy hands the croupier cleared away all losing bets, stacking the chips in columns of tens on the rack alongside her. She nodded her head to Rhodes and like the submissive bride, coyly she acknowledged his mastery over the gaming table.

'A commendable win, Mister Rhodes,' as was customary,

she covered the smallest bets first, 'four corners pays thirty-two pounds; thirty-five for your win straight-up on the number.' She counted out the amount in grey, one pound chips and again, in orderly columns pushed a total equivalent of sixty seven pounds across to Rhodes. Not without some play acting, Rhodes cut three chips from his winnings and tossed them back to the dealer.

'*Pour la croupier*!' he delighted in the opportunity for him to indulge his vanity with a smattering of casino French.

'*Merci beaucoup*, *Monsieur*. If there would be anything else, anything at all that might take your fancy?' Like her lips, her eyes were heavy with innuendo. However, Rhodes served only to smile at the implication; there were other, far more important attractions available to him than those being flaunted over the gaming table.

'One more bottle of Bollinger and my night would stand as to be complete. I would be obliged if you saw it to our table.' He looked to Kathleen. 'Our winnings, Ma'am, I'll leave you alone to cash them in. A fifty-fifty split I would see as fair, less the cost of our champagne. What do you say?'

'I say you're mad, Rhodes, but then again, I have known that all along.' Rhodes pocketed the remaining chips and with warm affection patted Kathleen's shoulder before disappearing back through the inter-leading doorway; it was then, Kathleen felt the empty space to her right hand suddenly refill.

'You should have stayed out your time on the goldfields, lassie.' The voice was edged with Scottish intonations, but only slightly; time spent amongst the colonists, the Zulus and the Afrikaners had wilfully diluted his accent. However, to Kathleen's ears it was more the bass snarl of a rabid dog. Her eyes flicked over the crowd, but there were no familiar faces for her to call upon. Her revulsion was the sudden rising up of the jack pike to the surface of a quiet river.

'Who are you, sir?' She forced her head around. 'I've

384

never seen you before, what do you want?'

'No more games, woman. What you took from me, three years ago.' He reached passed her and pointed out his winning bet to the croupier, with his free hand he found the small of Kathleen's back and easily he held her there, hard up against the table edge. Unable to move, Kathleen braced herself to turn away, but the strength in her assailant's arm was that of a powerful man.

'Cry out and I will hurt you, lassie. Put on that pretty smile of yours for our dealer lady and don't forget, not a wrong word or it ends here, right now.' His hand moved down to the warm cleft between her buttocks. 'You are who you are, Kathleen O'Rourke; long hair, short hair, makes no difference, I will always find you out.'

With the insistence of a careless lover, he caressed the innermost parts of her thighs. Through her clothing, Kathleen felt his fingers search and tremble; perverse insistent creatures crawling over her flesh.

'We will talk again, O'Rourke, no word of our re-acquaintance to your chums out there, or one at a time they will find themselves a permanent place in Blanckenberg's burial ground. Now pick up your winnings and go on back to your friends.'

He withdrew his hand, having turned sideways-on he made space for her to manoeuvre away from the table. As Kathleen squeezed on through, McKinnon dropped his mouth to her ear.

'And don't forget, O'Rourke, you and your Mister Rhodes, I know what you stand for; more akin to one another than either of you realise. Play me foul and the whole of Kimberley town will hear about it.'

Within the shadow line of his brow, she glimpsed his eyes. Deeply set to his skull, they were indeed those of the devil. He relished the shocked expression on Kathleen's face and leaned in closer – now the brutal wolf ready to tear out her throat.

'Hurry on back to your guardian, lassie, and no word of

385

our meeting, mind; my knowing the way he is, your foppish friend may well be fretting over your empty chair.'

# -36-

Kathleen sat with the back of her chair pressed hard up against the wall; through her paranoia, bearded men who came and went via the hotel's front door were all of them, Blackie McKinnon. What he had said tumbled around inside her head; every single word she recalled and within each recollection she searched unsuccessfully for some insight to McKinnon's intent. Across the table, Rhodes and the Barnato brothers were now entrenched in a permanent state of deep discussion, the air above their heads thick with cigar smoke, those slender, fluted glasses which were once filled with expensive champagne had been left abandoned and replaced with squat, thick-walled tumblers flooded with strong whisky. Kathleen stayed quiet, her ears cocked for the gist of the conversation, but her eyes were for every single second, glued to the hotel's front door.

'Without control, the diamond industry will collapse,' Rhodes' cigar was now the instrumental baton, 'the more stones found and sold on without any restriction on quantities, the further the prices will fall. Supply and demand, gentlemen, two more years of flooding the market and we will all be working for nothing.'

'So what are you saying?' Barney pushed for more in-depth reasoning behind Rhodes' portentous warning. 'Claim holders have the right to dispose of diamonds as and when they see fit, that's the way it has always been; without money, they will starve. Restrict their selling off of what they find and you will be faced with chaos, the diggings will be thrown into turmoil.'

'Rhodes is right,' Harry interjected, 'someone with a lion's heart and hefty clout is needed to take control of Kimberley's diamond output; the status quo has to be maintained. Mark my words, gentlemen, that someone is already out there, like some bloody hyena waiting to snatch away the kill.' He swallowed a mouthful of whisky and screwed his eyes at the pleasurable bite of raw spirit. 'The question is, who will it be? Who, from out of this pit full of desperate men will be powerful enough to pull in all the loose ends and govern the flow of diamonds from out of the diggings?' He shook his head and rolled his eyes to the ceiling. 'Damned if I have any ideas on that one.'

Rhodes smiled at the truth in Harry's realisation. Through the smoke he assessed the worth of those sat opposite and it was then, at that very moment that Barney Isaacs Barnato saw the first grandiose, spark of heady aspirations come alive in Rhodes' eyes.

'It will take more than grit and a few thousand pounds for any man to fit that billing, Rhodes. There will be far bigger fish to play, certainly those a hundred times bigger than any one of us sat here at this table.'

Rhodes nodded his head at the fact.

'And that I agree with, Mister Barnato, however, when the time is right, luck will favour those who are well in the thick of things, men with insight, experienced men who have seen the diggings grow from a prospector's yard-long trench on Gilfillan's Camp to what it is today.'

Rhodes leaned forwards against both elbows and, from her place outside the conversation, Kathleen recognised that deep, indomitable look in his eyes – that same, unwavering determination she had first seen all those years ago aboard the *Eudora*. She watched him carefully and like the flare from a hundred lighted Vestas, his thoughts strengthened and conjoined.

'It will be the hands-on entrepreneur who will eventually take complete control of the diggings, not some opportunistic wolf from behind the subterfuge of his

387

Mayfair gentleman's club. Without any doubt, money will prove to be the obvious essential, but not without a goodly measure of hard grind to back it up, gentlemen.' Rhodes nodded his head, reflecting upon what he had said. 'Men with blistered hands and diamond gravel settled inside their gut are the ones who will see this through to the very end, not your London toffs and wealthy Jack the lads looking for auspicious ways with which to impress their women or burn big holes in their fathers' wallets.'

'The end of what exactly,' Barney interjected. Already the problem had doubled in size. 'How can it end? It cannot,' he added, 'it will not end, Rhodes. At least, not within the confines of our lifetimes. Science is of common opinion that the gems have been forced to the surface by an upwards surge of deep magma, through a natural process of volcanic activity.' He rolled the ash from his cigar and without disengaging the mental wheels from the rails of his conjecture, drained the last mouthful of Glenlivet from his glass. He left the empty tumbler on the table and wiped his lips with the back of his hand. 'You and I are at different levels of achievement, Rhodes, exact opposites, you might say. You, the well-established, prolific producer of fine diamonds, whereas I am still reaching out for a hold on that first rung. I need money, and the only way to get it is through bloodying my knuckles every Saturday night down at the Queens. How else might I eventually finance ownership of my first claim?'

'The chicken and the egg,' Rhodes acknowledged the harsh reality of the Londoner's state of affairs, 'believe me when I say how much I understand, I have been there myself. Without money, there is no claim fit for registration and vice versa; neither one can exist without the other. No money, no claim; no claim, no money'

Kathleen gestured to Rhodes for him to lean towards her. Shielded from the others by Rhodes' leonine head of hair, tentatively, she passed her ideas on to him.

Rhodes listened, and as though he were suddenly

touched by some unexpected premonition, sat upright in his chair. His expression slowly altered from one of usual indifference, to that of the bemused owl. Openly, he was taken aback by the by the magnanimity of Kathleen's offer.

'You would do that?'

Kathleen nodded her head. She needed access to Kimberley's high achievers and this was her way in, far enough at least for her to breach the periphery of that male dominated, inner circle.

'Without a second thought,' she told him, 'but only on condition of your being in full agreement.'

# -37-

A leaden sky quickened the onset of darkness over Kimberley, and now, emptied of miners, apart from those plaintiff calls of roosting starlings, the diggings were deathly silent. However, not too far from the workings, light from the Queens Hotel pulled in men with dust in their throats and a gleam in their eye, all were eager for a schooner of cool beer and a fat financial return from their wagering the outcome of a good fight.

'Thanks to your Barney Barnato's skill in the boxing ring, business is booming, Lizzie my love.' Rhodes had got there early and commandeered his regular place at the bar. Less than half an hour out from the barber's chair, on one elbow, he leaned on the counter and with critical fingers appraised the smoothness of his chin; shaved of stubble, his cheeks gleamed.

Lizzie Jardine paused from her work and considered the steady build-up of clientele.

'Best entertainment you will find anywhere in Kimberley, Rhodes. No one can blame them for spending their

Saturday nights at the Queens. Save for losing what money they make to Harry's light-fingered strumpets down at the London Hotel, there isn't much else of interest within a hundred miles of here.' She turned face-on to him and smiled wryly. 'Speaking of which, I believe you were there last night?'

Rhodes chuckled at her astuteness, nothing happened in Kimberley without Lizzie Jardine being privy to it; always up there amongst the town's front-running busybodies for a first sniff of any latest scandal.

'An eyeful down at Harry's place can barely hold second place to his whisky and roulette wheels, my dearest Lizzie. My loss or gain of a few shillings you should look upon as remedial treatment for all things mining, even I need a break, sweetheart. The permanence of my standing day in and day out up to my neck in dust and hot sun, waiting for something worthwhile to show up is enough to drive even the strongest of men to the point of flinging themselves into the deepest, darkest part of that cursed pit.'

Lizzie shook her head at his grumbling; Rhodes, her ultimate sparring partner, seldom let her win. However, for whatever reasons, Rhodes always appeared as to be more at ease in the sole company of men; in his eyes, women had been put on the planet purely for the perpetuation of mankind, a natural annoyance which he was obliged to tolerate. Apart from his friendship with Lizzie Jardine and his platonic affinity with Kathleen O'Rourke, his disregard for women, alluring or otherwise was obvious. For a long time, Lizzie had been aware of Rhodes' personal leanings, but she had hinted at nothing. To the experienced woman, the truth in him was only subtly veiled; perhaps one day the pretentious charade that he hid behind would catch him out. She lightened up the conversation.

'I heard mention that you beat the table out of more than seventy quid with a single spin?'

'That I did, but your Kathleen is the one to take all credit, she chose the winning number, thirteen black. Her eye for a lucky number netted me more than most men make from a full day's work at the sorting tables.'

He looked past her and found Kathleen making her way through the crowd, she moved with confidence and with the brashness of a man, shouldered a route between the diggers. She smiled at those who were pleasant and just as easily, growled her threats at those who got in her way. Rhodes allowed her time to settle behind the bar before broaching the subject of their last night's conversation.

'I take it you are still of the same mind as last night, reference our discussion over your future interests in the diggings?'

'Nothing has changed, Rhodes. I meant what I said.' She glanced across at a ceiling to floor redoubt of heavy curtaining; behind the velvet facade, as before, final adjustments were being made to the hotel's makeshift boxing ring.

'Have you still to pass on my proposition to Barnato?'

Rhodes nodded his head to her.

'After the fight; then I will tell him. Now is not the time for me to fill his head with pretentious ideas, the less he has to think about the greater his chances of winning.' He winked an eye at her. 'I have wagered ten pounds on all three bouts; too much for me to lose, my friend.' He sprung the lid on his watch. 'Ten more minutes before the off, time for another hair of the dog.' He slid his glass across the bar counter. 'Whisky, my auburn-haired beauty and better we make that a double, one of your better blends. I need a goodly dose of Dutch courage before our champion struts his stuff.'

Kathleen reached down a bottle of GlenDronach single malt from the highest shelf and with a damp cloth, wiped it clean of dust. Without speaking, Rhodes watched her break the wax seal, draw the cork and pour. Armed only with modest expectations he lifted the glass to his lips.

The whisky had been matured in casks of American oak, once reserved for the ageing of fine, Oloroso sherry.

Decanted into bottles, it had been shipped to the colonies from that faraway valley of Forgue, somewhere deep within the Scottish Highlands. To Rhodes, it appeared as a mixing of gold and russet brown, the colour of winter grass from along that arid rim of the Great Karoo. Once inside his mouth, it exploded with all the vibrancy of Africa, robust and fiery, and though having been sweetened by the subtle contaminants of aged oak and old sherry, it came across as more the liqueur than the whisky. Peppery scents of a hot Karoo wind conflicted with those of turned peat, purple-carpeted crags and crashing mountain streams secretive of the wild Highlands. It was a coming together of both lands so that he closed his eyes and let the confusion take his senses wherever it willed. Rhodes gave chance for his throat to clear itself of fumes before he spoke.

'The bottle...?' He looked at Kathleen. 'How much?'

'Take it as a gift,' Lizzie called over to him, 'been up there on the shelf for nigh on two years, why the special interest?'

'An affinity,' Rhodes replied, 'suffice to say we were born to like one another.'

The room had almost filled; without effort, Lizzie counted off more than a hundred diggers, though by the minute, others poured in through the hotel's double doors. Already, besides the winner takes all fixed purse of fifty pounds a fight, fair amounts of money had been wagered.

'What are we up against?' Rhodes looked to Lizzie Jardine for the latest updates. On the strength of her champion's predicted success, Lizzie herself had covered all three fights with twenty pounds apiece.

'Can't say as I recognise any of them, but our winning won't come easy; two of them I would put at over six feet.'

'Same as before then,' Rhodes smiled, 'David and Goliath, it matters not.' He emptied his glass and nodded to Kathleen for a refill, then he reached inside his jacket pocket. 'A favour of you, Lizzie, a slight change of tactics.

I need you to get this to Barnato,' he handed her a sealed, manila envelope, 'for all our sakes, make sure he reads it.'

Lizzie hurried her way through the crowd and slipped behind a curtain for the stage's rear access door, she barred it behind her and followed a dimly lit passageway to the back of the ring. Barney was finishing off coating his torso with tallow fat.

'Stops them grabbing hold,' he winked an eye at her, 'all's fair as they say, and I can't afford to miss out on my share of the prize money.'

Realising the envelope was for him, he gestured to Lizzie for her to open it.

'You do it, my hands are all greased up.'

She slit the envelope with her fingernail. 'It's from Rhodes, do you want me to read it to you?'

He shook his head and took the slip of paper from her. Within those same few seconds the note was read and folded away inside his breeches pocket; like crystals of frost along the pit edge at sunrise, his eyes glittered.

'Tell Rhodes I accept.' He leaned across and kissed her cheek. 'And one for Kathleen O'Rourke, God bless her.' He looped an arm around Lizzie's waist and slid his hand downwards, to below the small of her back. 'As for you my fair and toothsome wench, you will get your reward later,' he slapped her rump with the flat of his hand, 'over a couple of bottles of your house champagne and a plateful of best beef.'

'In my room?' she whispered, and pressed her mouth to his ear. With her free hand hidden from any onlookers, she raked his back with her fingernails. 'Straight from the fight, Barnato, steaming ripe and hot bloodied – the same as your steak.'

## 38

'Curtain goes up in five minutes gents, so get them ordered in before the shouting starts!'

Kathleen pulled beer with both hands; diggers broke off conversations and bullied their way through to the bar. Bottles of Smoke and supplies of thick cigars were snatched up in exchange for hard cash. Barely able to cope with the rush, Kathleen called out to her employer for help.

'Where in hell's name has Trixi-Marie gotten herself to? You said she was curtain raising?'

'Gone,' Lizzie growled. 'Permanent barmaid job down at the Digger's Rest, stupid girl doesn't know what she has let herself in for. Week at the most and she'll be banging on my door for her job back. Cope as best you can, sweetheart, good cash bonus for you to keep our beer taps flowing and your cash bell ringing.'

The diggers were restless. Hungry for the onset of that first fight, they milled like starved wolves close as they could to the velvet curtains. In a small room off the back of the stage, three raw-boned men leaned against the wall and listened for that first call.

The bar clock showed the top of the hour and with that low thrum of the wakened hive the crowd stirred; incited by impatience it ebbed and surged as a single living organism. Collectively, the crowd focused its two hundred pairs of eyes on the velvet curtain. Agitated by their missing out on Trixi-Marie's usual run-up of ribald entertainment, the miners stamped their boots against the wooden floorboards. Hundreds of pounds were hanging in limbo, and whoever was fated to win or lose, would, within that next half hour, stand blessed or cursed with their finding out.

Like the parting of low clouds, the curtains drew back

from the stage; extra lamps had been hung on ropes from the rafters, so that the boxing ring below was now completely veiled in yellow light. For a showing of greater authenticity, the corner posts had been anchored substantially to the vertical and the ropes themselves were drawn taught and doused with whitewash, making it easier for the crowd to pick them out from against the shadows of that rear wall.

'Gentlemen, Kimberley's illustrious diamond merchants, diggers et al!'

Joe Walsh had dressed to suit and was, through an earlier showing of hands now firmly ensconced as Kimberley's official referee. Through his best efforts he had taken on the extra responsibility with keen interest and, to compliment his status, had put together and perfected an appropriate repertoire. Dressed in fresh on breeches and white shirt cinched at the throat with a black silk long string tie, he was every bit the boxers' referee. With his arms raised, he stood at the centre of the ring waiting for the noise to subside.

'A total of three bouts; winner takes all!'

The crowd erupted. Support and obscenities flew at the ring from both camps. Those too drunk to care stared at Walsh through dead eyes.

'Same as before,' Walsh went on with his rulings, 'fighters will stick to London Prize Ring rules; the bout ends either by submission, or an opponent being knocked to the floor. If after a count of thirty the downed man is still unable to stand to the scratch line, he will then be deemed as the loser and forfeit his claim to any prize money.'

'So who's first out there on your fancy new stage, Walsh!'

'Bring 'em out, Walshy. No need to for all your ruling claptrap, get the buggers out here where we can see 'em!'

Walsh smiled at the banter; it was as he expected. A lot of the men he knew by name, though few of them would dare go head to head with him in a fistfight.

'From London's East End, a man who walked every inch of the way from Cape Town to Kimberley!' he waved Barney out from the backstage doorway, 'with the heart of a lion and fists to match those of the legendary, Jack Broughton, Yankee Sullivan and the great Tom Cribb!' He lifted Barney's bare fist above his head. 'I give you the diggers' champion – Whitechapel's bantam rooster – our Champion of the Kimberley Diggings, the undefeated Cockney Cockerel – Barney Isaacs Barnato!'

Whistles, catcalls and derogatory cockerel related innuendos flooded the arena. However, ignoring the bombardment, Lizzie's hungry eyes fell upon her champion. Bared to the waist, the cocky young Barnato was as quick on his feet in the ring as he was flat on his back in the bedroom. To her, the ultimate obsession; flat across the gut and limber as a hunter's dog, he stood foursquare to the lamplight and not without contempt did he look down upon the crowd. As though he had sensed her watching, Barney turned his head and smiled in Lizzie's direction, and even at that distance she felt her breathing catch.

'From the Klipdrift river diggings and originating from Liverpool, I give you the first of three contenders, the scouser, Massey Thompson!' Walsh continued, 'big in the belly and hopefully, for his sake, at least half as big in the brain!'

Like Barney, Massey Thompson had stripped to the waist and with the finesse of a boulder freed from the slopes of a granite kopje, on thick legs he lumbered forwards into the centre of the ring. From her place behind the bar, Kathleen compared the giant's stature to that of Barney's and nothing she saw could put to flight, her fear of a bad result.

'Thompson makes up two of Barney, one blow from that ape and his head will come off!'

'But twice as fat,' Lizzie countered her fears, 'look at Thompson's face, the man has barely walked a dozen steps and already he's sweating like an overworked pit pony.'

The referee brought both men to the centre of the ring, one man to either side of the scratch line.

'No butting with the head and no striking of an opponent when he is down, or the offender will be declared the loser.'

Walsh stood between them and nodded his head to Barney.

'Where is your second, Mister Barnato?'

'There isn't one, Walshy. Let's get on with it.'

Massey shook his head and grinned at the referee. Like his opponent, he had foregone the luxury of a supporting umpire. He wouldn't be needing one, the fight would be over before it started.

'Then come to scratch and shake hands. No fouling gentlemen and may the best man win.'

Walsh stepped out from between them. In his right hand, as a sounder he carried a shortened length of jumper steel, and the gong for him to strike was a piece of cocopan rail fixed to a single strand of steel wire suspended from a roof beam. He reached upwards and struck it twice, and through the silence of an expectant crowd, like the sounding of a ship's bell it echoed back from the furthest corners of the room.

Thompson never saw it coming. Straight from that customary touching of hands, Barney's balled fist cannoned upwards at a steep angle. Massey Thompson was still grinning when what seemed to him as the crack of a digger's pick steel sparking off solid rock, exploded inside his skull.

## 39

'One down two to go,' Rhodes enthused, 'a quick return old girl, what do you say, Lizzie? Or did you forego the chance to back our champion?'

She laughed at his supposition and shook her head.

'Like my mother always told me, never miss out on a dead certainty, and bet your hat and drawers if you're short on money when needs must.' She rolled up a sheaf of five pound notes before pushing them down inside the cleft of her bosom. 'No one gets their hands on these beauties, not without my saying so.'

Rhodes frowned and playfully he chastised her.

'You're incorrigible, Jardine.'

'And I suppose, you are not?' She felt the devilment rise up from inside her stomach. 'By the way, Rhodes, how is your Mister Paterson keeping these days? The pair of you are normally inseparable.'

As though he had not heard her, Rhodes turned his attentions away, focusing instead on Kathleen O'Rourke.

'Did you see that, Kathleen? A single punch from Barnato and that Thompson fellow was laid out flat to the floor, ready for the undertaker.'

'Still two more to go,' Kathleen reminded him, 'maybe the best of them has held himself back for last.'

'Nonsense, girl, Barnato is lightning fast. The best there is and slippery as an eel; no one else out there can divvy up to him.'

'Hope you're right, Rhodes, the next contestant looks to me as harder to break than the padlock on your money belt.'

The crowd was in full voice. Support had swung away from the cocky champion and now favoured the lesser-known underdog. However, as he had done with the first, so did Barney send the second digger from Klipdrift diggings spinning into the ropes, knocking him off balance before dispatching him with a perfect horizontal hook to the side of his head. Nonchalantly, Barney leaned with his back pressed against the ropes, his breathing easy and there were barely half a dozen beads of sweat on his forehead. Then, as though he were suddenly aware of a wild animal watching him from the shadows, he looked back over his shoulder. Just inside the entrance to that inter-leading passageway, his remaining adversary struck a Vesta against the sidewall. Within those same few seconds, Barney glimpsed the man's face and it was then he felt the tiny insects of trepidation scuttle across his bare skin.

# -40-

Kathleen's hands stayed hard-pressed to the bar counter, and like her fingers, her eyes refused to move. At the centre of the boxing ring, the embodiment of all her hatred stood there, a dark colossus, rock solid.

Stock-still in the lamplight, like the others, the digger was naked to the waist and at a height of more than six feet from the floorboards, he towered head and shoulders over his opponent. Hardened by work in the diggings, the muscle above his belt was sharply set, rippled sand left behind by an ebbing tide. From behind his belt buckle, like moss to the north facing side of a giant oak, thickly the body hair had spread upwards to where it covered the full width of his powerful barrel chest. Merely through his being there, Kathleen felt an uncanny presence encompass the room; it was the reawakening of both her conscious fears and those deeper, more sinister introjections borne of past encounters.

The crowd as a whole fell silent and stared in awe at the third contender, as if it were not a man who had stepped out from the shadows, but the incarnate form of the devil himself.

'From the Kimberley diggings!' Walsh's voice rose up through the silence. 'The one we have all been waiting for, the third and final contender.' He raised the fighter's arm above his head. 'Uglier than your long-abandoned mother-in-laws, more dangerous even than a hungover grizzly bear from America's Rocky Mountains.'

'Go for the grizzly bear, Walshy – he's prettier than my mother-in-law!'

A roar of appreciation went up, Walsh held back with his introduction until the hubbub died down.

'Gentlemen, this will be the fight to top all fights.' Again he let the announcement hang in the air. 'I give you the moment, gentlemen. A moment for you all to contemplate your fears, hopes and aspirations, a moment, should you have backed the wrong horse, to grieve for the money you are about to lose, for the man standing next to me may well hold key to whether or not you eat steak, or for the remainder of the month, just plain old mealie bread and cold water.'

Again he held up the fighter's clenched fist, and now, with a twinkle in his eye, for one last time he looked down amongst two hundred or more drunken men and toyed with their expectations.

'Take a good hard look, gentlemen for this man holds the rights to your next half hour,' he opened his own fist to the gallery, fingers splayed, 'right here in the palm of his hand.'

'So what do we call him, Walshy? Or doesn't this pretty boy of yours have a name?'

'McKinnon,' Walsh revealed, 'Blackie McKinnon.'

'You must stop the fight,' Kathleen implored Rhodes, 'I know this man, he kills for the pleasure of it. Barney will not be able to hold him.'

'Not possible, girl, there's too much money riding on the outcome of this bout. Calling it off would incite a riot.'

'Then you shall at least agree to my warning him.'

'And get him to do what? Throw the fight?' Rhodes shook his head. 'Barnato is no man's fool, nor is he coward enough. A minute in the ring with the last contender and he will have the measure of him, let them be. Walsh will ensure them both a fair fight, anything untoward and he will stop the bout, the fight would be over.' He looked at Kathleen and smiled wryly. 'You intrigue me, woman, where is all of this coming from? What injustice has this McKinnon fellow ever done to you?'

'It does not concern you, Rhodes.' She shrugged off his meddling and turned to her employer. 'Spare me a minute or two, Lizzie. I need to fetch something from my room.'

'Couple of minutes, sweetheart, no longer,' she nodded her head to Kathleen, 'back as soon as you can, I need your support. This fight is going to get bloody and I am not sure I would want to be on my own when it does.'

From a locked drawer in her wardrobe, Kathleen lifted out her father's Colt from its wrapping; the oil was still fresh. In the corner of that same wardrobe, standing upright and partly bound with strips of oiled rag, her Yellow Boy Winchester rifle and the Sharps .50 calibre buffalo gun tempted her to stay longer. Just her looking at the Sharps rifle evoked in her strange feelings of déjà vu, and at that same moment, in her mind's eye, she caught that faint flicker of other happenings; some she did not recognise for they were as yet, still to come. From the open door on the stairwell, the combined voices of two hundred cheering diggers thundered in after her, the fight was about to begin. With hurried conviction she thrust the Colt revolver down inside her waistband and covered it with her shirt. She locked the landing door, pocketed the key and within the minute was back behind the bar.

It did not take Barney Barnato long for him to realise the physical power wielded by the man he was up against. McKinnon glowered at him, like a dog with a cornered rat, contemptuous of his smallness, berating him with his eyes.

The referee waved them both to the centre of the ring; both men stood to the scratch line. McKinnon, a bearded giant of a man, by a full six inches he towered above the London Jew; Barney, as the beleaguered fox, faced up to the mighty lion and with that fox's quick eyes probed McKinnon's defences for signs of weakness, but found none.

McKinnon leaned forwards and opened his mouth to speak. On his breath, the smell of old meat and dark rum poured from a hole in his beard.

'Soon, my little Yiddish friend, you will look upon this world from the other side; remember me to your slut of a mother and tell her the shilling I paid for her to suck my uncut dick was eleven pence over the odds.'

'Fight on!' The referee struck his gong and readied himself. Barney spun away to the right, keeping just out of reach of McKinnon's long arms. Every pair of eyes in the room was on them, every move and counter move was criticized, every feint, punch and counter punch dramatically mimicked by those cheering, cursing diggers.

The noise that surrounded the arena was now at its peak, baiting both men; merciless abuse that once would have been hurled down from the stone terraces of Rome's ancient Colosseum.

'Kill him, McKinnon! Give the smouse a beating he will never forget!'

'Watch that right hook of his, Barnato! Wear the big ape

down and then pummel the bastard's liver!'

Lizzie Jardine shook her head at Kathleen, her eyes wide with fear, pleading for an end to what was taking place. This was not just a fight, more the gladiatorial sacrifice; a clashing together of deadly swords. It would not finish before one or both lay bleeding on the floorboards. Lizzie leaned against the counter for support, the colour had fled from her face.

'Something I have to do,' Kathleen reached out for Lizzie's hand, 'fill in for me, will you.' She pulled out a fresh towel from the counter cupboard, doused it half through with clean water from the pail at her feet and then, with the wetted towel slung across her shoulders she forced her way through the crowd. On reaching the edge of the boxing ring, Kathleen swung up onto the raised platform and took her stance as Barney's second; close-in to the corner ring post. Walsh acknowledged her right to be there and it was then, infected by her sudden appearance that McKinnon's mannerism changed. Across the room, from behind the bar, Lizzie Jardine reached out over the counter to Rhodes.

'Something is wrong, Rhodes. The way she's looking at McKinnon, what has come over her – why would she do that?'

'She knew the pitfalls before the fight started.' Rhodes attempted to console Lizzie by covering her hand with his own; he felt her trembling. 'Get a hold of yourself, woman. She's worried over Barney taking a beating. The worst that can happen is Barney will lose the fight, perhaps a tooth or two and you and me our stake. The girl is up there either to nurse his wounds or to give the man encouragement, nothing more.'

Every move McKinnon made, Kathleen appraised; backed by formidable strength, his prowess was crude and unprofessional, dangerous as it was unpredictable, that of a low-life street fighter working some waterfront bar for the price of a drink and a dry bed. However, it was the way in which he prowled the ring which frightened her the most. Every movement McKinnon made was animal-like, devilish even; the fire that burned in his eyes, malevolent.

For him to stay out of reach of McKinnon's fists, Barney employed every single trick he had learned from his fighting the hardened scrappers of London's East End. McKinnon's stamina was relentless, every blow that Barney landed jarred against a solid wall of muscle; a towering human redoubt. Constantly on the defensive, time and again, Barney found himself forced up against the ropes and only through his own quick thinking and his agility had he been able to escape. However, less than fifteen minutes into the bout, once again, McKinnon herded Barney towards the corner post, but this time, with the slightest sideways flick of his foot, caught the heel of his opponent's boot and sent him down, almost to the floorboards. It was then that McKinnon saw his chance and like a cat coming over the trapped defenceless bird he fell upon the smaller man.

Turning his back to the referee and with his forearm locked about Barney's throat, like a battering ram to a castle's barred gates, McKinnon drove his right fist at the soft vulnerable flesh just an inch below the ribcage. Starved of air and shocked through by the force of McKinnon's fist impacting against his liver, Barney's eyes fluttered wildly, and then darkness engulfed him.

Walsh manoeuvred himself to come between them, however, overwhelmed by the fighter's superior strength he was closed out.

'Let him go, McKinnon! The man's out cold!'

McKinnon ignored him. The Jew was Kathleen's link with the diggings, her hold on the future, a foil for his own anger. The crowd went wild; rival supporters bated one another and bellowed for blood.

'Kill him, McKinnon and I'll split my winnings with you!'

'Finish him! Finish him!'

'Foul, Walsh! Get the bastard off of him!'

Most were so riddled through with Cape Smoke and whisky that they failed to differentiate between that which was real and that which was not, so that they cursed and cheered the goings on with the same breath. Whatever the rulings were, all had been discarded in favour of this final, full on open combat.

Without releasing his stranglehold on Barney's throat, again, McKinnon's free fist became the blacksmith's pounding hammer, and from the corner of his eye he watched the horror from what he was doing spread like fire over Kathleen's face and still, from outside the ring, the crowd screamed out for more.

Like hounds to their first scenting of the fox, every man in the room bayed for the ultimate excitement, only a quick kill would grant them surcease. Walsh fought to intervene, but as before, McKinnon blocked the intervention with his body and raised his arm above his head, priming himself for the *coup de grâce*; the drop hammer, ready to pound, bend and shape the heated metal. Lizzie Jardine covered her face with both hands, the spectacle of what was happening to Barney, now too much for her to watch.

'Sweet mother of God, Rhodes, do something.'

'Uncover your eyes, woman,' he reached behind and shook her by the shoulder, 'O'Rourke has stopped him. I'll be damned if she has not!'

Kathleen had vaulted the ropes and came up on McKinnon from behind; he felt the Colt's steel barrel settle between his shoulder blades. His arm froze mid-strike and on one knee knelt immobile against the floorboards, Barney's slack body still in the crook of his arm. Like the cornered lion, from within the shadow of his massive shoulders he growled at his attacker.

'You will pay for this, O'Rourke. Like your father – a thousand times you will pay the price for what you are doing.'

'Leave him be, McKinnon. Let him go.' Kathleen held

the Colt steady, hard into his back. 'Give me the excuse that I'm looking for, McKinnon. The hammer is at full cock.'

McKinnon released the pressure on Barney's neck and left him there on the floor. Kathleen stepped back, the angle of her aim now dead in line with McKinnon's throat. The entire crowd fell silent; every digger was struck dumb by what was happening. McKinnon turned around and from less than a yard distant, smiled down at Kathleen.

'You do not have the nerve lassie. Pull the trigger and have done with us both; me to Blanckenberg's Cemetery and you dear lady, straight to the gallows for the murder of Blackie McKinnon.'

Walsh took on the warning and though his feelings fell in line with Kathleen's, as referee he was forced to take back control.

'He's right, Kathleen. Put the gun away, you have made your point. Shoot McKinnon now and they will hang you for your trouble.'

Walsh had armed himself with the twelve bore double from behind the bar, he held the gun in line with McKinnon's stomach. 'Your fighting days are over McKinnon – you leave the same way you came in, with nothing.'

McKinnon stood up, he turned his back on Walsh and lowered his voice so that only Kathleen could hear.

'You should have stayed in Pilgrim's Rest, O'Rourke. Better you sleep with one eye open, you and me still have things that need finishing off,' he winked an eye at her, 'from our time back in Natal, girlie, I am sure you remember it well enough.'

With her free hand, Kathleen reached inside her shirt pocket and then, still with the Colt fully cocked, she held out her left arm at a full stretch. Between finger and thumb, suspended on slender, silver chains were three uncut diamonds; she flaunted them less than an arm's length from McKinnon's face.

'As if it were yesterday, McKinnon.' She twirled the miniature carousel, rotating the central, connecting chain with her fingertips, goading him with tiny reflected eyelets of lamplight. 'Recognize these? Keep them with me all of the time, never make it through any one day without feeling the need to remind myself of where they came from.'

McKinnon's face hardened, but before he could reply, Kathleen carried the torment further.

'From the look on your face, seems like your memory's just as good as mine, McKinnon.' She smiled at him, but solely with her eyes.

'So what do you say old man, an eye for an eye? Or maybe I missed my chance and should have killed you then, three years ago, that night on the waterfront.' She held back, allowing him the chance to recollect. 'I was only fifteen years old back then...' Her gun hand started to shake, for the hatred inside her was past simmering.

'Put down the gun, Kathleen.' Barney raised himself up onto one elbow. Through half-closed eyes he looked at her, barely able to speak, he shook his head and slowly the colour returned to his cheeks.

One by one, the onlookers realised that Barney was still able to move and again their shouts and whistles flew at the ring.

'What's going on, Walshy! How do we stand?'

The referee nodded his head to McKinnon.

'Better you leave now. Once I tell them the fight has gone to forfeit they will be baying for blood. Take the back way out, down through the stable yard.'

Walsh waited for McKinnon to disappear through the curtained doorway, only then did he turn to face the crowd.

'The fight is over, gentlemen.'

'What about our money, Walsh?'

Two hundred irate diggers surged forwards. Walsh was forced to shout above the uproar and as a warning, held the shotgun at the high port across his chest.

'Other than the purse money, all bets will be refunded. Make sure you produce written evidence of your wager.'

Kathleen gentled down the Colt's hammer and pushed the weapon back behind her breeches belt. She helped Barney onto a sitting position.

'You strong enough to walk...?'

'For as far as the bar, my lovely.' He hooked his arm over Kathleen's shoulder and without warning, kissed her cheek. 'I am indebted to you, Miss O'Rourke, you saved my life. Without any doubt, you saved old Barney Barnato's, worthless excuse for a life.' He reached for the ropes and tested his strength; the pain in his side was still the fire McKinnon had left him with. 'You and this McKinnon character, I heard enough of what was said to realise the severity of your predicament. You were right, McKinnon's worse than a dog, a bullet between the eyes would be too good for the likes of him.'

'Soon,' said Kathleen, 'McKinnon will pay for what he has done, but not tonight.' She steadied herself against the ropes. 'On your feet, Barnato, what we both need right now is a drink.'

# -42-

Barney drained his glass of whisky and then abandoned it to the counter. Rhodes handed him back his shirt and with painful effort Barney shrugged his arms inside the sleeves, he fastened up the buttons to a few inches below the collar.

'Today, the great Barney Barnato got his full and fair comeuppance; the beating of his life, Rhodes.' Tentatively, with slow fingers he felt along his ribcage for signs of any breakages. 'The bastard wanted to kill me, there is not a single part of my body which is pain free.'

'And he would have succeeded in doing so, had not our hero of the day thrown her courage into the melt. Though the means by which she saved your skin left us all in a sweat.'

'Heroine, Rhodes,' Barney corrected him, 'your Joan of Arcs, Florence Nightingales were heroines; men are heroes, women heroines.'

'Exactly what I meant, old boy, I blame my advanced state of inebriation for the misnomer; too much whisky has beggared my choice of words.' Rhodes' face was glowing from his profuse intake of GlenDronach. 'Twice in the same day, Barnato, the lady to your right has pulled you back from the brink.'

Barney nodded his head at the truth in Rhodes' words, he looked sideways at Kathleen and the smile on his face was playfully beatific.

'Obviously thinks I am worth the gamble.' His eyes softened, his expression now, one of unreserved gratitude.

Rhodes rolled his eyes skywards, allowing Barney his moment of self-indulgence before carrying on.

'Perhaps you have forgotten, Mister Barnato. My agreement with Miss O'Rourke was that of my taking up first option on the reacquisition of her one quarter share, should she decide to sell or pass on her part holding to someone else.' Rhodes pushed his glass across the counter for a refill, and unable to keep a straight face, he gave up on the charade. 'However, providing my glass is returned to an adequate state of fullness within these next few seconds I shall leave things as they lie.'

He fixed his eyes on Kathleen. Bounded by his red face the smile was soft lipped and infectious.

'I am impressed by your astute sense of fair play, Kathleen. Had your father been here today, he would have looked upon what you have done as something wondrous.' Rhodes lit a cigarette, his cheeks were those of a painted marionette, deep pink and laced with thread-like veins from the effects of strong whisky. At his temples, though he was barely past his twentieth birthday, strands of silver hair had already woven their sickly way inside his hairline. In all, his was the face of a man who was at best, looking over his shoulder from a point some twenty years on.

'However, our continuous reminiscing over today's happenings will not allow us to move forward. There are other stumbling blocks, bigger and bolder than perhaps either one of you are aware of.'

He waited for signs of their disagreement, but none came and he nodded his head to the pair of them.

'So, all three of us are of the same mind? Kathleen will transfer her part ownership of claim 339 to Mister Barney Barnato.'

Barney nodded his head to Rhodes and then turned to Kathleen.

'How could I not agree? A once in a lifetime opportunity, but only if you are doubly sure, Kathleen?'

'I am,' said Kathleen, 'though there are conditions.'

'Name them,' Barney invited.

'That the money outlaid with Rhodes for my share in the claim is to be settled in full, within a reasonable time and to include a levy of ten percent.'

'Twelve percent,' Barney upped the buyout price, 'a more than reasonable amount, considering what you have already done for me.'

'Within the first year.' Kathleen added. 'That is, from date of transfer. Plenty of time for you to clear the debt.'

'And what would you do in the meantime?' Rhodes asked her. 'Your foregoing control of any diamonds mined may well leave you short of funds?'

Kathleen smiled at the anomaly, Rhodes was neck and neck with her, every circumstance he had covered and taken apart, piece by piece, a dozen times in the space of those last few minutes.

'A stipend of five percent.'

'Five percent of what, exactly?' Rhodes looked at her for

answers.

'Of Barney's monthly turnover, after having taken into account his running costs, of course.' She folded her arms across her chest; the act flew as a flag of her insistence. She grinned at Barney Isaacs Barnato. 'Look upon it as my payment for manning your sorting table. How else can I guarantee a fair and quick return for having saved your life?'

Rhodes nodded his agreement to Barney; her working at the sorting table would benefit them all.

'You drive a hard bargain, O'Rourke.'

'I learned from the best,' she countered.

Rhodes reached across the bar for his dwindling supply of GlenDronach. With the fight over, the crowd was already dispersing.

'So as of now, the three of us are in agreement?'

Barney extended his right hand to Kathleen, his smile resolute. In less than a month he had risen from a penniless, bare-knuckle prize fighter to part owner of a diamond claim; that first rung on Kimberley's jealously guarded ladder had been aspired to.

'Monday morning, first thing; I expect to find you head down and hard at work at the sorting table.' He looked past her and pointed out a half emptied crate of champagne. 'Now, if you would be so kind as to chalk up a bottle of Bollinger against tonight's earnings, I would be most grateful, lassie. A certain young lady is waiting for me, fingers and liniment poised to repair any damage inflicted on yours truly by the McKinnon runaway steam engine,' He winked at Rhodes. 'God help me if she is still awake, by morning what bones are still intact will be well and truly broken, the rest of me reduced to the chewings of a woodworm.'

411

# -43-

Monday morning came upon the Kimberley diggings with the temerity of the grey wolf, sniffing the eastern horizon for a place into which it could sink its wet, though unseasonal fangs. Kathleen O'Rourke looked down from the pit edge and, like the wind-driven breeches that flogged her legs, so did a hundred remorseful memories flog the tattered canvas of her mind. Where she was standing, the ground was baked dry, though less than a mile away the dongas and ditches were already inundated; some ran half a yard deep with red slurry. Added to it were those collective remnants of human disregard; degrading cast-offs and the remains of diggers' excrement flooded out from a thousand makeshift latrines.

From his stance at the sorting table, Barney was forced to shout above the wind, for the first deep growl of wild thunder was already closing in on the diggings. The odd splattering of giant raindrops, those forerunners of the African storm sounded from off the dry earth, and with sharper, clearer reports, from off piles of discarded metal buckets, lengths of corrugated tin sheeting and that single throw of yellowed canvas stretched between two poles above the sorting table.

'This shouldn't be happening, not for another month at least. Best you get under cover before the storm breaks. Ten minutes and we'll be right in the thick of it!'

Kathleen stood her ground, the fingers of her right hand already tight to the topmost rung. The wind whipped her hair across her face and with pained expression, Barney willed her to step away from the ladder.

'What good could we do by going down there?'

'The men on the stagings,' she countered, 'they cannot hear the wind. They don't know there's a storm coming.'

Barney projected his confusion at the sky and from the

folly of his looking upwards, the wind threatened to tear his hat away.

'They should know to watch the clouds, but then again, it's the wrong time of year for thunderstorms.'

'What about old man Brown? He's alone down there.'

'We are not his keeper,' he reminded her, 'Thomas Brown makes his own decisions, he will know what to do.'

Directly below, men continued digging; tearing out lumps of virgin, diamond-bearing gravel. Sheltered by the pit's high wall, most were unaware of the deluge bearing down on them. However, those who worked above ground were gesticulating and shouting down from the pit edge, but their voices were small and lost to a wind, which was by each new minute increasing in strength.

Kathleen guessed the time it would take for her to reach the nearest staging; at exposed points along the pit wall, those who had at last realised the threat were fighting to make the ladders. She made her decision, nodded her head to Barney and without a second thought, levered her weight away from solid ground and onto that first rung.

By the time Barney reached the ladder head, Kathleen was only twenty rungs short of the halfway mark. Only once did she glance upwards and picked out Barney's head and shoulders starkly silhouetted against a growing maelstrom of dust and darkening storm sky. It was then, as if through some trick of the changing light, that the image of Cecil Rhodes appeared alongside him.

'Is it a cave in? A fall of ground? What have you seen, man?

'Kathleen!' Barney screwed his eyes at the wind and pointed her out for him. 'She's almost down on the staging. I tried to stop her but she wouldn't listen.'

Rhodes picked her out, hand over hand she made short work of the ladders.

'Damn her foolhardiness! I warned her about going down there, the wind's too bloody strong.'

Raindrops, fat as rotten windfalls splattered against his

shoulders. He glanced at the clouds and what he feared for the most he now saw inside of them. Mesmerised by that swirling core of white mist he shouted out a warning.

'Hailstones Barney. I've seen this before and sure as we're standing here now we are in for a pounding!'

Within the storm's turbulent heart, violent air currents rose up thousands of feet; vapour and droplets changed from water to ice, and, like magnetised iron filings they sought each other out, conjoining in their hundreds of thousands. It was because of this natural gathering together that some became as gnarled, fist-sized stones of solid ice.

'I'm going down there, Barney.'

'For God's sake, Rhodes, why put yourself in danger, there's nothing you can do.' .

Rhodes forced his way past and gripped the ladder's topmost rung with both hands; his inherent fear of heights now there at his shoulder and gleefully did it urge him closer in to the sheer drop.

'The least I can do is warn them, Kathleen has no idea of what's coming.' He saw the disbelief in Barney's face. 'And yes, Mister Barnato, if it adds credence to your argument, I am totally and irrevocably terrified of climbing ladders.'

'You are always one to consider the facts, Rhodes; besides the likelihood of your being blown off the ladders, you'll never get back before the storm hits!'

'I can try, Barney,' he smiled thinly. 'I know that I am not the world's best at this sort of thing, but I might at least see a way of cobbling together some sort of shelter. To me, good friends are worth more than diamonds, I treasure them deeply.'

Rhodes tried as best he could to hide his fear of the pit, but his limbs were shaking. Dust, whipped from the surface workings, coloured his skin to match his clothes, and his hair flew wild and red and confused about his ears.

'Do what you can to secure our equipment, Barney, before it follows me over the edge. Get it tied together and weighted down before the storm breaks. Use rope, wire, whatever will do the job, man!'

Through half closed eyes Rhodes located a lower rung and secured himself a foot hold, but his weakened heart and fear of the abyss was now the iron band around his chest. However, determined to reach the staging, with supreme effort he stepped below the lip and started down into the immensity of that man-made chasm.

Rapidly cooling air poured downwards from over the pit edge. Ahead of it, the warmer air was being displaced, forced upwards by the phenomenon, so that the sky above the workings began to alter. Churned inwardly, the dust towered upwards for over a thousand feet to meet the rain clouds, and, lifted from the abyss as if by the purposeful force of God's own hand, the air took on a strange and ominous colouring; that of watered primrose yellow, the colour of powdered Kimberlite. At its centre, where the uppermost clouds were at their darkest, from the opening of a pale eye, a super-cooled shaft of white mist had manifested itself, cutting through veils of storm rain with the insistence of iced sunlight, and from within it, thousands upon thousands of hailstones plummeted earthwards.

Hardened diggers abandoned their work at the tables and those without canvas tents snatched up whatever they could lay their hands on; offcut nine-by-threes or lengths of tin sheeting. Others took shelter beneath rickety lean-tos and even the spaces below the sorting tables were looked to for protection. Whatever men could find was hurriedly lashed together with rope and weighted down with rock from the waste dumps; fashioned as makeshift shelters, diggers and labourers alike crawled beneath them, huddled together like sheep, they waited for the storm to thunder past; that it might swing away to the west and run itself dry above some other far-flung part of the wilderness.

Just moments before Rhodes stepped from the ladder to the staging, the firmament darkened threefold. The sun had been blanked out and what was once, less than an hour ago a benign wash of pale blue, was now a heaving cauldron of cloud and yellow dust, engulfed from above by a deepening grimace of black sky.

'Kathleen!' Rhodes came up alongside her and took hold of her arm. 'We have to move! We're running out of time, get yourself onto the ladder before it's too late.'

Kathleen pushed his hand away and gestured for him to look down upon the adjoining claim. At a further depth of some twenty feet, the earthen platform was no larger than the floor space of a small room. Fixed to wooden pegs in the sidewall, a canvas sheet had been drawn part way over the digging, tightly strung against continual showers of loosened stones – only space enough for a ladder and the lifting and lowering of the old man's gravel bucket had been left open.

'Old man Brown's still down there!' she shouted through the thunder, 'I've seen him, Rhodes, but he cannot hear me!'

'Or chooses not to,' Rhodes countered, 'not many men have worked the pit for as long as Thomas Brown. Short of an earthquake or a case of good whisky, nothing on God's earth will move him off his claim.'

'What about the rain? The ground will be loosened; he could well be buried alive.'

'Not just rain, Kathleen,' Rhodes made a fist in front of her face, 'hailstones, some of them bigger than this. A clout on the head from one of these and you will finish up grist for Dyffed Jones' burial business.' He pointed to the ladders. 'We must leave now or pay the price.'

As if on cue, a single massive hailstone, crystal clear and

jagged-edged, the size of a blacksmith's four pound hammer head collided with Zingeli's steel shovel and sent it spinning from his hands. Slack mouthed, he left the shovel where it fell and with empty hands he acknowledged the futility of their still being there. Zingeli shook his head at Kathleen, he knew that their luck was running out and with growing trepidation, looked to the ladders.

'We have left it too late, *inkosazana*. Climb the ladder now and the *amatshe isichotho*, the ice stones, will dash the brains from our skulls.'

One man threw down his pick and, driven by his own fear ran for the ladders; his eyes now those of the panicked bullock. Above his head the thunder bellowed and lightning, like the devil's bony fingers, reached through the deluge to caress the very air above the diggings. Others started forwards in the vain attempt to bring the runner back, however, terrified by the chaos, the man's speed was beyond equalling.

'Let him go,' Zingeli shouted after them, 'when the buffalo runs from a burning forest, nothing will stop him. Already he is beyond our help.'

The terrified Zulu went at the ladders two rungs at a time, pounding the wooden slats with bare feet. Others now looked to their own survival and squatted close-in to the sidewall, as makeshift shields they put up their shovels and cowered beneath them.

From the small protection of an upturned loading platform, Kathleen and Rhodes watched the runner's determined attempt to reach the surface. Awestruck by the speed of his ascent, with morbid fascination they prayed for him to win the race, though both of them suspected otherwise and waited for the inevitable to happen.

'Please let him make it!' Kathleen willed the climber upwards and with her fingers locked to Rhodes' arm she held her breath.

Barely a yard from the ladder head, a single piece of ice,

the size of a small bird struck the Zulu's head with the lethal force of a hammer blow. Like a child's discarded doll, the Zulu slumped against the ladder; the expression on his face, that of bewilderment. For a long moment the weight of his own body held him there, and then, just as the full fury of the storm stepped out from the pit edge, his fingers slackened and like a wild pheasant shot mid-flight, he spiralled outwards into the abyss.

# -45-

Blackie McKinnon watched and waited for the worst of the hailstorm to pass overhead, then, without any feelings of remorse, turned his back on his claim and walked away from the western edge of the pit. Not once did he look over his shoulder, nor did he regret his selling off of that small patch of diamond-bearing ground to the best of twenty eager buyers.

Now the sky was heavy – encouraged by violent thunder and shaken of all its ice, the clouds closed ranks, the ground for more than a mile in any direction was covered over with hailstones, inches deep across the diggings. At every crash of lightning, the hail shone brighter than any starlight; electric-blue. Seemingly every glittering gem from Kimberley's Big Hole had been taken out from the earth and scattered there.

Men were back in the open, salvaging what they could from the devastation. The look on their faces one of disbelief that, in such a short period of time, so much fury could have been unleashed upon them. The rain was now incessant and those who were still inside the pit threw down their shovels and fought for a footing on the ladders, for the stagings were awash and ankle deep in treacherous, yellow mud.

McKinnon settled his hat against the downpour and from beneath the brim he sought out a way between the gravel heaps, close-in to the pit edge so that no one would question his being there. Before nightfall, he would be well outside the town's furthest limits, a good five miles beyond any last hint of whatever the town of Kimberley stood for. The two thousand pounds from the sale of his claim had made him a rich man; another boarding house perhaps, a drinking establishment or a whorehouse even, with pretty mulatto girls brought up from the Cape. Whichever one he chose it did not matter, but there was one last thing for him to put to bed before collecting his horse from livery, and he had sworn an oath against the forfeit of his own life that he would not leave Kimberley town with that day's work left unfinished.

He followed the pit edge to where a narrow causeway struck outwards from solid ground, to those claims at the very centre of the pit the causeway was their lifeline, an artery through which the life's blood of upwards of a thousand diggers flowed back and forth. Over it, at any one time, a dozen or more bullock carts carried newly mined gravel back to the sorting tables and to either side the drop fell away, sheer as Dover's cliffs, strung and pinned at ten yard intervals with the makeshift booms and pulleys of the diggers' hoisting tackle.

Under cover of the rain, McKinnon followed the causeway. He reached a prominent point in the track, a small outcrop of unmined ground that he was familiar with. Below his feet and at a sharp angle some hundred yards to the east, through a window in the rain, claim 339 stood out from the sidewall and it was upon it that he focused the full force of his hatred. Secured by a strip of canvas, from behind his shoulder he lifted across a tubular leather carrying case and flipped back the lid. The spyglass slid from its protective holder and with the draws fully extended, McKinnon soon found what he was looking for.

From a hundred different points, slurry splattered away from the pit edge and maliciously it covered everything below. Slabs of sodden earth slid silently into the pit. Prised from the earthen wall by the rain, most were less in weight than a shovelful, though others, flensed from solid ground by scores of undermining rivulets, were the weight and girth of fully loaded bullock carts. It was these gargantuan falls of ground that earned them the name of Widow Makers, and amongst the diggers, those who had mined the deepest, almost always paid the biggest price.

Forced from the ladders by lashing hail, two Zulu labourers had taken refuge close-in to the sidewall and it was this act of self-regard which had robbed them of their lives. They were now entombed, crushed to death by tons of saturated gravel, buried alive by that same diamond-bearing ground which had succoured them. Horrified, Kathleen stared down at the earthen mound which was now their tombstone. She had seen it fall and it was the uncanny lack of forewarning which had terrified her the most. On impact, the mud and gravel became a solid matrix and like a mixing of builders' mortar and stone, already it had become immovable. Kathleen shouted at the top of her voice to Zingeli.

'Get your men off the staging, Zingeli, the hailstones are gone. Use the ladders before the water breaks them free from the wall!'

The lighter, more agile went first and like rats to the rigging of a flooded ship, they scrambled upwards through the deluge. Only when the last man was well past the halfway mark did Rhodes and Kathleen turn their attentions back to the diggings. From the edge of the staging, together they looked downwards at the adjoining claim.

'Old man Brown, Rhodes! Where is he? I cannot see him.'

Rhodes cupped both hands against his forehead to shield his eyes from the rain.

'The canvas sail, Kathleen. Brown had it fixed to the sidewall, it's been flattened!'

It was then that Zingeli realised the unevenness of the lower staging. The canopy in its entirety had been caught by a fall of ground. Covered over with slip from the sidewall, only the head of one, single pick protruded from the mud.

'The earth has covered him over, *inkosazana*! We must hurry, there might still be life.' He reached out and swung his weight across the gap and onto the rungs of Brown's ladder. Like a snake from the limbs of a wet tree he slid downwards onto the staging.

# -47-

Thomas Brown lay on his side with his head twisted hard against his shoulder. From the waist down he was unable to move, held about the lower parts of his body by a vice-like girdle of heavy earth. The urge for him to scream climbed up from inside of him, but paralysed by fear, his throat was held immobile and like his legs, his voice was rendered impotent, only his panic enjoyed free rein. He closed his eyes against the darkness; the demons that held him down were there alongside him, and from within in that narrow space between the canvas sail and the kibble, vindictively they whispered to him. However, because of the nearness that same metal kibble and the tautness of the canvas sheet he was able to breathe what little air was left. Without them, the slurry would have killed and covered him completely.

With supreme effort, he fought his fear and listened for sounds – the sound of pick and shovel and the voices of men who were by now, he prayed, looking for him, but the sounds he could hear were small, that of his own breathing and the steady, drip by drip of water leaking in through a small tear in the canvas.

Zingeli vaulted from the ladders and onto the old man's staging and immediately he looked upwards for the others to follow.

Kathleen shook her head at Rhodes; he had neither the strength nor the will for him to make it across the gap. The rain had plastered his hair, flattened it against his skull and through the sodden texture of his flannel shirt, the girlish outline of his chest stood out clearly. Every breath that he took seemed to Kathleen as though it might well be his last.

'Stay here, Rhodes. You have done what you can. When you find the strength, get back on surface.' Without allowing him the chance to argue, like a cat stepping the gap between two buildings, she leaned outwards from the staging and, light on her feet, swung herself onto the ladder and followed Zingeli down.

The storm had slackened and the thunder, now a lesser growl was more the grumblings of an old man; the lightning, all but gone, mere flickerings above the western edge of the pit. Still, from that surrounding lake of sodden ground, the mud poured down from the pit edge. Zingeli braced his foot against the compacted mound of fallen earth and with all his strength, drew back on the pick. The wooden haft made a sucking noise when it came free. Kathleen put the depth of fallen ground at no more than a few feet. She prayed silently, that by some trick of fate the old man had been spared the agony of suffocation, that they might drag him from beneath the gravel, coughing and cursing them for having taken so long. She nodded her head to Zingeli; they had no choice, other than using the pick there was no other way of them reaching him.

'From the edge,' she encouraged, and pointed out the shallowest part of the mound. 'Dig like ten men, Zingeli! Dig as you have never dug before.'

Zingeli went at the gravel with the mindset of a lioness freeing her errant cub from an ant bear hole; each time the steel bit, Kathleen screwed up her eyes in anticipation of it finding soft flesh in place of hard gravel. However, Zingeli was a master with the miner's pick and with the skill of a surgeon plumbing the depths of a shrapnel wound, so did he gauge the depth and angle of his strike. Kathleen took up a shovel from where it had been abandoned to the sidewall, and when the loosened earth became too deep, she cleared it from about Zingeli's feet, timing her efforts as to match them with the upwards swing of his pick.

To Thomas Brown the total blackness of that tiny space between the metal bucket and his canvas roof was now the true worth of all his working life; an endless tunnel strewn with the debris of all his failures. Now, the acceptance of that fact was easier to bear and a strange silence settled over him, a feeling of peaceful resignation, for the air he now breathed was all but spent of oxygen and through the ache behind his eyes the images he saw turned fanciful. He saw the sky, the sun and the night with all its stars and the embers of that last night's fire. He saw many things, most of them a lie, but the stone he had reached from that break in the earthen wall just seconds before that fall of ground was real; cold as arctic ice it was still there, clenched hard in to the palm of his hand.

From the edge of the causeway and near on a hundred feet above claim 339, Blackie McKinnon watched the drama unfold. The rain had gone, so that now the images inside his telescope were pin sharp and the urgency with which Kathleen O'Rourke shouted her instructions rang out crystal clear from the staging. He focused the lens on the ladder; clinging to the slippery rungs like some bedraggled rat, Cecil Rhodes inched his way upwards. McKinnon smiled at Rhodes' inability to cope with any exertion and, from under his breath he mocked the man for his lack of masculinity.

'Yes, Mister Rhodes, you get on back home for a hot bath and a change of drawers whilst old Blackie here squares your friend O'Rourke for what she owes him.'

He inclined the telescope at a more downward angle and quickly he found the staging. He ignored the Zulu and instead, filled the lens with Kathleen's image. Openly, he marvelled at the power in her shoulders, though that same strength was not enough to distract him from her womanliness, rather than corrupt that latent femininity, her potency aroused in him a hundred separate fantasies. Aside from a need for him to set the record straight, it was her preferred needlessness for any man that drew him to her. Incessantly, she worked the shovel and without resting, matched the Zulu's efforts, one filled shovel to his every blow with the heavy pick. The sight of Kathleen's powerful forearms inflamed him; the outline of her breasts and that of her buttocks when she bent her back to shovel away the gravel. All of these things and more served as the drug which clipped at his breathing and quickened his heartbeat. She was to him, the want of life to a dying man.

From the desperate way with which Kathleen threw aside the mud and gravel, McKinnon realised that whatever she was after, it was not diamonds. He squatted against his heels and settled down to watch; an hour at the most was all that was needed. He smiled at the goings on inside his head – he was in no hurry, but the eagerness for what he had come for was already awake inside his breeches. However, satisfied to watch her from a distance, he held Kathleen's image within the lens; if needs pushed him beyond his ability to wait, then a few minutes at most and he could be down there on the staging.

'The canvas sail!' Kathleen shouted to Zingeli. 'If we are lucky....' She plunged the steel blade of her shovel beneath the edge of the downed awning and with all her weight levered downwards on the handle. 'It's moving,' she grunted under the strain, but only the first few inches lifted clear of the ground, 'there's still too much gravel, Zingeli, we must hurry.'

Zingeli hefted his pick and determinedly he stripped away gravel from off that canvas coffin. He broke up a further yard of compacted overburden and with his eyes, urged Kathleen to help him clear it aside and then, with both hands, he took a firm grip on the canvas.

'When I lift the sail, *inkosazana*, with all your strength push the shovel beneath it.'

Kathleen steadied herself. She glanced upwards, but only for a second. Rhodes was still on the ladder, by the time he raised the alarm, Thomas Brown would be beyond any help; it would be too late.

'I am ready,' she told Zingeli, and on his first lift she forced in the shovel's curved blade for as far as was humanly possible; with each subsequent lift she gained deeper access.

'I can feel something,' she looked at Zingeli, 'not stone, something softer.'

Zingeli released his grip on the sail and with renewed commitment tore away more ground. Now, more of the canvas sheet fell open and with their shoulders touching they went at the larger pieces with their bare hands.

425

'Thomas!' Kathleen shouted, with her face close to where they had cleared a path through the rubble. 'Damn you Thomas Brown, I know you're alive, speak to me!' She looked to Zingeli for him to try again. 'This time we lift together,' she told him and again, shoulder to shoulder, every last ounce of their flagging strength they threw into lifting back that final barrier.

At first, still pinned to the staging by hardening slurry, the canvas sail held firm, then reluctantly, some of the overburden gave way and toppled sideways.

'Again Zingeli!' Kathleen's adrenalin surged, buoyed by their small success. Like the circus strong man preparing to lift the heavy bar, they crouched down and took the strain with their legs. With their arms at either side they filled their lungs with clean air and prepared for the lift. 'With everything you've got my friend and this time, with the strength of ten men or the old man stands little chance of us pulling him out alive.'

# -49-

With the storm gone, slowly, the diggings came back to life, ox-carts lumbered forward and one after the other, they went back along those narrow causeways which spanned the pit. Diggers returned to their claims and the very air about the diamond diggings was again filled with the sounds of hurried activity. The sound of men shouting, the bellowing of frightened oxen and the roping in of a thousand scarified pulley-blocks; flushed of their grease by torrential rain, as steel upon steel the pulley wheels shrieked and clattered for a fresh dollop of tallow. Overseers checked their tipping ramps and sorting equipment for damage and their labour force for injuries, and they peered downwards inside the pit, praying for their men on the lower levels to have been left untouched. On surface, those who had been caught out in the open by the full fury of the storm now stood about like sheep, shocked and bewildered, unable to comprehend the violence reeked by the deluge. At pit bottom, knee deep in sucking, yellow mud, men searched with heavy hearts through the silence of the devastation.

The carnage was rife. There was no place on the lower levels which had been spared sufferance, what was once a dry digging littered with dust-covered men and discarded equipment was now the buffalo's wallow. With bare hands and blinded shovels, diggers tore at the mud for any hint as to where their comrades had been interred, but the mud had closed them in and had left no sign. It would take days, or weeks even for them to find and free the dead from the rapidly hardening matrix.

The hubbub suited McKinnon, insensitive to what had happened he picked his way over tenuous walkways. From staging to staging he jumped the gaps and jockeyed the ladders, and then, when he came to within earshot of claim 339, he crouched down behind a slip of fallen earth. With only his head exposed, like the anticipatory lion newly arrived at the waterhole, he settled himself for the wait.

Kathleen O'Rourke went down onto her stomach and waited for Zingeli to lift the canvas sheeting as high as his aching shoulders would allow. Like a snake inching its way beneath a slab of fallen rock, she slithered inwards to the depth of her breeches belt. By raising up on her elbows, she forced back the canvas sail. However, with her upper body now shrouded in darkness, the acidic stench of mud and old air came over her, and for that first moment she felt the fear of being buried alive crawl in close alongside her.

'Thomas!' She bellowed into the darkness. 'Can you hear me Thomas?' She reached out in front of her. Loose gravel blocked her fingers and out of frustration she lashed out and swept it aside. 'For God's sake Thomas – speak to me or make a noise so we know you're alive!'

To Thomas Brown, the voice he heard meant nothing. Poisoned by the re-breathing of his own oxygen-starved air, his mind had reached that befuddled state of heavy narcosis, the same hallucinatory world of the addict, that halfway house between life and death. In the light that swirled inside his head he saw so many things, so many faces, most of them long since forgotten. Then all of them were gone, taken from him, swirled away by mist and rain and inside of it all the stone he now held in his hand, by some unseen force, was being pulled inexorably from his fingertips.

'I've found him Zingeli!' Kathleen outlined the heel of a leather boot with her fingers. She braced her feet against the staging and by wriggling from side to side drove her weight further forwards, reclaiming a few more precious inches from beneath the mound.

Zingeli leaned backwards and with all the strength of his legs and shoulders raised himself another foot. Like a sodden hound, the canvas sail shook off some of its slurry, but where the gravel was at its greatest depth, only cracks appeared in its surface. Had he been carrying a knife, he could have easily slit the canvas and hauled it clear of the staging. However, the extra height he had provided gave Kathleen the chance she had prayed for and with her arms fully extended, she groped for a hold on the old man's ankles. Tightening her grip, she felt the warmth of living flesh. Like a terrier set to drag its prey from the burrow, she hunched her shoulders and then, having gathered in all her remaining strength, inched backwards towards the light.

'Zingeli! Pull me out, he's still alive!'

In exchange for the canvas sail, with his hands locked to Kathleen's ankles, slowly Zingeli took the strain of her dead weight and leaned back against his heels. Like an iron link in a taut chain, Kathleen felt herself been drawn to the point of her breaking in two and she knew it would not be long before she was forced into letting go. Then gradually, inch by inch, with her hands still to locked to just above the old man's boots, she felt that first backwards movement.

She prayed for the overlying weight of mud and gravel to hold off, and at the moment of her crying out from the pain in her shoulders, like the birthing of an awkward child, from amidst a rush of yellow slurry, Zingeli drew her out into the sunlight.

# -50-

Through his telescope, Blackie McKinnon watched Kathleen clean the old man's cheeks of blood and filth, but it was what Kathleen did next that held him spellbound. Knelt at Thomas' side, she checked his limbs and chest for breakages; she found none. Satisfied that he was still in one piece and that his airways were free of encumbrance, she prised apart the clenched fingers of his right hand.

'Sweet mother of Mary Magdalene,' McKinnon's voice hissed like steam from hot coals, 'damn you to hell McKinnon, get a hold of yourself, what you are looking at cannot be real.'

His heartbeat skipped, in the same way that hail had skipped from off the sorting tables, for the image inside his telescope was all of a thousand times more beguiling than anything he had ever dreamed of.

For long moments, Kathleen stared down at Thomas' open hand. What he had snatched from the sidewall just seconds before being engulfed, was a stone the size of a child's fist, the size of a small yellow peach. Thomas looked up at her, and though he was unable to speak with his mouth, he did so with his eyes.

From where he crouched behind the gravel heap, McKinnon struggled to steady his spyglass. His entire body trembled, and as had happened on that night in the Port of Natal, from his first glimpsing of Kathleen's naked body, on its hind legs that same perversity once again raised itself up, fearsome and wolf-like, and from its den behind McKinnon's eyes, it growled for surcease.

Kathleen nodded her head to the old man and took up the stone from his hand.

'The story you told me,' she reminded him, 'my first time on the diggings; do you remember it, Thomas?'

He nodded back at her, as yet unable to talk.

'No one believed you.' She smiled sympathetically and shook her head at the ridicule he must have endured, and like the victorious athlete lofting up the winner's trophy she lifted the stone in front of his face, just high enough for it to be infected with full sunlight.

Though the diamond was bigger than any other she had ever seen, still she felt no urge for her to shout the find across the diggings. What she held in her hand was the realisation of one man's private dream, one that had kept the old man going, a culmination of the months he had spent bending his back in reverence to that now, mile wide treacherous hole in the ground.

'The stone you lost to that storm, Thomas. Is this the very one?' Kathleen asked him, and he acknowledged her asking with a small nod of his head. 'Then trust me when I say that I will take care of it, you have my word.' Without her succumbing to the immensity of the find, she fastened away the gem inside her breast pocket. Instinctively, she looked about the staging for the means with which to keep him warm, but the act was fanciful.

'Zingeli,' she gestured to him, 'find Rhodes. Tell him what we have done here, but say nothing of the diamond. A blanket from the old man's bed, and brandy; a half bottle at least. As quick as you like, Zingeli, or the old man may not live to watch the sun go down.' She looked upwards to her own staging, the rest of the labour force was already out from the pit. Settling alongside the old man, she cradled his head in the crook of her arm and tried as best she could to protect him from the cold, covering him with her own body heat, but the shock induced from being trapped for that last hour beneath the ground fall was deeply set; by each new minute his shivering became more violent.

McKinnon watched the Zulu climb, and only after seeing Zingeli reach level ground did he break cover. With the spyglass slung across his shoulders, again he followed a latticework of rickety walkways and chain ladders; on the staging above where Kathleen was sitting, he crouched down and listened. Satisfied that she was now alone with the old man, as lightly as a leopard from its watch place in the treetops, McKinnon followed the ladder down to where Kathleen and Thomas Brown huddled together on the staging.

# -51-

'What're you after, McKinnon?'

'Whatever it is that takes my fancy,' he prodded her breast pocket with the barrel of his pistol, 'starting with what you have in there, lassie.'

He looked to Thomas Brown and his eyes narrowed, they showed no concern for the digger's injuries.

'Your race is run old man, what I'm after you'll not be needing anymore.' With thick fingers he flicked open the button on Kathleen's shirt pocket and took out the diamond, he smiled at his own fortuitous timing; an hour later and he would have missed out on the windfall.

'You messed up, Thomas. Should have got yourself out from the pit when you still had the chance.'

The old man tried to retaliate, vainly he attempted to right himself, but both the power in his arms and that of his voice failed him. McKinnon glanced upwards to the ladder head; save for Kathleen and the old man no one knew he was there. The decision came easily to him. The two thousand pounds he had reaped from the selling off of his claim, would, along with the Thomas Brown's last find see him on easy street for the rest of his life.

'You and me, old man, never did care much for one another and that's a fact. Not since my first day on the diggings.' He leaned from the waist and with the fingers and thumb of his right hand, grasped Tom by the throat and shut off the air to his lungs. 'By the time they find you, I'll be long gone. Bad luck, you getting covered over by the mud and all. Got no choice, old man, wouldn't do old Blackie any good for you to go about the diggings bad-mouthing him for stealing your findings, would it now.'

The old man barely found strength enough to raise his hand. Kathleen sat immobile, unable to move, the gun barrel no more than an inch from her chest. She was being forced into watching the old man die and prayed for Rhodes or Zingeli to look down on the staging; either one of them would know that something was wrong and raise the alarm.

'You evil bastard, McKinnon, let the old man be. Take the stone and go. I give you my word that I will say nothing of your being here.'

'That's right, lassie, a black-hearted son of a bitch, sired by the devil himself, my wife once said,' he increased the pressure on Thomas' throat and watched the light go out from his eyes, 'but both you and I knew that it would come to this. Thomas Brown just got in the way. That's the way things are, lassie. Some men strike it lucky, others like your father and the old man here choose their own time to die.'

Without loosening his grip on Thomas' throat, McKinnon rolled his lifeless body over the edge of the

432

staging; the corpse slapped against a pool of deep slurry at pit bottom and quickly it was sucked down.

'On your feet,' he growled to Kathleen and pressed the gun barrel against her ribcage, 'do as I say or the old man will have himself a pretty girl for company.' He waved her towards the ladder. 'Go right from the staging and on your life, woman, give me only the slightest reason to doubt your intent and I will kill you.'

For every step Kathleen took, every footfall to the ladderways which linked the different stagings, McKinnon matched her progress, never further behind than a few yards. On reaching the causeway, McKinnon purposely steered Kathleen amongst the bullock carts and crowds of labouring diggers; she looked back across the pit and desperately searched the stagings for any sign of someone following.

'They will come after you, McKinnon. Barnato and Rhodes will soon figure out what has happened.'

'I would thank you to keep your mouth shut, missy. By the time that happens I'll be well on my way to the Pniel diggings, or who knows, maybe I'll forego Pniel and ride the coach east to Natal and take up where I left off with that thin-faced bitch of mine. I fancy she'll take me back as an equal partner in the boarding house if my price is right.'

He closed the gap between them.

'That night in your bedroom, the boarding house...? You took something from me, I want it back.'

'I don't have it with me.'

'But you still have it in your possession, as sure as I'm standing here now,' McKinnon insisted, 'and I'll not be leaving Kimberley without it.' He looked to her for an answer. 'Better for us both if you weigh up the consequences of you're not telling me. Make up your mind, woman, but do it quickly, my patience is wearing thin.'

He allowed her a moment and then pushed hard for what he was after.

'One last time, woman. Where do you keep the fob chain?'

'Either way, McKinnon, I am already dead so why would I tell you?'

'Your choice, O'Rourke. Your life for the bauble. Hand it over and on your father's grave I swear I will set you free.'

'You're lying, McKinnon. Aside from your murdering my father, I am the only one who witnessed what happened to the old man. I can find no reason as to why would you let me live?'

'Because I can,' he told her, 'give me back the chain with the diamonds intact and I will be out of your life forever, it will all be over. No more looking over your shoulder. It ends here, today, in Kimberley; no proof of my finishing off the old man, no witnesses, aside from yourself.'

His smile was that of a Bedlam inmate and like those few remaining pockets of bright hailstones, his eyes glittered.

'As for your queer inclinations for the company of other women,' he shrugged his shoulders, 'means nothing to me, we all have our needs and like I said, lassie, you makes your own bed.'

He waved her onwards and glanced up at the sky.

'Another hour and it will be dark. Your lodgings at the Queens – from the stable yard, take the back stairs to the upper landing, on your life, O'Rourke, make sure that no one sees us.'

## 52

Rhodes moved in alongside Barney Barnato and stared down inside the pit. He searched for movement, anything, however small which might point to Kathleen's whereabouts. However, for fifty yards to either hand of the staging, the diggings were silent, devoid of any activity; only from the deepest parts were men and equipment being dragged both dead and broken from the mud. Rhodes angled the brim of his hat against the glare of low sun, and he strained his eyes for any sign of Kathleen and the old man.

'They have to be there, had they climbed the ladders we would have seen them.'

'No one has come up from the staging,' Barney insisted, 'Zingeli said the old man had suffered badly, that he was barely alive. Kathleen could never have moved him, not without help.' He looked across to Brown's tent. Zingeli had stripped a blanket from off the old man's dilapidated iron bed frame and across his shoulders he slung a canvas miner's bag. He draped the blanket around his neck and came back to the ladder head. Rhodes stopped him from climbing onto the first rung.

'Leave the blanket and the brandy, Zingeli. It would appear they have gone; there's no one on the staging. Quick as you like now, get on down there, try your best to find out what the blazes is going on.'

Zingeli took the rungs in twos and threes and was soon ankle deep in mud; aside from discarded picks and shovels the staging was empty. He crossed to the adjoining ladder and climbed down to where he had pulled Kathleen and the old man from under the canvas sail; again, other than a confusion of boot prints and his own pick marks, there was no other sign of anyone having been there. He looked upwards to where Rhodes and Barnato were watching from the pit edge and he spread his arms out wide, highlighting the futility of him being there; both stagings were empty.

'They've gone, Barney, the both of them. Don't ask me how or where to because I don't bloody well know.'

Barney didn't hear him. His eyes were fixed to the high causeway, a distance of over two hundred yards stood between the narrow access road and where he was standing.

'Rhodes, top of the causeway, a few yards left of centre. What do you see?'

Again, the sunlight's low angle forced Rhodes into drawing down the brim of his hat, almost to the point of it covering his eyebrows.

'Kathleen,' he answered him, 'I would recognise that walk from double the distance.' He screwed up his eyes to tight slits and strained for better detail, but the images blurred and mingled in with those of other miners. Long shadows made it even harder for him to tell who she was with. Barney hurried over to Brown's tent and returned with a battered pair of brass field glasses; he handed them to Rhodes.

'Saw these earlier, better than nothing, Rhodes. Give them a try.'

It wasn't long before Rhodes picked out Kathleen's boyish frame jostling between scores of diggers and bullock carts, and then, as though she had sensed him watching her, she turned face-on to where he was standing, and for a few seconds stared outwards from the causeway.

'Definitely our missing O'Rourke. She has to have climbed the chain ladders between the stagings. No sign of old Thomas Brown, though, and damn me if I'm wrong, Barney, but I'll back an English tenner against your pound, that the man walking behind her is our mutual friend, Blackie McKinnon.'

## 53

Robbed of choice, Kathleen waited for McKinnon to follow her through from the stairs landing, and it was McKinnon who closed the door, turned the key and slid in the extra locking bar.

'The curtains,' he nodded his head at the open window, 'draw them closed.' Kathleen set the lamp down on the table and did as she was told. 'And candles,' McKinnon insisted, 'as many as there are, too damn dark in here, can't see what you're up to.'

Kathleen held a paper spill above the open lamp glass and when the flame caught hold she carried it from candle to candle. The added light and the familiarity of her own room gave chance to the gathering in of her thoughts. The shadows fell back and apart from places where the light was unable to reach, contrary to her mood, her bedroom flowed and filled with gentle colours. For a small moment, the urge for her to fight back seemed fair exchange for what she knew was going to happen, so that she contemplated the wardrobe door. Behind it, the Colt lay with all six chambers primed and loaded with powder and ball, the Sharps and Winchester rifles close alongside it.

'Your shirt...' McKinnon slumped into the nearest armchair, '...take it off.'

He levelled his pistol.

'No rushing mind – nice and slow now,' he stretched out his legs and his boots ground grit and dirt into the waxed surface of her centre table, 'we both have plenty of time, sweetheart, not like before.'

'The diamonds,' Kathleen reminded him. She made pretence of searching for them, but the contrivance served only to annoy him.

'In exchange for your life, my lovely, and the promise still stands.' He levelled the gun with her stomach and drew back the steel hammer to half-cock, 'but you're wasting my time. Start with the shirt, take it off. Shout for help and I might just be forced into changing my mind.'

'That night,' she chased back her fear and with extreme effort, disguised the loathing in her voice; the urgent need for her to delay McKinnon now paramount, 'Upstairs at the boarding house; last room on the right, end of the corridor.'

'What of it?'

'You knew I was in there, alone – naked even.'

Hungrily, he fed off the recollection.

'The moonlight was strong. I could never forget it.' He settled his weight to the chair – with his legs outstretched, the bulge behind his breeches fly now showed a life of its own. 'White as lilies you were. Like I said, the moonlight was strong that night – new snow, ready for that first treading.'

'You were watching through the keyhole?'

McKinnon nodded his head, he sensed her mood swing, the edge had gone from her voice.

'That I was, for a good ten minutes at least. Every move you made, old Blackie was on to it.' He had seen it happen before; from abject fear to lust or the need even for uncontrollable violence inside of a heartbeat.

'If I had known you were there...' She left him with the intimation, the sentence unfinished.

McKinnon dropped his legs from the table edge and leaned forwards on his elbows.

'Spit it out, lassie. Finish off what you were saying.'

With conviction, Kathleen pressed ahead with the subterfuge, but she knew that if it failed, being forced to fight a man of McKinnon's strength would at best, see her badly beaten and left for dead on the floor. She steeled herself and with laughing eyes enticed out his weakness for young girls.

'You were not the first, McKinnon.'

She encouraged his drinking in of her own, supposed

perversity. With the point of her tongue she moistened her lips, beguiling him with suggestive smiles and a narrowing of those green eyes, but cautiously, not enough for him to see beyond the limits of her trickery. Coyly, she portrayed herself as the lewd young woman, the pretentious coquette, though innocent enough for her portrayal to invigorate his imaginings.

'The ship's master, Mister Trevelyan,' purposely she softened her voice to a cat's purr and with suggestive hands she stroked the deep cleft at the juncture of her thighs, 'he was here more than once and over a month before you, McKinnon; had him all red in the face and blowing off steam like a railroad engine.'

McKinnon lowered the pistol, his eyes bulged in their sockets and a starlet of bright spittle rolled out from his lower lip for the voices inside his head were now in uproar. Where only minutes before there was little more than a hollowness left to him by his killing of the old man, now there was a rising up of extreme excitement, so strong and infectious that, like his eyes, his breeches bulged enough to match the widest span of his fingertips.

Kathleen loosened the buttons on her shirt and with the slowness of an erotic dancer, slipped her arms from out of the sleeves; with planned deliberation, she allowed the garment long moments for it to slide downwards to the floor. Her breasts, though small were pert, perfectly shaped, unblemished and pale as falling Dakota snow. In McKinnon's twisted mind, they were the untouched breasts of the virgin adolescent.

'Fifteen years old, McKinnon, most men would have suffered pain from their striving to get into me, but I allowed it to happen, helped him even,' she encouraged the lie and like the apprenticed whore, purposely thrust with her hips so that in McKinnon's eyes she was now the willing lover, 'the full grown bull with a half grown heifer. Hard as living rock between my thighs he was, is this not what men such as yourself can only dream about?'

## 54

'Kathleen came back twenty minutes ago, just after dark.' Lizzie Jardine grabbed a hold of Barney's arm, forcefully she steered him out of the room. Rhodes followed them into the private office at the back of the hotel's foyer.

From under the counter, she took out a bottle and poured herself two full fingers of London Gin.

'Can't be sure who's with her,' she looked at Barney, her eyes wide, her voice rasped and trembled, 'they went in through the livery yard, one of my stable lads saw them and on his mother's life swears that it was McKinnon, he remembers him from the fight.' She discarded the tumbler. 'I can't do this alone, Barney, the three of us can go up there together. There's trouble here, or Kathleen would have come in through the front door, not through my livery yard.'

Her hands were shaking. 'I can't put it off any longer. I'm going up to her room, with or without you.' Again, she reached below the mahogany counter top.

The gun had been pre-loaded with buck shot, an ageing 12 gauge, 32 inch double. With those wickedly hooked hammers it was the ultimate, formidable peacemaker. In the event of any head-on confrontation, the load was heavy enough to disembowel a running man at close range. By design, both hammers were at half cock, held back from resting against their primers. Barney caught hold of her arm and with his free hand took the gun from her. He nodded his head to Rhodes.

'Stay if you like, Rhodes, but I'm going with Lizzie. If Kathleen is in there with McKinnon, it will not be through her own choosing.'

'Have you fired a gun before?' Rhodes asked him.

'Only at ducks,' Barney confessed, 'one shot with a twelve bore single and I missed them all.'

'Then now is your chance for you to acquire a little more practice. Lead on, Barney my lad.' He nodded to Lizzie. 'We had best get on with it, McKinnon's a nasty piece of work, God knows what's going on inside that room.'

They took to the stairway in single file, Barney in front, the shotgun held at a high port. Every step creaked and groaned as if his weight alone were more than enough to send all three of them crashing through to the room below. From across the stairs landing, a weak sliver of yellow light bled from the foot of Kathleen's door, and the distorted growl of McKinnon's voice made for Barney to tighten his grip on the shotgun.

Behind the door, a dozen candle flames speared a pool of quiet light, stilled by the room's lacking in fresh air, for the windows were shut tight, the curtains drawn and the smoke from McKinnon's second cigar hovered wide and flat and mist-like close-in to the ceiling. The bottle McKinnon had left on the table was already at half-mast and his eyes were the same, dark slits of the leering river pike; black and empty of any remorse for what it was planning, encouraged to a point of dangerous euphoria by watching a gentle, sylph-like creature flirt within easy reach of its jaws.

From within that same fantasy and devoid of any compassion, McKinnon ordered her closer in to his chair.

'Come here, girl,' he held out his hand to her, 'something special for you – take up where we left off back in Natal, you could say.'

The gun came up, his hand was rock steady for the whisky had done what was asked of it. McKinnon saw nothing more than candlelight and Kathleen, nor did he want to, for at that moment, the sight of her young body wrapped in soft candlelight was enough. Her neck, long and sleek underlined a face which was to a fault, almost childlike. Her nipples were small; tiny rosebuds delicately cut from pink coral, and her breasts as a whole, though less than large were firm, unblemished; their purity of white was to Blackie McKinnon the colour of moonlit hail left behind by that last storm. But it was her hair, McKinnon now looked upon; cropped short, the aura it created was that of the fey, compliant cherub, threads of copper and gold, all of what he saw was enhanced by hard liquor and soft candlelight.

From below her throat the china-whiteness of her skin spread downwards, engulfing the flat of her stomach with pale hands. Only where her flesh had been purposely left uncovered had it been burned to a deep, mahogany brown by that incessant Kimberley heat.

McKinnon dropped his gaze and, unable to draw out the moment any longer, focused all his intent on that spear of flaming curls at the base of Kathleen's belly. She was the elfin virgin, and that which had grown thick and hard between his legs was now the punitive snake rising up from Eden's forbidden garden.

'I said for you to get on over here.' He warned her with those dead eyes and drew back the pistol's hammer to full cock. 'On your life, woman, do as you are told or I will gut you like a fish; same as I did your old man.'

Kathleen moved towards him and through her facing the bedroom door head-on, was suddenly aware of faint sounds filtering into the room; someone was out there, moving about on the landing. She raised her voice, though not enough for McKinnon to pick up on the ploy.

'One shot, McKinnon and you'll have twenty people banging at my door.'

McKinnon threw back his head and laughed at her reasoning.

'Or I might be out of here and headed for the river diggings before anyone knows what's happened.'

He reached for her, grasped her arm and pulled her towards him.

'Open him out.' He grinned at her and dragged down her right hand to the buttoned front of his breeches. Excited by the revulsion he had evoked in her, he pressed the pistol hard-in to Kathleen's side. 'Loose the devil out I said, or you'll get more than the back of my hand across that pretty face of yours.'

Kathleen fastened her eyes on the door behind him and, without looking down, freed the buckle on his belt; then, with numbed fingers, from his hairy belly to the crotch of his rancid breeches she slipped the buttons on Blackie McKinnon's fly.

From its nest of matted body hair and now, freed from any constraint, like nothing Kathleen had ever seen, it rose up cobra-headed from a fist-sized mass of genitalia; cowled in loose skin and with a life of its own, it convulsed excitedly. The veins that had engorged it were as the tenacious roots of the strangler fig, thickly knotted about their host, and though the blood inside of them was rich and bright red with oxygen, to Kathleen they appeared as sinister and revolting, dark blue, fed from the depths of McKinnon's groin to the where they dipped to behind the weeping eye of their shared prepuce.

'I can see from the look on your face, girlie, you two will get along just fine.'

He lassoed half the girth of it with his thumb and forefinger, at its base where the shaft was thickest.

'Your choice, O'Rourke, get yourself onto it. Whatever takes your fancy, mouth the beast or ride it, either way, best you get on down there.'

For a long moment, Kathleen stared down at the living thing in McKinnon's hand; in her eyes it was a creature fit only for beheading, a single stroke with a long knife. Bile rose up in her throat and she shivered violently.

'I would rather I died than do what you ask of me.'

McKinnon shot his hand upwards for her throat and with thick fingers, pulled her down onto her knees.

'And you might well get your wish, O'Rourke,' he forced her head between his legs, 'your mouth, girl – use it.'

He pushed the gun barrel hard against a pad of soft flesh, just an inch behind her ear. Very slowly, deliberately, he leaned over her and his breath was thick with malice and body heat.

'And bear in mind, lassie, bite down on me just once and I will blow out your brains.'

# -55-

'Kathleen, Two minutes, girl!' With huge effort, Lizzie controlled the timbre of her voice and rapped the door with her bare knuckles. 'Downstairs in my office, we need to talk.' Again, she knocked on Kathleen's door and continued the pretence. 'Cat got your tongue, O'Rourke? I know you're in there, damn it, I can hear you.'

Barney stood alongside her; the twelve bore double fully cocked, levelled at waist height. With worried eyes he focused on the brass door knob. Lizzie sensed his impatience and shook her head at him, the timing had to be right. Standing slightly to one side she reached for the door knob and at the point of one slow, full turn, it was then the door flew back on its hinges.

McKinnon stood with his arm outstretched, the barrel of a .44 calibre revolver less than a foot from Lizzie's face. With the strength of his left arm he held Kathleen across his chest; still naked, she was now the human shield.

'Inside!' He herded them through and like penned sheep they gathered together at the centre of the room. 'Your shotgun, Jew boy – on the table.'

Barney did as he was told and gave up the twelve bore. Like Rhodes, he avoided looking at Kathleen.

'Let her go, McKinnon. We are all of us, unarmed; for God's sake let her cover herself.'

McKinnon released his grip on Kathleen and slammed the door closed.

'Get dressed,' he told her, 'you're coming with me.' He

turned the gun on Cecil Rhodes. 'You would all do well to stay here; come after me, Mister Rhodes and be it on your head.'

'You're a fool, McKinnon, half the town will be after you. The old man, Thomas Brown, what have you done with him?'

'He killed him,' Kathleen chanced to speak, 'bottom of the pit...' McKinnon swung a backhanded blow at her head. The gun barrel cracked against her cheek and an arrow of bright blood leapt from the wound. The blow sent her reeling back against the wardrobe doors. Half stunned she stemmed the flow of blood with her hand; ignoring the pain, openly she taunted him.

'So what now, McKinnon, you kill all four of us?'

'Fasten yourself up and keep your mouth shut, or you'll get yourself a second piece of the same.'

He watched her dress, and when she had at last buttoned her shirt closed, he pushed her towards the door.

'Don't come after us, Rhodes, or on my word O'Rourke will not be around to see the sun come up.' He removed the key from the mortice lock, opened the door and inserted the key from the outside, and then tipped his hat to Lizzie. 'If ever you're down in Natal, sweetheart – ask about for Blackie McKinnon, your luck might be in; might just make time for you and me to catch up on some shenanigans.'

He pushed Kathleen ahead of him, slammed the door and threw the lock.

'The livery yard. Do what I tell you and speak to no one.' He Followed Kathleen down through the hotel's innards and out into the yard. 'Bear to the right,' he told her, 'the last stable.'

On earlier instructions, his horse had been saddled and bridled up. Outside, in the shadows dropped by the stable awning, his pack mule stood only half awake on a long tether; the stable boy was waiting for him.

'Everything you asked for has been done, my *baas*; pick

and shovel, everything I have tied to your mule and will not fall off.'

'My horse, did you feed him?'

'Enough for him to carry you a hundred miles; he will not want for more, not for two days at least.' He slipped the bolt on the stable door and went inside. McKinnon turned his attention to Kathleen; the shadow thrown by the brim of his hat all but covered his face, only his mouth and chin were visible in the moonlight.

'Tonight you were lucky O'Rourke. Your friends up there in your room, were it not for their interfering you could well have been lying dead by now.'

'Works both ways, McKinnon, one bite and you would have bled to death.'

'And I would have killed you for it.'

Kathleen shook her head.

'A small matter, McKinnon. You murdered my father and old man Brown, if it had come down to losing my life, I would have seen it as fair exchange.'

'And I'll bear that in mind, lassie, the next time we meet.'

McKinnon swung his arm through a wide arc and the pistol's steel drum caught Kathleen square on to the point of her temple.

# -56-

Rhodes wiped the last remaining smear of dried blood away from Kathleen's cheek whilst Lizzie examined the severity of the wound; she gestured to the stable boy, urging him in closer with the lamp.

'Here, on the ground, next to her head.'

Barney came back from the hotel's frontage, the shotgun at the trail.

'No sign of him; the Pniel diggings most likely, I can't

tell, Rhodes. Too damned dark, too many hoof prints.'

'She's coming round,' Lizzie breathed a sigh of relief and looked to Rhodes for assistance, 'we must get her inside; back upstairs to her room.' She glanced over her shoulder and with a nod of her head, gestured to Barney. 'Doc Williamson, next to the barbers. Fetch him out and don't take no for an answer, that bastard McKinnon has cut her deep and I want it seeing to.'

Kathleen opened her eyes and stared up at the faces hovering over her.

'McKinnon...?'

'He's gone, sweetheart,' Lizzie cradled her head on her lap, 'Lie still, Barney's gone for the doctor.'

Instinctively, Kathleen lifted her hand for the pain at her temple, but Lizzie gently held it off.

'Lie still. Do you know where you are? Can you remember what happened?'

'I remember my bedroom; McKinnon had a gun.'

'And he used it, girl. Knocked you out cold and left you out in the yard.'

'Zingeli?' Kathleen tried to sit up, 'where is he?'

'I am here, *inkosazana*. If I had stayed with you on the staging this would not have happened.'

Kathleen brushed his guilt aside, she was as much to blame for what had happened and now, the time she had left for her to put things right was running out.

'Find which road the dog has chosen. Go to where the road breaks west for river diggings, Zingeli. The spoor will still be fresh; one horse, one mule. The horse is shod.' She turned her head and picked him out from where he was standing in the shadows. 'Do this for me, Zingeli, but once you have found the road McKinnon has taken, then you will turn back. You must go no further. I need to know.'

'Enough talking,' Lizzie insisted, 'we must get you out of this cold air.' She looked to Rhodes. 'Help me lift her, I cannot manage her weight alone.'

Zingeli stepped past Rhodes and easily as he would lift a

sleeping kitten from its basket, carefully he lifted Kathleen from Lizzie's arms. Zingeli followed Lizzie upstairs and with a father's concern for his own child laid Kathleen out on the bed.

'I will go now *inkosazana*, when I have found what you are after I will return.' He left her side just as Barney came back with the doctor in tow; like an insistent sheepdog, Barney hurried Williamson into the room.

Williamson shrugged off his coat and rolled up his shirt sleeves; he cocked an eye at Lizzie.

'Nasty bang on the head, who did this?'

'Not your concern,' Kathleen growled at him, 'just fix the hole in my head and leave your bill with Lizzie.'

In the livery yard, Zingeli took up a filled lamp from the nearest stable and set the flame to its lowest burn. Barefooted, he went out into the street and turned westward for the river diggings of Klipdrift and Pniel, within that next half hour he had reached the last outlying homestead. Dogs barked when he passed and then the silence of the deserted road and the open veld came over him. For that next half-mile and with the lamp held low to the ground he scoured the track for sign, those eroded by the wind he discarded. However, where the road forked, here he found the first signs of fresh spoor, those of the shod horse and, directly behind, sometimes overlaying these deeper, more pronounced marks were the smaller natural hoof prints left by McKinnon's heavily laden pack mule. The pack animal had defecated as it walked and with the sole of his bared foot, Zingeli put his weight to crushing the mule shit; still pliant and moist it squeezed from between his toes.

A slight wind came out of the west, Zingeli picked out the smell of woodsmoke and when he strained his eyes at the dark, the tiniest pinprick of light, small enough as to be almost that of a distant star winked at him from just below the horizon.

## 57

The bandana-style dressing and the doctor's liberal use of the iodine bottle had endowed Kathleen with a bizarre air of hostility, that of the warrior fighter freshly streaked with ochre battle lines, and on her instructions, painstakingly, he had wound his bandages so as to leave her field of vision totally unimpaired. She moved to the side of the bed and sat upright, face-on to where Zingeli stood in the doorway. The dizziness had abated and her perception of her surroundings was once again, pin sharp.

'It will be light soon.'

'An hour at most, *inkosazana*; it will take no longer.'

They looked at one another and what needed to be said passed between them without the speaking of a single word. Zingeli turned for the door and without looking back, disappeared into the darkness. Expertly, he saddled and cinched Kathleen's horse, and in less than a minute returned to the stable carrying his blanket and spears.

Lizzie Jardine set a mug of tea on the table, within easy reach of Kathleen's hand.

'You're going after McKinnon?'

Kathleen nodded her head, fate was playing its final card and there was no preventing it from doing so.

Lizzie placed a canvas miner's bag next to the mug.

'There's enough food in there for three days.' She looked up from the table; the sadness of what was happening already there in her eyes. 'You'll be gone some time, then?'

'A while, I guess.'

'Your things...?'

'Just what I came with, the rest...'

'You will leave with me,' Lizzie insisted, the corners of her eyes already starred with moisture, 'on your word that one day you will come back for them.'

'I will.' Kathleen promised and looked past her to the

open doorway. 'Rhodes and Barney?'

'Waiting in the yard. They refuse to leave without seeing you off.'

'I'll be down shortly.' She smiled at Lizzie. 'A couple of minutes to collect my stuff together.'

＊

'I'm coming with you,' Barney announced and pulled himself onto the driver's seat of the hotel's Cape cart, 'for at least as far as you're catching up with McKinnon.'

Lizzie handed up her twelve bore double.

'Chances are you won't be needing it, but either way you keep it to hand, Barnato.'

With Rhodes' help, Kathleen climbed into the saddle and with her weight settled, drew a finger's width more slack from the cinch; it was then that the old familiar feelings of déjà vu swept over her, relief even. One way or another, her relationship with Blackie McKinnon would soon be at an end. Without any conscious effort, she lowered the brim of her hat just one more inch and turned up her jacket collar, enough for it to hold off the chill of the pre-dawn. East of the diggings, first faint colours were there above the Karoo; one more hour and the sun would be fully risen, hot and big and fiery yellow over Kimberley. It was time. Kathleen nodded her head to Zingeli, apprehensive though not afraid of what his decision might be.

'I would not think less of you for staying behind, there is work for you here, food and a place to sleep; where I am going, I can offer only hardship, cold nights and an empty belly.'

'And I have asked for nothing more,' Zingeli answered her without the slightest sign of any uncertainty.

Kathleen smiled at his decision and made pretence of clearing her throat of dust.

450

'Then you would do well to ride with the cart for as long as it takes to find McKinnon,' she glanced at Barney, 'that is, if you have no objection to my Zulu servant sitting alongside you, Mister Barnato?'

Without answering, Barney made space for Zingeli. Standing next to Lizzie Jardine, Rhodes gave his best efforts to banishing some of his solemnity.

'No heroics, Barnato. I need you back on 339, preferably intact; being limbless as well as brainless would not bode well for our business venture.' He turned to Kathleen. 'McKinnon has killed twice, perhaps there are others we do not know of. If it comes to a head-on confrontation, trust your judgement, Kathleen, but without any hesitation, you must do as you see fit. Heaven knows, Kimberley will be a far better place without the likes of Blackie McKinnon.'

'I will miss you all so very much,' Kathleen barely managed the words.

'Likewise,' said Rhodes, 'when you realise what you are after is no better than what you have left behind, then come on back to us. There will always be a place for you, O'Rourke.' He reached up for her and glanced sideways at the stock of her Sharps rifle. 'Remember to adjust your sights for windage, and on the advice I once took from an old Boer hunter, if at all possible, shoot with the sun behind you.'

'God bless you, Rhodes, I could not have come this far without you.' She leaned from the saddle and with a heartfelt gentleness, held her cheek to Rhodes' upturned face. 'Our meeting, on the *Eudora* – so meant to be – so long ago.'

'And so far away,' Rhodes added to the memory. 'Now please, before you un-man me completely take your smile and your horse and leave this saddened diamond digger in peace.'

At a point where the track to the Pniel diggings swung westward, away from Stockdale Street, this was the place

451

where Kathleen reined in her horse and gave up time to looking back. Sentiment and first sunlight, as warm hands came over her, and from now to the beginning of those last three years, all of a thousand memories were there, bared to the bone for her to rummage through.

'Second thoughts? Wouldn't blame you,' Barney called up to her from the cart, 'perhaps we should let things lie as they are? Start again from scratch, so to speak.' But he knew the suggestion would fall on deaf ears.

A pair of mule-drawn wagons crossed in front of the Queens and the dust rose up, thick and red and as a final curtain it ruffled outwards. For one last time, Kathleen picked out the shapes of Rhodes and Lizzie Jardine; both of them were waving, but the moment was short-lived and then they were gone.

'Stay if you must, Barnato, this is not your fight, I did not ask for your help.'

'You're stuck with me, O'Rourke,' he flicked the reins, 'we're wasting time. McKinnon has a head start and we will need all of our best speed if we are to catch up with him.'

Where the road narrowed, empty handed, Zingeli jumped down from the cart and went ahead on foot; in that early sunlight the spoor showed up as sharp shadows, the edges clean, each new impression he saw to be only hours old. Kathleen stayed back and only when the distance between them had opened up to near on a quarter mile did she urge her horse forwards at a slow walk.

## 58

From the shade of an ancient *kameeldoring*, Blackie McKinnon stepped out onto the track, the gun in his hand at a level with Zingeli's stomach. From the forward tilt of his hat, black shadow fell as a mask across his eyes, and his smile was thin, that of a man who would kill without feeling.

'Didn't expect you so soon, black boy. O'Rourke sent you on ahead to do her dirty work?'

Zingeli stayed silent.

'Last chance, kaffir boy.' He cocked the pistol. Where's that mistress of yours? Where'd you leave O'Rourke?'

'I came alone.'

McKinnon shook his head and sniggered at the deception. The Zulu was bared to the waist, powerfully built, but unarmed.

'You're lying, boy. O'Rourke knows that given half a chance I will put her in the ground. Where is she?'

'Close,' Zingeli admitted, aware that his own life now hung by the slimmest of threads, 'but she is not alone.'

McKinnon looked past him, the sun had barely lifted more than the width of two fingers above the skyline, but already a band of haze had settled itself to the track. From inside of it, the distorted shapes of a Cape cart and a single, mounted rider appeared as wraiths, almost mirage-like.

'Turn around, boy.' McKinnon re-seated the pistol's hammer and pushed the weapon back behind his belt; from the canvas sleeve across his shoulders he drew out his spyglass. 'Stand where you are and let's have none of your Zulu shenanigans or I swear I will kill you.'

He put up the spyglass and filled the eyepiece; one horse, one rider.

'The girl from Pilgrim's Rest,' he mused and smiled at

Kathleen's tenacity, 'come to square old Blackie McKinnon for last night's hard loving; chokes me up, she does.' He lowered the spyglass and pushed it back inside the canvas sleeve. 'We shall see, lassie, just how much it takes for you to pull the trigger on that Colt o' yours.' He freed the gun from his waistband and pressed the barrel against Zingeli's back. 'On your knees black boy, a hen to catch the fox is what we need and you'll do nicely; today will be a good day for me to square the debt. Time for young O'Rourke to share some time with her father.'

From up ahead, Kathleen caught a tiny glint of reflected sunlight, and it was then she glimpsed McKinnon. She reined in and reached for her saddlebag. Barney pulled the cart in behind and called up to her.

'What is it? What have you seen?'

Kathleen drew out her spyglass and with the sun behind her, the images blossomed crystal clear inside the lens.

'McKinnon; he's got Zingeli.'

Barney edged the cart alongside her and urgently he reached out his hand for the telescope.

'The bastard is sucking you in, girl,' he adjusted the lens and spoke without looking up. 'Move any closer and he will kill Zingeli. That's what he's after, Kathleen; he knows you will try to stop him.'

Barney froze in his seat.

'Mother of God, he wouldn't do it!'

'Do what...?'

In that clean air, a sudden, pale flicker of burned powder preceded the sharp crack from a single pistol shot. Like the breaking of a limb from a tall tree, or the cracking of a whip, the sound from that single discharge flew at Kathleen's ears, so that she winced and turned her head away.

'Zingeli is down!' Barney told her, and then he rallied. 'No, he's alive, Kathleen. McKinnon's playing fast and loose with you.'

Kathleen slid from the saddle, the act was deliberate and

at that distance would appear to McKinnon as the first sign of her backing off.

'The telescope, Barney,' she took it from him and steadied her arm against the cart. Zingeli was still on his knees, a trickle of dark blood streaked the side of his face; the bullet had clipped his ear.

She estimated the distance between the cart and McKinnon.

'A hair over five hundred yards, what do think?'

'There or thereabouts I should say, though may as well stand as more than a mile for what it's worth. The odds are with McKinnon. Zingeli would be dead before we reached the halfway mark.'

She handed back the telescope.

'Keep the glass on McKinnon; do not take your eyes off him, not even for a single second.'

'What are you doing?'

'What I should have done back in Natal, three years ago.'

Kathleen pulled the Sharps carbine from its scabbard.

'We must do this quickly. If McKinnon moves for so much as an inch you will tell me.'

Barney watched her ready the gun.

'You might hit Zingeli?'

'I might, but I have no choice. Given the circumstances, what I am about to do, I know Zingeli would see as the lesser of two evils.'

Barney put up the telescope and concentrated all his efforts on watching McKinnon.

Kathleen slid the graduated rear sight onto the five hundred yard mark. The air hung dead still – no crosswind. Thankfully, she ignored the windage screw and from the leather pouch at her side she drew out a single .50 calibre, brass jacketed cartridge. She lifted the hammer to half cock and cranked the drop-down lever. With a steady hand she fed the finger long cartridge into the breach.

'I need a dead rest, Barney, to lessen the risk of the bullet striking Zingeli.' The cart was unstable; the slightest movement, the twitch of a horse's tail and her aim would be thrown.

Barney abandoned the telescope and in desperation, reached behind him; urgently, he fought the upholstered rear seat from its framework and let fall to the track.

Even with the added stability of the leather seat, the clearance was barely high enough to give her proper line of sight. Kathleen spreadeagled her weight behind the makeshift support and nodded her head to Barney.

'McKinnon,' she refocused her attention, 'tell me what you see.'

Exaggerated by the medium of his telescope, the images Barney found appeared to him as distorted; the haze was strong now, sweat trickled down from his hairline.

'Still with Zingeli, same place on the track – not as clear though, the haze is getting worse.'

Kathleen closed the breech and bedded the Sharps stock against the padded leather; she narrowed her eyes for a tighter line of fire. At close on four hundred yards, McKinnon's outline showed up as little more than a trembling silhouette from against the scrub. A few more minutes and she knew the haze would swallow him completely.

'He's got a telescope!' Barney warned her. A sudden rush of excitement made him garrulous. 'He'll see the rifle and our game will be up. The pistol, Kathleen, he's put it to Zingeli's head. Either you hurry and take the shot or step away and let him go.'

Kathleen drew back the hammer and with the rifle now fully cocked, she settled the very tip of the foresight to the notch of its rear counterpart; at that distance, McKinnon's outline was only vaguely recognisable, almost ghost-like. The matched sights appeared to waver and tremble and her heartbeat was now a fervent, endless drumming inside her chest. She favoured the highest point on McKinnon's torso and with a prayer partly formed on her lips, as her father had taught her, gently she squeezed the trigger.

With solid force the butt stock kicked back hard into Kathleen's shoulder and for a long moment her ears were deafened; Barney watched for the strike. McKinnon was still standing and then, as if struck by a whipping branch, he jerked sideways and reached out for the point of his right elbow.

From between McKinnon's fingers, Barney saw the first bright spray of living blood.

'You hit his arm!' Barney shouted and vaulted down from the cart. Again, he lifted up the spyglass. 'He's running, Kathleen, he won't get far, not with a wound like that.'

Kathleen stood up and worked the carbine's loading lever; the spent casing fell to ground and with quick determination she refilled the breech. McKinnon jinked sideways into the scrub and within those next few seconds came out hell for leather on horseback. Barney dropped the telescope against his chest and watched McKinnon's horse kick up dust.

'He's away, Kathleen, that's the last you will see of him.'

'Alive, that's as may be,' said Kathleen and at a full stance adjusted the Sharps' sights to their maximum range of eight hundred yards, 'but as a man already dead, he will soon be forced to settle his lot with the devil.'

For a moment, a single fluffy cloud came between the sun and Kathleen O'Rourke. The haze weakened and even at that greater distance, McKinnon's shape was clear to her; sharp-edged to a blue sky. Barney shook his head at the impossibility of her fatuous intent.

'He's too far out my sweetheart, there isn't a man alive who could make that shot.'

'Perhaps not, Barnato.'

She widened her stance and under the Sharps' weight the muscles in her forearms trembled like reeds in the grip of a powerful flood. Like the American buffalo hunter, Kathleen O'Rourke leaned into steadying the Sharps

457

carbine. Strengthened by her own terrible loathing, easily she held the gun at the level. When it came, the shot was loud as any thunder; only when the sound had died did Barney see McKinnon lurch backwards from the saddle.

# -59-

Unwilling to venture further than the beginnings of Kimberley's main street, Kathleen reined her horse in close alongside the Cape cart. Sat astride McKinnon's redundant bay gelding and with the pack mule secured to a long tether, Zingeli hung back. From the shade of a lone thorn, he watched and let the solemnity of Kathleen's farewells run its course. Another hour or another day even, time would pass as before, slowly or otherwise it was of no concern.

Kathleen lifted her hat and mopped her brow with her shirt sleeve. She turned in the saddle and with her arm outstretched to Barney Barnato, offered him her clenched fist.

'This I leave for you Mister Barnato, but on condition.'

'You confound me O'Rourke,' Barney chuckled, 'but yes, whatever it is you want from me, unless it's money. That I have precious little of, as well you know.'

'That I have your solemn word on what is to me, a matter of great importance.'

Barney nodded his head and, acting out the part of the jilted suitor, tossed a pinch of cockney humour into the charade.

'I should have seen it coming, you're marrying Cecil Rhodes in preference to me?'

'I have yet to experience the serious side of you, Barnato.' She turned her fist, palm upwards, but still with her fingers tightly closed about what she was holding.

'Thomas Brown, the adjacent claim holder to 339...?'

Barney rolled his eyes skywards.

'You want me to bury the man?'

'That I do.'

'Burying a man does not come cheap, Kathleen.'

'Nor does this,' said Kathleen and opened her hand to let in the sunlight.

To Kathleen, the stone appeared as to be larger than before, though to Barney it was a hundred times even more than that. It was the manifestation of every digger's dream, a stone amongst stones, a diamond the likes of which he never knew existed, the fanciful imaginings of the perpetually drunk or the ravings of a man just returned from the wilderness, his mind still awash with the damning effects of the swamp fever.

'Where did you get this?'

'From the man you will soon be laying to rest. Before he died, Barney, I swore I would take care of it.'

He reached out and lifted the precious stone from Kathleen's palm; already his hand trembled. Not without some effort was he able to stop his voice from croaking.

'You have overwhelmed me, Kathleen O'Rourke; what would you have me do with it?'

'He has a wife. Promise me you will find her, Barney.'

Like a candle caught by a spiteful turn in the wind, his excitement guttered.

'The stone is hers, then?'

She shook her head. 'Half the sale price. The remainder is yours, more than enough to get you started – no more fighting for your supper down at the Queens.'

'And should I find the immensity of your kindness too intimidating?'

'Then I will give the stone to Rhodes and that will be the last you see of it.'

Quickly he interjected.

'I'll do it.' His eyes sparkled. 'I was jesting, sweetheart. Rhodes has long since accumulated more than he can cope with, time for him to share the pie.' He pocketed the diamond, looked up at Kathleen and his eyes softened. 'You have my word on it. Half the proceeds will be forwarded on to Brown's wife in Blighty, but why must you leave? We could work together, share the spoils, so to speak.'

Kathleen shook her head. 'Some other time, Barnato, I need to get away. I have swallowed enough Kimberley dust to last me a lifetime.'

'But you will come back?'

'When I'm ready; might well be in need of your help when I do.'

'Whatever it takes,' he promised her, 'both Rhodes and I will be here for you,' he cleared his throat, 'where will you go, Kathleen, at least tell me that.'

'North,' she told him, 'the Transvaal they're calling it. Story goes there's new gold to be dug, might even be tempted to chance my luck and stake me a claim. My father would have liked that.' She tipped her hat to him and like the horizon, in Barney's eyes her smile was filled with sunlight, but fleeting sunlight; soon it would be gone. She leaned from the saddle and kissed his cheek.

'Time for me to go.'

'Stay, Kathleen. The three of us can work together, for God's sake woman, I would even marry you if it that's what it takes to keep you here!'

She shook her head and laughed, but fondly, the laughter itself interlaced with sadness.

'My darling Barnato, I shall miss your absurdity and I suspect that by the time we meet again you will be well and truly attached to some Kimberley belle, so let me get on with looking for whatever it is I am after. Taking Barney Barnato as my husband would do nothing good for either one of us.'

She turned her horse for the eastward side of the Kimberley diggings.

'My love to Lizzie and Rhodes. Take care of yourself,

Barnato, I have one more man to bid goodbye before I leave.'

# -60-

Kathleen O'Rourke reined her horse sideways-on to the Big Hole, she looked down into it and for a long moment all her regrets and a hundred more were there, swarming the stagings, climbing the ladders and crossing that ruined expanse of coveted ground, eager to greet her, keen to hold her back. All of this she was leaving behind and beneath a Colesberg sky, with a peaceful heart, she could feel her aspirations dying. What she had come to do was done, dead and buried out there on the track and not for all those diamonds found, nor the money they brought, would she change one terrible, precious second of it. For one last time she absorbed the tempestuous, evil splendour of that plundered hole in the earth.

A thousand steel wires picked up the sunlight and in that late hour, against a backdrop of ochre-coloured earth, they shone not as wires, but as a thousand glistening threads of fine silk, shot to the wind from a thousand man-made spinnerets. Upon them, as they had always done, pulleys squealed and bucked at their fastenings, snatched taut by repeated heavy loads of Kimberlite. All these things and much, much more she looked down upon, taking her time that they might set themselves indelibly and forever inside those deepest parts of her memory.

From her breast pocket, Kathleen reached out a fob of sterling silver. Set about the silver chains were three uncut diamonds, and as a tiny chandelier, the trinket turned and tantalised the sunlight. She tried her best to speak, but like diamonds buried deep inside the pit, the intended words stuck fast inside her throat and in their place, the raw ache

461

of her grief rose up as a dark wind and settled there. She drew back her arm and with the full weight of her shoulder sent the trinket spinning outwards from the pit edge. She watched it fall; like a wounded silver bird it glittered and twisted and in a second it was gone.

Zingeli touched her arm, the slightest of physical contact, but enough to bring her back inside the moment.

'We must leave, *inkosazana*, we have far to go before night falls, or sleep alongside the pit with ghosts and goblins.'

Kathleen turned her horse about. Zingeli was right, they must reach the crest of the ridge before nightfall, light a fire and sleep. In the morning, they would go on, or perhaps they would not. Either way it did not matter.

\* \* \*

Printed in Great Britain
by Amazon

58420002R00279